TWILIGHT GUARDIANS

NEW YORK TIMES BESTSELLING AUTHOR

MAGGIE SHAYNE

WINGS IN

REBORN

THE NIGHT

TWILIGHT GUARDIANS
Copyright © 2014 by Maggie Shayne

Edited by Jena O'Connor
www.practicalproofing.com

Ebook formatting and Graphic Design by Jessica Lewis
www.authorslifesaver.com

Cover Model: Lisa Benson

Cover Photo and Photo Finishing by Paige Wissenbach
www.paigewissenbach.com

ISBN: 1500762954
ISBN-13: 978-1500762957

CHAPTER ONE

Killian Garone was the last of his kind. So yeah, he was
lonely. But he'd had no idea what lonely was until her.

He wandered, Killian did. Had ever since his building had
been torched by vigilantes back in the wars of 2011. When
humankind found out the boogiemen of Bram Stoker's
inkwell were real, they decided pretty quickly that they had
to return vampires to the realm of fiction. And they'd pretty
much succeeded.

Killian had survived the fire in his home, and the
extermination of his species. As far as he knew, he was the
only one left. So he wandered, and he avoided humans, and he
survived by drinking the blood of wildlife, rather than feeding
on humans. He didn't mind so much that animal blood left
him weak. A watered down version of a vampire.

And then one day, he'd dreamed of her.

He'd *dreamed* of her.

Everyone knows vampires don't dream. The day sleep is
death. It's nothingness. But he'd dreamed of her. Could two

years of isolation make a vampire go crazy? He didn't know, and who the hell was he going to ask?

She came to him in flashes. Hair as red as a new penny, lots of it, rippling down way past her shoulders. Huge blue eyes that held the world inside them. A white owl. And the feeling that she was in trouble and didn't even know it.

He knew two things about her right from the beginning. She was one of The Chosen. That is, she had the rare Belladonna Antigen every vampire had as a human. Only The Chosen could become vampires. They would bleed out easily if cut, and they tended to die young unless they accepted the Dark Gift. It would be almost impossible for a vampire to harm one of The Chosen. They were compelled to protect them, instead.

Charlie O'Malley was one of The Chosen. And Killian was drawn to her like he'd never been drawn to one of them before. There was something off about that.

The second thing he knew about her was that she was dreaming of him, too. He felt it in brief, strobe-like glimpses inside her mind.

What is this? Who is he?
Am I losing my mind?
God, I wish this was real.

He'd been trekking through the cathedral forests of northeastern Oregon when he'd started experiencing her. And he'd changed directions, because he couldn't help himself. She exerted some kind of force on him, pulled him to her. It felt like a long rubber band had been snapped around the two of themF and stretched to its limit. When he tried to go the other way, it was like he just couldn't stretch that band another inch.

He had to go to her.

And now he was as close as it was safe to get, but he knew he'd keep moving closer. He stood on a winding road, looking down on Portland, and he knew she was there. Somewhere in that mass of human beings who would kill him on sight if they found out what he was. But he didn't care. He had to get to her. He didn't know why, and he didn't know what he was supposed to do once he did. But he had to get to Charlie.

He pulled up his hoodie and headed into the forest to seek shelter. Dawn was calling. But when he woke tonight, he was going into that city. Maybe if he kept his head down and his mind open, he could get to her before the humans got to him.

Charlotte O'Malley caught a glimpse of the morning news's nonstop media coverage of what was being called *The Bloodbath of 2014.* The story even had its own graphic— the word "Bloodbath" in a scarlet font that appeared to be dripping. It had been a week since the bodies of seven people had been found in and around Portland, bloodless, with twin fang-sized holes in their necks. It was a deliciously gruesome story that was just what she needed to distract her from her... issues.

Namely a dream lover who was...well, haunting her. Making love to a phantom all night every night wasn't exactly restful. She was exhausted and frankly, feeling like hell lately.

Charlie's mother was in a state of panic about the circles under her eyes. But if it wasn't that, it would be something else. Trish lived in a constant state of fear for her only daughter and hovered to the point of near suffocation. All of which added motivation to Charlie's goal: get her own apartment before she turned 21 in a few weeks.

She glanced at the clock. Still twenty minutes before she had to leave for her job at the local Rent-A-Center. Plunking her ass onto the sofa, she reached for her coffee mug and thumbed up the volume.

"None of the seven vampires responsible for these slayings survived our tactical team's raid," said a man whose face was as saggy as a bulldog's. The text at the bottom of the screen identified him as Commandant Barnaby Crowe of the DPI. He had expressive brown eyes that seemed sincere, and he sat at the news desk across from morning show anchor and American cutie pie Sherri-with-an-i Jarrard.

"With all due respect, Commandant," Sherri said, "authorities assured the American people three years ago that vampire-kind had been wiped out. Obviously, that was untrue."

"Obviously," he replied, his eyes as steady as his voice. "If we missed even one, that was one too many. I hope the bleeding hearts bemoaning the extermination of a *race we know nothing about*" (in derogative falsetto) "will pay attention. They propagate like rats. But they're predators. And humanity is their prey. This is a matter of self-preservation, Sherri. It's us or them."

Sherri Jarrard kept her poker face intact, providing her eager viewers no clue where she stood on the issue. "The autopsy reports on the victims, which the government released to the press just this morning, show that every one of them shared a rare blood antigen called Belladonna."

Charlie sat up straighter. *Wait a minute, did she just say Belladonna? Hell, I have that!*

Sherri was still talking, though. "This is the same trait shared by people who claim to have been used as bait in a black ops plot to lure vampires in for the slaughter at the conclusion of the war of twenty-eleven."

Commandant Crowe nodded firmly. "We had a rogue agent trying to run his own show back then. He went too far. But the truth of the matter is that if there are *any* surviving vampires out there, then anyone with the Belladonna Antigen is in grave danger. They are the Undead's favorite...food." He thinned his lips and lowered his head a little, as if his words were almost unspeakable.

"Holy shit," Charlie muttered. "Hey, Mom?"

I shouldn't tell her. She's gonna freak.

"What is the government doing to protect these individuals?" the anchor asked.

Commandant Crowe lifted his head, looked her dead in the eye. "First, Sherri, know that this attack was an isolated incident. We have no evidence that there are any other vampires still in existence. Secondly, I must remind you that the United States government made a promise to the few thousand citizens with the Belladonna Antigen, that they would never again be monitored without their knowledge. We do have plans in place to protect those who ask for it, but participation is entirely voluntary. We've reached out to all of those that we know of to offer our assistance. And obviously, I can't tell you what that assistance will entail. The enemy could be listening."

"If there are any left. Which you've just assured me isn't likely."

"We could be wrong," he said, leaning slightly forward. "We were before." He took off the microphone that was clipped to his lapel as he got up, then slung it into his empty chair and walked off the set.

They switched to a story about a monster storm about to hit the Midwest, and Charlie clicked off the TV, picked up her coffee mug, her hand shaking so hard the coffee sloshed over the rim, and headed into the kitchen. She'd deliberately stayed out of range of her mom this morning, because she'd been such a basket case about Charlie's restless nights and sleepy days.

Or maybe, Charlie thought, Trish had already known that the murder victims had the Belladonna Antigen, that they were just like Charlie. That would explain a lot.

In the kitchen, her mother was holding an official looking letter and crying. That alarmed Charlie even more than the news report had. Dammit, she should've stayed in bed and kept having out of body sexual encounters with her imaginary friend.

"What the *hell*, Mom? What's wrong?"

Trish O'Malley looked up quick, met Charlie's eyes, and scrubbed her own with the heel of one hand. "I...we have to talk. I have something to tell you."

Charlie lifted her eyebrows and felt the bottom fall out of her stomach. She couldn't remember ever seeing her mother cry. Trish tended to be kind of cold. She loved her daughter, sure, but mostly showed it through her overprotective tendencies, not by any real display of emotion or affection. It was like she was afraid to love her too much. Or something.

"Sit down, Charlie." Trish's blond hair was as messy as perfectly straight hair ever got. She'd been running her hands through it.

Charlie sat down. "You're freaking me out, Mom. Is this about The Portland Seven being BDs like me? Because if that's it, I already know."

Her mother nodded. "Yes. It's about that." She looked past Charlie toward the living room. "It was on the news?"

Charlie nodded. "They said people with BD are vampires' favorite snack foods. You never told me that."

"I didn't see the need." She kept her eyes elsewhere. But that was normal. "They were supposedly all wiped out three years ago. You were only seventeen. Why scare the hell out of a seventeen-year-old for nothing?"

Right. Why tell me that I'm the favorite prey of a deadly predator that would like to rip out my jugular? Why not just argue with me every time I want to leave the house after dark instead?

"There's more to your...condition than I've told you, Charlie."

There was more? More her mother had kept from her? Charlie's knees were shaking, and the sarcasm she tried to inject into her tone fell flat. "It's not a *condition*, Mom. It doesn't have any effect on my health other than making me more likely to bleed to death than your average bear." Her lack of certain clotting factors were, she had always assumed, her mother's reason for treating her like a porcelain doll. No sports. No rough housing. No roller skating or ice skating or sledding down steep hills or riding a bike. Her childhood had been miserable.

Her mother lowered her head. "That's not exactly true. There's a lot more to it. There just aren't any...symptoms until later on. And there's no cure."

"Well, of course there's no cure. It's a blood type for crying out loud, why would anybody want to cure a blood type?" Her mother was scaring her, and she didn't like it.

"Don't get upset, Charlie. Sit down, I'll make you some tea and—"

"Jesus, Mom, just tell me what the hell is going on, will you? You're scaring me here." All these years, Charlie thought, treating her like she was fragile, like there was something wrong with her. In all that time, Charlie had never once believed that actually might be the case. The problem, she'd decided long ago, was her mother. She was the one with the *condition*. If Charlie had to give it a name, she'd call it chronic, paranoid anxiety with overprotective tendencies.

"What symptoms?" she asked. She was still half-convinced her mother would list something like hangnails or frequent bouts of the sniffles.

Trish opened her mouth, then closed it again.

"Give me that." Charlie snatched the sheet of paper from her mother's hand. Then she read it and felt as if her blood all rushed straight to her feet, leaving her dizzy and kind of disoriented.

Dear Mrs. O'Malley,

Due to the recent, tragic events in Portland, we are reaching out to all individuals with the Belladonna Antigen to offer our protection in an effort to prevent such a tragedy from ever happening again. According to our records, you have a daughter, Charlotte Antoinette O'Malley, who possesses this rare antigen and who might qualify for inclusion in a special program we have implemented for people like her. Your daughter is eligible as long as she has not yet begun experiencing the onset of symptoms indicating that her inevitable and tragic premature death is near, which is, at her age, highly unlikely. (If she has begun experiencing symptoms, we still encourage you to get in touch as we have a separate program in place for such individuals.) We've scheduled an appointment for you to discuss her safety this Friday afternoon at 1 PM at the Federal Building in Portland. We strongly urge you to attend, if only to learn more about the programs. Participation will, of course, be entirely voluntary.

Sincerely,
Commandant Barnaby Crowe, DPI

Charlie let the sheet of paper fall from her hand to the floor. It floated like a bird, landing lightly at her feet. "Premature death?"

Her mother blinked red-rimmed, wet eyes. "I didn't know how to tell you, Charlie."

"Premature fucking death?" She stood rooted to the spot, her hands shaking, her heart pounding. "I'm going to die? When, Mom? How long do I have?"

"I don't...know."

"Yes, you do. You do know. You've always known. How long?" Charlie wasn't crying. Why the hell wasn't she crying? Shock, she guessed. "The letter says symptoms are unlikely at my age. At what age do they become likely?"

Trish lowered her head, closed her eyes. "The life expectancy of people with Belladonna is mid- to late-thirties," she said softly. "But there are exceptions."

"Where? What exceptions? You just waited until I was twenty to tell me I probably won't live much past thirty?"

"I'm sorry. I just...I didn't know how to tell you."

"God." Charlie's whole world had been turned upside down in a single conversation. "I don't know what to do. I don't even know what to do. My God. My God, Mom."

Her mother touched her shoulder, looked her in the eye for once. It was rare. Now she knew why, maybe. Maybe Trish couldn't face her. Maybe she didn't show affection because she didn't want to get too attached to someone who was just going to croak in a few years anyway.

"I'll call work for you. You can stay home today, and we can talk about—"

"I'm going to work. I'm going...at least out. Somewhere. I need to...I need to go. I need to just...go."

She turned and walked almost blindly to the door, yanked it open, and startled someone who was standing on the other side, apparently just about to knock. Through blurry vision, Charlie saw an older woman with wild red hair, a multicolored kaftan and about six too many strands of beads around her neck.

"Excuse me," Charlie muttered, trying to duck around her to get out of the apartment.

But the woman put both hands on her shoulders, holding tightly, and scanning her face way too intently. "Charlotte?"

Charlie frowned and looked up slowly. "Who wants to know?"

"Roxanne O'Malley," she said. "I'm your grandmother."

"I don't *have* a grandmother." Hell, just cue the "Twilight Zone" theme already, she thought.

"Yes, you do. Let's go back inside so you can pack your things while I tell your mother how this is going to go down."

"How *what* is going to go down? Hey, let go of me!"

But the alleged grandmother had exchanged her way-too-personal shoulder squeeze for a death grip on her upper arm and was marching her right back through her apartment door, closing it behind her and turning the locks as if expecting armed hit men to show up at any moment.

Charlie's mom said, "Did you forget something, hon—" as she came in from the kitchen. But then she stopped and just stared at the older woman's face with her mouth open, that letter in her hand again, and whispered, "Roxy."

"Wait, you *know* her?" Charlie asked.

Her mother's gaze shifted back and forth between them and she nodded. "She's your grandmother. Your father's mother."

"Told you," Roxy said, snarky and sarcastic, but with a teasing light in her eyes. She released Charlie's arm, held out her hand toward Trish, palm up, and snapped her fingers until Trish handed her the letter. Then she read it as Trish said, "I don't know what to do. If she's in danger—"

"She's in more danger than you know," the redhead replied. "You have to let me take her, Trish. I can keep her safe."

"What?" Charlie took two backward steps away from her mother and the stranger. "No, now wait a minute, here. No one's *taking* me anywhere."

"Don't you think the government is more qualified to do that than you are, Roxy?" Trish asked.

"You telling me you trust those morons?" Roxy shook her head. "Don't. Not ever. Fortunately, they don't know you have any connection to me. I've been dealing with these government goons for a long time. You have to let her come with me. It's the only way to keep her safe."

"No." Charlie threw up her hands and sat down hard on the sofa. "No, I'm not going with some crazy lady I never met before just because she shows up with this line of—"

"God, you look so much like her," her mother whispered, her eyes darting from Charlie's face to Roxy's over and over.

"Pack a bag, Charlotte," the older woman said. "We don't have much time."

"I can protect her fine right here," her mother said. "They'll help us. The letter says—"

"It's what the letter doesn't say that you should worry about. You know what their help consists of? I shudder to think." She turned to Charlie, her bright green eyes beaming into her. "I've seen what they do to our kind, Charlotte. You don't want that. Believe me."

"Our kind?" Charlie frowned. "What do you mean, *our* kind?"

Her mom kept talking like she hadn't even heard her. "If she just vanishes, they'll know–"

"Not yet they won't. I just finished a lovely little hack job into their systems, removing your names from their watch list. I also did a global search-and-replace in all Charlotte's health records, changing her blood type to good old ordinary A positive. Sure, they might figure it out eventually, but by the time they do, she'll be off the grid. Like me." She sent Charlie a conspiratorial wink. "You're welcome."

"For what? Mom, what the *hell*?"

"You should come with us, Trish," Roxy said.

Charlie's mother looked at her sadly. Then nodded, as if she'd made a decision she had no right to make. "Go pack some things, Charlie. Anything you leave behind, I can have sent to you later."

"Bring everything you want, Charlotte," Roxy said. "Anything you leave behind, we'll replace."

Charlie shook her head. "You can't make me go anywhere. I'm an adult, I can make my own decisions."

Her mother didn't look her in the eye. So they were back to that, were they? "She's right, Charlie. It's for the best. You have to go."

"I won't. You don't want me here, fine. I'll get my own place. I'll bunk with a friend till my promotion comes through, but I am *not* going with her."

"Yes, Charlie," her mother said. She lifted her head, met her eyes, looked stronger than Charlie remembered ever seeing her look. There was determination in those eyes, and resignation and insistence. "You are."

She got to her feet again, rising slowly, facing them both, trying to make her voice as firm as her mother's had been. "I am *not* letting anyone take control of my life from me," she said slowly. "Especially not now that I know how little of it I have left."

Roxy's eyes turned sad. "So you know about the side effects of Belladonna."

"Only because I read the letter," Charlie said. "It's not like anyone seemed to think this was information I might have a right to know."

"She's still in shock," Trish pointed out. "She only found out a few minutes ago."

"You must be reeling, then." Her grandmother reached out, as if to put a comforting hand on her shoulder, but Charlie dodged it. Shrugging, Roxy dropped her hand to her side. "Don't be so sure your time is short, Charlotte. I have the antigen too."

Charlie frowned at her. "How have you managed not to die?"

She shrugged. "Clean living? Yoga? Or maybe it's genetic. I hope for your sake that's the case. I am the oldest living member of The Chosen, Charlotte."

"The Chosen? What the hell are The Chosen?"

"You are. I am. Everyone with Belladonna is. If you trust me, maybe there's a slim chance I can keep you alive long enough to become the second oldest."

At sundown, Killian woke to the startling absence of Charlie's essence.

That sense of nearness, that feeling that he was closer to her than he'd been since he'd started following her siren's call, was gone. It was just gone.

He'd jumped to his feet in the cave where he'd spent the day, and for a few seconds, he panicked, pacing in circles like a crazy person, hands in his hair. And then he stopped himself, realized what he was doing. He was the most laid back person he knew. He didn't freak out.

I have to get to her. I have to.

Still, he forced himself to take a few deep breaths, stop acting like a human and use what he had. He didn't often have to. Oh, once in a while to avoid humans. Never to find one.

He moved out of the cave, out of the woods, onto the road where it was open and he could feel more. Then he stood there, closed his eyes and opened his mind.

Charlie. Charlie. I know you're out there somewhere. Charlie O'Malley. Make yourself known to me.

Suddenly he stopped, because he felt her. Not near. Far away and getting farther, but he felt her. She was still there, inside his head, just not as strongly as she'd been before.

Are you real? she whispered inside his head. *If you are, come and find me. I want to see you. Touch you. Know that I'm not losing my mind.*

Killian was stunned. Never had any human being ever spoken to him telepathically. He hadn't thought it was possible.

I'm coming, he told her, though he had no idea if she could hear him.

Now, hours later, he was following his sense of her along a mostly deserted stretch of forgotten road that ran more or less adjacent to I-84. He stopped in a spot where the trees thinned out and exposed the vast expanse of sky. There were crickets chirping like a symphony, birds calling out here and there. He heard an owl hoot, then a nighthawk's triumphant cry and the squeak of the mouse it had captured. He felt the breeze on his face and smelled a dozen piney scents and a thousand others. Tipping his head back, he looked at the stars. Galaxies upon galaxies.They made him feel small. And they made him feel alone. More alone than any person could ever have been.

He'd never been this lonely before her. He'd been so close... so close to her, only to have her run away.

But he was close again now.

A car door slammed, and a girl's voice, raised in what felt like frustration more than anger said, "Are you kidding me? This is the middle of *nowhere*."

And then he felt that very familiar buzz of awareness vibrating through his psyche, the one that was jacked up, more powerful than any he'd felt before.

"Is there even cell service out here?" asked the girl. It was Charlie. He was closer than he'd ever been, hearing her actual voice for the first time. The buzzing intensified, high pitched and vibrating in the base of his skull. He tipped his head back and shivered. What the hell *was* this?

Killian opened his senses wide, smelling, tasting the air, feeling her energy and honing in on it to the exclusion of everything else. He knew he'd be better off staying far from her, far from every human. But he couldn't help himself. Her emanations were racing up and down his spine in a rush of awareness that was sensual. Delicious. Arousing. Even more than they had already been, because he was so much closer now.

He followed his sense of her off the road and across a field of buttercups and Indian paintbrushes and tall lush grasses that brushed the legs of his jeans and sent puffs of pollen into the night air as he passed. Then he headed through a copse of small evergreens. Red pine, he thought. Their scent was so powerful, and his sense of smell so expanded that it nearly overwhelmed him—that redolence, that tang. He could *taste* it, the smell was so potent. But it was her smell that drew him.

He kept moving forward, but he was far from stealthy as the essence of *her* grew stronger the closer he got, until suddenly, she was everywhere around him and all through him. Her scent. The sound of her voice. The frequency of her soul, like a radio signal he was tuning in to. He was driven, like a hound on the scent, ignorant of everything else around him, walking through briars and not feeling their thorns, plowing through undergrowth instead of picking his way around it. He had to get closer. To see her. To touch her.

To taste her.

The bloodlust came to life inside him, so closely tied to sexual arousal in his kind that there was no separating the two. Feeding was an orgasmic experience for a vampire. Drinking blood from her, that would be explosive. And so he crept nearer to get a look at her and, he told himself, that was all he would do. But it felt like a lie.

CHAPTER TWO

"How long do you want me to stay here, anyway?" Charlie asked. "I mean, even you have to admit, Roxy, it's...kind of primitive." And she was afraid she would lose her fantasy dream guy by moving away from Portland. Hell, she'd been half-convinced he was going to show up on her doorstep at any moment.

Crazy. It was crazy. But he just felt so *real*.

They had driven all over the state of Oregon, by her estimation, only to end up here, a couple of hours east of the city at just a little after sundown. The roundabout route, Roxy said, was to make sure they were not followed. She was beginning to think the lady was a little bit crazy.

They parked her grandmother's aging gray pickup truck in an abandoned barn at least a mile away and then hiked through the forest to get to a small log cabin that blended into the surrounding trees so perfectly, you couldn't see it until you were on top of it.

Charlie's grandmother just kept unlocking the front door—

which took some time because there were so many locks on the damn thing. She didn't even respond to Charlie's question. Her hair was the color of a blood orange, Charlie thought, and a riot of curls. She had a killer figure under that kaftan, and until she'd shown up at her mother's apartment to take her away, Charlie hadn't ever even heard of her before.

She'd never known her father. Trish said he'd died before she was born. Cancer, she'd said.

Now she wondered if it was something else. Maybe he'd had Belladonna, too.

Roxy turned while putting away one key and fishing out another. She didn't smile, but she didn't scowl either. "Over the years, I've found that the more remote a location, the less likely someone's going to find me. But if you don't like it, just say the word. I've got several other places. This is just the closest one." She dropped the second key into her bag, then fished out a third.

"Hell, how many keys do you have for this place anyway?"

The ageless redhead leaned closer so Charlie could see the crow's feet at the corners of her eyes and the stripes of blue and green in her irises. "I know you don't want to be here, and you probably resent me for browbeating you into coming. But it's for the best."

She hadn't browbeat her into coming. Mainly, Charlie had agreed because she wanted to know why her grandmother was alive, and how she could beat this death sentence she'd just been handed. Period. It was worth serving a little time in the wilderness if it would save her life. The only conclusion she had reached since learning that her condition was fatal was that she was going to do whatever it took to make it not be. But the older woman was still talking, and she thought the pc thing to do would be to pay attention.

"You have the antigen, Charlotte. We both have it, and that makes life a whole different hill of beans for us. This place is in the middle of nowhere because if it wasn't, I'd be dead by now. Dead, Charlotte. As in rotting in the ground. And that's where you'll be before you can whistle Dixie, unless you do what I tell you."

Charlie was stunned. She opened her mouth, closed it again, blinked at this woman who could've been an older, wilder-haired version of herself, and nodded.

"Good. Now let's get our asses inside before we're seen." She pushed the wide wooden plank door open.

Charlie felt something–that unmistakable shiver-up-the-spine feeling you get when someone's staring at you, and immediately thought of her fantasy lover. She turned around and squinted into the dark forest, but of course she didn't see anything. Probably couldn't have if there had been an army out there.

But she still felt it. Eyes on her. Watching her. Her stomach clenched up in that funny, turned on way it did whenever she dreamed of him. Or thought of him.

If only he was real.

She hefted her bag up onto her shoulder and followed her grandmother inside.

The living room was alive with plants and birds in cages. Not parrots or cockatiels but regular birds, like you'd see flitting around outside. Robins and sparrows and the like. And in a giant, man-sized cage in the corner, there was an owl who stood as tall as a toddler. It perched on a broken limb that had been wedged into its cage and stared at Charlie with huge golden eyes. As she stared back, the creature blinked sideways, making Charlie jump a little.

"Who?" asked the owl.

"Charlie, that's who," she told it, with a wry look at her grandmother.

Roxy did not appear to get the joke. "It's all right, Olive, I'm back. And I'm sorry. I was as quick as I could be." She looked back at Charlie, still standing just inside the door staring at the owl. The owl stared back.

"Well, go ahead and take a look around," Roxy said. "My room's at the end of the hall. Yours is the door on the right, just before it. The one on the left is the bathroom. The basement's off limits until I say otherwise. Things down there require explaining. Got it?"

"Sure. Fine. Dare I ask if you even have internet out here?"

Her grandmother laughed softly, like some kind of rustic villain. "You'll be surprised at what I have out here. Go on to your room and unpack or something. I've got to feed the birds and make us some dinner. And then...then we'll talk."

Charlie sighed and walked through the living room-slash-aviary into a hallway filled with photographs of boys and men...and then she realized they were all the same person. A baby, a toddler, a little boy, a teenager, a young man. She knew him. He had brown hair and brown eyes with thick lashes that didn't change, no matter how old he was in each shot.

She blinked at the photos and felt a lump in her throat.

Then she heard soft footsteps in the hall and turned to see her grandmother looking at her from the end of it. "Your father," she said softly. "He had the antigen, too. Died young from it. Too young."

"My father." Charlie stared at the most recent looking shot of the beautiful man. She'd seen his face only in the very few photos her mother had of him, and they were all pretty much the same. She knew his name was Charles. She'd been named after him. Her mother didn't like to talk about him.

"Are you okay, Charlotte?"

She turned her head, looked at the grandmother she'd never known about, and felt a little bad for being ungrateful and uncooperative. "I don't know what's going on. I'm an adult. I need to know why all this is happening. It's my life, after all."

The older redhead nodded slowly. "You're right. It is your life, and you do need to know. A lot of things. We'll have a long talk about it as soon as I've fed the birds and thrown some dinner on for us. You like steak?"

Her stomach rumbled. "I guess."

"So unpack and we'll eat. And talk."

Charlie nodded. "Okay." She started down the hall, then turned and said, "What should I call you?"

"Gram, or Roxy. I'm not particular, as long as you never call me old." Then she turned in a flutter of her kaftan and a jingle of jewelry and headed back into the living room.

Charlie continued down the hall pausing in front of the doorway of her assigned room. Holding her breath in case it was horrible, she turned the knob and went inside.

But it wasn't bad at all. The cream colored carpet was so thick her sock-feet left prints in it. There was a great big window on one end, covered by cheerful curtains the same color, and the walls were a soft green. Charlie slung her backpack onto the comfy looking bed and opened the closet door. Racks of jeans, blouses, sweaters, and jackets filled it, and there were a half dozen cubby holes on one side, every one of them holding a pair of shoes.

Frowning, she closed the closet and turned to check out the giant dresser, opening one drawer after another. Underwear, bras, socks, pajamas, workout clothes, sweats. You name it, her brand new grandmother had apparently thought of it. And she'd apparently had some time to plan for Charlie's visit. She picked up one of the bras and looked at the tag. Her size. Exactly.

Okay, so her Grandmother had made an effort. But this was still going to be hell, and she just didn't think it was necessary. The vampires were probably all dead. The government said so. And if she really needed some kind of protection, then weren't they the best people to do it?

She went to the window and pushed open the curtains. Moonlight spilled through, but it was broken up...by the bars on the outside.

"What the hell...?"

And then she damn near jumped out of her skin, because there was someone out there. He ducked out of sight when she first glimpsed him, but she was sure he was there, just inside the edge of the woods, beyond the little clearing that passed for the cabin's lawn. Could it be him? Could he be real, after all? And if he was, how had he found her way out here? And how was it possible to have a dream love affair with someone she'd never met?

She opened the window but couldn't lean out. At least the fresh air could waft in. And it smelled heavenly. Breathing it in, she searched for him, her heart yearning to see him out there. And not just because that would mean she wasn't going crazy. But because she wanted to see him. In person, not just in her dreams.

She saw no one.

And yet she *felt* someone—him, she thought—out there. And that sense of longing for him stirred to life again inside her, stronger than ever before. She strained her eyes to see him again. But nothing. Nothing. And still, she sat there, staring into the darkness, and kind of lost track of the time ticking by.

"Charlotte?"

She didn't turn right away, didn't answer, still enthralled, sort of. Then her grandmother was tapping on her bedroom door and calling her name again. Sighing, she closed the window and went to open it. "Why are there bars on my window?"

Her grandmother sighed. "There are bars on mine, too, and the bathroom. The ones on the front of the house haven't been installed yet. They're for protection, Charlotte. I need to keep us safe. Now come on and eat."

Apuseni Mountains, Transylvania

A few survivors of the Vampire Armageddon had taken up residence in a haven that had first been a castle and later a hotel. Abandoned and left to fall to ruin, it stood amid the black, craggy mountains overlooking a Transylvanian village so small and remote that Rhiannon didn't know its name. She wasn't sure it had one. The mountains did. They were the Apuseni to some. The Occidentali to others. In English, the Mountains of the Sunset. A fitting refuge for a group of night-dwellers. Fortunes had been spent hiring mortal workers to restore the place to its earlier splendor. The rumor they'd leaked to the locals was that it was owned by a wealthy family from the Middle East and perpetually filled with guests seeking seclusion. People left them alone. No one suspected the castle housed a horde of the Undead.

But now, some of the residents of what the fledglings jokingly called "The *Real* Hotel Transylvania" were becoming restless.

Rhiannon stroked Pandora's soft fur, standing at the railing of the hotel's second floor and looking down over it into the Great Room where a crowd had gathered. The chandelier in the center, higher, even than the railing where she stood, was both priceless and beautiful. A half ton of Austrian crystal teardrops glittered and threw rainbows everywhere.

Roland stood beside her, and while she tried to watch the goings on below, she had trouble keeping her gaze from him. She never tired of the sheer male beauty that was her beloved. His hair was raven's wing dark and pulled back into what he still called a queue. He wore a suit, a formal one, and whenever he went about by night, one of his dramatic black cloaks embraced him and wafted out behind him like a dark comet's tail. He bore the strong jaw and aristocratic nose of his forebears, nobility, all of them. Indeed, Roland looked noble. He looked like a prince with striking blue-black eyes that were almost electric and lashes so dark one could easily believe he wore liner and mascara. He wore neither.

And he was the only man Rhiannon had ever known who was worthy of her.

Reluctantly, she shifted her gaze again to the group in the former lobby below. They all stood around Devlin, a mere century old pup who thought himself a pit bull. "It's enough, I tell you," Devlin said to the crowd of relative fledglings gathered around him. "Enough of hiding out here in these barren mountains. Enough of letting the mortal bastards tell the world they've wiped us out entirely, then resurrect us in the minds of all just long enough to blame us for their crimes against their own kind!"

Around him, the other vampires murmured, nodding hard.

Devlin was a big man. His mortal ancestry had been Samoan, African American, and Polynesian, and the combination was, Rhiannon had to admit, sexy as hell. Of his immortal ancestry, she knew nothing. He wore his hair short, cropped close to his head, and his skin was coppery and taut. He could've been a body builder or a movie star. And he had the charisma to go with his looks. Not that he held a candle to her Roland.

"I say we fight back," he went on. "I say we come out of hiding and retake our rightful place in the world of night. Let the mortals keep the day. The night is ours!"

The muttering around him grew louder.

"What makes you think it will be any different this time?" Roland asked the question in his usual strong, but utterly calm tone, drawing every eye upward to where he and Rhiannon stood. "As soon as the mortal world realizes we haven't all been extinguished after all, they'll put every resource they have into finishing the job."

"Maybe not." The voice was from one of the females. A mere fledgling, created in the days just prior to the war of 2011, in which most of her kind had been killed. She looked up at Rhiannon, her face lily white against her short, dark hair. "Even before I found you all, there were a lot of people questioning the morality of that war."

"Only," Rhiannon said, "because the idiots murdered so many of their own." During the war, anyone with nocturnal tendencies was at risk of being burned alive while they slept. Many, many humans had been killed in that way.

"No, it's more than that–" The girl, Rhiannon thought her name was Larissa, clapped a hand to her mouth and widened her eyes, shifting them between Rhiannon and the black panther at her side.

Rhiannon smiled inwardly, glad she hadn't lost her touch. The youngsters were impulsive and naive. It was good they feared her a little. It kept them in line. And keeping them in line kept them alive. "Go on, fledgling. Complete your thought."

The girl swallowed hard, nodded. "You were already here," she said. "You couldn't have known. But the media were lamenting that our entire race had been wiped out before mankind had a chance to know us, to talk to us, to study us."

"Believe me, child, they've *studied us* quite thoroughly." Rhiannon had been a DPI captive. She knew what they were capable of inflicting in the name of their science.

"I'm just saying that not all humans are out to annihilate us. We might have more allies among them than we think."

Rhiannon looked at Roland. *What do you think about that? Could the fledgling be right?* She spoke mentally but kept her thoughts shielded from the others in the room.

He said, aloud, "That might be the case. But if it's true, those humans are certainly in the minority. And the way for us to find them isn't to reveal ourselves so their fellow humans can kill what's left of us."

"You're right," Devlin called. "The way to find out is to fight back. We strike those who were responsible for the war in the first place. Those who are now murdering The Chosen and blaming it on us." He shook the newspaper that he held in his fist as he said it. The story of the Portland Seven had only just reached them there in the wilds of Transylvania.

"We must send a powerful message that we will not run

and hide!" Devlin said. "If there are supporters among the mortals, we offer our protection. If there are detractors, we feed on them until there are no more."

A shout went up from the crowd. Rhiannon's blood stirred, and she had to clench her jaw to keep from joining in the rapidly growing bloodlust. Because for all her beloved's confident caution, she felt, down deep, that Devlin was right.

Roland held up his hands until they quieted. "The elders will discuss your suggestions, Devlin," Roland said. "We're already considering every possible response to what's happened, and we're in the process of gathering intelligence now. We will let you know what is decided by this time tomorrow evening."

"With all due respect, Roland, I don't remember asking *the elders* to decide anything for me," Devlin said. A few gasped. A few others nodded in agreement.

There was mutiny afoot, and that was dangerous to all of them.

"We hide here in this desolate place," Devlin went on, "living on animal blood and growing weaker month after month, while you and your fellow *elders* rest in your penthouse suites and decide what's best for us. We're *vampires*, damn it. We have a right to decide for ourselves—"

"Enough!" Rhiannon moved her hand ever so slightly, and Pandora leapt the railing and hit the rebel like a wrecking ball, knocking him flat and holding him by the throat, growling softly.

To her shock and surprise, though, Devlin flung the cat off him, sprang to his feet, and stared into Pandora's eyes until, after a long tense standoff, Pandora sat down. Rhiannon rolled her eyes. *Even my cat thinks he's right,* she told Roland, carefully keeping her thoughts shielded from the others. And yet she could not tolerate rebellion.

Aloud, she said, "If you'd like to leave here, then leave. If you'd like to stay, then learn to respect your Elders."

She snapped her fingers and Pandora got up, ran to the

nearest of the two curving staircases and up them to retake her place at Rhiannon's side.

Everyone was looking at Rhiannon as Devlin stared her down. "We're still at war," he said. "We can't just let them murder The Chosen. We're supposed to protect them."

"And protect them we will," Rhiannon said. "Acting as one. United. With a plan of action in place. Not by fighting among ourselves and going off half-cocked, without a clue as to the outcome."

Roland placed a calming hand on her shoulder. "The elders will discuss your suggestions, Devlin," Roland repeated. "We feel hasty action would be disastrous. We're only delaying in order to gather as much information as we can to avoid doing something that could prove to be the end of us. That outcome would leave no one to protect The Chosen." Then he turned, taking Rhiannon's hand. She walked with him along the semi-circle hall that overlooked the great room. It had a door on either end that led to the guest rooms. Theirs was a corner suite.

"I should have let her kill him," Rhiannon said.

"Except that you agree with him."

"Not the point, my love," she replied. "He's stirring up revolt. He has no respect, no manners and a fiery temper. You're right about him. He's going to be trouble."

"It's a rare occasion when you tell me I am right about anything," he said softly.

"Enjoy it, then," she suggested with a kiss on his chin, which turned into a playful nip before she released him.

"The sooner we decide what to do about the humans' latest offenses, the better." Roland paced, deep in thought.

"I don't think Devlin will wait for us to decide," she said softly. "He fancies himself a leader, and he's stirring up a hornet's nest. I made matters worse, I suppose."

He nodded. "Probably. But it's good he knows he's not the only one with a fiery temper. He'll wait the night, I think. He'll wait to see what we decide. And then if he doesn't like it, he'll make his move."

Roland had an irritating habit of often being right about things, though he never insisted Rhiannon acknowledge that. Sighing, she said, "Have we heard back from any of our mortal contacts? Max and Lou Malone? Or Roxanne, by chance?"

"Not yet," Roland said. But she knew he felt the emotions of the others within the castle walls, just the same as she did. And he added, softly, "I hope they get in touch soon."

"I hope so too. And I hope Devlin doesn't push me too far," Rhiannon said softly. "There are too few of us left for me to relish having to kill one of our own."

CHAPTER THREE

Charlie dug into her supper with gusto. She couldn't remember when she'd been so hungry. Then again, she couldn't remember the last time she'd sat down to a rare steak. The meat was pink, going on red in the center, and she'd been prepared to complain about that, but Roxy had interrupted before she'd said a word. "One bite. *Then* tell me you prefer it less rare."

Charlie's usual diet consisted of anything microwavable, any kind of chips, and vats of diet soft drinks. Her mom, overprotective as she was, had never been the domestic goddess type. She didn't cook, hadn't taught Charlie to cook either. And really, junk food was good. So why bother?

What her grandmother had put in front of her was a giant hunk of rare meat with a salad on the side.

She took the first bite, though, as instructed, thinking she'd have to make the woman a grocery list if she was going to survive out here. And something inside her seemed to wake up and growl for more.

She took another bite, and another, and stopped herself after the third, because she realized she was eating like a starved pit bull and her grandmother was watching her with a smile on her face. Embarrassed, she finished chewing, swallowed, took a sip of water, and sat back in her chair.

"Your body knows what it needs. You haven't been getting enough protein," Roxy said.

Frankly, Charlie was amazed. Hell, she'd dabbled in vegetarianism only two years ago.

"It's important you get as strong as you possibly can. I know you don't realize how much danger you're in, Charlotte. But I do. If you have to fight, I want you able to do it."

"Fight?" She blinked, tried to resist finishing off the steak, and took a dainty bite of the salad instead. "I haven't got a clue how to fight. Mom freaked out if I even got my hands dirty."

"She lost your father. She's afraid of losing you, too." Roxy shrugged. "But don't worry. I'm going to teach you."

"To fight." She said it flatly, didn't make it a question.

Roxy nodded.

Charlie said, "And all this?" She waved her fork in the air. "All this off the grid living is just because you have the antigen?"

Roxy nodded. "Yes."

"I was born with it, though, and I've been doing just fine *on* the grid," Charlie countered. "Why are you suddenly so concerned about my safety? If I've been safe out there living my own life with my own mother for the past twenty years, why is it suddenly different?"

"Because things have changed." Her grandmother sighed. "You saw the letter from the government that requires everyone with your blood type to come in and register with them?"

Charlie had popped another piece of steak into her mouth. She was listening and chewing. She remembered how scared her mom had looked when she'd read the letter. "It was more of an invitation than a requirement," she pointed out. "And they didn't say anything about *registering*."

"It was an order. Had you replied with thanks, but no thanks, you'd have learned that the hard way."

"Yeah? So what would've happened if I'd said yes, instead?" she asked, unable to resist one last bite.

"Then when you showed up for that appointment, they would've inserted an electronic chip into your body, allowing them to track your location and monitor your vital signs."

The meat slid down her throat and stopped. Charlie started choking. Roxy got up, came around behind her chair, and slammed her back until the chunk flew from her mouth. Charlie held up a hand to signal her to stop and guzzled more water. When she could breathe again, she said, "Are you shitting me?"

"No, Charlotte, I'm not shitting you. This is what I've been hearing from my...sources. A few have dropped off the map, and no one's saying where they've gone. Young, strong ones, like you. That's why I hacked into the government's system and changed your blood type to A positive."

She set her glass down. "Then what happens to me if I get hurt or need a transfusion or something and they give me the wrong blood? Wouldn't that kill me?"

"They always type and cross-match before giving transfusions. I've worked as a nurse before. Trust me."

"You're a nurse?"

Roxy tilted her head to one side. "I said I'd worked as a nurse. Not that I am one."

So she'd impersonated a nurse? What the hell? It dawned on Charlie that her grandmother had claimed for the second time now, that she knew how to hack into government mainframes. "How do you know how to do that?" she asked. "Hack into systems, change data?"

"Experience," she said. "And necessity."

Who the hell *was* this woman? No typical grandmother,

that was for sure.

"I did the same to my own government records."

"Because you have the antigen, too," she whispered. Then she swallowed hard and asked the question that was foremost on her mind, the one she'd been itching to ask ever since she'd first met the woman. "Mom said that people with the antigen never live much past their thirties."

"People with the antigen *rarely* live past their thirties," Roxy replied. "But you can see that I have."

"Why?"

Roxy shrugged. "I don't know. I wish I did."

"Does that mean that I will, too?"

"I don't know that, either. But I do know there's a reason I've lived this long. A purpose. And I think that purpose might've been you, Charlotte. I believe the reason I'm still alive is to make sure you survive and thrive. To keep you safe. And everything I do, hacking your records, bringing you here, the bars on the windows and the trip wires outside of this house, all of it, is to that end. Understand?"

"So wait." Charlie put down her fork. "Are you saying that you're protecting me from...from the government? Not from some stray surviving vampire that might hunt me down for a tasty snack?"

Roxy said, "That's right."

"So I'm just supposed to stay here, hiding in the woods for the next ten to fifteen years and then drop dead? I'm supposed to stop living now instead of then?"

Roxy smiled. "We only need to keep to ourselves for a few weeks. Just long enough to be sure no one noticed my little updates to your records. Once we're sure of that, it'll be safe for you to reintegrate into your life again. It's not forever, Charlotte. It's just for now."

Charlie thought any time away from her life was time she couldn't afford to give up. If she only had thirty-five years, she wanted to live every minute of it. She opened her mouth to make that argument but saw her grandmother's green eyes go very wide, and followed them to see what she was looking at.

A red light was flashing on and off over the front door and a *soft bing-bing-bing* was sounding.

"Someone's out there!" Roxy jumped out of her chair so fast it tipped over behind her.

Maybe it's him, Charlie thought. Maybe it's him.

Roxy ran into the living room, opened a closet and pulled out a shotgun.

A freaking shotgun! And that wasn't all that was in there.

"There's a safe room in the basement. Go. *Now!* "

She couldn't. God, she couldn't let her shoot him! "You said not to go to the basement."

"Go, dammit. Lock yourself in. Don't wait for me." Then she opened the front door and stepped outside in the dark, all alone. A grandmother with a shotgun.

Maybe Roxy was crazier than Charlie had even begun to think. Then again, Charlie thought, she was the one who was afraid her grandmother was going to shoot her imaginary lover. Maybe craziness ran in the family.

Killian had ducked into the forest when Charlie had glanced out her barred window at him. He'd stood with his back pressed against the bark of a tree, his hand pressed to his chest, and watched her looking for him. And God, it was such a rush to see her, in the flesh, rather than just feel her invading his mind. It was so good. Pale skin like porcelain. Vivid red hair.

He could not be seen, he knew that. If the humans knew he was alive, they would hunt him down and kill him. Just like they'd done with every other vampire in the world. And yet, he couldn't stay away from her.

He stayed there, pressed to the towering sugar pine for

a full minute, feeling the bark against his back, smelling the pines and a thousand other scents wafting his way on the night. There were squirrels and chipmunks and deer and bear. There were flowers and berries and the leaves and needles of a dozen different trees. And there was her. Above all else, there was her.

He'd never felt anything as powerful as his sense of her. Like a magnet, she drew him. And it was stronger now that he was closer.

When he thought enough time had passed, he'd peeked around the tree's massive trunk again. His jacket peeled away from the bark in a way that told him it had sticky pine sap on it. God, it smelled good.

The barred window was empty now. And he couldn't help but move closer. He wanted to see her again. He should leave, he knew that. Avoiding humans at all costs was the only thing that had kept him alive this long. But he had to see her again before he did. Maybe up close. Maybe close enough to touch her. Or more. It didn't make any sense, it wasn't safe. It was suicidal, in fact.

And yet he had no choice. He could not resist this power, whatever it was, pulling him to her. It was like the lure of a drug to an addict. And it dragged him just as surely, just as recklessly, closer.

He smelled red meat, guessed the women were eating. He could get closer to the cabin if he approached from the side of it where she'd been looking out the window at him. Maybe he could slide to another window and get a glimpse of her inside. He decided he would move rapidly across the clearing between the redolent pine forest and the log cabin. He wouldn't be seen. He wasn't an old vampire, and he'd had nothing but animal blood for months. There wasn't a lot of strength in him. But even minimal speed in a vampire rendered them invisible to the human eye. He crouched beside the tree, taking one last look around him and at the house to be sure he was undetected.

And then he ran.

He barely felt the trip wire graze his shin before it snapped beneath his power. He skidded to a stop so suddenly that his feet sent topsoil folding up in front of him, then switched directions and sprinted back into the woods.

The humans inside the house were emanating fear and alarm. Well, one of them was. From Charlotte, he felt eagerness, worry about him, and a longing that sang to his soul. And then the front door opened, and a woman came out. Flaming red curls, a mature face, and the heart, he sensed, of a lioness. She cradled a double barreled shotgun.

She was one of The Chosen. Which was bizarre, because they didn't get to be her age. They always died young, unless they were turned.

He tore his eyes from her and looked toward the spot where his carelessness had torn up the lawn. It was around the side of the house. If she came out to explore, she would see it. Backing into the forest, he opened his senses. He needed a scapegoat, and he needed it fast.

Charlie didn't go to any safe room in the basement. She went to that closet off the living room instead, and opened it and looked inside. It was lined with weapons. Guns hung in neat rows up and down its walls, crossbows in various sizes, stun guns, axes, knives and other implements she couldn't even identify. Shelves were piled high with ammunition. She closed the closet door, stunned, and went to the window to watch her grandmother tiptoeing around outside with that giant shotgun in her arms. Roxy was completely paranoid, and she was going to shoot her new boyfriend before Charlie even had the chance to meet him.

She went back to her bedroom, climbed up onto the bed

and opened the curtains, staring outside into the darkness. The bedroom light was off, so she could see the night and the forest a little better. There didn't seem to be anything out there except some torn up ground. But she was sure she hadn't imagined the person she'd seen out there earlier. Maybe she'd imagined that it was *him*, but there had definitely been someone.

Something came crashing through the trees so suddenly that she jumped to her feet, backing up a few steps. Then she saw that it was just a deer. It galloped halfway to the cabin and then stopped, standing there with its eyes wider than wide, breathing through a slightly open mouth and flaring nostrils. As she stared, it lifted one front hoof and slammed it into the ground repeatedly.

She heard her grandmother come back inside. At least she thought it was her grandmother. The front door closed. "Charlie?" she called.

Yes. It was her. Charlie reached up to close the window, but just as her hand touched it, she felt something. Just like before. An awareness of another presence, combined with a sensation like warm honey running down her spine, and a pull that was all too familiar to her. A pull that made her want to get closer. It was him, it had to be.

But there was no one out there except the deer, its coat deep red in the darkness, its eyes like brown gemstones, shining. One ear flicked twice. Then its white tail flashed upright, and it bounded on its way, past the cabin and into the woods on the other side.

"Charlie?"

"I'm in here." She closed the window and then the curtains. God, was she imagining all of this? It would almost be scarier to find out she wasn't. Because if this was real, it was fucking weird.

Roxy came to the bedroom door. "I told you to go to the basement."

"I was going to. I came to get...." She looked around the room, spotted a book on the bedside table. "Something to read," she said. "And then I saw a deer on the lawn and realized that's probably all it was."

Roxy narrowed her eyes. She looked kind of dangerous that way, and her voice was deep and low, but trembling when she spoke again. "Next time I tell you to get into the safe room, you damn well better get into the safe room."

Charlie couldn't find words to reply. Her grandmother's personality had shifted into someone she didn't recognize. Not that she knew the woman anyway, but up until now, she'd seemed...harmless.

This Roxy seemed downright dangerous.

Was she even sane?

Was Charlie really safe here at all?

Killian couldn't leave. He tried, three times he tried to turn and walk back through the forest to the stretch of highway to resume his endless wandering, but each time, he'd failed. So he gave in, and he went back.

There was a reason. It probably had something to do with being a vampire. He was painfully aware of how much knowledge he lacked about his own nature. None of his former gang had been old. None of them had known the secrets of their kind. They'd lived by trial and error, learning fast that the day sleep was inevitable and irresistible and that you'd better damn well find shelter before it took you, because sunlight burned. They'd learned through experience that any injuries they might sustain would heal during the day sleep as long as they didn't kill you before it came. They learned that bleeding out was a constant risk if you were cut, and that vampiric bodies were extremely flammable. He knew his senses, all of them, were a thousand times as honed as they had been before, when he'd still been a human. Pleasure was intensified. So was pain. Pain could become debilitating in his kind, and the older the vampire, the more exaggerated all of those things became. He was stronger and faster, too. And he could hear things, if he focused. The thoughts of humans near him, but they often came all at once, a cacophony that was impossible to bear. He could even take control of some creatures' minds, as he'd done with the deer. It was harder with people, and he'd had very little call to try it, but it could be done. And yet there he was, pacing the forest floor in the dead of night, watching that sleepy little cabin as if his life depended on it, longing for another glance of the beautiful redhead through the barred window of her bedroom. Its light had long since gone out.

And then, before his eyes, the cabin's front door opened, and she was there.

Her hair was long and wavy, with side swept bangs over huge blue-green eyes. She wore blue plaid pajama pants and a pink top that didn't meet them, so her middle was exposed. Soft flesh. He wanted to touch it. He wanted to taste it.

She stood on the stoop for a moment, rubbing her arms and looking around. And then she stepped into the grass, her bare feet sinking deep. He opened his mind and heard her thoughts, and they were so much louder and clearer than all the other sensations he usually blocked out, that it was easy for him to focus on her and her alone.

I know I saw someone. I wonder if he's still out here. I wonder why I can't stay inside like any sane person would. God, I'm in grave danger, if my alarmist, conspiracy theorist grandmother is to be believed. So why am I traipsing around in the middle of the night looking for someone who only exists in my dreams, as if he could be real and—Careful. Trip wire.

She stopped walking, got down on her hands and knees in the grass and peered closely. He was lured from his place within the trees as surely as if she was a magnet and he was steel. He moved slowly, silently, and then he stopped near her, spotting the trip wire easily in the grass with his preternatural vision.

"It's an inch in front of your pinky finger."

She gasped and sprang upright, then stood there staring up at him. She was short, barely five two, he guessed. The skin of her face was flushed, and he could feel the warmth of her.

He's real ohmygod he's real.

He smiled a little, hearing her thoughts just as clearly as if she'd spoken them out loud. And then she got a little scared.

Can this really be happening? What is this?

"It's okay," he said. "I'm not going to hurt you."

Her wide eyes lowered. "Pssht. You couldn't if you tried."

"Tough, are you?"

"The toughest."

He knew it was a lie. The words she said were things she wished could be true but knew were not. She'd always wanted to be tough. To be strong. But she believed herself weak and fragile instead. He got all of that as he stood there, connecting to her even more strongly than he had before, feeling everything she felt—including her attraction to him.

She looked at him intently, her eyes moving over his face like a caress. Inwardly, she thought, *He's the most beautiful man I've ever seen. Can you say that about a guy? There's just no other word. If I tell him I've been making love to him in my dreams, over and over, will he think I'm a lunatic and go back to wherever he came from?*

Aloud, she said, "Who are you, and what are you doing lurking around outside my grandmother's cabin?"

"My name is Killian," he said. He hadn't looked into a mirror in years and was self-conscious under her scrutiny. He knew his hair was curly and brown and longer than the norm. His eyes had been dark, dark blue, once. He didn't know if they'd changed. He'd seen other vampires' eyes glow red when the bloodlust was upon them. He feared his would do the same if he stayed near her much longer.

"I'm Charlie," she said. *I want to touch his hair. It looks so soft.*

He nodded. "I was passing by on the highway, and I heard voices."

"Passing by on your way to where?"

He shrugged. "Nowhere in particular. I kind of wander."

"Free spirit, huh?" she asked and smiled for the first time.

It took his breath away when she smiled. "You could call it that."

"So why are you lurking in the woods, watching me, Killian?" *Have you been dreaming about me too? God, please say you have.*

But he couldn't, not without giving himself away. Could he? "I don't really know that, either. Once I saw you I couldn't seem to leave."

I feel the same way. It's like we're connected, like he's someone I've known forever, someone important to me. Vital. Past life, maybe? Maybe that's why I've been dreaming of him.

"Wow. That's like the best line I've ever heard. You're good."

"I am," he said. "Good." He was trying to reassure her but wasn't sure it was working.

She nodded. "I can tell. I'm just glad you're here. I know that probably sounds..." She shrugged, let her voice trail off, then turned to look back at the cabin. "Listen, my grandmother has this place wired for sound. She's both paranoid and armed. Not a safe combination for guys who like to lurk in shadows. If she finds you out here, she'll probably shoot first and ask questions later."

"I picked up on that earlier," he said.

She nodded. "The trip wire. It was you, wasn't it?"

"Yes."

"I think she's a little bit crazy."

He had gathered that she thought so. And more. She was thinking that she didn't want him to go away, and she was wondering what it would be like to kiss him.

He didn't dare do that, though the notion set him on

fire. He hadn't fed tonight. His skin was cold to the touch. Any physical contact could give him away. And yet physical contact was what he longed for. She'd at least dreamed of it. His dreams, vampire dreams, had been a mosaic. Bits and pieces. Flashes of jigsaw puzzle parts, but they'd left him just as hungry for her.

"Why are you really here, Killian?" she asked him.

"I don't know." He swayed a little closer to her as if pulled by her force. "But I'm not leaving."

"Why not?"

Because of me, because of me, because of me, I know it is, he heard her think.

"Because of you," he said. He stared into her eyes and felt her reaction to that. Surprise, a little ripple of alarm that he'd said aloud exactly what she'd been thinking. But she was also glad. "Your grandmother thinks you're in danger?"

"Yes." She sighed, nodded, paced past him to the tree he'd been hiding behind, and then sat down, putting her back against it.

He sat down beside her, knowing she wanted him to, and his shoulder, his hip, his thigh touched hers. Everything in him sang with need and hunger and lust.

"You heard about the vampire uprising?" she asked.

Every cell in his body reacted with so much shock that he was sure it must show. He forced himself not to react, tried to school his face to reveal nothing, and keeping his eyes away from hers, he said, "I've been on the road. No TV, no newspaper. I thought...I thought all the vampires were dead."

"Yeah, so did we all. But seven people got their blood sucked out of them last week and a gang of vampires was hunted down and killed for it."

The joy, the elation he'd felt so briefly, came crashing down and shattered into a million glittering shards. There had been other vampires...and now there were not. They'd been killed.

"They're saying that was the last of them, but even the

government admits that if they were wrong once—"

"They might be wrong again," he said softly. "There could be others." His heart seemed to expand with hope. There had been surviving vampires. There had to be more. Had to be. He wasn't alone. He wasn't the last of his kind after all.

He looked at her, overwhelmed with joy and relief and hope. Not only had he found her tonight, but he'd learned that he was not alone. And she'd brought him that news. She was... a beacon in the darkness of his endless night.

And then he saw her frowning at his apparent joy and quickly looked away as he realized it was the vampires she was afraid of. "I don't understand," he said, to change the subject. "Why does your grandmother feel that you're in danger if the government says all the vampires are dead?"

"Because she's a fucking lunatic?" She averted her eyes. He tried to hear her thoughts, but she'd closed her mind as if drawing a window shade over it.

And yet it made no sense for her to be afraid. Vampires protected her kind. They didn't hunt them. This was all backwards. But maybe she didn't know that.

He sensed her grandmother stirring awake inside the cabin, and it interrupted his thoughts. He didn't want to cause Charlie trouble. And he didn't want the shotgun wielding crazy woman to find out about his presence.

"Charlie, I think your grandmother's waking up. You'd better get back inside."

She frowned, looking back at the cabin. "How do you know that? Did you hear something or—"

By the time she looked his way again, he was closer, and before he could talk himself out of it again, he grabbed her, pulled her close, and kissed her.

Charlie was stiff in his arms for about a full second. And then she just melted against him, wrapped her arms around him, and kissed him back. It deepened and lengthened until she was pressing her body tight to his, and he was grinding his hips against her as passion and bloodlust rose as one to consume him. He tasted her with his tongue, and she pressed even tighter to him, opening to him, wanting more, so much more, and telling him so with her body as well as with her mind.

And then she pulled away, blinking and gasping for air.

"I'm sorry," he said. He kept his eyes averted, sure they were glowing with hunger for her. Her scent twined around him, and the sound of the blood rushing through her veins thrummed in his head.

"I'm not sorry," she whispered. "I'm not sorry at all."

He blinked, stunned.

"Find someplace to get warm, Killian. You're freezing." And then she headed for the house.

Killian moved back into the forest then crouched in the shelter of the pines, invisible to her but still watching and still aroused to the point of near madness. He watched the sway of her hips as she jogged back toward the house. She turned to look back just before she opened the front door of the cabin. His eyes were riveted to the shape of her breasts underneath the thin fabric of her pink top, as she whispered loudly, "Tomorrow night, same time, okay?" Then she slipped quietly through the front door.

In the shelter of a giant sugar pine whose drooping boughs made a dome thirty feet in diameter, Killian lay down on his back on a mattress of aromatic needles. Every breath tasted and smelled of the tree. But on his lips, he still tasted her. Charlie.

He was not the last of his kind after all. If there had been one gang of vampires, even rogue bastards who'd murdered innocents, then there would be others. There had to be others. And he had to find them.

Just as soon as he could tear himself away from the girl in the cabin in the woods.

He was going to meet her again tomorrow night, he

told himself. He was going to feed just before, so his flesh would be warm with living blood and his hunger sated, so he wouldn't be tempted by the sound of her blood thrumming in her veins. He would touch her to his heart's content. And to hers. He would make her erotic dreams about him come true. There was no way around it. He had to have her.

The thought of it tormented him as he lay there. And then he decided that he couldn't wait for tomorrow night. He would visit her now, tonight, the minute she slept. He would visit her in her dreams, but this time, he would be fully aware of it, too.

CHAPTER FOUR

"Why were you outside?" Roxy asked.

Charlie jumped out of her skin. She had slipped back inside and was closing the door silently when her grandmother's voice came out of nowhere and scared her so badly she would probably have gray hairs by morning. Roxy was pulling on her bathrobe and coming up the hallway, and Charlie tried to wipe the guilty and slightly dreamy expression off her face and replace it with an indignant one.

"I couldn't sleep, and I went outside. Not that I should have to explain myself to you."

"Charlotte, I've told you how much danger you're in. If you don't listen to me, how am I supposed to–"

"I am an intelligent, adult woman, and if I want to get some night air and look at the stars, I'll damn well do it. You need to ease up on me, Roxy."

Her grandmother seemed taken aback by that. Pursing her lips, she brushed past Charlie to throw all the locks on the front door and re-set her silly alarm system, all the while staring through the door's window panes until her eyes should've bled.

"You don't trust me, do you?"

There was a chiming sound, and Roxy pulled a cell phone from her robe pocket, glanced at it, and then put it back. "No more than you trust me, Charlotte. Not yet, anyway."

Charlie hadn't been prepared for the blunt reply, and it hurt, even though it was probably deserved. She heaved the sort of sigh she hadn't heaved since she was sixteen and said, "I'm going to bed."

And that was what she did, not exchanging another word with her wanna-be jailer. If she didn't think Roxy might have some kind of inside knowledge about how she could extend her own lifespan, and maybe countless other things as well, she'd leave this place tonight.

Instead, she lay in her cell, tossing and turning until finally falling into a restless and fitful sleep. As soon as she did, he was there, invading her dreams.

Killian.

In the dream she was standing outside again, and he was there too, staring into her eyes. She could feel him reading everything that had ever happened to her and everything that ever would. And she was letting him and vaguely aware, in an abstract way, that she didn't have to. She could stop him, shut him out. But she didn't want to. She relaxed and let him explore to his heart's content. And then he withdrew from her mind, or that's what it felt like, and he was staring into her eyes again. And she could hear his thoughts, just as if he was speaking aloud, only...not. He said, *I've never felt anything like this before,* without even moving his lips.

She thought, *neither have I*, and he nodded as if he'd heard her.

Is this real?

Yeah, he told her. *Almost as real as it gets.*

He ran his hands over her face, through her hair, down her

neck.

I've dreamed of this before. Of you, of us, together.

I know you have, he told her. *I have too, but only in bits and pieces. This time I'm here. I'm here with you.*

You're real. I'm so glad you're real.

His hands were on her shoulders as they stood there, toe to toe, thigh to thigh, chest to chest. *I think we belong together,* his mind whispered to hers. *I think there's something bigger than either of us at work, here. There has to be for it to be this intense.*

I don't understand it, either. But I feel it too, Killian.

He kissed her, and it felt as real as when he'd kissed her outside, under the giant sugar pine. She was wrapped up in him, pressing against him, and suddenly they were both naked, even though they hadn't stopped kissing. Her breasts were crushed to his powerful chest, and her hands kept running over his shoulders and arms. They were strong. She loved the way they felt and wondered how it was she could feel something so physical in a dream, and then she decided to just enjoy it and stop questioning it. It was different from the other times she'd dreamed about him. Even more real.

His hands were all over her, her back, her thighs, her waist, and he kissed her like he was going to die if he stopped. She was sure she would. Bodies straining, they tumbled to the ground beneath the sheltering boughs of the big tree, their hips moving urgently, insistently And then she wrapped her legs around him, and pulled him closer, and felt him inside her, filling her, and it was real, dammit, it was more visceral than any dream had ever been.

I want this to be for real.

It is, Charlie. Trust me, it is.

How can it be? I'm dreaming. You're outside and I'm, I'm....

He moved harder, deeper, taking her breath away and leaving no doubt in her mind that this was real. She didn't know how, and she didn't care. It just was. And that was good enough. He was on top of her, and wrapped around her, and buried inside her mind and her heart, as well as her body. It felt like they were melding. She could feel everything he felt. His loneliness. His endless aching emptiness that only she could fill. His soul, she felt his soul, and it was the most beautiful thing she'd ever felt. And her physical sensations, her sensual pleasure, it was magnified a thousand times because it was mirrored back to her by his. Pretty soon she couldn't tell which feelings were his and which were hers, and he couldn't either. They were one.

It felt as if they always had been and always would be.

She screamed out loud at the pinnacle of it.

Her bedroom door burst open about the same time her eyes did. She laid there in her bed, naked under the covers, her whole body coated in sweat and shaking like a leaf. The rippling echoes of the orgasm that had just shattered her were still pulsing through her body. And her grandmother was standing in the doorway, looking at her with wide, questioning eyes and crazy hair.

"I'm okay," Charlie whispered. "It was a just a bad dream."

But it wasn't, she thought. It wasn't, it was good beyond endurance. And it wasn't a dream. It wasn't a dream at all.

Many hours later, Charlie woke to the sound of rain, and stretched her arms out to her sides, arching her back, smiling to herself, and slowly opening her eyes. She was surprised, for a nanosecond, not to find Killian in the bed beside her, his head on her pillow, smiling that sexy smile of his as the morning sun painted his face in light. Then she came more thoroughly awake and things became clearer. Her night with Killian had only been a dream, albeit the most vivid one yet. Because really, what else could it have been? And the rain she heard was actually the sound of the shower running.

She rolled over, pushing up onto her hands and knees in

the bed and opening the curtains, so she could look out the window, which she'd left open all night. Around her, the forest was coming alive. So many birds were singing so many tunes that it was chaotic and yet perfect. The captive birds in the living room were singing back to them, and it was beautiful and plaintive and filled with longing.

Like her longing for Killian.

Whatever this was, it was good for her. She'd slept like a baby for the first time in weeks. And she didn't wake up feeling groggy and hungover. She felt good.

The trees cast long shadows over the wildflower dotted clearing that was the cabin's lawn, the sun still low in the sky beyond them and inching inevitably higher.

There was no sign of Killian. And everything in her wanted to go running out there in search of him.

This whole thing wasn't exactly fair to him, though, was it? Not when he didn't even know how short a time she'd be residing on Planet Earth.

It was kind of stupid to think that way, though. It wasn't as if he could possibly be feeling this thing as strongly as she was.

Yes, he is.

Hell, *she* probably wasn't even feeling it as strongly as it seemed.

Yes, I am.

She'd only just learned she had a fatal condition and only a decade and a half to live, give or take. She'd been coerced into leaving her home and her job behind and coming out here to Cabin Goldilocks. And she'd been told she was in grave danger from something even worse than her deadly blood antigen, all in the space of a day.

But I've been dreaming of him for weeks.

It was no wonder her emotions were all skewed and overblown.

It's real. He's real. And what I'm feeling is real.

She got out of bed, pulled on the robe that had been

hanging on the bedpost, and then stopped to look down at the thing as she ran one hand over its sleeves. It was a black silk kimono with bright red flowers, and it was beautiful. Her grandmother must have bought it for her. Along with all the other stuff in the room. Could she really be all that bad?

No. But she *could be* completely insane.

Takes one to know one, right?

Charlie stepped out of her bedroom and saw that her grandmother's bedroom door, to her right at the end of the hall, was open. The bathroom door, directly across from Charlie's room, was closed and the shower was running. Roxy's phone was on her nightstand. Biting her lip, Charlie gave one last look at the bathroom door and then tiptoed into her grandmother's room, picked up the cell phone, and scrolled to the text messages to see who her grandmother had been talking to. She'd heard the text sound go off last night, so she knew there had been one.

Someone named Tamara who had no photo or avatar, had written, "What do u know?"

Roxy, who was identified as TOC replied: "Not a lot. 7 Chosen murdered. Gov enticing others to come in. Even claiming a cure."

Tamara: "Cure? For BD?"

Charlie's heart leaped at those words. A cure! Jeeze, could that be true?

TOC: "So they claim."

Tamara: "Reports of many of TC missing. We need 2 come in. Where r u?"

TOC: "Safe. In hiding w my Gr Dtr."

Tamara: "Granddaughter?"

TOC: "She's BD."

Tam: "Like u?"

TOC: "2 soon 2 tell. Maybe more."

Tam: "She know about us?"

TOC: "Can't tell her till she trusts me. She'll run. Already thinks I'm nuts."

The shower stopped running. There was more to the conversation, several more lines, but Charlie was out of time. She dropped the phone on the nightstand and jogged back into the hallway, making it just to her bedroom door when the bathroom door opened.

Roxy stood there looking at her, and then at her open bedroom door, and then at her again. "You're up early," she finally said.

Charlie forced a smile for the secretive woman, realizing how very little she knew about her. "Yeah, not used to all the birdsong. Especially when it's coming from the living room."

Her grandmother looked toward her bedroom again and Charlie looked too, noticing that the phone was nowhere near the same spot on the nightstand that it had been in before she'd picked it up. Did Roxy notice?

"I um...just love this robe," she said, heading for the kitchen. "Is there any coffee yet?"

"Not yet," Roxy said, but she didn't follow her. She went into her bedroom, and closed the door.

Charlie winced, certain her grandmother was checking her phone, and trying to remember if she'd closed out of the text message screen or left it open. Hell.

Texts from Roxy!
Tamara was rapping on the huge double doors of Rhiannon and Roland's suite, while sending her thoughts directly through them. Rhiannon rolled her eyes and imagined the curly haired wife of her husband's best friend Eric Marquand, bouncing up and down in her excitement. Tamara was not a fledgling, exactly. But she was childlike, exuberant and joyous enough to make Rhiannon gag from time to time. Family, though. She was family.

The sun had gone down half an hour ago, but Rhiannon had been in the mood to lie naked in Roland's strong arms for as long as possible before getting up to face another boring night in exile.

A message from one of her favorite mortals would at least break up the monotony. She slid out of bed, putting her bare feet on the freezing floor. As she stood and reached for her red satin robe, she felt Roland's eyes on her, felt his desire rising yet again, and smiled down at him.

"I love that you're such an insatiable beast," she whispered.

His smile was slow and sexy. "It's good I'm a vampire. You'd be the death of a mortal man."

"And have been. Repeatedly." She winked at him and walked into the suite's living room. Pandora got lazily out of her bed, a miniature of Rhiannon's own, canopy and all. She arched in a long and luxurious stretch, then padded along behind her. With a wave of her hand, Rhiannon opened the doors. "Come in, fledgling. We were hoping someone would interrupt our morning of sexual bliss with news from the mortal world."

Tamara took two steps into the suite, then stopped, her big eyes going rounder. "I'm sorry. I can come back later, if–"

"She's teasing you," Roland said, coming out of the bedroom himself, tying his own robe around him. "Come in. You too, Eric," he added, since Tamara's mate stood just behind her in the ornate hall.

Roland crossed to the French doors and opened them, then stepped out onto the stone balcony. "It's a beautiful night."

"It is." Tamara and Eric joined him, and Rhiannon followed last of all. Eric had an iPad in his hand and as he tapped its screen repeatedly, Roland caught Rhiannon's eyes and rolled his own, making her smile. She knew he'd prefer an *actual* tablet, the kind with paper, to the modern electronic devices called by the same name.

"Here it is," Eric said, handing the device to Roland. "The entire conversation."

"I reached her just before dawn, as we were lying down for the day sleep," Tamara explained. "Or I'd have brought it sooner. "She's in Oregon."

"Ten hours earlier there," Eric said, probably because he knew it from memory. The man was a genius.

Roland took the iPad, but carefully set it on the stone table. Then he read through the exchange, and Rhiannon read over his shoulder. Roland frowned, lifting his head. "Roxy has a granddaughter?"

"Apparently so. Though this is the first I've heard of it," Eric said. "Read on, Roland."

Nodding, Roland continued. "She thinks the girl doesn't trust her."

"Doesn't say why," Eric went on. "I believe the granddaughter must be by her deceased son Charles who died of Belladonna Syndrome at twenty-nine. I can only surmise that she's kept the girl's existence secret in order to protect her."

"It makes sense," Tamara said. "Roxy's helped us so many times, she's on the government's radar."

Rhiannon reached past her beloved to scroll lower, grinning inwardly that he probably had thought there was no more to see. "The government is trying to entice The Chosen into their care," Roland said. "Roxy has heard rumors they're even claiming they have a cure for the ravages of Belladonna."

"So do we," Rhiannon said softly.

Tamara obeyed Pandora's insistent head butting and pet the large cat. "We have to go back," she said. "If The Chosen are being targeted again, we have to–"

"Something's wrong!" Rhiannon went to the stone railing, bracing her hands on its surface and leaning into the wind. Sensations of fear, of agony, of death, reached into her senses, plucking discordant notes in the strings of her mind. She closed her eyes. "Do you feel it?"

Roland came to stand beside her just as the voices came

into her awareness. Human voices, screaming in pain and in fear, and a rush of bloodlust, not her own, but that of others of her kind. Vampires in ecstasy, gorging themselves on mortal blood.

"It's a massacre," Roland whispered.

Pandora growled deep and low, picking up on the energy of violence and death, and the smell of smoke rising now on the night wind.

"It's Devlin and his band of rebels," Rhiannon said. "They're attacking the village!"

Within minutes, they had dressed and raced on foot, at preternatural speeds, down from the mountains to the tiny village below. But there was no life left there. Others of their band were following behind them. But the four of them and Pandora arrived first. Rhiannon knew what she would find before she ever got there. Her senses told her there was fire and death. And that the vampires who had wrought it were already long gone.

The six or eight little houses along the winding, narrow street of the primitive village were going up in flames. Rhiannon shielded her face with her arms against the deadly heat of the fires and pressed on, walking amid the bodies that littered the unpaved road. Pale skin, poor clothes, gaping wounds in their throats. More than twenty, perhaps close to thirty innocent humans, dead. Devlin and his gang of vampires must have ravaged the poor villagers as they emerged from their burning houses. They lay in the dirt track of a road, their eyes wide and unseeing. They had not died in peace, but in terror.

The attack had been ruthless and savage, and it looked as if no one had been spared.

But then Rhiannon felt something. Life. There was fear, devastation, too, but mainly, there was life. She held a finger to her lips and the others went still and silent, following her as she moved away from the blazing village, toward the source of those feelings. The road was packed dirt. There was no sidewalk. The houses were mostly thatch-roofed cottages that could've come from another time. There were woods beyond the village, and the next one was miles away. But word would get out, if any had survived. Mortals would be coming. And soon.

Rhiannon moved silently, homing in on the life force that drew her into the trees, around the base of one, to a hollow formed by a big arching root. Quivering inside that hollow was a little girl, hugging her knees to her chest and shivering in the darkness.

The child didn't look up or sense her there, and Rhiannon didn't want her to. Though her heart was tightening into a hard little knot, she knew she was not the best person for this child to see when she opened her eyes again. Sometimes, her one and only regret stabbed deeply, and this was one of those times. She would never have a child of her own. A little girl to raise in her own image. It was a ridiculous regret. She'd have made a terrible mother.

Silently, she called Tamara, who looked more like a modern day teenager than a relatively young vampiress. Tam came to her side, saw what she saw, and made a soft "Oh!"

And then she was on her knees, gathering the little girl into her arms. "It's all right, honey. It's all right, I've got you. I've got you."

The girl babbled in a Romanian dialect. Rhiannon knew every word, not because she spoke the language, but because she could read the emotions behind it. *Monsters came. They killed everyone. But they didn't kill me and I don't know why.*

Everything in her wanted to hold that little girl close, to comfort her the way Tamara was doing. But that sort of thing was best left to the tender hearted. Not the fierce.

"She's one of The Chosen," Rhiannon whispered. "That's why."

Tamara nodded, holding the child close. "We have to take care of her, get her to some family, something."

Take her home, clean her up, raise her as our own, Rhiannon thought. But she pushed those thoughts aside. "What we *have* to do is go after Devlin and his gang. They've gone rogue. They will not stop at this."

"Yes, but first we must eliminate the evidence of vampire attack on this village, before other mortals arrive on the scene," Roland said.

Always the voice of reason, her Roland.

Eric nodded in agreement, encouraging Roland to go on. So he did. "Tamara, take the child back to the nearest human village, erase this nightmarish memory and plant something less frightening in its place. Yet something that would explain this. A storm. A freak lightning bolt. But erase the memories of the screams, the violence, the death."

"She'll remember a storm, being afraid and running away to hide. She'll remember lightning and no more," Tamara promised, stroking the little girl's hair.

"Eric, please remain here." Roland looked at the other vampires, arriving now from the castle, shaking their heads at the devastation. "Take charge. Have everyone throw the bodies into the burning houses, and make sure they are completely destroyed. We cannot have any mortals found bloodless with their jugulars torn open, or our haven will be a haven no longer."

Then he turned to Rhiannon. "You and I will go—"

"Wait." She held up a palm to stop him, because someone was speaking inside her mind. She pressed her fingertips to her temple. "Listen." Then she opened her mind to her beloved and to Eric and Tamara as well, and replied mentally to the young vampiress who was speaking to her from far away, her emanations weak due to the distance. A younger vampire might not have picked them up at all.

Larissa, isn't it? Rhiannon thought.

Yes, came the reply. *I left the castle with Devlin, but I swear I had no idea what he was going to do. If I try to leave now, I'm afraid he'll kill me. I need help.*

Rhiannon smiled slowly. *Actually, child, you are going to be the one helping us. Stay with Devlin and his rogues—*

"Rhiannon," Roland said, but she shook her head at him.

Stay with them and report to me, so that I can find them, rescue you, and stop them from killing any more of the innocent. Can you do that, Larissa?

I...I don't know.

Will you try?

Yes. I'll try. Right now we're traveling by car to the coast. The vehicles were stolen from that village. There are seventeen of us, including Devlin and me. Devlin says he'll gather more once we get back to the United States. Portland, he said.

Why Portland? Rhiannon asked, alarmed. That was near where Roxanne was. Could he know?

It's where those seven mortals were murdered. He says it's where DPI must be operating. He says we're going to wipe them out. We're traveling by cargo ship to New York and then by plane to Portland. We should arrive there in five days.

Good. Keep me fully informed. Do not try to stop him alone, Larissa. You're too young. He has a century on you. Pretend to go along, or pretend to be too terrified to act, but do not try to stop him. If you have to participate in order to survive, then do what you must. If you can last until we catch up to him in Portland, you will be plucked from his reach before I kill him. In the meantime, be very careful to shield your mind from all but mine when you contact me. Do you know how to do that?

Yes.

And keep it either shielded or occupied with other thoughts at all times in his presence, or he'll read you. Understand?

Yes, Rhiannon. I'll try.

Do more than try, fledgling. Do it. Your life depends on it.

CHAPTER FIVE

Charlie's grandmother made a huge breakfast consisting of bacon, eggs, and ham. The smells wafted into the bathroom while Charlie took her shower and made her hurry to finish up. She dressed quickly in jeans and a floral print blouse with lace at the collar and hem. As soon as she stepped out of the hallway into the living room, however, the huge white owl swooped over her, and she dropped right to her knees, arms covering her heard. "Jeeze, what the hell?"

"Olive, really," Roxy scolded. "You're scaring our guest." She came in from the kitchen, held up a bent forearm, whistled three melodic notes, and the owl came and landed right on her arm. Frankly, Charlie was surprised she could support its weight.

"Come here, Charlotte. Olive needs to get to know you, so she won't think you're an intruder."

"Yeah, I'll pass."

"Well, if you're too afraid–"

"I'm not *afraid*." Charlie made an exasperated face. "On the other hand, you know how fast I'll bleed out if those talons sink through to the bone, right?"

"Do you see any blood on me, Charlotte?"

Sighing, she gave in and moved closer. The bird really was pretty impressive. Snow white with some black barring on her back and wings. Eyes as yellow as the sun at high noon. They almost seemed backlit and way too knowing. Their stare was intense.

"Hello, Olive."

Olive blinked.

Charlie reached out a hand and touched the bird's back, which seemed the safest place, gave it a gentle stroke. To her surprise the owl seemed to push back against her hand, like a cat would do. "I think she likes me."

"She's not usually the friendly type at all," Roxy said. "Hold out your arm, like I'm doing."

"Um, maybe I should grab a long sleeved sweater first. Or, you know, some chain mail."

Roxy held her eyes. "You're not as fragile as your mother has raised you to believe you are. It's important for you to know that."

For some reason, those words made Charlie feel good. No one had ever suggested she might be stronger than she thought she was. Her entire life had been filled with the opposite. Warnings and protection and caution.

Charlie bent her arm and held it out.

"Now whistle, just like I did."

She whistled the same three notes in the same way Roxy had.

The owl extended her wings and hopped, flapping them only once, and then landing on Charlie's forearm. Her talons gripped, but didn't break the skin.

"She's lighter than she looks," she observed. And she pet the bird again, scratched the top of its head lightly. The owl closed her eyes, pushed her head against Charlie's touch, and made a cooing sound.

"Aw, that's kind of nice. Yeah. You're a nice bird, aren't you Olive?"

"Now when you're ready, just lift your arm like you're launching her. She'll take it from there."

Nodding, Charlie pet the owl for quite some time. And Olive opened her eyes and stared straight into Charlie's so intently she felt the bird must be reading her mind or something. Then she lifted her forearm smooth and fast, and the owl took flight, swooped around the living room and then right into her huge cage, where she settled onto that limb that was her perch.

"She'll get some sleep now," Roxy said, closing the cage door. "She was out all night hunting."

"She doesn't fly away?" Charlie asked.

"So far, she always comes back. The choice is hers. I don't believe in keeping birds in cages."

Charlie looked around the room. There were five other cages, each holding a bird. "Um, then what are all these guys doing here?"

"Rehabbing. The robin had a broken wing. The fox sparrow was fluttering on the roadside when I went for supplies one day. The cardinal was too young to survive on his own when something ate his parents. I found him in the nest crying. His siblings were already dead."

Her grandmother might seem harsh and edgy–*and crazy, let's not forget crazy*. But she had a soft spot for birds. "So you keep them until they get better and then turn them loose?"

"Of course. Olive just...never left."

"That's...kind of nice." Charlie walked into the kitchen, found a pot of coffee and poured herself a cup. Then she went to the table and sat down.

Roxy already had coffee at her spot on the opposite end, and sat there to begin digging into the food. "You'll start feeling better and better soon. I'm loading you with protein."

"You mentioned that. Is it a Belladonna thing?"

Roxy nodded.

"Well, you're the expert. However, if I get fat, I'll be pissed at you forever."

"Do you see any fat on me?" Roxy asked between bites.

"Hard to tell with those kaftan things you wear all the time." Charlie was lying. The kaftans moved with Roxy, hugging her body whenever the wind blew. She knew her grandmother was in excellent shape.

The older woman shrugged. She wore one today that was multiple shades of red in a paisley pattern, with a matching scarf tied around her riotous curls.

Charlie ate for a while, then she said, "Do you think it's the high protein diet that's let you live so long?"

"Maybe. Partly. Or maybe it's the yoga, or maybe I'm too mean to die." She smiled after she said that. "I only know I've never had any of the typical symptoms that usually come to people with our condition."

"What kinds of symptoms? Mom never said."

Roxy nodded. "Better not to focus on the things that scare you."

"I'm not scared." *I'm freaking terrified.* "I'd just like to know when my own demise is imminent. And if I don't know what the symptoms are, I won't."

Roxy pursed her lips. "I suppose you have the right to know. It's nothing so drastic, really. Most of us start feeling weak, tiring more easily. The lack of stamina grows steadily worse until we're out of breath just walking across a room. We sleep more during the day and find ourselves becoming insomniacs at night. It becomes more and more debilitating until...." She bit her lip, shook her head. "There's no point talking about it now, though. You have years."

Did she? She'd already become an insomniac, and felt tired and worn out all day.

Until she came here. She slept great last night.

"Charlie?"

She snapped to attention.

"You have years," her grandmother said again.

"Yeah, like fifteen of them. I'm fucking Methuselah." She wolfed another bit of ham, then said, "I can't believe my mother never told me I was going to die before forty. It's the kind of thing a person ought to know, don't you think?"

"Not the kind of thing a child ought to know. She probably still thinks of you as a child."

"She's certainly been treating me like one."

"Don't blame her for that. She's terrified of losing you. That's all."

Charlie guessed that was probably pretty close to the truth. Neither of them seemed to have much more to say after that. They finished their food, and Charlie helped clean up after breakfast, then accompanied her grandmother outside with two of the birdcages in hand. One held a nearly pigeon sized bird, black with a white chest that she identified as a grosbeak, and the other, a tiny yellow goldfinch who looked like he was wearing a black cap on his head. When she opened the cage doors and the birds flew free, Charlie's heart soared with them.

It was beautiful in the forest, cozy in the cabin. Maybe life there wouldn't be so bad. Funny how one night of fantasy sex with a guy who'd stepped right out of her dreams could change her attitude, wasn't it? He was here. That was all that mattered. And if Killian was here, then here was where Charlie would stay.

If she could get her grandmother to stop keeping secrets from her, to trust her with the whole truth, it would be even better.

They watched the birds flit and flutter and land in the closest possible tree. The little goldfinch tipped his head back and sang for all he was worth, a high pitched, chirping song that made Charlie smile. She tore her eyes away to scan the trees for Killian, wishing he could see this with her, but there was no sign of him. And she'd known that, she realized, before she even looked for him. She could *feel* him when he was close.

Then Roxy said, "All right, time for the grand tour."

"I've already seen the whole cabin."

"Not the basement. It's time."

"Ah, the mysterious basement," she said. Sure, just when her grandmother started to seem semi-normal and maybe even sweet, she had to go and whip out her crazy alter ego to ruin her image all over again.

Roxy led the way back inside, closing and locking the doors behind them, and then walked straight through the door beside that armory-slash-closet, down a set of stairs into a finished basement, with Charlie following close behind.

It was one big room, half of it holding ordinary basement stuff, like a furnace and a hot water heater. The other side held a long table with two desktops, three laptops, and a small mountain of cell phones. There was a mini-fridge in the corner and a closed door in one wall.

Frowning, Charlie said, "What *is* all this? Looks like you're some kind of super spy or something."

Roxy shrugged. "I use different computers for different things. Once the IP address has been detected, I change hard drives and start over. Everything's stored externally, and I keep them offline unless I'm using them."

Oh, boy. "And what's with all phones?" She was almost afraid to hear the answer.

"We have to be very careful with phones, Charlie. These are all prepaid. Hard to trace."

Right. Just like the terrorists use.

"I use them once, then remove the battery and get rid of them far from any place where I'm staying. I keep one number active, but I stay on top of it. The minute I feel it's been compromised, I trash it."

Holy crap, it's worse than I thought.

She turned, pointing at the door in the back. "Now, the

safe room." She walked over to it, opened the door. "It's always unlocked. Come on in."

Charlie followed her inside, her steps hesitant, her mind whirling. She wanted to stay here because it was where Killian was. But her grandmother was certifiable.

The safe room was stocked with food and water. Shelves full of weapons lined the entire back wall. Roxy grabbed hold of part of the shelf unit and pulled. It swung open on unseen hinges, revealing a dark hole in the earth.

"This is the escape tunnel," Roxy explained. "At the far end, there's a trap door. I have a car hidden on the other side, gassed up with the keys in it, just in case I ever need to make a fast getaway. Sweet ride, too," she said with a smile.

"Um, yeah. That's...great."

"I know what you're thinking."

"I seriously doubt that," Charlie said. She inched her way back into the main part of the basement.

"I'm not crazy, Charlie, and I'm not paranoid."

"I didn't say you were." *She totally is.* "Hey, can I have one of those phones?" Roxy had insisted Charlie leave her beloved iPhone behind.

"They're for emergencies. And I know you probably want to call your mother, and we will, but later. Not from here, though. They can trace the ping to the nearest towers."

"Okay," Charlie said, drawing out the word. "Listen, um... Gram...do you really think vampires are monitoring our phone calls?"

"No, I don't. I think the government is."

Yeah, Charlie thought. The government, who might or might not have a cure for the fatal condition in her own bloodstream. Her grandmother was protecting her from the people who could help her. And her mother was apparently buying into Roxy's delusions. It was bizarre. But she would find out the truth. She looked at all the computers, at the phones, at the external hard drive that her grandmother had pointed out. She was still trying to decide whether to stay, and spend hours sneaking around trying to go through it all, or to leave, and find her own answers out there somewhere.

But as soon as she thought about leaving, one thing came down heavily on the "staying" side of the scale.

Killian was here. And for as long as he was, she figured she was going to be, too.

Killian was eager, but he was also nervous. He was playing with fire, and he knew it. If he let things go too far....

But he wouldn't. He just wouldn't. Last night, making love to her inside her mind, God, it had been...it had been incredible. But it had only left him wanting more.

He'd hiked to the nearest gas station, cleaned up in the public restroom, changed into a fresh set of clothes from the oversized backpack that held all his worldly possessions. And then he waited in the edge of the woods for Charlie to come out.

She did, eventually. Twenty minutes later than she'd emerged the night before and just when he'd begun to wonder if she would even show. She came out of the cabin's little door, closing it slowly and quietly, and then looking around for him.

He gave himself a moment just to savor her. She was so beautiful standing there beneath the starry sky. Her hair was a wavy bronze cascade, falling far past her shoulders. Her eyes were as blue as topaz tonight, their onyx centers expanded against the darkness. Her essence was unfolding, her sense of who and what she was, expanding and evolving right before his eyes, becoming even more.

He'd seen her soul, felt it. He knew her, inside and out, already. They were connected, and it wasn't just because she was one of The Chosen. His kind would always be drawn to hers. But not like this. Never like this.

He stepped out of the sheltering boughs of the sugar pines, then waited there until she spotted him. Her smile came instantly, and he felt the rush of joy and anticipation as she hurried forward, slowing when she neared her grandmother's trip line and stepping carefully over it, then continuing to him again.

She didn't slow down until she was standing inches from him. Then she stared up and right into his eyes, and he prayed she could not see what he was. Please, he thought, just let me look—and let me feel—perfectly normal to her.

He had no way to judge things except by watching her face and listening to her thoughts. She was feeling nervous. Aroused, attracted, hot for him, and nervous as hell. She didn't say anything for a long moment, but then she did. "I've been thinking about you all day, and I don't even know why." But she did know why. And so did he.

"Me too," he said.

"It doesn't make any sense, does it?" she asked. "We don't even know each other." She needed to know if he felt the same. He heard the question emanating from her heart.

He was devouring her with his eyes. The curve of her cheek, the dimples when she smiled, which she was doing now, in a wistful, questioning sort of way. She had the most amazing lips. Thick and full and bow shaped. He wanted to kiss them.

I want him to kiss me, she thought, and he heard it.

"Maybe we're meant to be," he said.

"Do you really believe in that sort of thing? Love at first sight?"

"I didn't used to."

She lowered her head to hide the blush that colored her cheeks, but she couldn't contain her smile.

"I dreamed about you last night," she said softly.

"You going to give me the details?"

She lifted her head, then shook it. "I think I'd better not."

But her teasing smile died slowly, and her eyes turned smoky.

"Maybe you could show me instead." He slid one hand around her nape, underneath her hair, his thumb remaining just below her jawline, where he could feel the strong, rapid beat of her pulse. Blood rushed beneath her skin like a river, and a wave of hunger swept over him. Quickly, he closed his eyes, in case they glowed red with the bloodlust and gave him away. And then he lowered his head and pressed his mouth gently to hers.

She tipped her head back and parted her lips to deepen the kiss, twisted her arms around his neck as if she would hold him to her forever. He wrapped her up tight, pressing his body against hers, and kissing her harder, hungrier, deeper, all the while warning himself to be careful. Not to go too far.

Already, he was trembling with need. When her hips arched into his, it was almost too much to bear, and he had to tear his mouth away. He cradled her head to his chest, though, keeping her close and unable to see his eyes.

"It's powerful, whatever it is between us," she whispered. "I felt you, Killian. Before I even saw you out here lurking in the trees like some kind of gorgeous peeping Tom."

She was a little breathless, and he knew the kiss had set her on fire as much as it had him. He had to get it under control, though. It shouldn't be this difficult. He'd fed, so he wasn't hungry for sustenance. But he *was* hungry for her.

Starving.

She pulled back to look up at him, but he pressed her head to his chest again. "Give me a minute," he said.

So she relaxed against him. "I get to you, huh?"

"More than you know."

She nodded against his chest then pulled free and walked away. He almost panicked, but she went only a few steps then stopped with her back to him. "This is moving so fast. I don't even know anything about you."

And you don't know the truth about me, she thought, and he heard it. *And you have to. It's not fair, otherwise.*

Killian found it ironic that she was worried about what *he* didn't know about *her*.

"How did you end up...homeless?" she asked.

He smiled. "I've never thought of myself as homeless." Walking up beside her, he took her hand, and they walked to the giant tree he'd used for cover, venturing into its drooping boughs like walking through a pine-scented curtain and continuing to the trunk. Then she turned and sat down with her back against it, knees up, and patted the spot beside her.

He sat close to her, so close they were touching, from their shoulders, to their hips, to their thighs to their knees. One arm around her shoulder, pillowing her head with his, he relaxed there with her and tried to get a grip on himself. "I used to have an entire apartment building in L.A. I had a lot of friends who needed places to bunk, so I bought it for us."

She lifted her brows. "You just bought a whole building?"

He nodded. "But it burned down. So...." He just shrugged and let the word hang there.

"What is it that you...do? I mean, if you can afford to just buy a whole building in L.A.–"

"I'm not rich. I hold a few patents. Royalty checks come quarterly. My living expenses are small, so mostly it just piles up in the bank until I need it for something."

She was watching his face, clearly fascinated by his words. "You're an inventor? What did you invent? Tell me, I have to know."

He shrugged. "A mechanical prosthetic hand for amputees. A motorized walker that works as well on uneven terrain as it does on solid surfaces and helps patients move with less effort. A charger that plugs into a car's cigarette lighter for recharging electric scooters. A–"

"It's all stuff for disabled people." She tilted her head to one side. "Why?" She was truly curious and interested and impressed. He almost regretted that the only life he could tell her about was the one he'd left behind. He could tell her almost nothing about his new life. The life of endless night.

"I used to work in a rehab facility," he said, and he felt the past coming back to him. "It seemed like every day I saw the need for some kind of equipment that didn't exist yet. The ideas were coming at me too fast to ignore. So I started drawing up designs and building prototypes. I wound up selling several of them to big medical supply companies."

The look in her eyes would've made his ego swell large enough to be seen from the moon, except that he knew it wasn't deserved. He hadn't built anything in years. He wasn't *that* Killian Garone any longer.

"What about you?" he asked, to shift the topic back. There was something she wanted to tell him. Something she thought he had to know.

She shrugged but averted her eyes a little. "Not much to tell."

"Sure there is. Like, why are you out here with your grandmother, and where were you before this?" He already knew, but it seemed a safe topic of conversation. He didn't want to leave her side, but he had to resist having sex with her, because he knew where it could lead. He wanted to taste her blood, to feel the life force of her flowing through his veins. He wanted to imbibe her, to take her into him, to possess her that thoroughly. If they had sex outside of the dream realm, that was exactly what would happen.

Sighing, she relaxed her head on his shoulder once again, snuggling close. "I lived with my mom before this. We have an apartment in Portland. I work at the Rent-A-Center. Have ever since I finished high school. I always knew I'd do something more, something bigger, but I was kind of waiting to figure out what. I've never really done much of anything."

"Why not?" he asked, watching her face, feeling her emotions as she spoke. Regret. Lots and lots of regret.

"Mainly because my mother has always treated me like I'd

shatter in a strong wind. Overprotective." She took a deep breath, sighed heavily. "I have this rare blood thing. The Belladonna Antigen. Do you know what that is?"

He thought it would seem odd if he did. It was rare. But he didn't want to lie to her. "Tell me."

"Well, it means if I ever need blood, it's going to be hard to find a donor. BDs can only receive transfusions from other BDs, and there are only a few thousand of us worldwide."

And vampires, he thought. They could take blood from vampires, though not in the usual way. "That's gotta be scary for you."

"More scary for my mom than for me. The antigen messes up clotting factors, so if I get a bad cut, I could bleed to death pretty easily. She's practically kept me in bubble wrap my entire life."

"Do you blame her?" he asked.

"No. I did, but...I only just learned there's more to it than I knew. Most people who have this condition...don't live to see middle age."

He kept his head down, unsure how to react. Feigning surprise seemed too dishonest, but the thought of her death filled him with so much sadness that he didn't need to fake that.

"Before whatever is happening between us goes any further, I thought you should know that, Killian. I'm not going to be around, long term."

"You can't be sure of that."

"Sure enough," she said.

"No. Your grandmother has it, too, and she's—"

She shot him a look then, her eyes first widening in surprise then narrowing in something else. Suspicion? "How do you know my grandmother has it too?"

"When I overheard you two talking before—when I first heard your voice."

"We didn't mention that." She sat up straighter, as if no

longer content to sit so close to him.

"Then you must have mentioned it last night."

"I'm pretty sure I didn't."

"Well, I'm pretty sure you did," he countered, trying to sound a little offended that she was so doubtful. The best defense, after all....

Her frown eased, she exhaled and rolled her eyes. "Hell, maybe I did. Honestly, I don't know. The past few days have been...." She shook her head. "I'm sorry. I'm a mess."

"It's all right." He hated making her doubt herself, but damn that had been close.

"My grandmother is the oldest living person with the Belladonna Antigen. She says no one knows why." Shrugging her shoulders, she said, "I keep hoping I've got more of her genes than my father did—I never knew him, and he died very young. But I can't count on it. I just figured you should know that." She watched his face, awaiting his reaction. "So there you have it. I'm going to start getting weak and tired and feeling like shit in a few years, and then I'm going to croak. Not that being with me now means you'll still be with me then, but it could happen early. I didn't think it was fair not to tell you."

"It doesn't scare me away from you, Charlie. Is that what you were thinking would happen?" It was. He already knew it was.

"Yeah," she said. "That's what I thought would happen."

"Well, you can relax now. I'm not going anywhere."

She turned, smiled up at him, slid her fingers into his hair and kissed him again. And he kissed her back, and it turned into more as she turned her body toward his and traced his lips with her tongue.

He pulled back before she could go further, so she wouldn't feel his razor sharp incisors, and slid his mouth over her jaw, and then down to her neck. Huge mistake. Huge. He tasted the salt of her skin, and her pulse thrummed powerfully against his lips. He warned himself to be careful, to move away from that spot. He even managed to do it, too, holding her close as he eased them both away from the tree trunk so they could stretch out on the ground, even while telling himself that was a bad idea, too.

And then he was kissing her neck again, and her collarbones, and the upper part of her chest, above the little pajama top. Blue tonight. He nudged its thin strap off one shoulder with his mouth.

She pushed his chest, and he lifted himself off her, thinking this was it. She was stopping him and it was a good thing, because if they'd gone any further....

But instead of scurrying away, she just sat up a little and peeled the top right over her head. He knelt there, staring at her breasts, and he thought his eyes were watering.

Then her hands came to his head and she pulled him back to her again.

They kissed like they were starving for each other, and he stopped worrying about the razor edged length of his incisors, because passion was pounding in every part of his body and mind. He pulled off his own shirt before he could think better of it, and then they were lying skin to skin, were grinding against each other, lost in a haze of desire.

He pulled his mouth away, kept his eyes sealed, felt the fire glowing in them, the fire she must not see, and panted, "If we don't stop now–"

"If we stop now, I'll die," she said, breathless, her skin hot to the touch. "I dreamed of this."

"So did I," he admitted.

"I want to make it real."

"You don't know–"

"Then show me." She shimmied her pajama pants off without even moving out from under him, and then her hands were on his jeans, freeing the button, shoving them down over his hips.

"Dammit, Charlie, I can't–"

"Shut up," she whispered. She pulled him until he lay on top of her, naked now, and she was aching for him. He felt it. "I don't know how many years I have to live, Killian. But from now on, I'm damn well gonna live them." She wrapped her legs around his back, using them to press him closer.

He resisted for a solid three seconds, and then he let himself go, lowering his naked chest to hers, nestling his hips between her thighs, his erection finding its way naturally inside her. She gasped, and he tipped his head back, baring his teeth as passion and pleasure and need rocketed through him, all of them intensifying the bloodlust until it was beyond bearable.

Release in his kind, came in two ways. The usual one, and the sinking of fangs into flesh, the first swallow of the essence of life itself. And as his body strained toward the one, he was irresistibly pulled by the other.

She was straining too, and he felt it, her pleasure, the slow tensing of every muscle in her body, coiling ever tighter as her nails raked his back, and her teeth nipped his shoulder. She flung her head back, arching the length of her beautiful pale throat up toward him.

He was on the precipice, staring down at the strong powerful pulse in her neck. And just as he tried to turn his head away, her fingers threaded into his hair and jerked him down until his mouth was at her throat, and she was burying her face in his hair to muffle her cries of pleasure.

He felt her climax around him, and that was the end of his control. The lust took over. He drove into her hard and sank his fangs into her neck at the same time. The taste of her, the rush of her blood over his tongue–God, it hit him like heroin as he pumped into her, his entire body suffused in the most intense pleasure he had ever experienced.

A sip. A taste of her, was all he allowed. As his senses returned, he pulled away, shocked at what he'd done, averting his head, wiping at his mouth just in case. And then he looked down at her. At the two tiny punctures in her throat, and the tiny rivulet of blood that had run from one of them. She wouldn't bleed out. Not from those wounds. The bite of a vampire could not harm one of The Chosen, unless of course, one drank them dry. He didn't know why, only knew it was true. He hoped she would go straight to bed when she went back inside. He prayed she wouldn't look into a mirror and see those marks and know what he was.

Maybe he should tell her.

Maybe he should get away from her before she told her grandmother and the authorities what and where he was.

He fell back onto the ground, blinking up at the undersides of the lush pine boughs, covering them as completely as a dome tent would do. "I didn't mean for things to go that far."

"I did," she whispered, rolling onto her side and hugging him around the waist. "I can't explain it, Killian, but I've been dreaming of you for weeks. And last night...it was so real. I don't know what this is, but it feels even stronger now than before."

"Sex creates a bond." *And sharing blood, an even stronger one.*

"I think I might love you," she whispered. *I'm sure of it,* her heart sang.

He ran a hand over her hair. "I think I might love you back."

She sat up a little, smiling down at him, then jumped to her feet and rapidly pulled her pajamas on again. He could not take his eyes off her. She was glowing. And those damn marks on her neck. They would fade, of course, at the first kiss of sunlight. But until then, there they were, banners proclaiming his guilt and lack of self-control. He should've told her.

"I have to go," she whispered. "Tomorrow night? And really, we should use some protection next time."

He bit his lip, nodded slowly. Male vampires were sterile, disease free, but she had no way of knowing that. "I'll take care of it."

She'd finished dressing. He got up to his feet, naked, to say goodbye, and told himself it should be that. Goodbye. But who was he kidding? He couldn't walk away from her if he tried.

She pressed her body to his and tipped her head back, and he kissed her long and slow, like something out of an old movie. Then, smiling, she turned and hurried back to the cabin.

Killian held his head in his hands and whispered, "What have I done?"

When she got back inside, floating on a cloud of bliss, Roxy was waiting for her. She had two cups of tea and a stern expression on her face.

Charlie closed the door behind her and faced her grandmother, feeling guilty as hell and wondering why. Then Roxy's eyes dipped lower, narrowing when they focused on Charlie's neck.

"Oh, Charlotte. Oh, Charlotte, child, do you even *know* what kind of game you're playing?"

Charlie's hand went to her neck immediately. She'd felt the delicious pinch of Killian's teeth there. He'd probably left a hickey and blown her cover.

"It's not what you think, Roxy," she began. And then she shrugged. "Oh, hell, it probably *is* what you think. But there's just something about him. Something–"

"Oh, there always is," Roxy said with an exasperated toss of her head. "You know more than I thought you did, Charlotte. That's good. That'll make this all a lot easier."

Charlie frowned, not knowing what the hell her grandmother was talking about, but not wanting to prolong the conversation either. She wanted to go to bed, to dream of him again.

"Bring his ass in here tomorrow night," Roxy said, "and

I'll hide *him* as well. God knows I've got enough experience bailing his kind out of trouble. This will just be one more. Fortunately, he has friends on the way. Maybe they can teach him what's appropriate behavior toward the daughter of The Oldest Chosen, and what isn't. The rude little fuck."

Charlie stood there frowning and trying to make sense of her grandmother's words. Why would she want to hide Killian? And how could she know he had friends on the way, when she'd only just found out about him? She didn't even know his name yet.

"No more sneaking out, Charlotte. I mean it. We'll talk this out tomorrow. I'm going to bed." She picked up her tea and was down the hall and closing her bedroom door before Charlie could even construct a reply.

Frowning, replaying Roxy's words in her head, Charlie walked into her own bedroom, flipped on the light, and sat down at her nightstand. Her reflection stared back at her from the stand's oval mirror, and she searched her own eyes...and then caught a glimpse of a slight red trickle on her neck. Hell, had Killian nipped her that hard? Hard enough to draw blood?

She tipped her chin up, leaning closer for a better look at the hickey and then just stared at the two puncture wounds in her throat. There was no mistaking them.

Her breaths came faster as she stood up, backing away from the undeniable truth in the mirror.

Killian was a vampire.

That was why he could visit her in her dreams. That was why she could feel him when he was near. He was manipulating her mind! He was making her feel things for him that couldn't possibly be real. All...all for what? Just to get a taste of her blood?

She had Belladonna blood, the vampire's favorite kind. And her grandmother knew it, had looked right at those marks on her neck and hadn't even seemed all that upset. Her words replayed in Charlie's mind.

I'll hide him, as well.

I've had enough experience bailing his kind out of trouble.

He has friends on the way.

"Oh Jesus, Oh God," she whispered. Her grandmother was on the vampires' side! That's why she seemed so strange and outrageous. That was why she hated and mistrusted the government. She was aiding the enemy!

Charlie looked around the room, feeling suddenly vulnerable. "I have to get the hell out of here." She went to her window, made sure it was closed, made sure it was locked, pulled the curtains tight, then curled onto her bed, drawing her knees to her chest and hugging them.

And in spite of herself, tears came into her eyes. Killian had lied to her. He'd used her. He'd...he'd fed from her!

He was a vampire. And all he wanted was her blood. It was just like that military asshole had said on the news the other day. And her grandmother. God, her own grandmother was in on this. Did her mom even know?

She had to get out, but she was trapped! She was trapped here in the woods with a hungry vampire and a crazy old lady with an arsenal in her basement....

The basement.

As soon as she thought of it, clarity came. The safe room with the escape tunnel and the car at the other end with the keys always in it. Charlie *did* have a way out. And the minute Roxy had time to fall back to sleep, she was taking it.

CHAPTER SIX

Even knowing that at any second, he might be discovered, Killian couldn't leave. If Charlie saw the marks on her neck, if she told her grandmother and the authorities, then whatever. He couldn't leave until he knew.

After two hours had passed, he started to hope that she hadn't made that discovery at all. Maybe she'd gone straight to bed and fallen asleep. Maybe the marks would be healed, erased by the arrival of dawn, long before she woke again. Maybe he would have another chance to explain himself before she found out what he was and jumped to all the wrong conclusions.

But then he heard the unmistakable sound of a car's engine starting up. The sound came from the woods somewhere beyond the small cabin, which made no sense whatsoever. That was the opposite direction from the nearest road.

There was something else too, some kind of dread taking root deep in the pit of his stomach. Something that made him move quickly toward the sound. He ran at vampiric speed, his instincts guiding him around and between trees, beneath limbs, over fallen logs. He had perfect night vision, but that wouldn't help when racing full tilt through a forest. It was all about reflexes, all about focus. He reached a small clearing in time to see a magnificent car, a vintage powder blue Mustang, just rumbling away over a barely discernible track through the forest, with Charlie behind the wheel. Keeping up wasn't a problem. He jogged behind the car, wondering what to do. Shoot around it and spring out in front of her to stop her? Force her to give him a chance to explain that, yes, he was a vampire, but not a monster.

To her, he realized, the two were one and the same.

The car burst out of the woods onto that deserted stretch of road he'd been traveling what seemed like a lifetime ago. She cranked the wheel hard to the left and hit the gas. Tires spun, squealing and leaving black rubber on the road and the stench of it in the air. And then she was off like a rocket, speeding until she was out of sight around a curve.

But she wasn't beyond the reach of sound. Not to a vampire. So he heard the squealing tires, the crunching metal, the breaking glass. Her pain-filled scream was like a dagger in his soul.

Charlie had tears in her eyes as she sped away from her grandmother's hideaway. She told herself that it made no sense to cry. She didn't even know Killian. He was a stranger and not worth crying over. Everything she thought she felt for him had been fake. Vampires could do that, couldn't they? Mess with peoples' minds. He'd been stalking her, hiding in the woods and waiting for a chance to...to drink her blood. God!

And yet it had felt so good. The sex, the release, the gentle suction of his mouth against her throat. It had felt so incredibly, intensely good, it had damn near melted her brain. But that was how it was with vampires, wasn't it? They charmed you, they tricked you, they screwed with your head and made you think it was pleasant to be drained and left lying there, an empty husk. Dead.

But he didn't kill me. Why didn't he kill me?

She was stupid to have let herself be swept away by him. Stupid to have seduced him into having sex with her. Stupid to have believed anything he'd said, ever. It shouldn't hurt this much. She barely knew him.

God, then why did it feel like her heart had been torn right out of her chest? Why did it feel like the love of her life had betrayed her?

She'd pressed down harder on the accelerator, knuckling a tear from her check with one hand as she rounded a sharp curve. Then her heart froze when she saw an overturned truck and flashing lights. There was no fucking way she could stop in time.

She jammed the brakes, jerked the wheel left, and the car skidded, squealed, and then flipped over....and over and over.

The alarm went off and startled Roxy awake. She was a sound sleeper, something that had always bothered her, which was why she'd set so many alarms around the place in preparation for her granddaughter.

This particular alert was coming from the cell phone she kept beside her bed, and the indicator light showed that someone had crossed the boundary between the hidden access road and the highway.

Flinging back the covers, she sprang from the bed, grabbed a handgun from under her mattress, and ran to Charlotte's room. Two perfunctory taps, then she flung open the door. "Charlotte, get up. Someone's here."

No response from the rumpled bedding. Roxy flicked on the light, her heart in her throat, and saw why. Charlotte was gone.

"Oh, hell, no. Charlotte! Charlotte!" She went through the cabin, calling for the girl, but her backpack was gone, and the basement door was open. Roxy raced down the stairs, to see that the safe room door was open too, as was the secret entry to the escape tunnel. She ran through the tunnel in her night clothes, bare feet smacking over damp, hard-packed earth, goose bumps rising on her arms from the chill of it. The trap door at the far end had been flipped open, and as Roxy climbed out, she saw that the Mustang was gone.

Charlotte had taken the car and run away. Hell.

No choice but to go after her. Roxy jumped back into the tunnel, pulling the trapdoor closed behind her, and returned to the cabin that way, because it was the quickest route. She dressed hurriedly, tucked her handgun into her purse, and headed out to her pickup truck. She had no idea which way Charlotte would've gone. Much less why. Hell, she hadn't told the girl what she knew about vampires yet, because she'd been sure Charlie would think she was crazy and take off on her. She was hoping to gain her trust before springing it on her. But after she'd apparently made love to one in the forest, Roxy had assumed the girl must already know that they were the good guys, not the bad ones. That they loved and protected The Chosen, didn't hurt or kill them.

So why had she run?

And where? Back to her mother in Portland? Or the opposite direction?

Charlie had been visited by a vampire. Maybe *visited* wasn't the most accurate term, going by the bite marks on her neck. But she'd been fine. All dreamy-eyed and love-struck. Enough so that Roxy thought it wouldn't be so hard now to explain to her that the undead were her friends.

God, she should have sat her down and had the entire

conversation right then. Should've called her undead Romeo out too, made him a part of the discussion. She'd screwed up, thinking it could wait until morning. Thinking she wasn't going to tell the girl anything she hadn't already figured out for herself.

She'd screwed up, and royally.

Roxy drove the pickup to the spot where the hidden escape route met the road, got out and looked at the flattened grass and tire tracks where they crossed the shoulder, and at the rubber that Mustang had left on the pavement. Left. Charlie had turned left. Getting back behind the wheel, Roxy headed the same way Charlotte had gone.

And then she came on a scene that made her blood freeze in her veins. The Mustang was so thoroughly demolished that she didn't recognize it at first, and there was a helicopter just lifting off from a nearby field. Skidding to a stop, Roxy jumped out of the truck and ran to the nearest cop, who met her halfway. "That's my car! Where is my granddaughter?" she demanded.

"She's being airlifted to the closest trauma center–a clinic near Pendleton. I'm going to need some information from you," the officer said.

"Then you'll have to meet me there," Roxy said, and she didn't wait for an argument, but dove back into her pickup, drove into the field to get around the wreckage and emergency vehicles, and pulled back onto the road beyond it, driving hell bent for leather toward Pendleton, an hour away.

If they tested Charlotte's blood, and there was no earthly reason to think they wouldn't, they would find the antigen. All Roxy had done to protect the girl would be undone with the click of a mouse button. The minute they entered her blood type into the computer, some government pencil pusher would be alerted that what was in the system did not match what was in the girl. That she was Belladonna positive and apparently trying to hide it.

Dammit. Dammit!

Killian had come upon the accident too late to do much to help Charlie. The car was upside down in a field along the roadside, and the ground around it was untouched, as if the Mustang had been airborne before coming to rest where it had. It was half the size it had been before, crumpled, crushed. He couldn't see her, and his panic kept him from feeling her, as men in uniforms swarmed around the demolished car, tugging on its door.

There had been another accident, he gathered. He moved closer, cautious but frantic, staying out of sight, but close enough to hear the conversations of the humans on the scene, and far more focused on Charlie than his own safety. She was alive. That was something, at least.

The overturned truck in the road must have been what caused Charlie to veer too sharply and lose control. She'd been driving too fast. *Because of me*, he thought over and over. *All because of me*. Police and an ambulance had already been on the scene due to the overturned truck. Lucky for her, they kept saying.

Only it wasn't. He could help her, maybe, but not with all of them lingering.

Still, he could do something. He moved toward the opposite side of the car from where the rescuers were trying to open the door, and he knelt down to look in at Charlie. She was upside down, held to the seat by her safety belt. Her head was bleeding and her face, all cut up and illuminated by the dashboard lights that had somehow remained on. Headlights too, cutting an odd angle through the darkness.

"That door's impossible, son," one of the firefighters called. "We can probably get this one open with the jaws, though. It'll take a little while."

She didn't have a little while. He could feel her life force ebbing. She was going to bleed out.

Killian gripped the door's handle and yanked with his full strength. The door came free, and he tumbled backward with it, then shoved it off his chest, as the firefighters ran around to his side, swearing in surprise and asking how he'd managed that.

"It just gave," he said, getting to his feet, brushing himself off. Several of them were leaning into the car, where Charlie was now accessible. One man maneuvered a brace onto her neck, touching her with exquisite care. The beat of a propeller, and the wind it generated, blew dirt into Killian's eyes.

"Get the bleeding stopped. We need a tourniquet here!"

The medics were working on her. The gash in her arm was wrapped up tight, and the bleeding slowed.

"Where are they taking her?" He asked, torn between shouldering his way nearer, just to touch her, and keeping his distance from the mortals who could not, *must not* learn what he was.

"There's a trauma center near Pendleton," a paramedic told him. "It's the closest one. Are you family?"

"Just a bystander."

They were wedging a back-brace underneath her, men on either side holding her body to keep her from twisting. They were careful. They had better be. The chopper had landed nearby, lights blazing, prop beating, dust flying. Killian backed away, but no eyes were on him. Once he'd achieved the cover of the forest, he ran. It was forty-five miles to Pendleton. He could make it almost as fast as the chopper could. An older vampire could have beat it there.

Killian ran, he poured on speed he shouldn't have even had. He wasn't at his strongest. Animal blood was not the healthiest diet for a vampire, and he'd tasted precious little of Charlie's. But emotion drove him, in spite of that. And he arrived at the small trauma center where the chopper had already landed. His heart in his throat, he tried to calm himself, to listen and to feel and to find her. Slowly, he walked the building's perimeter from the outside, opening his mind to the riotous noise of human thoughts pouring from within.

He came through the surgery fine. It was very minor, and he'll be okay....

I'm so sorry. We did everything we could, but....

Patient in three is pressing his call button again. Jeeze, does she think we're nurses or waitresses?

She's lost too much blood. Where the hell is the blood I ordered?

That one, that thought. He homed in on it, closing out all the other noise as best he could, and let his senses guide him to where she was. Ground floor, east side. A room with a single window. Closer now, closer, and finally he could see her.

Charlie was lying, still and pale, in a bed, barely any evidence of life emanating from her. But she was alive. Her heartbeat was weak and erratic, but she was alive.

People were all around her.

"Doctor, the patient is Belladonna positive," a nurse was saying. "We're looking, but so far, we haven't found anything to give her."

"Did she have any ID on her? Maybe she banked some, knowing–"

"Charlotte O'Malley, twenty. She's unregistered. Her records say A Positive."

"That's not possible."

"We've triple checked it, Doctor."

Killian felt the man's thoughts, then. *She'll die without a transfusion. Belladonna positive, she can't even tolerate O-neg. Where the hell are we going to find a match for her this time of the night? In time?*

"Family?" he asked.

"We've phoned her mother in Portland, who says she was staying with a grandmother who might be a match."

"Did that show up in her records?"

"No, Doctor. The only grandmother listed in her

government file is also listed as A positive."

"Have we reached her yet?"

"Not yet."

There was silence. Then the doctor said, "All right, we've stopped the bleeding. Keep the fluids going and wait for the family to arrive. That's it. That's all we can do."

Killian closed his eyes, aiming his thoughts at the doctor. *Leave her alone. Just leave her alone. Just for a minute, that's all I need.* He sent his will with every bit of power he could muster behind it. He'd barely ever tried the trick of manipulating humans to do what he wanted them to do. It was not his strongest skill.

It took a while, but eventually it worked. The staff left Charlie alone and weak, barely clinging to life in her hospital bed. Killian went to the window, exerting his will again, this time to turn the lock from the inside without touching it, and then he slid the window open, and climbed inside.

Roxy ran through the trauma center's double Emergency Room doors with dread driving her. *Let her be okay,* she thought desperately. *Let me be in time, and let them not have run her blood type yet.*

"Thank God."

The voice was her daughter-in-law's. Roxy came to a stumbling halt, her eyes wide and searching the area behind and around Trish O'Malley. "How the hell did you beat me here? Where is Charlotte? Which room? Is she alive–?"

The slap across the face took Roxy by surprise. Her head rocked to one side with the impact, but she straightened up again, pressing her palm to her stinging cheek.

"I trusted you!" Charlotte's mother shouted. "You couldn't even keep her safe for two days? What was she doing in that car, Roxy?"

"Running away, Trish," she shot back, not missing a beat.

"And not just from me, but from you, too. She was heading away from Portland, not toward it. So fuck you. Now where the hell is she?"

"Excuse me, are you Charlotte's grandmother?" a nurse asked from behind her.

Roxy turned, met the woman's eyes. "Yes."

"She needs blood desperately, and we can't find a match because—"

"I know. I'm a match. Did you change her type in the system yet? Because if you didn't, then don't. I forbid it."

The nurse looked extremely confused. "Of course we did. We're required by law to correct mistakes like that. It could save a life."

Hell. The minute they had entered the information that an unregistered Belladonna positive patient whose records had been tampered with, had been admitted, Roxy knew that somewhere, an alarm had gone off. People had been notified. Teams had been dispatched. She knew how DPI worked.

Dammit.

"I have to get her out of here." She turned to Trish. "We have to get her out of here, *now*."

"Did you not hear the part where she's going to die without a blood transfusion, Roxy? What the hell is wrong with you? Bare your arm, now, bitch, or I'll do it for you."

"You don't understand—"

"We'll have to type and crossmatch," a nurse said.

"No you will not." Roxy pinned the nurse with her eyes. "And you will not *touch* my computer file, because I'm not your patient and you have no reason to, do you hear me? Get a needle and a bag and come and take as much blood as she needs from me. I'll be in with my granddaughter. Where is she?"

"Ma'am, we can't just—"

Roxy leaned in close, nose to nose, but didn't touch the woman. "Where. Is. My. Granddaughter?"

The nurse nodded toward a closed door at the end of the hall.

"That's where I'll be. Bring what you need to save her and do it fast." She looked at Trish. "And as soon as the blood's onboard, we have to get her out of here. We *have to*."

Killian leaned over the hospital bed and pressed his lips to Charlie's forehead. She was near death. Not at the brink, not yet, but close enough so that he could feel Death's presence in the room, cold and heavy...and waiting. But he also knew what to do about it. She was one of The Chosen. She could take blood from a vampire and survive it with no side effects. Well, no negative ones, anyway.

She was so beautiful, nearly as pale as the bed sheets. Bruises were forming on her cheekbone, her jaw. She had cuts and scratches from the flying glass. Her head had been stitched up and bandaged heavily.

She was dying. And there were people outside the room. He had to act, and act quickly. He pulled a pocketknife from his jeans, flipped open the blade, and made a small cut on his forearm. When the blood began to well up in the wound, he pressed it to her beautiful mouth, and gently teased her jaw with his free hand. "Come on, Charlie. Drink. It'll save you. Just drink. Come on."

The blood filled her mouth and ran from the corners of her lips down to her neck, and dripped onto her pillow.

"Swallow, Charlie. Please." Then he focused his will, closed his eyes, and commanded her. *Swallow. Drink. Live.*

She swallowed immediately. Exerting his will worked far faster on her than it had on the medical staff.

Her body went rigid for an instant, and then her hands snapped around his arm, holding it to her hungry mouth as she went wild, sucking at his wounded arm, drinking all she could get from him. As his blood shot through her body, restoring it, he felt everything she did, everything she ever had or ever would. In those moments of complete connection, he experienced her as if he'd known her for her entire life. In a rush, her childhood, her adolescence, her teenage angst, all of it rushed through him in a blinding flash of brilliance that was pure Charlie.

She drank only a little. Not enough to save her. Not yet. She needed more, he thought. But the people outside were coming closer. He felt their intent, heard their footsteps. He yanked his arm free, and Charlie fell back onto the pillows, thrashing and twisting now as the powerful vampiric blood raced through her body, rejuvenating every part of her, sending powerful energy zinging through her organs, sizzling into her cells, jolting them into action. Killian grabbed a role of adhesive tape from a nearby shelf, wrapped it around his arm and tore it free with his teeth.

The door was opening. He couldn't leave her now. She needed more. He gathered Charlie out of the bed and into his arms, and lunged for the window with her.

"What the hell are you doing? Put my granddaughter down!"

He recognized her grandmother's voice, but didn't slow, just poured on the speed, leaping out the window and running, carrying Charlie in his arms. She was struggling against him, but still weak, her head lolling from side to side as he ran. He had to get her away from all these mortals, had to feed her more blood to make sure she'd had enough to survive. To recover. Tearing the tape from his cut forearm, he pressed it to her lips again, and again, she drank as if dying of thirst. In a way, she was.

Two black vans skidded to a stop in the parking lot in front of him, and men piled out of them. They had guns–rifles of some kind, and they were pointing them his way, ordering him to "Let the girl go!"

Behind him, the girl's crazy grandmother had apparently climbed out the window after them and was shouting, "Put my granddaughter down right now, vampire, or I'll shoot you where you stand, I swear to God."

Charlie opened her eyes wide as a jolt zapped through her. She felt like she'd stuck her finger into a live socket, and every nerve ending seemed to be vibrating. She blinked her vision into focus. Everything was weird. Different. Like the world had gone hi-def. Her head was buzzing. She could feel the night air touching her skin and smell every blade of grass, every tree, every human, and every vehicle along with about a million other things.

Killian was holding her in his arms, and she felt him, too, more acutely and completely, she thought, than ever before. Whatever the hell that meant.

And then she heard her grandmother say, "Put my granddaughter down, vampire...."

Vampire!

Frowning, she looked back. Her grandmother stood in the grass outside a building—a hospital or clinic, her mind whispered—pointing a gun at Killian.

She looked up at him again, and then she remembered. "You lied to me. You're a vampire."

He glanced down at her, and his eyes were glowing red.

"Holy shit. Put me down!"

"I'm only trying to help you. To save you—"

"Put me *down*!" She struggled, twisting herself in his arms, pushing against his chest and eventually falling to the ground.

"Charlotte, come to us!" a male voice shouted urgently. "We'll keep you safe."

She turned her head toward the man, and saw what was apparently a SWAT team. A bunch of guys in black with vests and helmets and guns. God, what was going on here?

"No, Charlie, don't listen to them!" Roxy yelled. "Come to me."

Charlie jerked her head back Roxy's way, then looked up at Killian again.

He stared down into her eyes, and she could've sworn he spoke without saying a word. *Trust me. I'm not going to let any harm come to you. You're everything to me.*

She heard a soft hiss, and then Killian jerked, swore, looked down. There was a dart in his arm. He staggered a little. She took advantage of the moment and got to her feet. Killian dropped to his knees.

"Charlotte, you come here right now," Roxy said.

But before she could answer, one of the SWAT team guys rushed forward, grabbed her by the arm, and was running with her toward the waiting vans. "There are more of them, Charlotte. We have to get you to safety."

"But my grandmother—"

"She can't protect you. That should be obvious by now."

She let him pull her alongside him while a thousand questions spun through her mind. Her grandmother was insane, possibly in league with vampires. And Killian had tried to feed on her. What the hell was she supposed to do?

She looked back over her shoulder. Roxy was sprinting across the grass to the parking lot like an Olympian or something, and Killian was dragging himself toward a clump of shrubs. There was a dart sticking out of his shoulder.

The soldier or cop or whatever he was, pushed Charlie into the back of a waiting van and jumped in beside her. The door slammed and the van jerked into motion. Then her rescuer pulled off his helmet and smiled at her. He looked like a movie star. Clean cut, thick dark brown hair, big brown eyes, a killer smile. "You're safe now. I promise you, Charlotte. It's okay if I call you Charlotte, isn't it?"

"Ch-Charlie," she said. She tried to look out the windows

behind them, but they were tinted almost black, and she couldn't see a damn thing. They'd shot Killian with something.

Because he was a vampire.

And her grandmother had raced away into the night. Probably after her truck. Probably she'd be giving chase, soon. She wished she could see.

"Charlie," her companion said. "I like that. Here. You've got something on your face." He handed her a clean white handkerchief. She took it, then dabbed the spots he indicated by pointing them out on his own face. When she looked at the hanky, it was bloody and her eyes went round.

"It's all right. I don't think it's yours."

"Then whose?"

He didn't answer, just shook his head. "I'm just glad we got to you in time. I don't imagine you even know how close you came to...." Then he stopped, bit his lip. "I'm getting ahead of myself, though." He took back his hanky, handed it to someone in the front seat, passenger side. She couldn't see them from her angle. "My name is Lucas," he told her. "Lieutenant Lucas Townsend, to be specific. I'm with a special ops unit of the Division of Paranormal Investigations. DPI for short. I'm also Belladonna positive, just like you. And you can trust me. That's the first thing. Okay?"

She nodded and figured she had no reason not to believe him. He *had* just saved her from a vampire, after all. "Where are we going, Lieutenant Townsend?"

"Somewhere safe. I promise. Then we'll make sure you're okay, and then...then I'll explain to you what's going on. You must be so confused you don't even know which end is up right now. Am I right?"

"I'm pretty confused."

He nodded, looking her over from head to toe. "Yeah, you must be. You're looking pretty good, though for someone who was near death a little while ago. You always heal this fast?"

She frowned and looked down at the cuts and scrapes on

her arms, they looked a week old already. Then she shook her head and met the lieutenant's eyes once more. "What the hell is happening to me?"

"That's what I'm going to help you find out, Charlie. You just hang in there, we'll be at Fort Rogers soon."

She sighed, but settled into her seat and closed her eyes. Maybe she was going to get some answers. Finally. It was about freaking time.

CHAPTER SEVEN

Killian yanked the dart from his shoulder and threw it, then dragged himself to his feet behind some shrubbery and watched Charlie running off with the soldier. Others were coming his way, though, dart guns pointed, and he was weakening by the minute.

One burst of speed was all he could manage. He poured it on fast and hard, and he knew that to their human eyes, it would've looked as if he'd vanished, when in fact, all he'd managed to do was race into the parking lot and fall to his knees between two cars. He didn't have enough strength left in him to pull it off again. He didn't even know if he could walk very far. Whatever had been in that dart was going to put him down for the count soon. Maybe even kill him.

Charlie was put into a van. The door closed on her, and the vehicle sped away. He watched it go, and his heart bled. She was with the enemy now. They had her, and God only knew what they'd do with her.

Then a pickup truck pulled to a quiet stop in front of

him, the passenger door opened, and Charlie's grandmother whisper-shouted at him, "Get in, fast, or they're going to have you, too. And *you*, they'll kill. Move it, vampire."

He didn't see that he had a choice. The goon squad was still searching the grounds around the hospital. They were not even looking his way at the moment. He got upright, stumbled forward, and gripping the open door, pulled himself into the truck.

"Shut the door nice and easy," she said, "Don't make any noise, and stay low." She was pulling away while he obeyed. She didn't floor it, didn't spin her tires or leave rubber on the paved parking lot, just rolled slowly to the exit, then eased onto the street and into traffic. As she drove, she pulled a cell phone from her pocket and fired off a text. He didn't know what it said or who it went to, and hoped to God she wasn't informing some vampire-execution-squad that she had captured a live one.

Killian sat up enough to look behind them.

"They didn't follow," Roxy said, dropping the phone back into her pocket.

"How can you be sure?"

"Me? I can't. You can, though. Open that preternatural brain of yours and feel for them."

Embarrassed that he hadn't thought of that himself, he closed his eyes, opened his mind and sifted through the chaos in search of their pursuers. But he didn't find them. "I'm not picking up on anything."

"We'll have to drive around aimlessly for a few hours to make sure, then. They've probably been taught how to block."

"How to block?"

"God, you are a young one, aren't you? What's your name, kid?"

"Killian."

"And you've been undead for how long now? Ten years?"

"Almost thirty."

She smiled. "Gotta love an eighties model."

Self-consciously, he pushed a hand through his thick hair, shoving it back from his head.

"Humans can shield their thoughts from your kind. Vamps can shield them from each other. Did you know that?"

He shook his head slowly.

"Who made you?" she asked. "Where do you come from?"

"I didn't get her name," he said, remembering the night vividly. He'd been riding his Harley, and she'd pounced on him at about 60 miles an hour. Just leaped on him from out of nowhere, taking him off the bike and onto the shoulder of the road. He'd skidded several yards with her clinging to him, already latched onto his neck, crazed, draining him.

He'd thought he was dying when she pulled away, wiped her mouth with her forearm and blinked down at him. Big black eyes, dark brown hair, long bangs that hid her eyebrows. A walking anime vampiress.

"Don't die. I didn't know you were Chosen!" she'd said.

But then he had died. Or he thought he had. He'd been gone, for sure. Into something. Darkness. Nothingness. But when he'd awakened again, she'd been feeding him from her own wrist. She pulled away, wrapped her wrist in a bandana so tightly he thought she'd lose the hand, and then just walked off, saying, "Find shelter before you pass out. If the sun hits you, you'll burn alive."

And she was gone.

He told Roxy none of this. Just remembered as she drove, and finally said, "I used to live with a few others in L.A. where no one thought much of our nocturnal tendencies."

"Smart to join with a group. Where are they now?"

"Dead." He kept his eyes straight forward. "Three years ago, humans torched our building while we slept. I woke up in a drainage ditch. No idea how I got there. The building was gone, not a survivor in sight."

"Doesn't mean there weren't any," she said. "You give me

their names when we get back to my place. I'll add them to the list."

That drew his gaze her way. Up close, he saw a lot of Charlie in her. She was a beautiful woman, older, but there was no evidence on her face of how old. And yet, she was also one of The Chosen. And he knew they tended to die young. "What list?" he asked.

"The list of those of your kind who are still missing and unaccounted for since the Vampire Armageddon." She shrugged. "I've been calling it Varmageddon, but it hasn't really caught on. Too soon, I guess."

She'd turned the truck onto the highway and was heading west, toward her cabin in the woods.

"We shouldn't be going this way. We should be going after Charlie."

She stomped the brakes and pulled the truck onto the shoulder. It came to an abrupt stop in a cloud of dust. "Can you sense where they took her?"

"No. No, I haven't been able to feel her since they closed the van's door."

She nodded, didn't look surprised. "Then we go back to my place. We gather some intel, we make a plan, and we call in some reinforcements."

He looked at her with his brows raised. "Reinforcements?"

"Vampires. I know a lot of vampires, Killian."

He stared at her, sure she was playing some kind of cruel joke. "There are others? There are others still alive?"

She nodded. "Lots of them. Did you think you were the last?"

Everything in him seemed to come to singing life at those words. "Up until the murders of those seven people in Portland, and the vampires that were killed as a result of it, I thought I was the only one left."

"The murder of the Portland Seven wasn't what it seemed. And I suspect the gang of vamps they killed for it never even existed. It was all faked by DPI to convince The Chosen they needed government protection."

He frowned. "DPI? What's—"

"Your former gang, they were all your age or younger, weren't they?"

He nodded.

"So you don't know diddly squat about what you are, or the history of your kind. Do you?"

"I know enough to get by."

"Yeah. Yeah." She lowered her head, rubbed the bridge of her nose. "Did you give Charlie your blood? Did she drink from you?"

He nodded. "It was the only way to save her life. She was so close to death. I could feel it." He looked out the truck's window at the towns behind them, the rural terrain and forests unrolling in front of them. She was back there, somewhere, and he had to get to her. "I don't understand why I'm so drawn to her, so in tune. I've been around others of The Chosen before. And you, now. But it's never been that...powerful."

She didn't reply, just kept glancing at him with wide, knowing eyes.

"You know why, don't you? Tell me."

She lowered her head. "For every vampire, the natural bond with The Chosen is super-charged with one particular person. There's a powerful link. No one ever told you this?"

"No. I didn't know."

"So then you probably also don't know that sharing blood empowers any bond still further. It'll be ten times more intense than before, Killian. But it will also help you to track her."

"It will?"

"Yes, it will." She looked at the sky, sighed. "It's going to be dawn soon. Can you drive, Killian?"

"Of course I can drive."

"Then take over. I need to make some calls and then ditch this phone. You can spend the night in my safe room. No harm will come to you there. They don't know where I live."

"Unless Charlie tells them," he said softly. "What if they torture her?"

"Easy, fella. Your eyes are glowing." She got out and came around to his side. He slid over behind the wheel and pulled the truck into motion.

"We should turn around," he said. "We should go after her now."

"We need to get to my computers so I can find the nearest DPI owned properties. That'll give us a clue where to begin searching. We have two hours until daylight. That's not enough time for you to do any good. And if you roast, you'll never find her. Trust me, okay? I've been around the block a few times."

He narrowed his eyes on her, then focused on the road again while she dialed her phone, and waited. "Who are you, anyway?"

"I'm Roxy," she said. "I'm the oldest living Chosen. And I'm on your side."

The van stopped at a tall gate that slid open slowly. Lieutenant Townsend was watching her face as she looked through the windshield at what seemed to be a military base. There was no sign giving its name, though, and it was in the middle of a forest, along a rutted path they'd been following through the towering trees for almost two hours.

"We call it the Area Fifty-One of the Pacific Northwest," he said after a second. "It's really called Fort Rogers. It's a top secret facility. Very few people even know it exists. You *will* be safe here."

She nodded. "We should get my grandmother, then. She's in danger, too."

"She's one of The Chosen?" he asked.

Charlie lowered her eyes. No matter how looney she was, her grandmother did not want the government to be aware of her blood type. She didn't think she should blow that. "No, of course not," she said softly. "She'd be dead by now if she was."

"What's your grandmother's name, Charlie?"

"Charlotte," she lied. "Same as mine. But...the whole grandmother thing is more an honorary title. My actual grandmothers are both dead."

"I see."

He didn't, but she didn't know this guy. She wasn't going to go spilling her grandmother's secrets to him.

Then again, Lieutenant Townsend *had* just saved her from a vampire attack.

She couldn't believe that was what Killian was. A vampire. He hadn't been drawn to her, or attracted to her, or turned on by kissing her, or falling head over heels in love with her, no matter how true and real those things had felt. He'd been stalking her and planning to make her his next meal. He'd played some kind of mind trick on her to make her feel the things she'd felt–still felt–for him. Fucking bastard, trying to bite her when she was already all but dead.

Images, hazy and broken like pieces of colored glass from a shattered mosaic, flipped in and out of her mind. Killian, leaning over her hospital bed, whispering something. Opening her eyes and looking up to see him, and realizing that he was carrying her away, through the night.

She remembered her grandmother shouting at him to stop.

She remembered him jerking and dropping to his knees, staring after her as she ran away with this Lieutenant Lucas Townsend.

She remembered wondering if Killian was dying and worrying about him.

She'd barely known him. Why did it feel so much like someone she'd trusted forever had just stabbed her in the back?

It made no sense.

"Charlie?"

The van had stopped in front of a long metal building. Green metal siding. Gray metal doors and roof. It didn't have windows that she could see. There were other buildings along the solid dirt road, all very similar. The lieutenant took her hand. "Hey, Charlie, you there?" he asked

"I'm here. I need to let my mother know I'm all right."

"We've already taken care of that. She asked us to keep you here until we've caught that rogue vampire that tried to kill you earlier."

"I don't think—" she cut herself off.

"Go on," Lieutenant Townsend said. "You can tell me anything. You don't think what?"

She blinked and looked him in the eyes. They were warm and completely sympathetic. "I don't think he was trying to kill me."

His sad eyes grew sadder. "I know they can seem...almost human. But Charlie, there's only one thing a vampire ever wants from a person like you or me, and that's a meal." She frowned at him, and he said, "Everyone here has the antigen, too. Well, with the exception of a few staffers. You're safe here."

She looked around. The camp was quiet, dark. "What is this? Some kind of BD internment camp?" she asked.

"Not internment. Training. You're not like everyone else with the antigen, Charlie. You're stronger than most. You have a unique and powerful healing ability. The scrapes and bruises you sustained in that car accident are already healing. You're smarter than most, too. You're a rare and special individual. That's why you're here. You can help us."

"Help you do what?"

He smiled. "Protect others like you. People like your grandmother, Roxanne O'Malley.

She looked at him with a gasp.

"Yeah, we know who she is."

"Then why did you ask me?"

"To see if you'd lie." He shrugged. "I don't blame you. You're protecting her. That's admirable. I'm going to help you learn how to protect her even better. Okay?"

She swallowed hard, feeling suspicious of this guy, and this camp, and whatever the hell was happening here. "How long do I have to stay?"

"Only as long as you want to." He looked behind them. "I just hope you won't leave quite yet. That bastard won't give up easily. He's probably lurking outside your mother's apartment or your grandmother's place, just waiting for another shot at draining every ounce of blood from your body and leaving you dead where you fall."

She shivered and followed his gaze, but of course saw nothing through the tinted glass. "I'll stay for tonight," she said.

"Good." His smile was as white as any she'd seen. "Come on, I'll show you to your bunk."

"We're here," Roxy said.

Killian heard her, vaguely, as if from a great distance, told himself to open his eyes, but had a hell of a time doing it. "Wake up, Killian. It's still nighttime. Not time for you to sleep just yet. And I'm gonna need your help, so let's go. Shake it off."

Nighttime? Then why was he so....?

He forced his eyes open, lifted his head, looked around him. He was still in the pickup truck, outside Roxy's little log cabin in the woods. He'd driven for a few miles while she'd made her calls, but then Roxy insisted they switch places again. Once they did, he'd slept all the way back from Pendleton. At *night*.

"It's the drug," Roxy explained. "They have this tranquilizer that works on vamps. It was developed in the nineties by DPI."

"DPI?" Right, she'd mentioned them. The Division of Paranormal something or other. Idiots maybe.

She was already out of the truck, hurrying around to his side, opening his door. "I usually park farther away and hike in, but special times call for special measures, or whatever that saying is."

He gave his head a shake. "Tell me more about this...DPI."

"They used to be a secret sub-division of the CIA. They're not so secret anymore. They're the government's top players in the games of vampire misinformation, fear mongering, and eventual extermination. If they have their way, they'll wipe your kind out of existence. There are, however, some of us mortals who intend to see to it that they don't. I'm one of those. Now get out of the truck and come on inside so I can fix you up."

He wanted to ask a dozen questions. How she knew so much, why she would take the side of his kind against her own, when they were going to start searching for Charlie–that was topmost on his mind.

He slid to the ground, wobbled a little. Roxy grabbed his arm and steadied him to the front door and then through it into a living room full of plants and birds in cages. The entire place smelled of Charlie. It made him ache for her. Then the giant white owl in the man-sized cage stared at him and ruffled her feathers all up in alarm.

Animals knew a predator when they met one. He tried to send her his harm-free intent with the power of his mind, and thought he might have succeeded when her feathers settled again and her head bobbed up and down.

"That's Olive," Roxy said.

"I know. She just told me."

"A bit of animal communication? Nice talent, Killian."

The sofa was where he thought he was headed, because he

needed to get off his feet, but Roxy tugged him past it. "This way. Fortunately, there's an antidote for the drug they shot into you. Even more fortunately, I have some on hand. So buck up, you'll be yourself again in no time."

She had an antidote for a drug that worked on vampires? Who the hell *was* she?

He followed her through a door and down into her basement. There was a long table against one wall with three computers on it. There were weapons all over the walls, ancient ones as well as modern, and there were books, a hundred of them at least, some of them apparently very old. On the table was a small mountain of cell phones.

Off to one side there was a separate room with its door standing open.

"That's the safe room," Roxy said when she saw him looking. "It's where you'll sleep. You can lock it from inside. No one can get in once you do, and there's a tunnel to the outside if you need to make a quick getaway." She frowned. "Used to be a cherry '68 Mustang at the other end. But my stubborn granddaughter made short work of that."

Killian followed along, peering into the safe room where there were shelves of weapons, crates of supplies and a couple of cots. Behind him, Roxy was tapping a message into a cell phone. He frowned. "Who are you texting?"

"Reinforcements. Don't you worry about it. Come here, sit down." She tossed the phone aside and pulled a rolling chair away from the bank of computers. "Roll up your sleeve for me."

He obeyed, watching the woman open a tiny refrigerator, and he glimpsed clear plastic bags inside it that made his body tense and his eyes heat. "Is that blood?"

She was drawing fluid into a syringe from a vial. "That it is, my friend. Human, even. I try to keep a little on hand in case of emergencies." She replaced the vial in the fridge. "You'd be surprised how easy it is to slip a few pints into a large purse when you show up at a blood drive. They think you're there to make a deposit. No one's expecting you to make a withdrawal instead. I'm a frequent donor." She took a bag from the fridge and tossed it to him. Killian caught the blood in his hands, feeling the hunger come to life inside in a way it had rarely done. Human blood. God, how long had it been?

"You can warm it in the microwave if you want," she said, holding up the syringe and snapping a finger against it to remove the air bubbles. She glanced his way. Saw the empty bag in his hand and probably the red glow in his eyes as well. He'd bitten through the plastic and downed the pint in about two seconds. "Well, I guess you must've needed that. Now give me your arm."

He took off his denim jacket and then his T-shirt, turning a shoulder her way.

"My goodness, aren't we ripped?" She swabbed him with an alcohol wipe, which was completely unnecessary, then injected him. The needle prick hurt like a knife wound would've hurt, him being a vampire and super sensitized, but he clenched his jaw and bore it well, he thought, then put his shirt back on when it was over.

"I don't think we can safely stay here," he said. "What if they make Charlie tell them where you live?"

"We're moving at sunset. You need to sleep and heal. Let that blood and the day sleep do its work today. I'll pack what we need and do some recon. I have other places. We'll be out of here by sundown." She pawed through the pile of cell phones, chose one and dialed it, clicking the speaker button so he could hear both sides of the call. "Charlotte's mother," she said. There was ringing, and then a woman's voice answered.

"If your phone is being monitored, hang up now."

"It's not...that I know of anyway. What the hell happened to my daughter, Roxy? What have you done with her now?"

Roxy rolled her eyes, probably at the woman's use of her name on what might be a monitored call. "You saw what happened, same as me. That government goon squad took her, which is exactly what I was afraid would happen."

"No. They *tried* to take her, but then that vampire came back and got her away from them."

"Oh did he now?" Roxy met Killian's eyes, her own a little angry, but not at him.

"They came over here a few hours ago, the same damn commandant that's been on the news every day since the Portland Seven. Crowe. He's got eyes like one. He was asking if I'd heard from her, said the vampire ambushed the SUV on the way to some safe house where they were planning to hide her. He got her, took her away with him. They said I'd probably never..." her voice broke. "...never see her again."

"Well that's complete–" Roxy stopped herself as an odd mechanical hum came and went through the line. Killian saw her eyes widen, and then she went on. "That's completely tragic. I'm devastated. But don't give up hope, Trish. Not until we know for sure."

"I'll never give up hope, Roxy. But you...you can help. You know these–"

"You know I'll do all I can," she said. "I'll call you soon. Goodbye Trish." And she hung up, shook her head, and said, "God that woman is too dumb to live. Calling me by my name, and she was just about to mention how well I know the Undead on a tapped line. That a girl as intelligent as Charlotte managed to emerge from that gene pool is beyond me."

"Maybe she got more from her father's side of the family," Killian said. He was more than halfway to admiring this woman. But he still didn't trust her. Not entirely. "Why are you helping me, Roxy?"

She took the empty plastic bag from him, crossed the basement to the furnace, opened a burner door and tossed it inside. "I've got a whole list of reasons."

"Such as?"

She shrugged. "Mainly, because I'm going to need help

getting my granddaughter back from the government. Preternatural help. And right now, you're the only vampire close enough at hand."

"Ah."

"And because I've been a friend to your kind for more than twenty years. And because in this world of grays, there are still such plain and simple things as black and white. Right and wrong. And what's been done to the Undead and what I suspect is now being done to The Chosen is just simply wrong. I've never been very good at tolerating wrong."

"So you're an ally."

"I'm a blood-relative, Killian."

He nodded.

"And there's one more reason."

"What's that?"

"You are Charlotte's destiny. Part of it, anyway. I have reason to believe there's a lot more. But you and she...you're bound. Fated. You might not know it yet, and neither does she, but I know it."

The words rocked him. He had been alone for so long that the idea of being anyone's destiny was alien to him. But he felt the validity of those words right to the core of him. They resonated with the unmistakable vibration of truth. He was bound to Charlie from before he'd even met her, and he didn't think it was because she was one of The Chosen, or even because she was the one with whom he had the most powerful link. It was because they were two parts of the same soul, torn apart during some previous incarnation and seeking each other ever since. That's what it felt like. She was a part of him. The part he'd been missing.

Killian felt the pull of the sunrise tugging him toward slumber. His eyelids were heavy, drooping.

"Come on, before you fall asleep where you are, and I'm forced to lug your carcass into the safe room." Roxy went in before him, and he followed, watching as she unzipped a plastic storage bag and pulled a blanket and pillow from it. She put them on the nearest cot, then went to the shelf unit on the back wall and pulled it open to show him the tunnel she'd mentioned. She closed it again. "I'll go check the other side, make sure the exit is still camouflaged. You're safe here for the day, Killian. Rest. You need it."

"Thank you, Roxy. I want you to know that I'll do everything in my power to help you get Charlie back."

"I know you will," she said, and then she left and closed the door behind her.

CHAPTER EIGHT

Charlie woke so suddenly she sat bolt upright in her bunk, eyes wide, heart pounding, dreams still hovering around the edges of her mind.

Soft and wavering, like a mirage, those dreams. Killian, bending over her in a hospital bed, pressing a wet sponge to her mouth. She remembered how thirsty she was, how she latched on to that sponge to suck the moisture from it as if she'd been dying of thirst.

But wait, it hadn't been a sponge, had it? What, then?

"Welcome to Fort Rogers. Hope you don't plan to sleep this late every morning."

The girl doing the talking wore green cargo pants and an olive drab tank top. She was ripped. Her black hair was pulled back into a tight ponytail and her skin was the color of caramel.

"I was told to let you rest till you were ready. So? Are you ready?"

Sitting up in the bed, still in her hospital gown, Charlie tried to decide what to make of the girl. "Ready for what?"

"Breakfast. Then the grand tour. And then you get to decide if you want to stay or not. Be a part of something bigger than you. Something important."

"I get it now. You're what? Some kind of recruiter?"

She shook her head. "Nope. Just another BD like you. Well, maybe a *little* different."

She came closer, scooping a neatly folded stack of clothes from a nearby three-drawer stand. There was one beside every bunk, ten bunks in the room, five on each side. "I'm Mariah." She held out the clothes.

"Charlie," Charlie said, taking them. They were the same clothes the other girl wore. There were socks, a sports bra and a pair of underpants as well.

"Shower's through there, Charlie." Mariah pointed to a door at the end of the barracks. "There's a footlocker under your bed. Everything you need is provided for you here. Get yourself cleaned up and dressed, and I'll take you to the mess hall for some breakfast. LT's gonna meet us there."

"All right." Charlie took the clothes with her and headed into the bathroom, which had six private stalls. Three of them were showers and three were toilets. There was one sink and a mirror, and she thought if all ten bunks were occupied, there should've been at least five of each.

Didn't matter. She wasn't staying here. She'd rather languish at her grandmother's middle-of-nowhere cabin in the woods than join this troop. Or whatever it was.

She was buzzing and nervous, and yet hyper-aware. She had no idea how she could feel the way she did after nearly dying from blood loss. She felt good. Strong. And it seemed to her that her senses had sharpened. She'd noticed that last night, but thought it might be shock or something. But it was still with her.

She took her shower at record speed and emerged dressed in what was apparently the uniform of this place. But she left her hair down, because she was feeling slightly defiant.

She saw Mariah notice it, but the other girl made no comment. She just opened the door into bright morning sunlight. They fell into step side by side, walking over a winding strip of pavement amid other barracks and across a central yard where Old Glory waved and snapped from a giant flagpole. It was situated in the center of a circle of lawn and flowers, which was surrounded by a loop of pavement. Like a hub. The pavement went in four directions, including the one from which she'd come. Buildings lined three of them. The fourth seemed to veer off into wilderness. A group of men and women dressed just like she was, were jogging off in that direction. This place was far bigger than she'd realized at first.

"That big square that looks like a warehouse is the mess hall," Mariah explained. Charlie would've known that without being told. She'd been smelling the food since they'd left the barracks. "Breakfast is over, but Cook had orders to hold a plate for you. Bear in mind, this is a one-time deal. You stick around, you get up at reveille like the rest of us, or you don't eat."

"Good thing you're not a recruiter. You're lousy at it."

The girl looked at her sternly. Charlie smiled, but she didn't seem to get it. "Hey, I was joking, okay?"

"Yeah. Okay." Still no smile. She pushed down the bars on a big set of double doors and sailed through. "Cookie, you got something for the newbie?"

"Cookie" was another girl, around the same age as Charlie and Mariah. She was blond and unsmiling as she took a plate from somewhere with a pot holder and set it on the counter that separated the kitchen from the cafeteria. "It's hot." Then she put a mug beside the plate, and pointed. "Coffee's over there. I think there's still a cup or two left."

"Thanks," Charlie said. She plucked a few brown paper napkins from a stack and used them to pick up the plate. It burned her fingers anyway before she dropped it onto a table. Mariah had two mugs filled before Charlie even got herself seated, and she put one in front of her, then slid onto the bench seat directly across from her and pointed at her plate. "Steak and eggs. We're all about high protein here. BDs need more than ordinary people do. And BD-Exers need more yet."

"What's a BD-Exer?" Charlie asked.

Mariah just smiled. "LT will explain that to you before the day is out."

LT for lieutenant, or maybe for Lucas Townsend. Either way, same guy. Charlie noted that her grandmother had said the same thing about a high protein diet, then she tucked into the food, hungrier than she'd been in a month, and surprised by how every bite made her want more. The flavors exploded on her tongue in a way she'd never experienced before. Apparently Cookie was a world class gourmet who could make ordinary steak and eggs taste incredible. She'd intended to chew, swallow, sip, and ask questions. Instead, she wolfed the food, barely taking a breath in between bites. She was embarrassed, and her plate bare, by the time she managed to get a grip again.

Lifting her head, she must have looked apologetic, because Mariah said, "It's okay. When you haven't been getting enough, it's like that. We're all the same here, Charlie. We understand each other."

She nodded slowly. Maybe they did. "What is this place, exactly? I mean, I thought it was some kind of safe house for people like me, but it looks more like a military base."

"Not military. We don't belong to any branch. We're a special unit in training. A vampire attacked you last night, didn't it?"

She nodded, once again haunted by the hazy memory of Killian, gathering her upper body in his arms, bending over her, feeding her...something.

"One got my whole family," Mariah said. "My mother. My baby sister." She closed her eyes. "I wasn't home when it happened. Out drinking with some friends. I thought I was being kidnapped when LT and some other officers took me as I stumbled out of a bar. But I found out later they'd been tipped off. They were trying to protect me, to get me to safety. Another team was sent to rescue my family, but it was too late."

"God." Charlie no longer wondered at the other girl's lack of lightness or humor. It was a dark tale. "How long ago?"

"Two months."

"I'm really sorry."

Mariah nodded. "Cookie was married to her childhood sweetheart. They got him, too. All of us have lost someone to those bloodsuckers. Where's your family?"

"I was staying with my grandmother, but I think she can handle herself." She wondered, though. Would Killian go after her mother? She'd be an easy target. Not Roxy, though. Not Roxy with her cache of weapons and her alarms and her eight-hundred and two cell phones and all her precautions.

Except Roxy was deluded. She wasn't afraid of vampires at all. She was more afraid of the government.

"I'd like to call her." As soon as she said it, she knew it would be impossible. Roxy changed phones like most people changed socks. But maybe she could call her mother and find out how to reach Roxy. She needed to be warned, at least.

"You take the tour, you make the decision, we take you back if you want to go. No calls from base. It's not safe. Can you imagine if the vamps found out about this place?"

"I thought they were all dead. Or mostly all."

"You thought wrong. There are more of them out there than anyone knows. That's not for public dissemination, by the way. Gotta keep the populace from panicking. And besides, we're the ones in danger, not them."

She nodded, not liking that truth, but accepting it.

"The people here have had enough of hanging around waiting to be vampire food. I don't like being a victim. This unit is giving me a way to fight back. And there's more, too. I can't even tell you the stuff you get by staying here–"

"That's right, recruit, you can't."

Lieutenant Townsend stood in the doorway. His cargo pants were camo print, and his green shirt was a T, not a tank. No insignia anywhere, but Mariah jumped to her feet and saluted when she saw him. "I wasn't going to, Lieutenant Townsend, sir."

"At ease. I know you weren't. I'm gonna take over the tour from here. Go change up and join the others on the obstacle course, on the double."

"Yes, sir!" She headed out of the mess hall like her boots were on fire. "Yeah, see, that's not gonna be me, *LT*," Charlie said. "Not in this lifetime. I've never called anybody sir in my life, and I don't intend to start now."

He smiled. "That's your call. But there's a lot to see, Charlie. Come on, let's get started."

She hadn't stood up, and she didn't. She was feeling rebellious, tired of being told what to do, taken where people wanted her to go, protected and kept in the dark about God only knew how many things. So she sat there, instead. She finished her coffee, and noted with regret that Mariah hadn't had a chance to finish her own. When her mug was empty, she got up, walked to the doorway where Lieutenant Townsend stood waiting, and said, "All right. I'm ready now."

"Good."

The private jet's pilot was one of Rhiannon's regulars, a human completely under her thrall. Weak-willed mortals were invaluable assets to the Undead. Of course, Roland often disagreed with her about the ethics of using them. (Her mate was sometimes far too ethical for his own good.) But this was an emergency situation that would save lives. Even *he* hadn't argued this time. Oh, he might have, until they'd received an urgent text message from their mortal friend, Roxy.

They'd flown the night through with the sun behind them, as if in pursuit. Dawn was pushed back with every time line they passed, flying westward from a private airstrip in Brasov, Transylvania to one in upstate NY. There, they refueled and then continued on across the US, landing at last on a hidden runway within a cathedral forest outside Portland, Oregon.

Rhiannon watched their pilot go off on foot, heading into the city with a hefty wad of cash and a set of false memories to explain how he had arrived there. He would emerge from his dazed state enough to use the cell phone she'd tucked into his pocket and call one of the numbers she had programmed into it for him—a Portland cab company, a nice hotel where a room was already reserved and paid for in his name, and his home number in Albany. He would find commercial airline tickets back home awaiting him at the hotel's desk. His disappearance would be blamed on a temporary lapse of cognitive function, possibly stress related, and he would go on to live a happy life, never knowing the service he had provided to his own kind, as well as hers.

Rhiannon smoothed a soothing hand over Roland's tense shoulder. "It's over now, darling. Your feet are once again firmly planted upon solid earth."

"I hate flying in those contraptions. It's unnatural."

"If you'd only allow Vlad to teach you shapeshifting, you could fly without them."

She was teasing, and he knew it. Not every vampire could master every skill, and there were precious few who could manage to change their form. Vlad was one. He could become bat or wolf. Vixen was another, but she'd been a shapeshifter before she'd become a vampire. Rare individual, that one. Rhiannon wondered if she'd survived the war of 2011, and hoped so. Reaper and his little gang of vampires were dear to her. She hoped they'd all survived, but hadn't heard from any of them since she'd been forced to flee to Romania.

"Come, Pandora," she whispered as she turned to walk back into the woods. The trees were huge, bigger than she'd seen anywhere, and she'd been almost everywhere. Never here, though. The forest must be virgin, the trees, thousands of years old. Older than she was, perhaps. Had they been saplings in this wild and untamed land when she'd been a little girl in the temple of Isis in Egypt? Had they seen as much as she had?

Rhiannon had a feeling of camaraderie with the arboreal giants as she walked among them. Seldom did she feel small or insignificant, but in this great forest, she came close to that. Even the lush ferns were higher than her head, and the smells, the scents of the trees, their needles and cones and sap, were an olfactory feast.

"Darling." Roland's hand curled around her nape, sending shivers of pleasure right to her toes.

She tilted her head in catlike pleasure. "I'm sorry, my love. The majesty of this forest is overwhelming my sense of purpose."

"And your purpose is?"

"To get to Roxy, of course. We should have plenty of time to help her recover her stolen granddaughter before Devlin and his gang of killers even arrive here. Cargo ship." She rolled her eyes. "Amateurs."

"Agreed. But if those are our goals, then why are we traipsing through this forest, back toward the plane?"

She turned around and smiled up at him. Rhiannon was tall for a woman. Particularly for an ancient Egyptian woman. Not that there were many of those walking around today. Roland was taller. She loved that he was taller. "To camouflage it, of course. It won't take long."

"Ahh. The *Glamourie*?"

"It is my specialty." They emerged from the sentinel conifers to the edge of the clearing where her speedy little jet awaited their return. Rhiannon stopped, stepped her feet a bit farther apart, and gave her hands and arms a shake. Roland gave her room to work. He loved watching her use magic. He'd told her so a thousand times. And she loved practicing it. The magical arts had been a part of her since long before she'd become a vampire. She had been taught by the priestesses of Isis, after all—the most powerful magical practitioners there had ever been.

Arms to her sides, palms turned outward, Rhiannon stared at the jet, and then past it, at the trees that were its backdrop. In her mind, she conjured an image of those trees that came all the way down, rather than stopping where the jet began, so that the space the jet occupied vanished, and the trees were all there was to be seen. Near the bottom, she imagined the grasses and wildflowers, the giant ferns and berry briars, also continuing. Once her vision was firm in her mind, she closed her eyes and slowly raised her hands outward and upward. As she did, the grasses, flowers and ferns rose up in her mind's eye. The tree trunks, limbs and leaves, lowered down like a curtain over the plane. When her hands met over her head, she twisted her palms outward again, and brought both arms down fast. Then she opened her eyes and looked. "There. Since inanimate objects give off very little discernible energy, that should hold until I reverse the spell."

Roland stood beside her, shaking his head. "You never fail to amaze me. Even after all this time."

"I hope I never shall," she told him, and she trailed a forefinger down his cheek, to his neck, leaned up and kissed him slow.

His arms came around her waist, pulled her hard against him, and he bent over her neck, nibbling and nipping until her body yearned. "Later, my love," she whispered. "Roxy first. Remember?"

One sharp bite made her wince in pleasure, then he lifted his head. The glow in his eyes was for her, and she knew it, relished it. "All right, my love. But I'll hold you to that promise."

Rhiannon pulled out her cell phone in its glittering, beaded case, and looked again at the text message she had received just before leaving Romania. It had come from a number she did not recognize.

"Granddaughter abducted. Desperate Prayers Invoked. TOC."

She'd deciphered the simple code easily. "Desperate Prayers Invoked" clearly referred to DPI, the Undead's most hated enemy. TOC was Roxy's way of identifying herself. The Oldest Chosen.

"Where is she?" he asked.

"That's what we're about to find out, my love." She typed in a text. "We've arrived. Send coordinates."

Within seconds, the map feature on the small but amazing device, took over the screen, showing an X that was highlighted. Rhiannon clicked the "find route" command, and the screen changed to one showing how to drive to the spot. Of course, they wouldn't need to drive, and there was still an hour or so until daylight. She turned the phone to show Roland. "It's less than twenty miles."

"Eighteen point seven," he said.

"Even you must admit to the amazing capabilities of this little handheld computer."

"I'm not a fan. No one has to remember anything anymore, or even learn anything. Computers are a crutch. They weaken the mind. But conveyances bother me more."

"I think you simply hate to admit to such a human weakness as motion sickness."

"You think wrong."

She smiled and fluttered her lashes. "I'm never wrong. But I won't make you admit it just now. We can make it in no time on foot, taking a direct route through the forest. We don't even need to liberate a car."

He brought her hand to his lips for a lingering kiss, met her eyes, and together, they crossed the road, entered the woods on the other side, and sped off too fast for even animal eyes to detect.

"This is my favorite part of the base. Look."

LT was awfully attentive. The kind of attentive that told Charlie he was into her, which was okay. She was wary, though. The last guy who'd given her shivers up her spine had turned out to be a hungry vampire out for a quick meal. Even if it felt like he was the soulmate she'd been searching for all her life. So she told herself to just play it cool for now.

Lucas had shown her the company gym where people had been working out on every imaginable piece of equipment. He'd shown her the Dojo where martial arts training was going on. He'd taken her through the infirmary where empty beds with clean white sheets were lined up, and the only activity was in a sectioned off portion near the back that held a lab on one side and an office on the other. There had been several people in white coats and goggles in the lab, messing around with beakers and test tubes doing she had no idea what.

And now they were standing at the Combat Training Field, according to the sign, where men and women in olive green shorts, T-shirts, and running shoes were tackling an obstacle course like a bunch of athletes in training. There were three groups taking turns on a course. The obstacles included sawhorses they had to jump, a mud pit they had to traverse using a long pole, and some razor wire that required a twenty foot belly crawl. And there was a tall wooden wall at the far end that she presumed they would climb over when they reached it.

As she watched them, Charlie felt an old familiar longing in her gut. She'd always wished she could be one of those people. The strong, active, muscled types who could jog for miles or do fifty push-ups or play sports adequately enough to be on a team. But she couldn't. She'd never been strong.

The sun was high, and it was a gorgeous day, cool but bright with just enough of a breeze to be perfect. The wooden wall caught her attention again as the first group of recruits reached it. It had knotted ropes dangling from it, and one recruit after another grabbed the rope and scaled the wall more or less like Spiderman.

Charlie shook her head and looked at LT. "I'm not athletic. There's no way I would ever be able to do that. Any of this."

"Neither could most BDs, Charlie. None of them could begin to tackle this course when they arrived here. The Belladonna Antigen begins making you weaker than normal humans long before you're aware of it. Just keep watching, though."

The second group had reached the wall, and one by one they grabbed the rope, placed one foot on the wall, and launched themselves over the top. Charlie's jaw dropped. "Are you kidding me?"

"Wait. Just wait."

The third group came to the wall, and didn't even touch the ropes. They just jumped, springing into the air as if they'd been launched there, and landing on the other side easily.

She frowned, not taking her eyes off of them. "That wall has to be fifteen feet high. How is this possible?"

"It's twenty. And that's the part I haven't told you yet."

"I don't get it," she said. "They have the antigen, just like I do, right?"

"Yes."

"And you just said it makes you weaker, even before you're aware of it, didn't you?"

"Yes, I did. And you already know that most BDs don't live much past thirty-five. Almost none of them in fact. The average lifespan used to be around forty-two, by the way. We don't know why it's getting shorter, but it is."

That distracted her momentarily. "*Almost* none live past thirty-five. That means that some do?"

He nodded. "Yeah. There are one or two exceptions that we're aware of. But it's rare, Charlie."

"Do you know why some live longer?"

"Like your grandmother, you mean?"

She didn't confirm or deny it.

"We don't know. We're trying to find out. That's part of what we do here. Research is as much a part of Fort Rogers as training is. It's even named after one of our first and most ground breaking researchers–Curtis Rogers. But your grandmother...well, she's...not a person who's likely to cooperate with us in those efforts."

"I know. She's stubborn."

"It doesn't matter, though. We've found an answer."

Charlie frowned and watched as the three groups of recruits returned to the beginning of the course and started again. They were smiling, laughing, animated and high-fiving one another. "What do you mean...an answer?"

"A cure," he said.

Her heart jumped in her chest. "A cure?"

"More than that, Charlie. We have developed a drug called BDX. We give a series of treatments that not only cure the side effects of the Belladonna Antigen and remove that sentence of an early death, but make you stronger in the meantime. *Way* stronger."

Blinking slowly, she searched his eyes, trying to tell whether he was lying or not, but she'd never been much good at reading people.

He looked away, focusing on the recruits again. "Group One has only had the first treatment. Group Two has received two of them, and Group Three has had the full series. Three intravenous treatments over three days, and you'll be jumping that wall like they are."

She *wanted* to be strong and healthy and vibrant, and she *really* wanted to live past thirty-five. She almost told him so right then, but there was something holding her back.

"If this is true, then why aren't you distributing this formula far and wide to every BD in the country by now?"

He gazed out at the course where the recruits showed off their skills. The sun gleamed off his dark hair. "FDA. We're lucky they're even letting us run these trials."

"So it's experimental."

"Yeah."

"How long have you been experimenting on human beings, Lieutenant Townsend?"

He didn't even flinch, didn't try to deny it. "Since the war. Three years now."

"So then how do you know they won't die around the age of thirty-five?"

"Because they're no longer growing weaker. They're growing stronger. Every physical test indicates—"

"But you're not sure."

He pressed his lips. "I'm as sure as I need to be."

"And you want something from me, from them, in return for this miracle cure, right?"

He stared at her for a long moment, then smiled shaking his head rapidly. "Man, you're something aren't you? No small talk. Cut right to the chase. Am I right?"

"It's usually the shortest path to the truth. So you're offering me this drug, this treatment that will make me able to leap small garden sheds in a single bound. What is it you're asking from me in return?"

"Fair question. I want you to stay. To live here. To train here."

"And what would I be training for? Some kind of re-run of the Vampire War?"

He nodded. "That's right. This camp, and these trainees— this is how we prevent mankind's extinction, Charlie. This is humanity's last line of defense against the next wave of vampire attacks. And it is coming, believe me, it is coming. We didn't get them all the first time. They've had two years to propagate, and they are pissed."

She drew a deep breath, looked around her and nodded. "I want the cure. But I don't want to be a part of whatever this is, and I sure as hell don't want to fight vampires. I don't want to fight at all. I just want to live out my life in peace. So I guess my decision is...thanks, but no thanks. I'm not into playing guinea pig, and I'm not into violence or genocide."

"Charlie, aren't you hearing me? We can *cure* you."

"Yeah, I got that. But um, I'm not all that near my expiration date yet, so I'm just not feeling the urgency. A little more testing, a few more years to make sure this cure of yours actually works can't really hurt anything, can it? I'm not warrior material, LT. Never have been. So you have my answer. I get to go home now, right?"

He blinked, clearly surprised. It must not have been the response he was expecting, she thought. Apparently, most BDs didn't say no when offered this sort of a trade. Well she had. Now she would find out if he'd been telling the truth when he'd told her the choice was hers. Somehow, that was the part of this whole scenario that she didn't quite believe. And maybe that was because she'd spent a little too much time in the company of her paranoid, conspiracy-theory nut of a grandmother, but whatever.

"Fine. We'll have you home before sundown." He didn't look her in the eyes when he said it.

Charlie was not relieved. She would believe it, she thought, when she was home. With her mom, not Roxy.

CHAPTER NINE

Killian awoke at sundown, blasting into life from a state of nothingness so suddenly that it felt like a powerful current jolting through every cell of his body. He would never get used to that. Such an abrupt awakening. Like electrocution. It almost hurt, and he considered it one of the least pleasing aspects of being what he was.

He sat up on the cot and tried to quiet his mind and let his muscles unclench for a moment. But instead of peaceful tranquility, he found something else. The buzzing charge to the air that had his hair rising with static, and goose bumps dancing over his forearms. A presence he hadn't sensed in years.

There was another vampire nearby! And the air was thick with the scent of human blood.

"Roxy," he whispered with an alarmed look at the door. He surged to the safe room's door, quickly unlocking it, swinging it wide, and lunging through, ready for battle.

Roxy stood in the basement with a big tray. Warmed mugs

held freshly heated blood, and two vampires stood beside her. Two vampires, living proof that he was not the last of his kind. He was not alone. His mind worked rapidly to process all the sensations ripping through his awareness, but it wasn't easy with the scent from those heated mugs bringing the bloodlust to screaming life in him. He got *powerful* and *ancient* and *hungry*, and that was about all.

"Oh for heaven's sakes, feed him before his head explodes," said the female. She had jet black hair that gleamed like onyx and reached her waist. She was tall, lean except for the swell of her breasts in the V-neck of her black blouse. It had long sleeves that draped loosely at the ends, and she wore tight fitting leggings and shoes that had heels at least three inches high.

"Stop ogling my bride and drink up, Killian. We have much to discuss." That was the male. He wore a suit. Black and white. Formal. Narrow lapels, no tie. His hair was as dark as the woman's but pulled straight back and held behind his head with a band. His eyes glowed red as he took a mug from the tray, brought it to his lips, and drank it straight down.

The woman did the same, smiling with her eyes, and Roxy held a mug out to him. "Take it, Killian. We need you all in top form if we're going to save Charlie. Drink up."

He took his mug from her, said "Thank you," and chugged it. Then he replaced it on the tray and waited for someone to tell him what the hell was going on.

"This is Roland," Roxy said, nodding to the striking man. Killian shook his hand, and Roxy went on. "And this is—"

"Rhiannon," the vampiress said. "Born Rhianikki, daughter of Pharaoh, princess of Egypt, and undisputed Queen of the Undead."

She offered a hand as well, but he wasn't sure whether she expected him to shake it or kiss it. He opted for the latter, and she beamed in approval.

"Rhiannon and Roland are elders among the Undead,"

Roxy said. "Leaders. And friends of mine. They've come to help us."

"Among other reasons," Rhiannon said softly.

Roxy frowned, shooting her a look that said she had not known about any other reasons.

"I'm Killian," he said. "I thought I was the last, until that attack in Portland."

"That attack in Portland was perpetrated by humans," Roland said. "No vampire can harm one of The Chosen."

"That's what I thought. But what about the band of vampires they said they killed in retribution?"

"I don't believe there ever was a band of vampires," the elegant Roland said slowly. "I think it was simply a story made up by DPI to frighten and control the public. Especially The Chosen. The very notion that *they* are our preferred prey is ludicrous. Clearly DPI is after something. They have a hidden agenda."

Roxy nodded. "They want to track and monitor us," she said. "But since Americans aren't crazy about that sort of thing, they have to convince us that it's for our own protection."

"Oh, The Chosen need protection, certainly. But from DPI, not from us," Rhiannon said softly.

There was something happening to Killian. He was feeling a surge of emotion. Of connection. Of relief and something like joy just at being in the presence of other vampires when he'd been so alone for so long.

Roland clapped a hand to his shoulder. "There are others, Killian. We've reclaimed a hotel in the most clichéd place you could imagine, and survivors have been making their way to us there ever since."

"Including a handful of rebels intent on re-starting the war of twenty-eleven and taking vengeance on humanity," Rhiannon added. "But they won't be here for a few days, so we'll deal with your issue first. And then, I'll deal with Devlin and his rogues."

Killian didn't get the feeling he'd like being in Devlin's shoes when Rhiannon caught up to him.

"Roxanne has told us a bit about your past," Roland said. "We'd like to know the names of the others in your band."

"Quickly, of course," Rhiannon said, pulling an iPad from a bag and running her dagger tipped forefinger across its screen to open the program she sought. "We can go over it while Roxy and Roland finalize our plan for locating Charlotte." She looked around the basement. "But honestly, let's do it in a bit more comfort than this." She turned toward the basement stairs, snapped her fingers beside her, and suddenly a huge black panther emerged from the shadows, leaping to her side.

Killian's eyes widened, and he stepped quickly and firmly in between the animal and Roxy. Rhiannon saw the reaction and smiled. "Pandora, this is Killian. He's a brave one. Try not to eat him."

The cat looked at him and made a chuffing sound, flicked its ears, and then looked away. Killian stared into her eyes and silently told her he was a friend, and he thought she heard him.

"Just keep her in the living room," Roxy said. "I've moved all the birds into the bedrooms." She took the stairs and headed up.

"She wouldn't hurt them," Rhiannon said.

"No, but she'd terrify them. Most of them are well enough to be released soon. I don't want anything causing any setbacks."

"What about the owl?" Roland asked. "I noticed her as we came in this morning. What a beautiful creature."

"Thank you, Roland. Her name is Olive, and she's become a companion of mine." Roxy opened the door at the top of the stairs and led them into the main part of her cabin. "I've released her twice now. The second time, thirty miles away. But she just keeps coming back."

Roxy went to the coffee table where a laptop computer sat. There was a half-filled cup of cold coffee in front of it and a small plate with some crumbs. "I've been doing research while you've been resting today. The men who took Charlie were clearly DPI but also some kind of militia type unit. I knew what to look for. There are precious few military bases in Oregon. A few National Guard Reserve Posts way too transparent to be hiding much. Coast Guard stations all along the coast, naturally, and two air bases, both on the property of commercial airports, Klamath Falls and Portland International. And then there's Umatilla Chemical Depot where they used to store chemical and biological weapons. All the weapons have been safely disposed of, or so the government claims, and that base is closed. Nine thousand acres, complete with underground bunkers. We should check it out, but I have a feeling it's too obvious."

"I agree," Roland said, nodding.

"What about federally owned lands that are not military? National parks and so on?" Rhiannon asked.

"National parks are too frequently visited by tourists to be feasible, but you're right about federally owned land. There's quite a lot of it that's labeled 'Wilderness.'" Roxy got up and went to a corner table where a printer held a stack of sheets. She picked through them, brought one. "I've got a map of all of them, and some aerial photos of a few."

"Well, that certainly simplifies things," Rhiannon said. She reached behind her neck to unfasten the chain she wore. It held a pendent that was made of shining black stone and came to a point at the end. "Bring your maps and photos here, Roxanne, along with something your Charlotte recently held in her hands. We'll do this the old fashioned way. Meanwhile, please, Killian, tell us about your former gang. Roland will take notes." She handed her iPad to Roland. He made a face and pulled a pen from his jacket pocket. Smiling, Roxy handed him a yellow legal pad instead, which he accepted gratefully. Then she quickly cleared the coffee table to make room for all her printouts.

"There were seven of us," Killian said. "I was the oldest."

"And how old is that, Killian?" Roland asked. "How long have you been Undead?"

"Since eighty-five. I had an apartment in LA. One by one, others found me there, and pretty soon we'd taken over the whole building. There was a street tough kid who called herself Krystal. Maybe fifteen when she was turned. She had short brown hair, but she liked to dye it all the time. Purple and blue were her favorites. She was small, skinny, and moody. George and Rys were older, early twenties, twins I think, though they never said. Looked alike. Blue eyed blonds who loved makeup and leather and chains. Musicians, both of them. And there was Robert, a monster-sized man. I have no idea of his age before he was turned. He was off, you know? Like he'd been mentally stunted as a human and still was as a vampire."

Roland was writing it all down, but he was still watching Rhiannon. She was leaning over the maps, dangling her jewelry from its chain so the stone was suspended over one of them and sitting very still.

After a moment, she snapped the chain upright, catching the stone in her palm, and switched to a different map.

"And you're certain they all perished when your building was burned by human vigilantes?" Roland asked.

"I don't know how anyone could've survived," Killian said, lowering his head.

"You did," Rhiannon commented without looking away from her once again suspended pendant.

"I don't know how. I woke in a culvert, underneath the road with ice water flowing over my lower body."

"Nonetheless, you woke," Roland said. "You escaped. That means they could have as well."

"If they had, they'd have contacted me by now."

"Have you tried to contact them?" he asked.

"No."

"No. Because you believe them to be dead. Perhaps they

haven't contacted you for the same reason. Because they believe you to be dead."

"Ahh, here we are," Rhiannon said softly. She was staring at the pendant, which was swinging in a series of ever-widening circles over one of the maps. Killian moved to look at the map. It was a National Wildlife Refuge that consisted of forests and wetlands, about seventy-five miles south of them, as nearly as he could tell.

"That's it?" he asked. "You're sure she's there?"

Rhiannon's brows bent closer, and the look she sent him made him think she wasn't used to having her opinion questioned. He didn't give a damn, he needed to be sure. Otherwise, time would be wasted. Time that could be spent tracking Charlie down. Saving her.

"If Rhiannon says she's there, she's there," Roxy said, putting a hand on his shoulder.

"Then let's go get her out," he said, and he got to his feet, eager. "Let's load ourselves down with some of Roxy's collection of weapons and go get her. Right now."

Roxy nodded hard and left the room.

Roland met Rhiannon's eyes, and something passed between them. Some secret knowing, laced with affection. "First," Roland said, returning his dark gaze to Killian, "we'll get close enough to conduct a bit of surveillance and find out what we're dealing with. And then we'll make a plan, and *then* we'll get her out."

Killian was about to argue, but Rhiannon said, "Or, we do it your way and end up dead, and no one is left to get her out."

He closed his eyes, told himself to be patient. "Let's just get there. All right? Can we just go? Now?"

"I'm with Killian," Roxy said. She had come back into the room, arms loaded down with weapons and a plastic bag in one hand. She was dressed in jeans, a skin-tight, camouflage print T-shirt, and an olive drab fishing type hat. She unloaded the weapons onto the sofa, marched to the front door, opened it, and tossed the bag outside. "That's a five pound rump roast," she told Rhiannon. "For the cat."

"Pandora, eat," Rhiannon said, pointing.

The cat loped out the door and tore into the bag. Roxy closed the door and turned. "We'll load the truck with weapons, the computers, and anything else that ties Charlotte or me to this place. We can't come back here. Just in case they've made her talk."

Killian felt a chill go up his spine at those words. "I've been thinking about that. And I just don't believe Charlie would tell them where you are. Do you, Roxy?"

Rhiannon said very softly, "There are not many mortals capable of withstanding DPI's...methods. Roxanne is right. You cannot come back here. Just in case." She looked at Roxy. "Nor can you risk missing anything, so much as a microscopic dust mite, that can give them a clue where you've gone."

Roxy nodded, a look of grim resolve crossing her face.

An hour later, the pickup was loaded full, and the four of them were crammed into the front seat together with Roxy driving over the rutted path through the woods to the highway. Poor Olive was in the back, her six foot tall cage wrapped in a dark blanket to keep her from having heart failure at the sight of the black panther who was sharing her ride.

Killian looked into the rearview mirror at the burning cabin, tongues of flame licking into the night sky. The vampiress Rhiannon had set the fire with no more than a long, intense stare. Nothing would remain of the place. That was for sure.

But it scared him that all three of them believed this was necessary.

And something deep inside him rose like a dark demon, unfurling in his chest with a hatred and a need to do violence that he had never felt before. Not even when his old gang was burned alive while they slept. Not even then.

If those bastards hurt Charlie, there would be hell to pay. And he would be the one doing the collecting.

"Your grandmother still isn't answering her phone," Lucas said. "But we've left messages with both her and your mother."

Of course she wasn't answering her phone, Charlie thought. There was only one of them whose number she knew, and Roxy had probably tossed it the minute she saw her granddaughter leaving with these people.

"Mom will call back," Charlie told him. "She works nights. Can't check her phone till her first break." They'd been trying since mid-afternoon when her grand tour had been complete and their irresistible offer firmly turned down. She'd had lunch with the BD-Exers, then dinner, then free time which she spent in an on-site bowling alley with Mariah and several other recruits. It had been fun. But she hadn't changed her mind. She wasn't cut out for this. She just wasn't warrior material.

"If we don't hear from either of them by morning," LT said, "we can send Portland PD out to find your mother and let her know where you are."

"Yeah." Her mom really should've called back. They'd been trying her all day. Yes, she slept part of the day, but with her daughter missing, one would think she would pick up. Something was wrong.

Or else they were lying to her, and they hadn't been calling at all.

Right. And is paranoia genetic?

"You could just give me a ride back into the city. You know, me being an adult and all."

"You're not twenty-one. You're twenty. Legally, I have to release you directly into your mother or grandmother's custody. Especially given the recent attack."

She rolled her eyes, but figured it was probably true.

"I especially wouldn't want to just drop you off somewhere

at night," LT went on. "Vampires, once they fixate on a target, don't give up. He'll try again, Charlie. You need to be ready for that. He'll do anything it takes to have you, and he'll kill anyone who gets in his way."

She shivered as Killian's face came vividly into her mind. The deep, deep blue of his eyes, like oceans full of feeling and experience beyond anything she could fathom. The way she felt like she knew him better than she'd ever known anyone, and loved him more than anyone had ever loved anyone before. And yet he'd lied to her. He'd tried to drink her blood. And the rest...just mind games.

"I really don't think he'll try for me again," she said, and she wasn't even sure why she said it.

"You don't know them like I do, then. They're brutal. Vicious. Tenacious."

Killian didn't seem brutal or vicious to her. He seemed determined, but gentle. He seemed caring and kind and beautiful. When he kissed her....

For a moment, she relived that first kiss. The tender pressure of his lips on hers. The tentative exploration. The burgeoning passion of it. The way it felt perfect and right and inevitable.

It had left her knees weak. Hell, they were weak again now. And if she started remembering the rest, the lovemaking under that giant sugar pine tree, she'd probably need to sit down.

"Why don't you get some rest, Charlie?"

"Yeah, um, I'm sorry, LT, but I'm not going to rest until you let me use your phone to make those calls myself. To my mom. To Roxy. Because then I'll actually believe you."

Sighing, he lowered his head. "I knew you were going to ask." He pulled a cell phone from a pocket and handed it to her. "We're not supposed to make personal calls from the base, but I'm gonna make an exception for you. Because I need you to trust me."

She frowned and thought it would be a long time before

she trusted any male again. "Do I need to dial anything special first?"

"Just the area code and number. Go ahead."

She tapped the screen, dialing Roxy's number first. There was endless ringing, but no answer. She wasn't surprised. Then she tried her mother's phone. It went straight to a robotic computer voice telling her "The caller you are trying to reach has a voicemail box that is currently full. Please try your call again later."

She frowned hard. "That's messed up. Mom's a nurse. She gets emergency calls all the time. Not to mention that her daughter is currently missing." She narrowed her eyes on LT. "Are you playing some kind of game with the phones, *Lieutenant?*"

He took the phone away from her. "I saved your ass from a vampire, or have you forgotten that?"

"I haven't forgotten. I'm just not all that convinced he would've actually hurt me."

"That's not how it looked when you scrambled out of his arms and ran straight into mine."

"I was pulled into yours. And I panicked, I admit that. But I'm telling you, the more I think about it—"

"The more you rearrange your imagination to suit your romantic daydreams. Am I right? I've seen it before, Charlie." He snatched the phone away from her. "Get some rest. Just get some rest. You'll know I'm telling you the truth when we drop you off at your mother's place in the morning, alone and unprotected. And if you don't, then you'll sure as *hell* know it when that vampire returns to sink his fangs into your neck and bleed you dry."

The 'fangs into the neck' part sent a shiver of blatant carnal lust up her spine and stirred up the memories she'd been trying not to recall. Probably not the reaction the good Lieutenant had been going for.

LT stormed away, leaving her standing alone outside the

barracks where she was supposed to "get some rest."

She put her hand on the door, but then gave her head a shake. Who was she kidding? She was wide awake, and there were a trillion thoughts ricocheting around inside her skull. All the things LT had told her, the little bit Roxy had told her, the things Killian had said and how he'd seemed. All of them were at odds. At war. Battling for her belief, and she had no idea which side was winning.

She wasn't going to sleep, that was for sure.

She decided to take a walk instead, and rather than using the roads all through camp, she went around behind the barracks and walked along the inside of the tall perimeter fence. The night was serene, the air heavy and still, and the warmth of the day still lingered on the air. It was cooler than it had been, and the temperature seemed to drop a degree at a time as she walked along. The forest outside the fence was a lot like the one where her grandmother's hideaway was nestled. Tall conifers, so big you had to tip your head straight up to see their steeples against the starry blue-black sky. They smelled like heaven. And the air around them just tasted better. Cleaner than it did in the city. She'd noticed that at Roxy's place, too.

Her walk took her near the center of Fort Rogers where the flagpole was. The flag had been taken down for the night. "Taps" had long since played and all the obedient little recruits had marched off to their beds. It was quiet now. She looked in at the base's heart from the brushy backside of the mess hall and saw no one. Picking a direction, she decided on the road out to the training grounds where she'd seen the recruits on that obstacle course. It had been quiet out there. No buildings, just woods.

She stayed to the fence line, not walking on the road at all. The span of woods between the tall, powerful fence and the well-worn dirt road grew wider the further she walked, until she couldn't see the road at all anymore. Just the fence. It was made of tall metal poles, titled inward at the top and lined with razor wire. Heavy metal cables ran horizontally from one pole to the next, held in place by fixtures.

It must be electrified, she realized. Then she put it to the test by throwing a pine cone at it. Nothing happened. She reached out a hand to touch it, and someone grabbed her arm and said, "Wait."

CHAPTER TEN

"Mariah! Jesus, you scared the hell out of me!" Charlie pressed both hands to her chest.

"Yeah, well, better than letting you touch that fence," Mariah said. "Watch." She looked around, picked up a length of tree branch that had fallen, then carefully positioned the bottom of the branch on the ground, holding it perfectly upright near the fence. She leaned the branch slightly toward the fence, then let it go.

It fell. It made contact. A shower of sparks and smoke made Charlie jump backward, one hand gripping Mariah's arm to pull her back, too. The limb bounced off the wire and hit the ground, its top six inches black and smoldering.

"There. See?" Mariah asked.

"I see, I see. Jeez. Next time just tell me."

"You don't seem to be the type who hears words. You have to see things to believe them."

"Do I?" She hadn't thought about herself in those terms. It was fascinating to hear how others perceived her upon first meeting her. "You think I'm a skeptic?"

"I think you've got some kind of deluded star-crossed notions about vamps as romantic, exciting figures. I think you're in denial, maybe because you're in love with the one who tried to kill you."

"You've been talking to Lieutenant Townsend, haven't you?"

"Yes, I have."

"Well he's wrong. I'm not in love with a freaking vampire. Don't be dense. I just don't think he was trying to kill me."

"The hell he wasn't." Mariah turned away, started walking the fence in the same direction Charlie had been going. "Come on, I'll show you something I just love."

She didn't answer, but she did follow along. It was too nice a night, and she was too wide awake to be in the barracks. Something about the night was calling to her, teasing her to stay awake and embrace it.

She and Mariah walked in silence for quite a long time until the perimeter fence turned sharply right, cutting through the woods. "This is the end of the line. And this is what I wanted you to see, right up here, just a few more yards." She picked up the pace, jogging a little. It was pitch dark outside, but Mariah was somehow anticipating every upthrusting root and vine, jumping them easily. Charlie realized she wasn't going to be able to keep up after about three jogging steps, when she tripped and almost caught herself on that high voltage death trap of a fence. After that, she took her time, and when she finally caught up to Mariah, she was the only one out of breath.

Mariah had stopped and was staring through the fence. There, in a perfect circle of pine trees, was a little pond. On the far end, a deer was leaning down to sip from the clear water. Bullfrogs croaked deep, somehow rhythmic songs, and an owl hooted in the distance. Charlie thought of Olive and Roxy, and there was an ache in her chest. God, could she actually be missing that crazy woman and her bizarre pet?

Mariah said, "I want to sit by that pond. Maybe put my feet in the water, you know?"

"Why don't you?"

Mariah looked at her. "We don't really get out of here much, and especially not alone. I mean, if the vamps knew about us, they'd hunt us down for sure."

"Has that always been the reason? 'Cause, I thought up until that attack in Portland, everyone believed they were all dead."

"Everyone else, maybe. These guys, our commanding officers, they never believed it. They know stuff."

And lie about it. And conceal it from the public, Charlie thought. Maybe Roxy wasn't such a wild-eyed conspiracy theorist after all.

"But I'm gonna do it anyway. I almost can already. Watch this." Mariah bent her knees, crouching until her backside almost touched the ground, and before Charlie could even ask what the hell she was doing, she sprang up. And up. And *up*. And then she came plummeting back down again, landing right back in the crouch where she'd started. She bounced upright again, her eyes sparkling. "How high did I get?"

"I...." Charlie had to shake the shock away before she could even think clearly enough to answer. "I think your knees got level with the top of the fence. Maybe even a little above it."

"Yeah, that's about what I thought. I come out here and practice all the time. And I work hard to get stronger. One of these times, I'm gonna be able to clear it. And when I do, I'm going swimming in that little pond."

"I'll bet you will, Mariah," Charlie said.

Mariah sighed. "Oh, I *know* I will." She looked around, pointed at an area where a fallen limb the size of a sofa lay. "I usually sit here for a while, watch the animals come and go and the fish jumping up to eat mosquitos. You want to?"

"Sure. Why the hell not?"

The four of them, Killian, two elder vampires, and one ageless mortal, stopped at the edge of the Oregonian Wilderness area, where the road they'd been following just abruptly ended. Signs everywhere proclaimed that this forest was protected from hunting, fishing, logging, and motorized vehicles of any sort. The sky above it, Roxy had found with a little more Internet sleuthing, included a very small no fly zone with a notation that nesting eagles were often disrupted by low flying aircraft.

Right.

Killian had felt Charlie's essence more and more powerfully as they had driven to the edge of this forest. She was close, and everything in him was aching to just run to her. Yet the practical part of his mind knew that would be foolish and possibly even suicidal.

"The no fly zone is so far into the forest, there's no way anyone would ever be likely to make it there on foot," Roxy observed, looking at her map. "But if there's a facility in these woods, that's where it must be. Directly beneath it. Twenty miles, southeast."

"She's in there," Killian said. "I feel her. It's strong."

"Then we have to go on foot," Roland told him.

Rhiannon stood beside him, stroking Pandora, who was sniffing the air and looking excitedly into the forest. She'd jumped out of the pickup the second it had come to a stop. Poor Olive was still stuck in the back, in her cage.

"We can't walk twenty miles on foot in any reasonable amount of time," Roxy said.

"*You* can't," Rhiannon told her. "But we can."

"She's right," Killian said, turning to Roxy. "I know you want to see for yourself that she's okay, but you can't go that far on foot. We'll have to pour on the speed and run all the way."

"It won't take long to reach the facility, if it exists," Roland said. "Give us time to surveil the place and then get back. Two hours at the most. If we haven't returned by then, Roxy, you should leave. Staying here too long might attract unwanted attention, and you don't need that."

She nodded. "Especially not with a truck full of computers, untraceable cell phones and weapons."

Rhiannon's eagerness faded, and a worried look marred her brow. "She's right, Roland, we cannot risk her being caught with all of that. She shouldn't wait here at all."

Roland nodded. "Go to the farmhouse you told us about, then. It's a far better plan. We have the coordinates. We'll meet you there once we've found what there is to find. All right?"

Roxy nodded, went to the truck, then returned and handed a matchbook to Killian. He opened it and looked inside, where there was a phone number. "Call me if you need anything. I'll keep this phone with me."

"Perfect. Good thinking." Killian tucked the matchbook into his pocket, and turned to face the only vampires he'd seen in more than two years. "What about Pandora?"

"Pandora goes where I go," Rhiannon said. "Don't worry, she'll keep up."

He didn't want to argue with her, and probably wouldn't have even if he did. Rhiannon was the oldest vampire he'd ever encountered, and therefore the most powerful. He didn't need to ask anyone to know these things. They emanated from her body like sparks from a Fourth of July sparkler. Roland gave off the essence of great power as well, but his was calmer, steadier. More like a glowing light than a shower of sparks. And yet Killian didn't feel threatened or intimidated by either of them. They were like a reflection of what he was. And what he could be, if he survived as long as they had. And he liked what he saw. The grace and the confidence. The power. All of it.

Roxy went to the pickup and Killian followed, taking Olive's cage out of the back and moving it into the front for her. Poor bird had probably had enough of jostling around in the bed. Roxy nodded her thanks to him, then with an unsteady smile, hugged him.

"Charlie's special, you know."

"I know."

"To everyone, not just to you." She looked past him at Roland and Rhiannon, deep in conversation at the edge of the forest, then up into his eyes. "I had a recurring dream that told me I was unique and important, but that the blood of my blood would be even more so. She would be stronger, wiser, faster, a great warrior destined to save many lives. I had this dream over and over and over, ever since I was a little girl. Now, I'm the oldest living Chosen. That part about me being special came true. So I have no reason to doubt that the rest of the dream will come true as well. I have only one grandchild. Blood of my blood. She is a female, just as the dream predicted. There's something more about her, Killian. She must be saved."

He blinked, stunned by Roxy's words, but he nodded firmly all the same. "I'll save her," he promised. "Because I love her."

She nodded hard, patted him on the cheek, and then got into her pickup and drove away, her red taillights bouncing over the dirt road until they were out of sight.

Killian faced the towering pines, the immensity of the forest, and he thought of Charlie. He saw her face in his mind and felt his heart whisper, *I'm coming for you, Charlie. I'm coming for you, soon.*

R oxy drove her old, reliable truck along the winding road, amid forests so pristine you'd have thought them untouched by mankind. The towering conifers were more holy than church spires, she thought, and she tried to take some comfort in the power and beauty and longevity of them. They'd seen centuries of mankind's petty troubles come and go. And they all must seem petty from the point of view of one so mighty, so ancient.

It felt wrong to be driving away from Charlotte instead of toward her. Every instinct in her was urging her to turn around, to march through that forest to the secret base, storm the gates and take her granddaughter out of there. But she knew that was a job better left to those more suited to it. Hell, they'd probably have Charlie in hand and be back at the farmhouse before she could cover half the distance to that hidden base on her human, mortal feet. No, it was best she get her hind end out of there before she was seen and aroused suspicion. She trusted Roland and Rhiannon. And she trusted Killian. Not because she knew him or due to any sort of gut feeling. But because he was bound to Charlotte in a way Roxy would never fully understand.

It was said that every human with the Belladonna Antigen had a vampiric protector with whom the natural bond was stronger, more potent than anything else known to exist. She'd seen it before. If usually resulted in a close friendship that would last beyond lifetimes. But when it was coupled with a powerful physical attraction, much less the tender buds of new love, it was a force beyond human imagining. She was convinced that Killian and Charlotte shared such a bond. They might not be aware of its strength. Certainly, Charlotte wasn't. But she would be. It was unavoidable.

Roxy had yet to experience that sort of thing herself. No vampire she'd ever met, and she'd met a lot of them, had felt like her own special one. No preternatural hand had sizzled on contact with her own. No mental bond. Nothing.

Maybe she didn't have a special guardian among the Undead. Maybe that was yet one more way in which Roxy was unique from others of her kind. Charlotte did, though. Her guardian was Killian. Roxy knew how this worked. He would do whatever it took to save Charlotte. There was no question. She didn't think he could help himself if he tried.

She contemplated these things as she drove down the forested mountain onto the narrow, still-deserted road that circled its base, and turned right. It was twenty miles to the new safe house. Roxy had several houses, cabins, cottages, even an apartment or two, in rural New York, in Maine, on the gulf coast of Louisiana, and here in Oregon. They were places she'd reclaimed for owed taxes, tumble-down houses that were all but abandoned. She'd bought them under many names not truly her own, because false identities were another thing she had in abundance. She knew how to stay off the grid. To fly by night. Mortal or not.

With time and elbow grease, she'd fixed most of them up into livable quarters, and a few even had passable security systems. This wasn't one of those few. It had been a turn of the century farmhouse, situated in the middle of a cleared meadow in the shadow of the nearby Blue Mountains. Because she'd spent the last several years here in Oregon, she'd visited it often, so the power was turned on, and it was within range of some of the strongest 4G signals in the state. That, of course, had been a requirement. She needed a reliable and fast internet connection at all times, Roxy did. Her hacking skills rivaled Homeland Security's. She'd worked hard to learn what she needed to know to keep tabs on DPI. Not just to help the vampires who'd survived the US led worldwide effort to wipe them from existence, but for her own sake. And for Charlotte's. Because when the Undead were eliminated once and for all, the governments would train their sites on those humans who could become vampires. The Chosen. It was inevitable. They would want to make sure vampire kind could never again become a threat.

She thought it was happening right now, far sooner than she'd expected. They'd taken her Charlotte. They'd taken others. Their offers of protection were nothing but bait for their cruel trap.

The farmhouse was only a few miles further now, and she was starting to relax a little. She'd released the birds who were ready to return to the wild before they'd torched her cabin. The rest, she'd dropped off on the front step of a wildlife rehabber who would take care of them. Olive was out of her cage now, sitting on the front seat, waiting impatiently for her dinner.

Roxy rounded a corner and came upon two cars, one with its nose planted in the other one's front fender. They were blocking the road, but she would've stopped anyway when she saw that while one vehicle was empty, the other had someone inside–a woman, slumped over the steering wheel. Maybe the other driver had gone for help.

Roxy brought the pickup to a stop but didn't get out right away. Instead, she pulled up her current cell phone to call 911 in case no one else had. But she never finished making the call, because a man in a suit came up to her door with a giant of a gun aimed right at her head and another was on the other side. The woman who'd been slumped over her steering wheel got out of her car, also pointing a gun and walking forward, and when she glanced in her mirror, Roxy saw a fourth person approaching from behind.

"Get out of the vehicle, Roxanne!" That was the guy on the driver's side. Sagging jowls and all, the commandant himself. She'd seen him on the news. She must be hellishly important, she thought. "Don't make us shoot you." He was shouting, and not just so she could hear him through the closed window.

She nodded and put her hands up, but pressed one foot to the truck's door. When the man started to open it, she shoved hard, slamming the door into him, knocking him flat on his ass. "Fly Olive! Go!" she yelled.

The owl didn't hesitate. She leapt onto Roxy's thigh and pushed off from there into the night sky. Roxy shifted into reverse and hit the gas simultaneously. The truck lurched backward and the suit behind it dove to one side, somersaulting into the ditch to avoid getting hit. The other two started firing. Roxy's passenger side window exploded, then the windshield did too, but by then she was speeding backward down the road. She hit the brake and yanked the wheel to spin around 180 degrees, shifted into drive and stomped it. But she knew she wasn't going to shake them. The truck was coughing, probably from bullets in the wrong places. The rear tires left rubber on the pavement before they caught. She grabbed the cellphone, hit the voice memo button, spoke rapidly into the phone.

Something landed in the back, and another shot went off, shattering the rear window, and then a gun barrel pressed against her temple.

"Stop. This. Truck." A female voice, deep and dangerous. Roxy dropped the cell phone and kicked it underneath her seat. She shot a look in the rearview and saw the woman who'd been in the phony accident, one arm anchored inside the busted out rear window, her body braced against the cab. "Brake, Roxanne. Now."

Roxy wrenched the wheel instead, and the woman went flying across the pickup bed, hitting the side hard. She fishtailed, whipping the wheel back and forth to try to shake the woman off, but the bitch just kept coming and finally got a grip, thrust the gun through the rear window again and fired.

Searing pain burned through Roxy's thigh, and she drove smack into one of the majestic trees she'd been admiring only moments earlier. Blood pulsed from her leg as if it was a fountain. She needed both hands to press against it. She was Belladonna positive. She'd bleed out fast. There would be no stopping it. Her hands were slick with blood as she pressed, one on top of the other.

Her door was yanked open, a needle was jammed into her shoulder before she even whipped her head around to see

Commandant Crowe. Then he faded into the color of his hair, and there was nothing.

Charlie heard Killian's voice as clearly as if he was standing beside her and whispering into her ear. Except he wasn't. He was whispering inside her head, and shivers of desire and awareness and something like joy flooded through her at the sound of it. She reminded herself that he was the enemy and shot to her feet from the log where she'd been trying to enjoy the serenity of the night.

"What? Did you hear something?" Mariah got up too, looking into the woods, her eyes narrow and searching.

"I thought, I...I thought I did, but...." Charlie shook her head. "I guess I imagined it."

But Mariah wasn't relaxing. She was still looking around, wide eyed. "They can talk mentally, you know. Vamps, I mean. I don't think humans are supposed to be able to hear them, though. Is that what it was? That vampire that's after you?"

"I don't know. I don't know what it was." She looked into the trees outside the fence, thinking she knew exactly what it was, and who it was, and rubbed the goose bumps off her arms. "Let's get back, okay?"

"Yeah, sure, okay. But you need to tell me what you heard. A twig snapping? A voice? What?"

"A bird. I think it was just a bird." But she knew better. It had been him, it had been Killian, and it felt as if he was close by. He said he was coming for her. Was that a threat? Was he going to try to get in here and finish what he'd started? She tried again to recall the events of that horrible night of her accident. Not waking in his arms outside the hospital and panicking and twisting free and running from him, but before that. He'd been with her, *inside* her hospital room. He'd leaned over her, and he'd been squeezing that wet sponge into her mouth because she was so thirsty and she knew she was going to die if she didn't drink.

Drink, he kept telling her. Only not out loud.

Inside her mind. Exactly like what he'd said to her just now. And like the dreams, especially that most recent one. It was real, then. It was real. He was close. He could speak to her with his mind. And he was coming for her.

She thought back, fighting to remember. If he'd wanted to kill her, he'd have just sucked her dry right then, wouldn't he? Why would he feed her water from a sponge?

Only...it hadn't been a sponge.

It had been...it had been his arm.

She blinked rapidly, searching her mind as the memory came.

He'd held his arm to her lips while she sucked eagerly, hungry for every drop. It had been his arm, and the liquid she'd been gulping so greedily hadn't been water at all.

Oh my God, it was blood!

What did it mean? What did that do to her? She wasn't a vampire, that was for sure. She'd been out in the sun all day today, after all. She poked at her incisors with her tongue just to be sure. And yes, they were still their normal size and shape. She didn't slice her tongue open on them. They had not elongated or grown razor sharp the way his had been when he'd tasted her.

Oh, God, passion rippled through her body again just remembering that...him inside her, that delicious pinch on her neck, and the way he'd sucked her skin between his teeth.

He drank her blood. And then he fed her his.

What had he done to her then? What did it mean?

She'd been dying in the hospital, she was sure of that. She'd felt herself teetering on the edge of oblivion and unable to find a foothold. She knew she'd lost a lot of blood in the accident. Bits of conversation from the paramedics, the ER nurses, the doctors, came floating back to her, disjointed, but real.

...lost too much blood...

...rare type. Nothing in stock.

....checking with the Red Cross and local hospitals...

Maybe someone else in her family....

Why wasn't she registered? Aren't they all supposed to be registered?

Did you hear about that bystander who ripped off the car door, when none of the firefighters could get it open?

Yes, she'd been near death. But afterward, when she'd run from Killian to that dark van with LT, she'd been awake, alert, and strong. Stronger by the minute. No longer dying.

Charlie came to a complete halt in her rapid-paced march back to the barracks and stood there, blinking in shock. Could it be that Killian had not come to the hospital to *take* her life, but rather to *save* her life? Had he been the stranger who'd torn off the jammed car door so they could get her out?

It was at that precise instant that she felt him close to her, like a warm finger tracing a path up her spine. She turned to look beyond the fence and found him without even hunting for him. He was crouched behind a tree, looking right at her. Their eyes locked, and everything in her seemed to lean toward him, to reach for him. Her body craved his like...like his craved blood, she thought.

"We have to cut back through the trees to the road," Mariah said suddenly. "My pager's vibrating. LT must be looking for us. I'll be in trouble for sure."

"I um...I think I need to sit for a while. I'm all worn out. Not strong like you."

"You can be, though."

She nodded, not wanting to get into that discussion right then. "Go ahead, Mariah. Tell LT I slipped out and you came looking for me. I'll back you up. Besides, it's the truth."

Mariah frowned at her and looked around as if she expected to find someone else lurking in the forest. Charlie sensed Killian's withdrawal. He wouldn't be seen, not if he didn't want to be. Mariah finally seemed satisfied that no one else was around. "I can't just leave you here."

Charlie wanted her out of there, and she wanted it now. Her temper sparked to life in a way completely unlike her. "I'm not one of you obedient little recruits, Mariah. I'm going home in the morning. And I didn't ask your permission. I'm staying put, and when I fucking feel like coming back to the barracks, I'll come back to the barracks. Now get out of here."

Mariah's face turned angry. "You're too stupid to be one of us," she snapped. "You wouldn't make it a day. I hope your Goddamn vampire comes back and eats you."

So do I, Charlie thought.

Mariah stomped off through the trees. No sooner was she out of sight, than something seemed to fall from the darkness and hit the ground right beside Charlie, making her jump backwards, trip over a limb and land ass-first on the ground. Heart racing, she watched Killian as he straightened up. His eyes searched hers as he grabbed her hand, pulled her to her feet and flat against his chest, wrapping his arms around her. And then he kissed her like there was no tomorrow. No hello, no preamble, no apology or explanation. Just the kiss.

And she responded, because the touch of his mouth was too much to resist. Heat rose through her while he held her against his cool body. His tongue tasted minty and sweet all at once. They devoured each other for a solid minute. Maybe longer. And then he pulled back, stared down at her. "Wrap your arms around my neck, and I'll get you out of here."

"Charlie!" That was LT's voice, shouting through the woods, no doubt being led right back to her by that back-stabbing Mariah.

"You have to get out of here." She pushed his chest, backing him away from her and regretting it with everything in her. No time to ask the questions burning in her mind, no time to ask him to explain. She didn't know if he was good or evil. She only knew her body ached for his, and that they would kill him if they found him. Every recruit in this camp was trained to kill vampires. "Go, Killian, hurry."

"Not without you." He was beautiful against the night and the giant trees. As natural as if he was a part of the nocturnal forest. That long, swept back, mink brown hair mimicking the swirls and twists of the rugged bark, his eyes gleaming like stars in the night sky. Her hands were running up and down his back and arms like they had minds of their own, her eyes devouring his face.

"They're letting me go anyway, Killian," she managed to tell him. "First thing in the morning. But if they catch so much as a whiff of you, they'll search the woods until they catch you. And then they'll kill you. Please, just go."

"I can't–"

"Charlie?" LT called. He was closer now. Too close. "I've heard from your family, Charlie. Where are you?"

She looked toward where his voice was coming from and could hear his crashing footsteps through the woods and undergrowth now. "Just jump back over the damn fence, will you? You can come right back in again once I get rid of him. Please?"

He shook his head, but he did back away, vanishing into the nearby trees and brush like a ghost. She strained her eyes, but it was impossible to see. He was too well hidden. And everything in her ached with the loss of his nearness. How could she want someone this much? It wasn't normal. It was supernatural. It had to be.

LT came out of the trees behind her. "There you are! What the hell are you doing out here?"

Charlie turned his way and told herself to be casual. Not defensive. Not sarcastic. Not rebellious. Just casual. "I was walking. Getting some air. I don't sleep well at night. But you know that. It's a BD thing, isn't it?"

He sent her a skeptical look, then scanned the trees all around her, not even trying to hide his suspicions.

"What, you think I'm out here meeting someone? I've only been here a day, LT. And while a man in uniform is a guaranteed chick magnet, even I don't work that fast."

He nodded, but he didn't crack a smile at her little joke. Though he did, apparently, choose to believe her. His face was grim, though. "I have news about your family. It's not good, Charlie."

All her defiance left her like air from a punctured balloon. "What do you mean, it's not good?"

"Just come with me, all right?" He took her arm, not firmly, just gently. Like he was a grown-up and she, a little girl in need of guidance. It pissed her off. She'd spent her entire life being treated like a fragile child. She'd had enough of it. If all of this bullshit going on lately had done anything positive, it was to show her that. She was done being protected. Finished letting other people tell her what to do, and how to live her life.

But for Killian's sake, she let LT lead her back through the woods to the road where a Jeep was parked. Mariah sat in the back, waiting.

"What's going on, LT?" Charlie asked. "Why the big dramatic build up? What have you heard from my grandmother?"

"Nothing. She's missing. We have reason to believe she's been taken–"

"Taken?" Her skepticism rang clear in her voice, but it was followed rapidly by a shiver of fear. "Taken by whom?"

"The vampire that tried to kill you. Who the hell do you think?"

The one she'd just seen, not five minutes ago? The one she'd been kissing like she wanted to swallow him whole? *That* vampire? No fucking way.

LT jumped into the driver's seat, and Charlie took the spot beside him. "If my grandmother is missing, trust me, it's because she *wants* to be missing. She has this thing about staying under the radar. You already know that about her."

He quickly turned the Jeep around, then punched it so they

were bounding over the road back toward the camp's center, then he stopped sharply in front of a building she hadn't been inside before. He got out, reached for her hand to help her out as well, and Mariah jumped out of the back.

Charlie crossed her arms over her chest and sat where she was. "I'm not moving until you tell me what makes you think some vampire has kidnapped my grandmother."

LT lowered his extended hand. And his head, too. "I...I don't know how to tell you this. Your mother...." He looked up again as her stomach tied itself into a knot. And then he said it, the words that changed everything. "Charlie, your mother is dead."

Her soul turned to ice, she could feel the crackling coldness forming all through her. His words didn't sink in too deeply, because she refused to let them. Her brain sealed itself in frost and bounced them right back to their sender, registering only that they made no sense. They did not compute. "That can't be true," was all she said. It was a knee-jerk response. She didn't choose the words, they just erupted. "There's no way that's true. There's no way."

"I'm sorry, but it is. We've been trying her cell phone all day. The last time I did, a police officer answered. He was in her apartment. When your mother didn't show up for work, a co-worker went to check on her and found her."

The words were penetrating now, still not making sense though. "Found her?"

"Lying dead on the floor of her apartment, two puncture wounds in her neck, her body drained of blood."

"No. No, that doesn't make any sense. Why...? She doesn't even have the antigen. Why her?"

"Because of you," Lucas said. "It was him, Charlie. There's no doubt."

"No."

LT pulled out his phone. "I knew you wouldn't believe me. So I had the officer send proof." Then he showed it to her.

Hands shaking, she took the cell phone from him and forced her eyes to focus on its screen. There was a photograph of her mother, lifeless, lily white, on the familiar beige carpet of her home. She recognized the coffee table and sofa nearby. Her mother's eyes were slightly open. There was no faking the sunken, drying look of them. The look of death.

Nor was there any mistaking the marks on her pale neck. She'd seen them before, after all, on her own.

Charlie's hands went numb. The phone fell from them, landing on the ground with a dull thud. Tears welled in her eyes.

"A man matching the description of the one who took you from your hospital bed was seen leaving the building. The landlord gave us a positive ID when we showed him a photo we took that night," LT said. He spoke slowly, like he was giving his words time to sink in.

"Are you sure?" she whispered, and turning slowly, she looked back toward the woods where he'd been. But Killian wouldn't be there now. Not now.

"There's no doubt. I'm sorry, Charlotte."

Tears welled in her eyes. Tears for her mother and for her own guilt. My God, what had she done?

She should tell them where he was.

But no. If she told them she'd been meeting with a vampire inside their supposedly secret camp, they might withdraw their invitation to join them. Bending her knees, she recovered the phone, looked at the photograph again, this time searching for any signs it had been faked. But no. Her mom's mouth was slightly open. The gold cap on one tooth was there in plain sight. This wasn't a doctored image, because they wouldn't have known to include that detail. And the book on the coffee table was one her mother had started reading only the day before Charlie had left with Roxy.

Lucas took the phone from her. Mariah came closer, put her hands on Charlie's shoulders, her earlier anger apparently forgotten. "I'm so, so sorry. I tried to tell you. But we'll get him for this. We will, Charlie. And *we can*."

Charlie nodded, shock and grief, regret and shame warred with anger for control of her mind. She looked down at the cell phone in Lucas's hand, its nightmare image still filling its screen. Her mother's lifeless eyes stared back at her, silently begging for justice.

Anger won.

She looked at Mariah, then at LT. "I'm in," she said. "Give me the damn drug. How long will it take to make me strong enough to kill him with my bare hands?"

"Not long," LT said. "Not long at all, Charlie."

CHAPTER ELEVEN

Killian followed the Jeep that carried Charlie away, keeping pace while remaining out of sight. The camp didn't have a lot of exterior lighting, probably to keep its existence secret. The wooded areas ended, and he was forced to jog behind and between buildings to keep Charlie and the others in sight, but he managed it. Moving rapidly and all but silently, he managed it. And finally the Jeep stopped, and he crouched a few hundred yards away, concealed by shadows, far from their range of sight or hearing, keeping his presence masked even from Charlie by drawing an invisible shield around himself. He could see and hear them perfectly.

And *what* he heard sent a chill straight to his bones.

He couldn't see the image on the cell phone as the Lieutenant showed it to Charlie, but it must have been a convincing one, and he could feel her reactions. Devastation. Guilt. Grief. Her mother was dead, the Lieutenant had told her. And then he'd shown her proof.

When the idiot went on to blame her mother's murder on

him, when he finally convinced her it was true, Killian felt the hatred that emanated from Charlie like a shockwave. It hit him full on, rocking him almost off his feet. And then something in her changed. Hardened, closing around her like a shell, one he could no longer penetrate. The only thing she allowed to come through it was fury and rage, all of it directed at him.

"Give me the damn drug," she'd said. "How long will it take to make me strong enough to kill him with my bare hands?"

Sickened by the force and purity of her anger, Killian staggered back the way he had come. Within moments, he heard Roland and Rhiannon, shouting mentally at him. Instead of replying, he sprang over the fence, landing hard on the other side, letting his knees buckle, and staying where he landed, bent on the forest floor, not even trying to summon up the will to move.

They were standing over him in seconds, Rhiannon looking furious. "We agreed to do reconnaissance first! To make a plan! You could have ruined everything by jumping in there that way," she whispered.

"Everything is already ruined."

"What are you talking about?" Roland asked. He came closer, put a hand on Killian's shoulder. "What happened in there, Killian?"

He shook his head slowly, but kept it level, at least. "That jackass who took Charlie just told her that her mother is dead and that I'm the one responsible."

Rhiannon's face darkened. He saw it and was glad that storm cloud expression wasn't directed at him. Beside her, as always, the panther Pandora seemed to sense her anger, and emitted a soft, truncated growl. "No granddaughter of Roxanne's would be gullible enough to believe such an outrageous fairytale."

"Horror tale," Roland said. "Did she, Killian? Did she believe?"

Killian nodded. "He showed her something on his phone. Her dead mother, I presume. Told her there was an eye witness who identified me from a photo."

"Everyone knows we can't be photographed," Rhiannon said.

"Charlie doesn't," he said. "And whatever she saw on the cell phone must have been pretty convincing." He looked from Rhiannon to Roland. "Do you think her mother is really dead?"

"I think we'd better find out," Roland said.

"The Lieutenant told Charlie that Roxy is missing, and that I'm the most likely reason for that, too."

"Roxy isn't missing, she's waiting for us at the farmhouse." Rhiannon frowned, sending a look at Roland that turned from fury to concern. "At least, she's supposed to be."

"We'd better get back there," Roland said. "We'll figure the rest of this out once we've ensured Roxanne is all right and checked into this claim about Charlotte's mother." He clapped Killian hard on the shoulder. "Take heart, my friend. She's young, she's mortal, and she's crippled with grief at the moment. The truth will be revealed, and she *will* see it."

He nodded. "She said something else...something that worries me even more than her believing I would murder her mother. She said, 'I'm in. Give me the damn drug.' And then she asked how long it would take to make her strong enough to kill me with her bare hands."

Roland sent a horrified look at Rhiannon.

A muscle worked in Rhiannon's jaw as if she clenched it. "DPI is up to its old tricks again, isn't it? They've always loved playing mad scientist. Experimenting on vampires. And on The Chosen."

"We can't let them do that to Charlie. She's nobody's guinea pig," Killian said.

"We'll stop them," Roland said. "But tonight, it's not an option. She saw you and now believes, no matter how temporarily, that you killed her mother. She's going to tell them you've been here. And they're going to come looking.

We have to go, Killian. Find Roxy, make a plan, and return. If they find us, there will be no one to save your Charlotte."

He couldn't argue with them. They were right. He was surprised the forest wasn't crawling with searchers already. They took flight, all three of them, pushing their bodies effortlessly to speeds beyond human ability, but not beyond Pandora's, arriving near the farmhouse a short while later. But not *at it*. What they saw stopped them before they made it that far. Roxy's pickup truck with its nose wrapped around a large tree. There wasn't a piece of glass remaining in the thing.

"Good gods," Rhiannon whispered.

Roland held up a hand. "You two stay back. I'll get a closer look."

"To hell with that." Killian pushed past Roland's outstretched arm and walked right up to the pickup. He was furious. Roxy had been kind to him, had saved his life, given him shelter, taken him in. These bastards had taken her? The same bastards who had taken Charlie and maybe even murdered her mother? No way was this going to go unanswered. No fucking way. Lieutenant Townsend was going to have his ass thoroughly kicked before Killian drained him and left his sorry dry husk for the crows. He didn't give a shit that the man was also one of The Chosen. He would find a way.

He kept watch around him, kept his senses open, but didn't cower or hide. Let them come for him. Let them try to take three immortals if they were stupid enough to think they could.

"That's all well and good, Killian, but they have the tranquilizer," Roland said. He'd come up beside Killian without a sound, startled him a little. "They dart us, and it's over."

He met Roland's eyes, knew the man was as angry as he was. Maybe not enough to broadcast his thoughts at full volume, but still—

"You should shield your mind," Rhiannon said, from his other side. "There are a few humans who can pick up on vampiric telepathy. No point taking undue risks."

"He had no one to teach him, Rhiannon," Roland said. "He might not know how."

"Of course," she said. "Killian, imagine an impenetrable wall—"

"I know how to block my thoughts," he said. And he did, but only because Roxy had told him. "I was angry. I slipped. And I know about their tranquilizer. I was darted with it, after all. Roxy has an antidote."

"*Had* an antidote," Rhiannon said, looking at the truck.

Killian turned his focus back to the pickup. Its contents, all the things they'd packed and loaded from the cabin in the woods, were scattered all over the road, computers smashed, not a weapon in sight. "Those windows didn't break in the accident. They were shot out. Look." He pointed at the bullet holes that riddled the truck's body. Then he leaned inside to look around, expecting to see Roxy dead inside, and probably poor Olive with her. But the driver's seat was empty, the cage door open. Olive must have escaped. There was a scent though, and there was no mistaking what it was. "There's human blood in the truck," he said. "Roxy's blood. She must have been shot."

Roland was walking along the road, looking at the skid marks, the torn up shoulder, the piles of spent bullet casings.

"Her handbag is still inside," Killian said, reaching in to get it. But as he did, he spotted the phone, just one corner sticking out from under the seat. Frowning, he pulled it out, tapped it to bring it back to life. The screen lit, and the most recently used app was still open. Voice Memo. He clicked on the latest recording and heard gunfire, and Roxy's voice.

"They've got me, Killian. They won't kill me. Been wanting to study The Oldest Chosen for a long time. You leave it be and get Charlotte. I mean it, Killian. Tell our friends I've got time. Get Charlotte away from these DPI bastards."

He turned, holding up the phone to tell Roland and Rhiannon about the message, but he saw by their stunned expressions that they'd heard it. Of course they had. They held his gaze for a moment, then got back to work, inspecting the crash site.

"Take anything important," Rhiannon told him, looking around, almost sniffing the air. "This happened very recently. They might send back a team to collect all of this. We need to move the vital things and leave the rest. Keep the place looking as undisturbed as possible. No point announcing our presence."

Killian nodded and took Roxanne's purse, dropping the phone inside, then thinking better of it. What if they'd left the phone deliberately, hoping he would take it so they could track its signal?

He deleted the message and put the cellphone right back where he'd found it. Then he went through the inside of the truck. He looked up every few seconds to watch Roland, who was walking from one pile of bullet casings to the next. Bending, he picked one up, then frowned and went to examine another and another. "Four shooters," he said. "If they'd wanted to kill her, she'd have been dead."

"We should check the farmhouse," Rhiannon said softly. She wasn't examining the scene the way they were. She was, instead, keeping her back to them, every sense scanning the tree line in all directions and the road as well. Watching their backs. "It's a few more miles. Maybe they still don't know about it."

"I don't think we can count on that," Roland replied, but he also nodded his assent that they ought to check it.

The three of them scoured the debris, gathering up a laptop that looked to be in one piece, the cooler that contained Roxy's remaining supply of blood in sterile plastic bags bearing red crosses on them. They found a few weapons, some under the truck's seat, and a few in the bed.

While they were gathering things up, Olive soared silently down and landed on the truck's hood, blinking and looking around, probably for her friend.

"We'll find her, Olive. Don't worry." Killian spoke with his mind as well as his words, unsure whether the owl could understand either of them. "Come with us, okay?"

They returned to the woods to get out of sight, leaving the scene and Roxy's poor truck looking pretty much exactly as it had before. To Killian's surprise, Olive flew overhead, keeping pace with them until the farmhouse came into sight. Then she flew straight to it, landing on the roof and hooting repeatedly. "Apparently, Olive's been here before," Killian said.

After scouting the area thoroughly, minds wide open to sense any living presence and determining there were no humans about, they made their way to the farmhouse to join her. It was situated in the middle of a meadow that was alive with wildflowers and the nodding heads of yellow grasses heavy with seed. The woods ended where the meadow began, a wide open expanse they would have to cross to reach the house. As soon as they started in that direction, Pandora took off ahead of them, leaping through the meadow grasses toward the house as if she knew that was where they were going. The three vampires made their way more cautiously. They walked inside the woods that bordered the meadow. Then they ducked low, using the tall grasses for cover until they were directly behind the house to keep out of sight from the road. Still, they sensed no one.

Killian looked at Rhiannon when they reached the rectangular, white house's back door. Her eyes were intensely focused as she felt for any presence, human or otherwise. He'd been doing the same.

She gave him a nod, reassuring him that she wasn't sensing anyone either, and so Killian took the keys he'd pilfered from

Roxy's bag and started trying them in the locks. Three keys, three locks, and they were inside.

Something swooped out of nowhere, damn near taking off his head, and Killian ducked fast, arms raising up to fend off the demon.

But it was only Olive, whose target had been the black panther, not him. Pandora crouched, then sprang onto her hind legs batting at the bird as it swooped again.

"How the hell did she get in here?" he asked, looking around and deciding there must be a window open somewhere on the second floor.

Pandora's tail swished in agitation as Olive landed on the back of a chair and stared unblinkingly at her.

"Pandora," Rhiannon said, her tone sharp and authoritative. "Olive is a friend."

The cat looked from the owl to the woman, then back to the owl. She licked her lips.

"Friend," Rhiannon said sharply.

The cat looked her way again and gave a short, sharp growl that left no doubt as to her feelings on the whole "friend" matter. She clearly had been hoping to have owl cutlets for dinner. Hanging her head, she laid down and sighed.

"You'll be safe, Olive," Rhiannon said, speaking directly to the owl.

The barred white bird looked at her, blinked twice, once with each set of eyelids, and then hooted. Then she launched herself from the chair with a heavy push of powerful wings and swept through the kitchen, into another room and out of sight.

"I'm not sure having those two in the same house is a very good idea," Killian said.

Roland opened the fridge, the cabinets, but Killian saw only empty shelves behind the doors. "Pandora always obeys Rhiannon," he said, "though she doesn't always like it. Don't you, cat?"

The cat chuffed at him almost indignantly.

"Precisely."

"No humans have been in this house since the last time Roxanne herself was here," Rhiannon said.

Killian walked through the house. It was in good repair. Dusty, with no sign of recent habitation. A warped dining table in need of refinishing and a few folding chairs occupied the dining room. The power was on and the water worked, hot and cold.

He continued on to the second floor, found an open panel in the hall ceiling that led into the attic, and jumped easily through.

There were some boards, a few loose bricks, an antique trunk, some pieces of pink insulation. And on each end, a round window, one facing the road, the other facing the meadow and the woods behind the house. The front window had a broken pane—that, he presumed, was how the owl had made her way inside, though it must have been a squeeze, and not, he thought, a very safe one. He worked on the window until he could pull it free from its frame, making a safer passage for the owl. Then turning, he whistled just the way he'd heard Roxy do it.

He didn't think it had worked until the owl flew up and joined him in the attic, balancing on a beam and blinking down at him.

"I took the window out for you," he said, and he poked his hand through the opening to show her. "You can come and go as you please, and if there are mice up here, they're all yours. Also, there's no way for Pandora to get up here. I don't think she can jump high enough. So you're safe and sound."

She just stared at him, but he knew she was understanding, because he felt her gratitude.

"You're welcome." Then he went back to the opening and jumped down through it into the hallway.

Rhiannon and Roland were at the bottom of the stairs,

looking up at him, "So what's our next move?" Killian asked, heading down the stairs and taking a seat on a nineteenth century radiator as tall as Olive. "How are we going to get Charlie out of there if she thinks we're all killers?"

"We might have to take her against her will," Roland said.

"Then that's what we have to do. As long as we get her out of there."

"And we will, Killian," Roland said. "But I need to talk to you about something else, if you'll indulge me."

Killian gave him a nod and hoped he'd be brief.

Roland went on. "In a few days, a band of rogue vampires is going to arrive here in the states, and they're going to make all the government's lies about us look like a weak prequel. They're out for blood, Killian. Human blood."

"You mentioned that," Killian said. He was willing to listen but not for long.

"They want to wage war on mankind," Rhiannon said. "They want vengeance for every vampire those bastards murdered in twenty-eleven. Frankly, I don't disagree with them."

"They're led by someone named Devlin, you said."

"And he's a brutal bastard," Rhiannon raged. "More dangerous than I had realized. He murdered every human in a small village near where we've been staying, then headed here to do more of the same."

"Devlin and his gang total seventeen," Roland said.

"Sixteen, in truth. Larissa is with them but working for me. Keeping me informed," Rhiannon explained. "They found a faster ship, she told me most recently. They could be here already, for all we know."

"And there are only two of us to stop them," Roland said. "Three, if we can count on your help."

Killian nodded, taking it all in, but still having only one goal on his mind. "I'll help you. Of course, I'll help you. I'm one of you." God it felt good to say that. To know it. "I'll help you with this rogue gang and anything else you need," he promised. "But only after Charlie is safe."

His eyes were beginning to feel heavy. He glanced at the window in alarm.

"Dawn approaches," Rhiannon said. "As much as it pains me to say it, Killian, we must sleep. The day will pass, and we'll begin again."

"Dammit!" He searched Rhiannon's eyes, then Roland's. "You're right that I know nothing of my own kind, that I had no one to teach me. Tell me that in all this time, all these centuries, you've found some way to resist the day sleep."

Roland sent a sideways glance at his woman. Her eyes flashed just a little wider. "There is a drug," he said. "My friend Eric Marquand created it. But there are side effects."

"It makes you aggressive and violent," Rhiannon said. Then she winked at Roland. "And amazing in bed."

"I nearly killed you, my love."

"But what a way to go." She gave him a sexy smile that made Killian feel like he ought to leave the room.

"At any rate," Roland said, after clearing his throat and tearing his eyes off Rhiannon, "we have none of it on hand, so the point is moot. We sleep. And await nightfall."

At eight a.m. Charlie was wearing the cargo pants and tank top that seemed to be the uniform here and sitting on the edge of a cot in the sick bay. The other cots were empty. She was the only patient in the place.

LT stood nearby. She'd have liked Mariah there for moral support, but she was with her unit on the firing range this morning. Charlie wasn't sure she was going to like this military lifestyle bullshit, but she knew she would like the strength and the power the others had. And if there was a cure, she'd like that, too.

But mainly, she wanted vengeance on the vampire who'd played her for a fool and then murdered her mother.

Do I really believe that, though?

Pictures don't lie, she thought, answering her own question.

Her mother. As many times as she'd resented the overprotectiveness, the hovering, the smothering, Charlie had always loved her mom. And now she'd been taken from her, violently and cruelly, for no reason whatsoever.

"Relax, dear. It's not good to take the treatment during emotional times. Try to let it all go." The man who spoke was so pale he had to be either sickly or an albino wearing tinted contacts. He wore a white coat that wasn't much lighter than his skin, and he prepared a spot on her arm with an alcohol wipe, then stuck her with a needle and inserted an IV line. She assumed he was a doctor, then decided that it was stupid and ignorant to presume anything.

She'd *presumed* that Killian's feelings for her were real. And that her grandmother's crazy, off the grid lifestyle and booby traps and escape routes were unnecessary and ridiculous. And that her mother was perfectly safe from the boogie men of childhood nightmares.

She'd been wrong on all counts.

"I thought it was just a shot," she said.

"It's a little more involved than that," LT said. "But not a lot."

The "doctor" taped the IV line to her arm, then went to the clear plastic bag of fluid hanging from its pole beside her and made adjustments, talking as he did. "We've found that the formula is too powerful to inject directly. So we've altered our delivery method. Now we give the first dose slowly over a longer period of time. Two hours seems to be the minimum. After that, two booster injections and a chemical that makes your blood impossible for–"

"Let's get started," LT said.

She wanted to ask about side effects, and what it was going

to feel like, and how the hell they found out it was too powerful to inject directly and what happened to those recruits who'd been given the drug that way.

But more than any of those things, she wanted to rescue her grandmother before Killian, or someone else, killed her, too. She wanted the chance to apologize, to admit she'd been wrong to run away and cause all this chaos. Roxy had done nothing but try to help her, even if she had trusted the wrong side. And now *because* she'd tried to help her, she was imprisoned by monsters. Maybe even dead.

Charlie wanted the cure and the power that came with it. And then she wanted out of here. Because once her grandmother was safe, she had another mission on her mind. Revenge.

"I'm ready," she said, then she eyed LT. "But I'm holding you to your promise. I get to go home long enough to bury my mother."

"The arrangements are already being made, Charlie." He put a soothing hand on her shoulder. "It's not your fault, what happened to her."

"It's entirely my fault," she told him. Then she watched as the bone-thin doctor picked up a huge syringe filled with something the color of root beer and injected it into the saline. Deep brown-red swirls of liquid invaded the clear fluid, twisting and twining. The doctor removed the needle, shook the bag a little bit to mix it better, then checked the flow. She followed his eyes, spotting the steady drip-drip of the brown colored liquid, and then following the flow down the tubing and into her arm.

She swore she felt the first drop that entered her body. A warm sensation that seemed to travel up her arm, along the highway of her vein.

"Lie back, Charlie. Relax." LT put a hand to her forehead to ease her back onto the pillows. Dr. Deathly was fiddling around near her right wrist, and she glanced down just as he buckled a leather strap around it.

"Hey, whoa, that's not even—"

"Stay still, Charlie." She'd sat up fast but LT pressed her flat again, his hands on her shoulders. "Don't fight it. This is for your own protection." He held her still while the doc buckled a restraint around her other wrist, and then one around her chest, once her arms were imprisoned and unable to fight.

"This is bullshit. You didn't tell me about this—" Something hit her heart like a wrecking ball, and then white heat engulfed the center of her chest. It knocked the fight out of her as she lay there, wide eyed. "Oh, God, what is this? What's happening? LT, what is this?"

"It's all right. I know it feels alarming. But this is how it is with everyone."

Her heart was beating so hard she could feel it reverberating through her body. She could feel it pounding from within. "I'm gonna die. I'm gonna die. Take the needle out. Stop the IV. I withdraw consent." She kicked at the IV pole, but it was out of her reach, and the only result was that LT grabbed both her legs and held them while the doctor strapped them down.

"Easy, Charlie. It will pass."

Her pulse was thrumming in her ears. Inside her head. Deafening. Painful. And her entire body was engulfed in that odd white-hot sensation. "I'm dying, I'm telling you, it's killing me. I'm allergic or something."

LT was looking a little alarmed himself, sending the doctor silent questions with his eyes while the doc watched the monitors that were supposed to show her heart rate and God only knew what else. The lines were a series of sharp spikes like the blades of a saw. Way too close together, shooting higher and dipping lower than she thought was normal.

"You're killing me. I'm telling you, you're killing me!" She strained against the bonds holding her down. The room began to shake. Instruments fell off of tables around her as a red haze clouded her vision. A dull roar filled her ears.

"She's strong, LT muttered, holding onto the bed as the entire room quaked. "Stronger than any of them."

"We're going to have to tranquilize her," the doctor shouted, coming at her with another syringe. He plunged it into her shoulder just as she broke the restraint on her opposite arm, reached around and gripped his wrist, squeezing until he dropped to his knees. Then she plucked the needle from her arm and flung it.

LT grabbed her free arm and pinned it back down. "It's not working! Get something stronger, dammit!"

The doctor got up as LT climbed onto the table, straddling her, his legs pinning her legs down, his hands on her arms. That pale faced medic held one arm bent at the elbow, his hand close to his chest and dangling loosely from his bruised wrist. He scrambled to a locked cabinet while Charlie thrashed and tried to throw the lieutenant off of her, twisting her head from one side to the other. Sounds were coming from her body that were not her own. They weren't even human sounds. Growls, snarls, deep and powerful. LT was sweating. "Hurry, up, dammit!"

Finally the doc came back and sank yet another needle into her arm. She tried to pull away, twisted her head and snapped her teeth at his hand but couldn't reach.

And then her body seemed to deflate like a balloon. She went limp and her mind turned languid. She let herself drift away, because it was easier than fighting. She was dying. She was going to be with her mother again.

LT got off her, watching her carefully. She could still see him, but he was hazy. Her focus was off.

"It's working. What did you give her?"

"The vampire tranquilizer."

LT frowned. "Shouldn't that kill her?"

"It would have killed a normal BD. But she's not. I've seen a similar reaction to BDX only once and not this strongly. Before we acquired the subject, he had nearly bled out due to an accident, and his vampiric protector had fed him from his own veins."

Vampiric protector? What does that mean?

"We knew this, of course, so we were prepared for his reaction to BDX to be different. His strength would've been enhanced by the preternatural blood. According to my calculations, a subject with vampiric blood in his veins would react in one of two ways. He would either die on the table or he would survive and become the strongest BD-Exer on the team. Possibly the strongest human being alive."

"A super weapon against the Undead."

"Or a dead one," the doctor said. "That first subject didn't survive the transfusion. And the rest is no more than an unproven theory." He looked at Charlie, and she saw a hint of sympathy in his bone china face.

She struggled to form words, sought LT's eyes. "LT– Lucas....stop the...IV. Please. I'm dying."

He didn't answer.

The doctor's voice came from very far away. "I recommend we stop the IV, Lieutenant Townsend."

LT stared into her eyes for a long moment and said, "She's different from that former subject," he said softly. "She's the only descendant of the oldest living BD. She's special. Stronger than any of them, even without the blood of one of those animals coursing through her veins. Get a fresh restraint for the right arm. Get another dose of the tranquilizer ready to go, just in case, and crank that IV flow up as high as possible. We're giving her all three doses, right here, right now. She can handle it. And we need her ready to fight."

"No," she whispered. "no, please...*please*–"

But the doctor hustled, first to a drawer to pull out a fresh leather strap for her arm, which he handed to LT. Then, as Lucas buckled it tightly around her arm, anchoring it to the bed, the doc went to the cabinet for another needle full of vampire tranquilizer, which he laid on a tray nearby. "What about the additive?" The doctor asked.

"Just the BDX," LT barked. "Now."

The doctor brought two more syringes full of the drug they were pumping into her–BDX–and injected them into her IV bag. Then he bent to the IV's digital panel, and started pushing buttons.

The drip drip of the rusty fluid became a stream, and the heat inside her body was cranked up to full power and burned as if there was acid running through her veins. She screamed and screamed, and the pictures of peaceful landscapes fell from the walls in the sterile white room, as if earthquakes had suddenly ravaged each setting.

"More of the tranq," she heard LT order. "And don't forget to harvest the usual samples once she's out. They'll be the best of the crop."

CHAPTER TWELVE

Killian came awake all at once with a more jolting shock than usual. He sat up before he was even fully conscious, the sounds of Charlie's screams echoing through his mind. And more. The impact of her hatred. Hatred for him.

He hadn't expected that. And he couldn't have expected it to hurt this much. He sat for a moment, looking around the room where he'd awoken. A hidden section of the basement. Roxy, or someone she trusted, had erected a new wall a few feet in front of the original one. It didn't look at all out of place, and short of measuring the house above and below, no one would notice. One section of the wall resembled an aging wooden shelf, complete with mason jars, antique milk bottles and coffee cans. That shelf was actually a door. Behind it was a space about four feet wide that ran the length of the house and the height of the basement. It held four cots, with just enough room so you could walk past them. A double bed took up the full width of the space at the far end. That was where Roland and Rhiannon had slept. Beneath each bunk, sealed plastic bags held fresh bedding and soft pillows. For a walled off section of basement, it wasn't half bad.

"You do not look like a vampire fresh from the day sleep," Rhiannon said. She was sitting up in her bed, gazing steadily at him. Roland lay still, his eyes wide open, but he wasn't moving just yet.

"I kept hearing Charlie. I know that shouldn't be possible, but with her...it is. I've heard her in my sleep before. Dreamed of her."

"It's been said that vampires do not dream. That the day sleep is impenetrable," Rhiannon said. "But I know differently. For every rule, Killian, there are bound to be exceptions. Never take anything as absolute."

"What did you hear of her?" Roland asked.

Killian lowered his head. "Screaming. She was screaming. We have to get her out of there."

"This is freaking *amazing!*" Charlie shouted. She stood on the top of the 100 foot high, rock climbing wall that she and the other recruits had been ordered to climb. She'd scrambled up it like some kind of spider-girl. The others were coming up now, and climbing faster than any normal person could, but she had smoked them all. As she stood looking down from a dizzying height, her blood pumped madly through her veins. "I can't believe it."

"I told you it would be worth the discomfort, didn't I?" LT, who'd been waiting for her at the top, could not seem to contain his own smile. "Didn't I?"

She sent him a hateful glance. "I don't remember. I was too busy screaming in agony."

"But you're not screaming now."

"I *told you* to stop. You did it to me anyway. That's not right, LT. I'm not going to let you get away with that, and I don't care who you work for." She supposed she should be respectful, do the "Yessir, Lieutenant Townsend sir" bit, but fuck that. She was strong enough to rip out his liver, and he knew it.

She had never felt like this before. She'd run five miles today in about 10 minutes. Only hours after the treatment. And she hadn't even been out of breath. She could've done it again.

LT had a notebook with him, and he marked down the time it had taken her to make the treacherous ascent.

"How'd I do?" She didn't need to ask, but she did anyway.

"Just under a minute. The fastest it's ever been done was five thirty-four. You shattered the record."

"I'll shatter it on every course you've got," she told him, and then she closed her eyes as some of the sadness she was trying to keep sealed inside her leaked out. "But you'd better not break your promise. I'm attending my mother's funeral."

He nodded. "Tomorrow night. Nine p.m. I've taken care of everything and believe me, Charlie, we spared no expense. We got the Methodist minister you requested, the flowers you said were her favorites, the musical selections, the readings. Everything will be just the way you said she would want it."

She nodded. "That's...thank you."

"You're a huge asset to the cause, Charlie. We want you to realize how much we appreciate having you as a part of the team." He lowered his eyes, then raised them again to look into hers, and she got a little trill of alarm shooting up her spine, because he didn't look like her commanding officer anymore. "And I want you to know how much *I* appreciate you, too. On a personal level."

"I..." She didn't know how to answer that. She had decided, somewhere between begging them to stop, and hearing him order the doc to crank it up to high gear, that she hated Lucas Townsend. She had got what she wanted. The cure, the strength. And bonus, it had worked on her like it had never worked on anyone before, maybe because she'd imbibed vampire blood before the treatment.

But she thought there might be something more. Something her grandmother had hinted at. After all, Charlie did have the same genes as the oldest living BD.

"It killed me to let you go through all that pain, Charlie, but I knew it would work. I knew it would make you stronger than any recruit yet. But more than that, I knew it would save your life."

She looked away, out at the sky, the forest with all its tall trees completely blocking the camp from the view of anyone outside it. She didn't need to exact vengeance on the Lieutenant, she reminded herself. She was already getting it. Using him, sticking around here for the information. This was the best place to find out what she needed to know. Where Killian was, and where he was keeping her grandmother. If he was truly the one who had her. The minute she found out, she was out of here.

But she couldn't be too obvious about that.

"So I'm going to live past thirty-five now? You're sure about that?" she asked.

"I'm sure. And once the scourge of vampirism has been wiped out of existence, you'll have the rest of your life to do whatever you want with it." He smiled a little. "What do you think you'd like to do?"

"Kill the bastard who murdered my mother. Find my grandmother, if she's still alive, and get her home in one piece. That's as far as I can think right now."

"For now, that's enough." He looked past her, down at the recruits still climbing the wall, some of whom were nearing the top now. Taking her arms, he pulled her back a few steps, onto the platform beyond their line of sight, and then he bent his head and he kissed her.

And she let him.

Killian felt a hot blade searing straight through his heart, opened his eyes, and met Rhiannon's. She had helped him calmly reconnect to Charlie's mind for a few brief seconds. Long enough to know that he wanted more than ever to kill Lieutenant Lucas Townsend.

"She'll be at her mother's funeral," he said. "Nine P.M. tomorrow night. But I don't think we should wait." He got up, turning to the false door and pushing it open, stepping into the basement and then moving through it and up the stairs to the first floor. Pandora lay at the base of the second floor staircase, watching the hallway above where the entry to the attic was. She had refused to bed down with her owner the night before, unable to let go of the notion of that giant white owl as a snack, he thought. Olive seemed happy as hell having the attic to herself and was taking full advantage of the open window to hunt.

Rhiannon stopped to stroke her cat and then opened the front door for her. "Go, Pandora. Hunt yourself down some breakfast. I'm in the mood to do the same."

"We're going to need something soon," Roland said. He'd wandered to the kitchen and was holding the door of the refrigerator open. They'd moved their supply of blood from its travel cooler into the fridge. "We're down to the last three bags." He took out the bags, emptied their contents into tall glasses, and then set them in the microwave.

"At least it's human," Rhiannon said softly. "We're strong again."

"I *said* I don't think we should wait," Killian repeated. "Do you two have anything to say about that?"

"And we won't," Rhiannon said. "Are you still sensing that she's in pain?"

"No," Killian admitted. "But there's exhilaration about her

own strength, which is baffling to me. I connected with her long enough to hear part of a conversation she was having with that Lieutenant asshole. They gave her some kind of a drug. It made her stronger than ordinary humans. Its effects on her have been more powerful than they've been with any other recruit. And it cured the other effects of Belladonna."

"Cured it?" Rhiannon asked, shooting an alarmed look at Roland.

"Yeah. She's not going to die around thirty-five now. At least, not according to that bastard Townsend."

"Oh," Rhiannon said then. "Jealousy. *Now* I see why you're so eager. Did Townsend attempt to seduce your beloved?"

"Yeah, and if he touches her again, I'll kill him."

"You can't kill one of The Chosen, Killian," Roland said. The microwave beeped, and he took the glasses out and handed them around. Then he looked at Rhiannon. "And before you judge Killian too harshly, my love, put yourself in his shoes. If some eager mortal female were to put her lips to mine–"

"If another woman kissed you, darling, I would tear her open from neck to groin and read the future in her entrails." She downed her liquid breakfast in a single, long draught.

"As I suspected. That said, Killian, prepare yourself. Charlotte has been drugged. We do not have any way of knowing the effects of it. And beyond that, she is being systematically brainwashed by her captors."

"Brainwashed?"

"They've cured her of a fatal condition and blamed you for her mother's death and grandmother's disappearance. What else would you call it?" he asked, sipping from his glass as they spoke.

Killian nodded slowly, drained his glass, and set it down. "I want to go after her now."

"Then let's go." Roland finished his drink as well. "We need to get a sample of this drug they gave her, if we can, to send to Eric for analysis."

"We need to wipe DPI from existence," Rhiannon said, and there was a darkness in her voice that sent a chill down Killian's spine. "I'm afraid the rogue Devlin was right about that all along."

Charlie had to force herself not to gag and push LT away. She allowed his kiss but didn't respond to it. She couldn't bring herself to go that far.

"Do you know how to shield your mind, Charlie?" he'd asked her after a long and awkward silence.

"I don't think so, no."

"Imagine the hardest shell you can think of taking shape around you. It begins at the ground, forming a sphere in which you are the center. Can you see it?"

She closed her eyes and tried to imagine a sphere around her, going along with the "lesson" because it was better than pretending not to have minded his kiss. "Yes. I see it."

"What color is it?"

"Steel underneath. But on the surface, blue, deep dark blue." Like Killian's eyes. "And streaks of red. A lot of red."

"That's very good. Now I want you to understand that this is your shield. Nothing can get through it, in or out, without your specific say so. Do you feel it's strong enough?"

"Yes. I feel it."

"Very good. You can open your eyes now."

She opened them and had to blink, because for just an instant, the shell around her was real. Translucent, but there. And then gone, although not really. She still felt it, just no longer saw it.

"What does this shell protect me from?" she asked.

"Vampires are powerful telepaths. They can read the thoughts of most humans. This keeps them from reading yours."

She frowned, wondering if Killian had been able to read her thoughts earlier, when she'd been wishing him dead, imagining his murder, and a wave of regret washed over her. Had she really meant any of it? Could she really kill him?

He'd murdered her mother. Of course she could kill him.

Don't believe anything anyone tells you, including me, until you've seen irrefutable proof. Her grandmother's words rang in her memory. But she had seen proof. She'd seen the photos of her mother–

No, she couldn't think about that. And yet, she should, shouldn't she? She should hold that image in her mind's eye above all else and channel every bit of horror it created in her into vengeance. Into retaliation against Killian and his kind, so that no one ever had to lose a mother again.

"Did you hear me, Charlie?"

She shook out of her thoughts and refocused on LT. "No, I'm sorry, I drifted."

"I said, there's no question in my mind that the vampire who attacked you will try for you again at your mother's funeral tomorrow night."

"He will?" She processed that, then realized that he was right. Killian would come to that funeral, whether he'd killed her mother or not. Innocent or guilty, he would try to see her again, and he would know she would be there.

And why was she still thinking in terms of innocent or guilty? He did it. What, like it could be coincidence that she'd banged a vampire, and her mother got killed by one within the same twenty-four hours?

She focused on LT, and did the thought blocking visualization in her head, just in case. "What if he does? Do you have a plan?" Whatever it was, she thought, she didn't care, just as long as he didn't get in her way.

"Of course I have a plan. You don't have to be afraid, Charlie. I won't let anything happen to you."

"How are you going to prevent it?" she asked. Let him think she was afraid. She wasn't. She was so strong now, she thought she could take on both him and Killian if need be.

"Come to the office after you've showered up. I'll show you."

She nodded, but thought she picked up a hint of something besides business on his mind when he said it. Didn't matter. She could handle him.

"You need to rappel back down the rock face now." He picked up a rope that was anchored to a chink in the stone, and helped her get it fastened to the harness she wore. "Are you ready?"

"I'm ready." Standing on the lip of the rock she'd just ascended, a few feet from where the other recruits were still climbing, she leaned backward, balancing the balls of her feet on the brink. Then she pushed off, and let the rope slide through her gloved hands.

CHAPTER THIRTEEN

Charlie. God, I hope I can make you hear me. I need to talk to you. I need to see you so badly that I'm risking everything to get to you. I'm coming, Charlie. I'm coming.

Charlie's eyes popped open. She was in her bunk. It was after midnight, and the other recruits in her barracks were asleep, as far as she could tell. But that voice–Killian's voice–had been speaking clearly and passionately inside her mind. Had it been a dream?

She thought of Killian, saw his face in her mind's eye, and whispered, "I'd like to see you, too."

Charlie? You can hear me?

She had thought it was a dream! But she was awake now, and it was just as real. It was actually him, Killian, speaking to her, mentally. She must have let her protective shell slip while she'd been sleeping. Not that she seemed able to muster up the desire to shut him out. Not really.

Yes, it's real. Charlie, I know what they told you about your mother, but it's a lie. I was nowhere near Portland that night. I wouldn't hurt you

184 | MAGGIE SHAYNE

that way. You have to believe me.

Her heart beat faster. Every little thing seemed to kick it into high gear, since the treatment. Excitement, anger, impatience, sadness. Every emotion sent it rocketing. Sometimes it scared her, how fast and hard her heart would pound when she wasn't even exerting herself.

She wondered if it was a side effect of the BDX, and whether she was the only one to experience it.

I have to see you again, Killian went on. *Meet me by the fence, where we met before. I'll be there waiting.*

She closed her eyes and tried to listen to the practical part of her mind for a change. He was a vampire. He'd attacked her in the hospital. He'd probably killed her mother and kidnapped her grandmother. She couldn't trust him. He'd been trying to kill her that night...he'd been trying to....

No, he fed me from his own veins in the hospital. That wasn't an attack. He didn't even try to...to bite me. Except that once, when we had sex. And that was...it was...ecstasy.

LT said he'd killed her mother. That he'd been seen, or someone who looked like him had been seen. That they'd identified him from a photo taken the night he was abducting her from the hospital.

God, she wanted to believe it was all a lie. And maybe that was selfish. Maybe she just wanted to believe that because it would ease her guilty conscience. After all, the vampire she'd had sex with had murdered her mother.

No. She couldn't believe him. She had to kill him. She was strong enough now. She could do it.

Couldn't she?

"Okay," she whispered. "Give me a few minutes. I have to be careful."

Thank God. Thank God. I'll be waiting, Charlie.

She took a breath, had second thoughts, and wondered if she was out of her mind to be doing this. Meeting him like this. But she knew LT's plans for tomorrow night. He'd told her on the way back to the barracks, apparently too proud of his plan to keep it to himself. Her mother's funeral would be surrounded by armed guards, government types, not BD-Exers who were, for some reason, deemed "not yet ready" for battle. A squad of hired guns would be waiting for Killian to try to get to her. It would be an ambush, a slaughter. They would be armed with automatic weapons as well as tranquilizer guns. The funeral home had been chosen for its location. They would let him get in, him and anyone who might be helping him. But they wouldn't let him get out again. The orders were to kill him by whatever means was necessary and to bring the body back to Fort Rogers. Killian wouldn't stand a chance. If there was any possibility he was telling the truth....

She had to be sure.

And if she wanted his explanation before he died, this would be her only chance to get it.

Pushing back her covers, she slid out of her bunk, wearing only her panties and a tank style undershirt. She grabbed her pants from the top of her strongbox at the foot of the bed, and carried them with her as she tiptoed quickly to the bathroom at the end of the barracks. In case anyone saw her, going to the head wouldn't look as odd as walking out the front door. Once inside the little lav, she pulled the pants on, then opened a window and jumped out, landing in the weeds behind the building. She closed the window almost all the way, leaving a crack so she could open it again to get back inside later on. And then she paused to look around, to listen, to feel.

No one. Nothing. Good, she was good. Turning, she ran as fast and as lightly as a fox, landing on the balls of her feet and making almost no sound, yet moving rapidly along the boundary of the electrified fence, through the wooded area, past the center of camp and onward, beyond the parade grounds and obstacle courses to the very end.

He was there. He was there, just inside the perimeter fence, waiting in the shadows. She felt him even before she saw him and walked right up to him, stopping only a foot from where he stood. So close. So very close. Everything in her was itching to move even closer. To touch. To press herself to his body, to melt into his arms.

It sickened her that she could still feel such a powerful attraction to a killer.

Hold firm, she told herself. She had to know the truth. She had to be cool. Distant. Objective.

"What happened to my mother?" she asked, eyes fixed on his chest instead of meeting his.

"I don't know. I only know that it wasn't me, Charlie."

She tried to see the lie in his eyes, but all she saw was longing.

"That night at the hospital...I wasn't trying to hurt you. I was trying to save your life. You'd lost so much blood–"

"You were taking me somewhere. Kidnapping me." She had to interrupt him. His voice stroked her nerve endings like a bow over violin strings, making her shiver and hum all over.

"That's right, I was taking you somewhere. Away from them. The goons who brought you here shot me with some kind of tranquilizer. They're the ones who kidnapped you. Took you away. Brought you here. They'd have probably killed me, if not for Roxy. She found me dragging myself along the ground, trying to get away. She told me to get into her truck, and I did. She took me home. To the cabin. Gave me a safe place to sleep, even had an antidote for the tranquilizer darts."

She frowned, distracted from wanting him for a moment. "Roxy... *helped* you?"

He nodded.

"Prove it." She glanced behind her, back the way she had come. "And hurry, you don't have much time. Tell me something you wouldn't know if you hadn't spent time with my grandmother."

"There's a recording. She left us a message. They shot up her truck and they took her, Charlie. They have your grandmother."

"Who?"

"The same people who are behind this...this secret death squad you've joined. DPI."

He seemed to be searching his mind and spewing anything he could think of. She felt it happening, felt him searching his memory. It didn't feel like he was making things up.

"Roxy made me sleep in the safe room that first night. On a cot. The blanket was blue and sealed in a plastic bag in there. She had blood in a mini-fridge in the basement. And three computers and a pile of cell phones."

He was convincing her. And that was terrifying. What if she was wrong? "You'd know all that if you'd been inside the house. Doesn't mean she helped you."

He spoke fast, holding her eyes with his. "She had the truck's radio tuned to a country music station. She has a pet owl named Olive. It comes when she calls it by whistling." He puckered his lips and whistled the same three notes, and for the first time, Charlie's doubt of his guilt became bigger than her certainty of it. "She's the oldest living Chosen," he went on. "She helped us find this place, too. Her computers, satellite photos. I wouldn't even begin to know how to get the intel she did, but she found this secret camp, and we all drove out here. She was supposed to meet us after we'd checked it out, but when we got back there, she'd been taken. Not by me, Charlie. By these assholes you're working for."

"Is she alive?" She searched his mind with hers as she asked the question, wishing she knew whether what she sensed there was real or wishful thinking on her part.

"I don't know. Rhiannon thinks so."

"Who's Rhiannon?"

He lowered his eyes, the first sign of a lie. "A friend of your grandmother's. She and her husband came to help us find you. Get you back." He reached out for her, and she didn't duck away, but let him slide his arms around her and pull her closer.

Then she panicked because it felt so damn good to be pressed against him that way, and because when he touched her, she couldn't think of anything else. In a knee-jerk reaction, she flattened her hands to his chest to push him away.

He flew backward like he'd been hit by a wrecking ball. His feet left the ground and he hit a tree, splitting its trunk, and then slid to the ground. "Holy–!" Pushing himself up, rubbing the back of his head and shaking it as if to clear it, he said, "What in the hell did they *do* to you, Charlie?"

"They cured me. I won't die at thirty-something now. I'm strong. As strong as you, maybe. Stronger than anyone here, that's for sure."

He frowned. "Why would that be?"

She averted her eyes.

"Look at me, Charlie."

She didn't. But then he said it again, and this time it was inside her mind, echoing, commanding, irresistible. *Look at me.*

And she couldn't refuse, she turned to look at him.

He moved closer, slid his arms around her waist and pulled her hard against him. "I couldn't hurt you if I wanted to. Vampires cannot harm The Chosen. Even if we tried it would be impossible. I want to kill your Goddamn lieutenant more than I want to wake up tomorrow night, but he has the antigen. So I can't. It's in our DNA."

Her eyes were captive now as his held them, and his will wouldn't let her look away. "God, I've been dying to hold you like this," he said. "To kiss you...like this...."

And then he did, he kissed her, and the heat between them rose up like a living thing, a ravenous flame that would devour her if she let it. And she wanted to let it, in spite of herself. His hands moved, one crawling underneath the shirt and up over the small of her back to press her against him, the other, sliding over the pants to cup her backside and hold her tighter to his hardness. His hips moved in a mimicry of sex that made her blood turn molten. She clutched at his shoulders, arching her hips in time with his, her fingers threading into his hair, her mouth opening to his hungry invasion.

"I have to have you," he muttered. "I have to have you now, Charlie." He grabbed the edges of her shirt and pulled it up, and almost off, but she pulled free as her heart launched into a full gallop inside her chest. She turned away from him, bending with her hands braced on her knees, fighting to catch her breath as her heart thundered like never before.

"Oh God. Oh God," she panted.

"Charlie?" He went to her, clasped her shoulders, turned her around, and then his face clouded with fear. "Charlie, what's happening to you?"

"My heart....I can't catch my breath...."

He didn't need to touch her chest, she thought, not when she could hear her own pulse thundering in her ears. But he pressed his hand there anyway. "It's the drug, isn't it? Jesus, Charlie, what the hell did they give you?"

"Just go." She had to stop to try to catch her breath, speaking only a few words at a time. "They'll miss...me soon." She clutched his shirt. "The funeral...it's a trap." Panting, panting. "Don't go there."

"I have to get you out of here. I'm not leaving you here, Charlie, not again." He wrapped his arms around her, scooped her up, turned toward the fence, bending his knees to jump it. But shots came out of nowhere, all but silent, like puffs of air, and darts stabbed into him in so many places that Charlie couldn't count them all.

He tried to jump, but already the drug was obviously flowing through him, and he landed again, sinking onto the grass and letting Charlie fall from his arms.

She sat up, then scrambled to her feet, staring down at him, her eyes wide. Her mouth was agape as she fought to catch her breath. Her heart was pounding so hard she thought it would break her ribs. She pressed her hands to her chest as if she could slow it down.

"Well done, Charlie. Well done." LT stepped out of the trees, waving a hand at a dozen recruits who surrounded Killian, their guns aimed at him.

She tried to see him, tried to tell him with her eyes that she had not done this on purpose, had not set a trap for him. She envisioned opening her mind wide to his. But there were too many recruits surrounding him, blocking him from her eyes, and then she dropped to her knees, too dizzy to stay upright.

"Charlie?" LT rushed to her side, kneeling, hands to her shoulders. "What is it, Charlie?"

She patted her chest with one hand, still straining to see Killian around the recruits. They were picking him up now, carrying him off somewhere.

LT pressed a hand to her chest, swore at what he felt there, then picked her up and carried her back through the woods to the road. He set her on the passenger seat of a Jeep, and she was allowed an all too brief glimpse of Killian, limp and barely conscious, being thrown into the back of another one that quickly sped away.

Gasping for each breath, she asked, "Wha-what are they... doing...with him?"

"Not what you were about to, Charlie. We don't deal well with traitors, you know. But right now, we've got to keep you alive long enough to hear what you have to say in your own defense." He looked at her, shook his head in disgust. "I had high hopes for you. I really did. What a waste." Then he put the Jeep into gear and stomped the gas.

Just before he shifted into second gear, Charlie felt a distinct sensation. The kind she'd only felt when Killian was near, but not as pronounced. Frowning, she looked back in the direction they'd come from. There was another vampire... maybe more than one.

Oh my God. He'd brought others here. Had he fooled her yet again? Was she planning some kind of an attack or....

But no, she'd felt something when he'd kissed her. She'd

felt *him*. His mind, his emotions, his thoughts, they'd twisted around and melded with her own. There'd been nothing of betrayal, of trickery or deceit. Or murder. Only passion, only longing. She'd felt as if she'd known him always, as if she'd seen his soul and recognized it, knew it intimately. Why couldn't she just trust those feelings and let all the rest go?

Closing her eyes, she tried to send a message as she had done with Killian, but she had no idea whether the vampires she sensed nearby would receive it.

Killian's been darted and taken prisoner. Save him. Save Killian.

CHAPTER FOURTEEN

Rhiannon and Roland waited outside the perimeter fence, near the center of the secret base. Only a few yards of scrub brush and trees stood between them and the place where the road formed a loop around a mound of greenery with a flag pole in its middle. No flag hung from it by night, though.

The plan was simple, and they'd gone along with it because Killian would've come alone if they hadn't. Killian was supposed to take Charlie out of the camp, with or without her cooperation–he was a vampire, after all–and once he had her in the clear, he was supposed to create a diversion by pushing a tree over on the electrified fence, sending a shower of sparks into the night. The recruits would all rush to the lower end of the base, leaving Rhiannon and Roland free to slip in, unnoticed, find the lab or infirmary where the drug was kept, steal a sample and get out again. Simple.

Rhiannon was just starting to worry that things were taking a little bit too long, when apparently something happened, because several Jeeps and more soldiers on foot, took off, heading in the direction they had wanted them to head.

"Odd, I didn't hear Killian's diversion," she whispered to Roland.

"I didn't either," he said, taking her hand. "Too busy reading the thoughts of those still awake in camp. Particularly The Chosen. Nearly all of them, Rhiannon. Except for the medical personnel, but I've been eavesdropping on them, too. Let's go."

Together they bent their knees, then pushed off, clearing the electrified fence and landing on the inside. "You know where they're keeping the drug?" Rhiannon asked excitedly.

"It's in the infirmary. There's a laboratory in the rear." He still pronounced it la-BORE-a tory, which brought a slight smile to Rhiannon's lips. "This way," he said, still holding her hand. They crept through the trees, emerging in the rear of some of the camp's buildings. Peering around the side of the nearest one, they could see the camp's center. "We have to cross in the open," he said. "It's on the other side of the road."

"I'm ready," she told him.

He gave a nod, and they released hands and exploded in a burst of speed. When they stopped again, they were behind the infirmary. And there was a door.

"There are bound to be patients inside."

"Sleeping patients," Roland assured her.

"And staff."

"Human staff," he said.

"Human staff that have been treated with a drug that's supposed to make them super human," she corrected. "We have no idea whether our powers will work on them."

"They're still The Chosen. We have no choice."

Roland tried the doorknob. It turned, unlocked, and he opened it easily. The room they entered was some sort of supply room. Locked cabinets, stocked shelves, boxes and crates lined it. Only a pair of long, light green curtains closed it off from the rest of the building. Moving silently, Rhiannon parted the curtains to peek into the main part of the medical unit, then ducked back again. She spoke to Roland mentally. *Beds line both walls. There are two rooms, though, on the other side of this curtain, one to the left and one to the right.*

You take the right, I'll take the left, Roland told her. He squeezed her hand. *The drug we're looking for is called BDX. Be careful, my love.*

There was something in his voice. Something like nervousness. He was sensing something. *Roland...?*

On three. Fast and silent. Get the BDX and get out. One, two, three!

On three, they both slipped through the curtain, straight to their assigned door. It was dark inside, and they moved without a sound. Rhiannon gripped her doorknob, found it locked, and twisted harder. The lock snapped, and she slipped through the doorway without incident.

In the utter darkness, she looked around the room. It was an office. No refrigerator. No test tubes or vials. There was, however, an oversized laptop computer on the desk. She picked it up and looked for another exit, but the place had no windows or doors. She'd have to go back the way she'd come.

She opened the door just a crack, peered out. *Roland? I have a computer. No vial.*

Something's happening. Get out now, Rhiannon.

Already she heard the vehicles out front, the voices. The front doors of the infirmary burst open, and a man in camouflage fatigues strode in, carrying a woman in his arms. The woman's scent bore a hint of Roxanne's DNA. This had to be her granddaughter.

"Tell them to throw the vampire into the brig!" the man carrying her shouted to a young woman with short dark hair and lean powerful muscle tone who ran along beside him. "Make sure he's bound good and tight. We want him alive, for now. But keep him sedated. The minute he starts to rouse, you shoot him up again. You hear me, recruit?"

"Yes, sir, Lieutenant!"

"Go. Now!"

The female looked worriedly toward Charlotte, but obeyed, turning and running back the way she had come, nearly colliding with an all but albino mortal in a white coat who was on his way in. The lieutenant lay the girl on a bed as Rhiannon got her first look at Charlotte O'Malley. She was a beautiful creature—hair the color of copper, falling in soft waves onto the pillows. Skin as porcelain as if she'd already been transformed. She was small, everywhere. Short in stature, slight in build, even her nose was tiny, but her eyes, when they opened wide in panic, were huge.

"What's happening? What's happening to me?"

Rhiannon could feel Charlotte's heart beating at a dangerously powerful rate.

"It's fine, you'll be fine, Charlie," the lieutenant said. "It's a side effect of the BDX. You got too excited, that's all. Doc?"

The doctor looked grim as he hurried from the bedside toward Rhiannon. *He's coming this way, Roland! Hide!*

She ducked back into the office, backed into a shadowy corner between a bookcase and a wall, and visualized herself blending into the darkness. But the doctor didn't come in. He entered the room across the hall. The room where Roland might still be. He was concealing his energy from anyone who might be able to sense it. She wished he would answer her.

She held her breath, listening, waiting, sending her power out to cloak her love from eyes unworthy of looking upon him. And in a moment, the door across the hall closed again and the doctor's footsteps returned to the girl's bedside.

Cautiously, Rhiannon opened the door again to watch what was happening without. She could still feel Charlotte's heartbeat. It was pounding more rapidly, and more powerfully than she'd ever heard a human heart pound.

Roland, where are you?

Still in the lab. Across the hall from you. He didn't see me.

Do you have the drug?

Yes. But they have Killian. And Charlotte.
There's something terribly wrong with her, Roland.
I know.

She watched the doctor inject Charlotte with something. Within a few seconds, her heartbeat began to slow. To soften. To ease. The girl herself slipped into unconsciousness, and Rhiannon was surprised to see genuine relief on the face of the so-called Lieutenant. The man's back bowed with it as he sank into a chair and took hold of her hand. It wasn't false. She could feel it in him.

Did you see what drug he took from the lab just now, Roland? Get some of it, if you can.

"We need to talk," said the doctor.

The Lieutenant nodded. "In the office," he said.

Bloody Hell. Hide, Rhiannon.

Rhiannon put the laptop back on the desk where she'd found it, and returned to her shadowy corner. Invisibility was not a physical state, but a mental one. She had to believe it and see her body vanishing, becoming a part of the wall behind her, a part of the bookcase beside her, a part of the shadowy darkness. It wasn't hard. But it did require her constant focus to maintain. She was not an inanimate object. Living energy was harder to conceal. But she knew how. She'd trained with priestesses of Isis, after all, from the age of five. She knew about magic.

While they're in here with me, Roland, you have the chance to slip out. Find this brig where they've taken Killian. I'll keep my eye on Charlotte while you do, and as soon as they leave the office, I'll make my own exit.

If they see you....

Darling, really? How long have we been married?

She felt, rather than saw his sexy smile, then quickly had to refocus her energies as the two men came into the office.

Killian came awake to some kind of acid trip. Everything around him was wavy and out of focus, and he could hear a million voices, some physical and some mental, all talking at once and none of them making any sense. He was on a hard surface. He saw people standing outside a wall that he could see through. Bars. It was a wall made of bars. Okay, he was in a cell. And the people were guards, and there might be two of them or six or eight. They kept multiplying and then unifying again.

They'd shot him with the same damned tranquilizer as before, then, hadn't they? And there was no Roxy standing nearby with an antidote, this time.

A female voice said, "LT says to shoot him up again if he starts to come around. Those darts we shot him with were practice loads. Not the full dosage. Here, these ones are more potent."

He was a prisoner. He wondered about the side effects of repeated use of their tranquilizer, but figured he probably wouldn't live long enough to find out.

Where was Charlie? Something had happened to her out there. Something about her heart....

He searched his scrambled up mind and told himself not to move, or moan, or do anything to reveal that he was slowly regaining his senses. He needed to stay perfectly still and give his strength time to return. And then he had to find Charlie in this maze of super-soldiers who would do everything they could to stop him. All of them, The Chosen. He could not fight back, not effectively anyway.

"It's funny, isn't it?" the girl said softly. "He looks just like an ordinary guy. Not a bad looking one, either, aside from being a little pale."

She sighed and then he heard her footsteps moving away.

Then there was a soft sound from her, like a little squeak of alarm, and a voice that said, "There now, just do as you're told, and I won't have to snap your pretty neck."

Roland!

The guards, however many there were, jumped into motion, but in a second they were still again, and Roland, or three Rolands, stood there with the girl held to his chest. "Gentlemen, if you'd be so kind as to unlock the cell, I'll leave you alive."

He couldn't hurt them, and he knew it. Fortunately, though, they did not, and the sight of him standing there with his dark hair slicked back, in a suit with a freaking black cloak of all things, was enough to scare them half out of their wits. He could feel their fear.

"Not gonna happen, sir," said one of them, but there was a tremor beneath the words. The guards aimed their weapons. No, one of them did. Just one, while the other one stood there looking from his comrade to Roland over and over. No one was paying any attention to Killian. "Let her go, or I'll shoot," the first guy told Roland. "It's point blank range. I won't miss."

Roland flung the girl aside, lunged forward and yanked the weapon from the recruit's hand before he could blink. His eyes probably hadn't even followed the movements. Roland whirled around, cloak flying dramatically, hit the other guard with the rifle butt, sending him to the floor, then bent the weapon's barrel into a kinked right angle.

He reached for the bars, but the soldiers, who should have been unconscious, if not dead, sprang to their feet again, the female included.

"Impressive," Roland said. It wasn't. Killian knew Roland could barely bring himself to shove them around, much less actually hurt them.

They attacked, and he defended himself. Weapons were drawn, and Roland knocked them away, punches were thrown, kicks. Roland blocked and dodged, but his return blows were deliberately mild.

Killian couldn't believe Roland was having as much trouble as he was with three mere mortals, even if he couldn't hurt them much. He pushed himself up onto his feet, tried to move quietly, one hand on the wall for balance, and got up close to the bars. He met Roland's eyes. *Throw one my way, Rolly.*

No one calls me Rolly. But Roland half-heartedly plowed a fist into the chest of one of the men, sending him reeling until his back slammed against the cell bars. Killian snapped his arms around the mortal's neck, and squeezed, but then suddenly, he couldn't keep squeezing. He had to let go. He couldn't hurt the guy.

Dammit, I can't hurt them even now!

They're unnaturally strong, Roland replied silently. *Just disable them, if you can even manage that.*

I'm trying!

It took a supreme act of will, but he managed to choke the young man until he lost consciousness and slumped to the floor. Then he gripped the bars and tried to bend them apart.

Roland shoved his two attackers off him yet again. The male hit the block wall, and his head took a blow. Then he, too, slumped to the floor. Roland surged to the bars, then, gripping them, helped to pull them apart. The girl scrambled to her feet and made to run for it, but Killian lunged out of the cell and grabbed her, clapping a hand over her mouth.

"What the hell are we going to do with her?" he asked as she struggled in his arms, amazingly strong and hard for him to hold.

"Take her with us," Roland said. "I'd take them all, if we could." Bending, he picked up one of the darts the girl had dropped to the floor.

Her eyes widened, and she struggled hard in Killian's arms, as he strained to hold her. "I heard her say that was full strength, Roland. Be careful."

He brought the needle to her arm, gritted his teeth,

grimaced in effort, but in the end, flung the dart to the floor. "I can't. Dammit, I can't do something that could harm one of The Chosen, no matter how I try."

The girl frowned, but Killian still had his hand over her mouth.

Roland gripped her chin angrily. "Look into my eyes," he told her.

She closed her eyes hard.

Killian rolled his. "Look into his eyes, woman, or I'm going to have to bite you and drain enough blood to make you pass out. *That* I think I can manage."

She shook her head. Killian moved her hair off her neck and snapped his finger against her skin like a nurse in search of a good vein for an IV.

She muttered what sounded like an urgent "okay, okay" behind his hand and opened her eyes, staring straight into Roland's.

Roland, his voice deep and low, said, "No harm will come to you in our care. Sleep, woman. And do not wake until I command it."

And she went. Just like that. Out like a light.

"I have *got to* learn how to do that," Killian said. "Where is Charlie? Did you see her?"

"Infirmary, last I saw. As was Rhiannon. Now we need to find them and make our way out of this den of super-charged Chosen. If we can," Roland said. "Tie this one up and leave her near the fence. We'll pick her up on the way out."

Rhiannon was pressed into the shadowy corner, completely relaxed, feeling herself meld with the wall and the wood and the shadows. Until the doctor said, "Like everything else, the side effects of the BDX are exaggerated in her."

That drew her attention away from the invisibility

meditation, not a good thing. She tried to relax back into the spell while keeping herself mildly attuned to what the men were saying.

"Then treat her." The lieutenant replied. "Just the way you do the others."

"I have and I am. I'm just warning you that it might not work as well with her to postpone the inevitable. Especially if she goes into battle. But this is the fate that awaits them all. You know this."

The lieutenant lowered his head. "I was hoping it would be different with her. She's so much stronger."

"It *is* different with her. It's more severe. While the others last six to eight months, this one will be lucky to make it through one. But it's not about them. It's never been about them. It's about the offspring. You know that, Lieutenant."

"I know."

The doctor said, "They should all be injected with Protectol. They won't survive the stress of combat without being properly prepared."

"I don't think there's time for that. The vampires have found us."

A radio crackled. A voice spoke rapid, static laced words. *Vampire. Break. Brigg.*

The lieutenant picked up a handset. "Repeat that, and key your mike appropriately this time."

"Sorry, sir. The vampire has escaped the brig. There was another one helping him. And they've taken Mariah–I mean, Recruit Senate."

"Has anyone gone after them?"

"Three recruits are trailing them, sir."

"Good. Sound the call. Wake the recruits. I want them armed and assembled in three minutes. Two if possible. Tell them this is not a drill."

"Yes, sir, Lieutenant!"

He clipped the radio to his hip, got to his feet. "Doctor

Mariner, this base has been compromised. We're initiating Bug Out Protocol One."

"Sir?" The medic looked puzzled.

The lieutenant was already heading for the door. "Gather every trace of what you've been working on here, pile it into a Jeep, take two armed recruits, and get yourself directly to Site B. Do not stop anywhere or go anywhere else. And *do not be followed.*"

"Yes, sir."

The lieutenant slammed out of the room.

The scrawny doctor grabbed the laptop from his desk, opened and closed several drawers, taking things out of them, an external hard drive, a couple of notepads, a thumb drive or two. He shoved all of it into a small black satchel that had been sitting nearby. Then he went out the door, leaving it wide open behind him. Rhiannon could see him as he headed straight across the hall and into the lab.

Now was her chance. She emerged from her corner and moved silently to the door. He was in plain sight of her, but not looking at her as he took racks of capped vials from a glass-doored refrigerator and stacked them carefully in a styrofoam picnic cooler.

She stepped out of the office. He looked up. "You! Stop!"

"I think not," she said, and she ran into the infirmary where three mortals occupied beds. They were wide awake, the lights were on, and they saw her and shouted at her to stop. She ignored them, heading straight for the still unconscious Charlotte. She slipped the IV line from the girl's arm and covered the pierced flesh with a piece of adhesive tape from a nearby stand. Then she bent to scoop her out of the bed.

Two of the three patients came charging from their beds at her, and when she spun around to face them, ready to do murder, she realized she could not. They were Chosen.

They paused in a ready-to-fight crouch right in front of her, only Charlie's bed between her and them. Behind them, coming closer, shaking like a dead leaf in a strong wind, was the doctor.

"You're not taking her anywhere, vampire. Just back off," said one patient.

She titled her head slightly to one side. "You've been deceived, misled, and you're being used. I'd take you too, if I could." Then she launched herself over the bed so fast, she was but a blur to their eyes. She landed between them, grabbed each by the nape, and picked them right up off their feet. They kicked and fought, but they were no challenge for her. She strode toward the office, where the doctor blocked her path.

"I can't harm these two, doctor, as I'm sure you know, you lying piece of refuse. But you? You, I can shred. And I will. Get into the office. Now!"

He backed into the office. She strode in behind him with the lads in tow, then dropped them. "I'll just take this," she said, snatching the black satchel. Then she withdrew like the wind, closing and locking the door behind her. She ducked quickly into the lab, opening the cooler and removing a rack of vials, because she didn't have room to abscond with the whole cooler full. She got some vials labeled BDX, and some labeled "Protectol." Adding them to the black bag, she raced back into the infirmary.

The third patient still remained in his bed, looking conflicted and scared. He was young, early twenties, with blond hair cut close to his head, military style. Rhiannon gathered Charlotte out of her bed, sent him a quick look. "Come with me if you want to know the truth about what you are, and what it means."

He blinked rapidly then got out of the bed and grabbed his clothes from a drawer. He was a big fellow, powerfully built and taller than Roland. Rhiannon carried Charlotte to the back while he was pulling his clothes on, then through the curtains, past the storage unit, and outside.

Roland and Killian appeared from the shadows, both of

them breathless. "We gave them the slip," Killian said, "But they're after us." He took Charlotte from Rhiannon's arms, staring down into her face, his own twisted in worry. "Charlie? Charlie?"

"She's unconscious and would probably fight us otherwise. It's to our benefit." Rhiannon lifted the satchel. "I have everything we came for," she said.

"So do I." Roland took the satchel, adding vials from his pocket to the rest.

"And this one is coming with us," Rhiannon went on.

The big blond patient, just now pulling on a shirt and stumbling out of the infirmary, looked terrified. "You-you're *all* vampires?"

"And you are one of The Chosen," Roland said.

"I don't know what that means."

"It means, you ignorant child, that you have the Belladonna Antigen. We couldn't harm you if we wanted to," Rhiannon explained. "Which is why not one of you has been harmed since we've been here. Don't you know we could've wiped you all out by now? BDX or no?"

Recruits came around the building, guns leveled. "Run," Roland shouted. "Go that way, leap the fence and get clear. Killian, don't forget the package we left on the other side. Go, now! Get the drug to Eric!"

Before Rhiannon could voice her objections, Roland ran toward the recruits, arms in the air. "I surrender! Don't shoot!" he called, and Rhiannon felt him willing them not to fire.

She nudged the others into motion, and they melted into the trees and weeds, heading for the perimeter fence. There was not a moment's hesitation. Rhiannon handed the escaped mortal recruit the satchel, wrapped her arms around the patient's waist, and jumped. Right beside her, Killian did the same, clinging to Charlotte. They both landed safely on the other side. "Get them out of here," she said. "Go to the farmhouse. Roland and I will join you there."

"I can't leave you—"

"Contact Eric Marquand. There's a number in my phone. Go, now, or your woman will die! And don't forget my cat!"

"Rhiannon, I can't leave you and Roland to—"

"Go now, or I'll kill you myself! And get Pandora!" She ran, top speed, leaping the fence again in a different spot, hoping and praying Killian would do as she told him. Then she crept around the mess hall, peering into the center of the camp.

Roland was surrounded. His hands were raised high. The recruits all aiming weapons at him were The Chosen, every last one of them. He could not harm them. He couldn't fight back, and neither, she realized, could she.

Lowering her head, she closed her eyes. "By the horns of Isis, how am I to save him? Is there even time to cast a decent *glamourie?*"

Something stung her left hip, and she spun around to see a dart sticking out of her flesh. "Oh, for the love of the Gods, this again?" She plucked it out, it had barely penetrated and she doubted any of the drug had made its way into her, but the lieutenant was the one standing nearby, holding his gun, ready to plug her again, if need be.

She dropped to her knees, acting weak and dizzy. He came and stood over her. "Tell me your name, vampire."

"Tell me yours," she whispered. She didn't contact Roland, blocked him, in fact, so he wouldn't get himself killed trying to save her. She was the one who would save him, she thought.

"Lieutenant Lucas Townsend," he said.

"You are one of The Chosen," she whispered. "Yet you have not partaken of this drug you're giving to the others. Why?"

"How do you know that?"

She shrugged. "They give off a different energy. I can sense it. But you haven't answered my question. Why them and not you?"

"Because those are my orders."

She let her head fall forward, hair curtaining her face. She lifted her eyes again, finding his. "You're wrong about us, Lucas. We are not your enemy. We are your...."

He came to her, put his hand under her chin and lifted it. "What? Finish the sentence? What are you to me?"

"Protectors," she whispered. "We are your guardians."

CHAPTER FIFTEEN

Killian carried Charlie as he ran through the forest, around the perimeter to the other side of the compound. The mortal recruit ran behind him, his camo-cargo pants and olive drab tank a dead giveaway that he was one of the enemy. And yet, one of The Chosen. They all were.

"I hear Jeeps heading out of there. We've got to get where they can't go if we're gonna outrun them."

"I agree," the recruit said.

He'd spotted Pandora, pacing the outside edge of the fence, chuffing and growling low and deep, in search of her beloved Rhiannon. He'd called her, but she'd only sent him an irritated look and returned to stalking the grounds in search of Rhiannon.

"Why were you in the infirmary?" Killian asked.

"Heart." He patted his chest as they ran. "It starts racing sometimes." Killian's brows went up. Was this the same as the problem Charlie had just experienced? He slowed his pace a little more. God, he could've been out of here by now, but he couldn't leave the recruit and the cat behind. He beamed a thought to Roland. *Can't pick up your package. Being chased.*

Rhiannon? was the only reply.

She went back for you, Roland. I'm sorry.

Roland said nothing more, either because he had no more to say just then, or because he couldn't. There was no way to tell.

"What's your name?" he asked the recruit.

"My name's Christian," he replied, rubbing his blond crew cut vigorously. "Christian Payne."

"I'm Killian. So how's your heart doing now?"

"It's okay at the moment. I'm...glad to be out of there."

"Yeah." He looked at the woman in his arms. "I don't think Charlie's gonna share the sentiment when she wakes up." Looking back, he called out mentally. *Pandora, come. Hurry now, we need you.*

Faintly, he heard another voice, Rhiannon's, mentally shouting, *Pandora, go with Killian! Now.*

They came to a ravine too steep for any sane person to try to descend in a Jeep, and Killian looked down into it, then back at Christian. "I've got to jump down there and hide Charlie. I'll come back for you."

"I can make that jump." Christian leaned forward, looked down into the ravine. "Yeah, I can make that easy." He met Killian's eyes, saw the confusion there.

"How?"

"The BDX."

Killian started to ask more, but the growl of a motor pulled him back on track. "If you can make it, jump. If not, hide for Christ's sakes."

Christian grinned at him, swung his big arms backward and sprung off the spongy forest floor. It was at least 60 feet to the bottom. From his periphery, he saw a lean black form running through the forest and leaping over the edge as well. Pandora! Finally!

Killian jumped after the cat, hit the ground in an easy crouch and sprang up still cradling Charlie in his arms as he searched for Christian's body. Then he saw it, alive and well and running at a speed Killian didn't think was possible for a human, into the thickest part of the forest beyond. He probably had no idea there was a black panther running full tilt behind him.

"What the hell is this shit they're pumping into people, Charlie? God, what did they do to you?"

Charlie didn't answer. Her full lips moved a little bit, but no sound emerged. He wanted to kiss them. But he had to get her safe first. He took off running after Christian and Pandora, caught up, but not without a bit of effort. The kid wasn't vampire-fast, but he was definitely beyond the speed of a normal human being. It had to be the drug. He looked at the satchel he carried. This mystery drug was inside. He had to go back, help save Roland and maybe Rhiannon, too. He had to help the others there, The Chosen, all of them brainwashed to hate and fear his kind and trained to kill them, but his responsibility, nonetheless. He was *compelled* to help them, like a goose is compelled to fly south in the fall. He didn't know *why* he had to help them, he just had to. It wasn't an option.

But he couldn't go back for them until he got Charlie to safety. And he had to contact this Eric Marquand person, arrange to get the vial to him. And he had to find Roxy. He hadn't felt her vibrant aura anywhere at that camp. Clearly, she hadn't been there. He had to find her, save her. She'd saved his life, after all. He owed her.

That wasn't why he wanted to save her, though.

He wanted to save her for one reason–to prove himself to Charlie.

Charlie came awake in someone's living room. There was another recruit running around, looking in closets and out windows, and someone was moving around upstairs. And then that someone came down the stairs with a huge black panther beside him, and Olive, her grandmother's snowy owl perched on his forearm.

Killian!

She sat upright, scrambling backwards into the sofa, like she could burrow inside it, then anger pushed back her fear. What the hell was Killian doing with her grandmother's owl?

The recruit said, "I don't think anyone's been here. And I don't think we were followed, either, so–" He saw Killian staring past him and turned Charlie's way. "Hey. Hey, Charlie, you're awake. Great. It's me. Christian. Remember?"

He put himself right in front of her, taking up all her vision, forcing her to look at him instead of Killian. "I remember you," she said slowly. "I beat you on the rope course."

"By a few seconds."

"I was holding back."

"Bullshit."

Her stress level dipped a little. Christian was good people. She wasn't alone with Killian, and since she still didn't know whose side the vampire was on, that was a good thing. "So Christian, what are you doing with a vampire?"

"Helping him," he said. "You should, too. They're not what you think, Charlie. Not what LT's been telling us, either."

Killian's hand, unmistakable to her hungry eyes, clapped down onto Christian's shoulder from behind, and Christian stepped aside, saying, "Just listen to him, Charlie. Just hear him out."

And then it was Killian standing there, looking down at her on the sofa. And for some reason, she didn't jump up and grab him around the throat. If she jumped up and grabbed him at all, it would've been to bury herself in his strong arms and taste his kiss again.

She couldn't think straight when he was near.

She sat up a little straighter, pushed her hair back off her face, and said, "What are you doing with my grandmother's owl, Killian?"

He sighed and lifted his arm so that Olive took flight. She swooped around the room, but came right back and landed on the arm of the sofa beside Charlie. Then hopped into her thigh.

Charlie forgot her questions for a moment, long enough to pet the owl, and just as before, Olive pushed against her hand. Her big eyes stared into Charlie's, and she could've sworn she was trying to ask her where Roxy was, why she wasn't here, and when she would come back.

She said, "I don't know, girl. But I'll tell you what, I'll stand in for her until she does, okay?"

Blinking twice, she ruffled up her feathers, gave them a shake, then settled down again.

"This is your grandmother's place," Killian said. "One of them, I mean. She says she has several. We were supposed to meet her here, but when we arrived, she'd been taken."

"And you expect me to believe that?" But she wanted to believe it. God, she wanted it so much.

He pressed his lips, shook his head. "Her truck's a mile or so down the road with its nose wrapped around a tree, riddled with bullet holes from all sides. Vampires don't use machine guns, Charlie. We don't need them."

Everything he said was like a fist to the gut, but he kept right on going, until she felt like throwing up.

"She was still alive when they took her. Olive was with her, but she must have got out of the truck and got away. She came here. I told you Roxy left a message. A voice memo on a phone she threw under her seat. She said it was DPI. She told me they would keep her alive. She told me to get you first and worry about her later. So that's what I did."

She frowned at him. "So let me hear the recording. That's

212 | MAGGIE SHAYNE

simple enough."

He lowered his head. "I deleted it and left the phone with the truck. I thought they might be tracking it."

"Maybe it's still there."

"Maybe it is. And maybe I can find the deleted file in the trash or something and prove what I'm telling you is the truth. But it's not safe to go down there right now, and we don't have time anyway."

"We don't have time? What pressing engagement do we have?"

"I have to go back to that camp," he said. "I have to help them."

Her brows pressed against each other. "Help who?"

"My friends. And The Chosen. The rest of the recruits. They're in turmoil. I can feel them the way all vampires always feel it when one of The Chosen is in pain or in fear."

"BDs, you mean."

"I mean The Chosen. Your grandmother. You."

"Me," Christian said from across the room, where he was leaning down, looking out a window. "Everyone at camp. Almost everyone, anyway. Even LT. The vampires call us The Chosen."

She turned on the sofa, putting her feet onto the floor. "And what is it we're chosen for?"

"I'm glad you asked that," Christian said softly. "I was wondering about that myself."

Killian nodded. "I don't have time to be gentle with you. I've already waited hours for you to wake up. We're short on time. So this'll be short and to the point. Every vampire was once a human who had the Belladonna Antigen. We were all what you call BDs. The only humans who can become...what I am...are humans who possess it. Humans like you."

The sentence hit Charlie like a tidal wave, sweeping away the ability to comprehend. She shook her head, struggled to the surface, took a breath. It felt true. It felt shockingly true.

"Vampires protect The Chosen," Killian went on. "We watch over them. We're like Midnight Creeper Guardian Angels. We don't have a choice, it's programmed into our DNA. We can't hurt you, which is why Roland and Rhiannon, two of the oldest vampires in existence, just risked their lives to help me get you out of that camp. That's why they're back there, right now, captured by a pack of trained killers who think it's us or them, and that's why they're unable to fight back even to save their own lives. And I don't know if I can go get them, much less the poor freaking recruit we left tied up near the fence. Not even now, because I'm afraid if I leave you here alone you'll run right back to them." He put his hands to either side of his head, looked at the floor and turned in a slow circle. "Jesus, I need more help."

"I'll help you, Killian," Christian said.

Charlie stood up slowly, shot a look at the black panther that was stretched out on the floor like it owned the place, wearing what looked like a diamond studded collar. Olive flapped her giant wings, jumped from the sofa to Charlie's shoulder, almost as if she was afraid to let Charlie out of her sight.

"I'll believe all this when Roxy tells me herself." She tried not to look Killian in the eyes, and wound up looking there anyway. They drew her like a magnet. There was no way not to look. "But in the meantime, I'll help you get your friends back. If you'll help me get my grandmother back. Okay?"

He gave her a half smile. "Are you sure you're up for it?"

She nodded hard. "I'm as up for it as you are, vampire."

Then he checked the phone he'd pulled out of his pocket. "I've sent the message Rhiannon and Roland asked me to send, with the formula for the BDX, which we found in that mad doctor's notes. And on the way here, we overnighted him a sealed sample with a small packet of dry ice. Thank God for 24-hour shipping centers. Those things were vital, Rhiannon said, and so they're done. We have three hours till daylight. We have to get them out first, because we know where they are, and because they can help us find and rescue Roxy."

"I was out longer than I realized," Charlie said, looking down at her clothes.

"It seemed like forever," he told her. The fear he'd been feeling all that time was clear in his voice.

"You're sure your friends will help us save Roxy?" she asked.

"They're her friends. I only just met them. She says she's known them for twenty years." His fear for her grandmother was clear in his voice.

Charlie heard it, even felt it, but pretended she hadn't. "I wish I had my jacket."

"Roxy brought some of your things from the cabin. I brought a few of them up from the pickup in case we found you. They're in that bag over there," Killian nodded toward a green trash bag he'd reclaimed from the wrecked truck.

She crossed the room, opened the bag, pawed its contents and pulled out a short black jacket. Fake leather.

He looked at her for a long moment. "Don't go back to them, Charlie. I'm telling you the truth about everything, I swear."

She didn't even blink but held his gaze. "I didn't plan to stay with them anyway. I'm not going back. I got what I wanted from them."

"And what was that?"

"To be strong enough to kill whoever murdered my mother," she said. She zipped up the jacket and walked to the door. And though she was talking as tough as she could manage, her heart was breaking inside and yearning for him so much it brought tears to her eyes.

Surrounded by weapons and recruits he could not harm, Roland lowered his hands, having just learned from Killian that Rhiannon was still somewhere in this camp. "On second thought," he said, "I *don't* surrender."

He poured on the speed, zipping from one of them to the next, yanking their weapons from their hands as he went, then springing upward, he landed on a rooftop, and flung the weapons over the fence, as the naïve, false soldiers pulled their side arms and fired at him, and not with tranquilizer darts, either.

He leaped over the peak and crouched low on the slope facing away from the gunfire, scanning the area below for any sign of Rhiannon. She was here. Somewhere, she was here.

And then he saw her. A man held a gun to her head and marched her into the center of the camp. She was shuffling her feet, hanging her head, drugged, no doubt. The lieutenant he'd seen earlier, one of the Chosen like nearly everyone here, spoke to Roland, his voice ringing through the camp. "Give yourself up, or I'll kill her. I'll shoot her and let her bleed out before the sunrise."

"What will you do with us then, Lieutenant?" Rhiannon asked, her voice weak, soft.

"Turn you over to my superiors. It'll be up to them."

She looked up at Roland, her eyes finding him unerringly, and the twinkle in them told him she wasn't as disabled as he'd thought. "You'll forgive me, Lieutenant, but I've been in the care of your *superiors* before. And you've already missed your opportunity to kill me."

She moved so fast he never had a chance, spinning away from him and kicking him in the head at the same time, though clearly holding back her full power. He flew into the side of the nearest building, hit it hard, and then hit the ground.

A hail of gunfire criss-crossed the entire center of the camp, and to Roland's horror, the recruits were shooting toward each other as they fired at Rhiannon.

"Leap, Rhiannon! Jump!" he cried.

Several recruits rushed her where she'd paused near the flag pole, but she dodged them with ease. The pain of the fallen, the pain of the others, and then Rhiannon's pain, hit him at once, as a bullet ripped through her. She was hit!

She alighted on a rooftop, and he went to her, dodging gunfire all the way. Pausing, furious, he watched her sink to her knees, bending and clinging to the roof as bullets flew over and around and–God, through her! Rage burned, and Roland let out a growling shout that shattered the overhead lights. When one exploded near him as he crossed rooftops to get to his love, he saw the pole was within reach between one building and the next. Never breaking stride, he leaped on it, toppling it like a felled oak and riding it to the next roof as it fell. Sparks exploded like fireworks and he landed, finally, beside Rhiannon, picked her up in his arms, prepared to keep on going, two more roofs, then over the fence, where he'd left that poor dark-haired soldier-girl, bound and gagged and under orders not to wake until he told her to.

He started to do just that, but there was a bloodcurdling scream, and a mushy, popping sound. And then a lot more screaming.

"What's happening?" Rhiannon cried. "I feel their pain!" She was pressing one hand to each of two gunshot wounds, one in her waist, another in her thigh. "Roland, I must know."

He stopped running with only one roof between them and freedom, and turned to look down at the men and women who'd been trying to kill them. They were running around, screaming. Some were lying on the ground in pools of blood, their chests torn open.

Roland stared. "What in the–" And then he saw it happen. One of the young people stopped mid-lunge, grabbed his chest, screamed in pain, and then his chest exploded.

"I warned you, Lieutenant," someone shouted. "They were not pre-medicated for battle! I warned you–"

He located the source of the words, a man in a blood spattered white coat, the doctor, yelling at the lieutenant.

Roland lowered his head. "There's nothing we can do."

"We have to, Roland, we have to."

He gathered her up and jumped to the next roof. "Send your will, then. I'll send mine. Calm them. Sedate them. It might be of some help. But whatever you do, Rhiannon, live until sunrise. Live, my love."

"Do not think...for one moment, that the death of Rhianikki...daughter of pharaoh, goddess among women, will come at the hand of a clueless, misled child, playing soldier." Then her eyes fell closed and her body went lax.

Roland carried Rhiannon rapidly through the forest. He'd expected to have to dodge recruits, but for some reason, he didn't. A hundred yards from the facility, he paused to lay her on the ground and examine the wounds that were pulsing blood at an alarming rate. Bleeding out was one of the few ways their kind could die. If he could stanch the flow until daylight, her body would heal itself with the day sleep. But if she died before then, it would be a death from which there was no return.

And that was unacceptable to him. So he searched all around him for items he could use and wished he'd thought to take a first aid kit from the infirmary. Settling for what he could find, he scraped the moss from a rotting log with his fingers, and squeezed and shaped it into a patch, then pressed it to one of the wounds in Rhiannon's flesh. The one in her waist was bleeding the most, so that was the one he attacked first. He took off his cloak, then his shirt, tearing strips of it with his teeth and knotting them together until he had a long enough piece to wrap around her twice. He bound it tight. She didn't even flinch from the pain. God, she was fading fast.

Quickly, he repeated the process with the other wound, the one in her thigh. It took less time. Then with a nip of his teeth, he opened a small vein in his own forearm and held it to her lips. For a moment, there was no response.

Drink, Rhiannon. Drink or you'll die. Come back to me, my love.

Her lips moved ever so slightly against his skin. "That's it. That's it, my darling. Drink, so you can live."

She latched on then, drinking from him until he pulled his arm free. "Any more and I won't be able to carry you out of here, Rhiannon." He quickly wrapped his forearm with another strip torn from his shirt, knotted it tight, then enfolded her within his cloak and scooped her up again. She was starting to wake up, but he could not afford to linger there any longer.

Three darts stabbed into his back on the third step. He tried to pick up the pace, knowing they'd been caught, but it was no use.

As he fell to his knees, he held Rhiannon close. "If you can run, my love, then run."

"Never would I leave you." She twisted her arms around his neck and pressed her lips to his. "Besides," she whispered, plucking a dart from her thigh, "They got me, too."

He looked behind them and saw a circle of The Chosen, all pointing weapons. "He wants them alive," said one.

In his head, Roland heard Killian calling out to him.

We're on our way. What's your situation?

He struggled to form a mental reply strong enough to reach the younger man. *We're caught, my friend. Drugged by those damnable darts. Rhiannon has two gunshot wounds, as well. They're taking us...I don't know where. I can't...stay awake....*

We'll come back for you at nightfall, Roland.

Get those samples to Eric.

I've already—

Get Roxanne. It's more important. I heard them say they want us alive. We'll be all right here a bit longer.

But Roland—

Roxanne. And the samples. Do it, Killian, for the good of our kind. You must.

The lad sent more, but Roland was beyond hearing.

CHAPTER SIXTEEN

Charlie hiked through a towering Oregon forest with the impressively muscled soldier, Christian, on one side of her, a black panther named Pandora on the other, and a vampire leading the way. And she wasn't afraid of any of them. She was pretty sure she could take them all, if it came down to it. Except maybe the cat.

If someone had told her a month ago that she would be in this situation and feeling equal to it, she'd have recommended psychotherapy. And yet here she was.

Olive had followed by air, and she was staying very close, never far from Charlie's sight, and every time she paused to take a look around, Olive came to land on her shoulder and soak up the attention Charlie gave.

Killian walked several steps ahead. They were not running, though she presumed they might be on the way back. Better, Killian said, to go slow and silent, in case the forest around the secret base was still crawling with troops, searching for them.

She felt strong. But she also felt desperate. She ached for

Killian. For his touch, his kiss, his arms around her. And yet she still didn't know for sure if she could trust him. So she was desperate for that, too. Proof that he wasn't the monster DPI said he was. Proof that he hadn't killed her poor mother or kidnapped Roxy.

As they drew nearer Fort Rogers, she was surprised that there was still no sign of recruits in the woods. It was as silent as death.

"Where do you suppose they are?" Killian asked softly, apparently thinking the same thing she was, though she'd taken pains to try to keep her thoughts to herself.

"I don't know, Killian." Charlie hadn't yet decided if LT and his military cronies were the good guys or the bad guys, but she was pretty sure that either way, they'd be plenty pissed off if they caught her and Christian with one of the enemy. She was no more eager to run into them than Killian was.

"Well, you both used to be one of them. Give me an educated guess, will you?"

Christian sent him a look that was a little bit wounded. "I didn't know they were the bad guys when I joined up, you know."

Charlie put a hand on his bulging bicep. "He knows that. He was teasing, I think."

The big guy sent Killian a look, and Killian nodded. "I know you didn't."

"I wish I didn't even have the damn tattoo," Christian went on with a look at his shoulder. Charlie saw the edge of what looked like a Celtic knot or some similar pattern showing beneath the short sleeve of his T-shirt. She'd seen them on a few of the other recruits. "I got it when I finished the first round of training," he told her, even though she hadn't asked. "Everyone does. You would've too, if you'd stayed long enough."

"Doubtful," she said. Olive landed on her shoulder, and she absently scratched the bird on the back of her head, where she seemed to enjoy it best. Then she looked ahead to Killian. He'd started forward again. "Maybe they figure you got away and gave up searching."

"*We* got away," he corrected. Then he nodded. "That could be it, though. Or maybe they already combed the woods enough to know we weren't out here." He was speaking softly, because Fort Rogers' fence was visible up ahead. "And they probably figured we'd have to be idiots to come back."

The panther stopped, and when Charlie glanced down at her, she saw her lifting her head, scenting the air. Her ears laid back and her tail switched.

"Pandora's picking up on something," she said. "Is that... possible?"

"Completely." Killian came back a few steps and put a hand on Charlie's unoccupied shoulder. "Stay close to me, just in case."

She looked right up into his eyes as he said it, and she thought he was either truly in love with her or the best actor she'd ever seen. That intense stare, the electric blue emotion swirling like an ocean behind his eyes. She told herself to look away but couldn't do it until he turned around again.

She stayed close, Olive riding along easily. No hardship there. Despite her lingering doubts about his motives, the attraction and whatever else she felt for Killian, was alive and well and even now gnawing at her stomach. Maybe it was because he'd given her his own blood. Maybe it was something else. But it had to be something supernatural, because these feelings were too big to be ordinary.

He led them further along the fence before moving close enough to look past it. Then they followed the fence line closely, heading uphill to the top of a significant rise with plenty of brushy cover. From there they crept right up to the fence to look down at the camp below.

The scene laid out before them was gruesome. A bloodbath. Charlie gasped, clapping a hand to her mouth and another to her belly. On her shoulder, Olive ruffled her feathers in agitation. There were bodies everywhere, all of them drenched in blood and gore. Charlie lost her breath and just stood there, riveted, unable to turn away. It looked like a massacre had taken place. And then she realized that every one of those bodies was dressed just like she was, Cargo pants and T-shirts. Recruits. BD-Exers. Her friends.

She looked at Christian's stricken face, put a hand on his arm as tears rose in his pale blue eyes.

"What the hell *happened* to them?" he asked softly, brokenly.

"Vampires," Charlie hissed. "This Roland and Rhiannon he keeps mentioning." She shot an accusing look at Killian, all but quivering with rage, furious with herself for continuing to believe vampires could be anything but monsters. "They were the only ones left behind. It had to be them."

"It wasn't them," Killian said, and he said it with certainty.

"How can you be so sure of that? Maybe you didn't know what their true intent was, maybe they–"

"It's not possible, Charlie. I've told you, vampires can't harm The Chosen."

The doubt in her heart flickered, he was that sincere, that convincing. She said, "Has there ever been an exception? Even once?"

His confidence wavered. "Once, that I know of. A rogue who managed to go against his own nature, somehow. Other vampires hunted him down and killed him. It's a well-known story among our kind. Everyone knows about it."

Charlie caught movement in her peripheral vision and, keeping one hand on Olive's soft, feathered back, she moved along the fence to get a better look. "Something's alive down there. Look." She pointed, crept along the fence closer to where she'd glimpsed the motion, and spotted a wriggling bundle near the fence, on the inside behind one of the barracks.

Christian saw it too and said, "Let's go check it out."

Killian nodded, and they made their way down the little hill, following the fence line closer to where the thing that had to be a person was. Pandora crept right along with them, but Olive launched herself upward, vanishing into the canopy of the towering pines. They started hearing motors, vehicles, coming closer, and by the time they got to the bottom, large trucks were spilling in through the front gates of the compound. Killian touched Charlie's arm and crouched low, so she did, too. They stayed still, watching as the vehicles poured through the gate. Men in disposable white suits, wearing goggles and big gloves got out the backs of the trucks, and began moving the bodies of the fallen. Her age, all of them, Charlie thought. Some even younger. One by one, their bloody bodies were slung into a gruesome pile.

As she watched, Charlie noticed that their wounds all looked very similar. Gaping, ragged holes in their chests. Every single one of them.

"No vampire did that," Killian whispered.

"Then what did?"

A muffled sound, like "mmf mmf" drew their attention back to the bundle just inside the fence, and they hurried closer as the bundle got itself turned around and upright. It was a girl.

It was Mariah! She was alive!

She was looking at them, wide eyed, and silently begging them to help her.

"I'll get her," Charlie said, and before Killian could say a thing, she sprang easily over the fence, landing right beside her friend. She put a finger to her lips.

Mariah nodded, understanding. Charlie gathered her friend into her arms and leaped back over again. Then they crouched near the fence, watching what was going on below.

The men inside hadn't seen them. They were paying no attention, apparently convinced everyone who remained in the camp was dead. The survivors, if there had been any, must've evacuated the base.

Of course they had. Vampires had found their location. They wouldn't dare stay.

As she and Mariah looked on, they started pouring gasoline over the mountain of bodies. Then someone struck a match, and the flames blasted to life with a whoosh.

Charlie had to turn her face away and thought she'd vomit. Tears were streaming down Mariah's face.

"It's okay," Christian was saying softly, coming up behind them. "You're gonna be okay, Mariah."

She shot him a surprised look as he bent, pulled a knife from his boot, and said, "I'll cut you loose."

"You do and she's gonna scream these woods down and get us all caught," Killian said, stepping out of the cover of the trees.

For the first time, Mariah saw him, and her eyes went huge.

"No she won't," Christian said. "Because she wants to know what's going on as bad as we do. Don't you, Mariah?"

She looked at Charlie. Charlie sighed, leaned close, whispered to her even though she was sure Killian could hear with his damned bat-like hearing. "I'm pretty sure he's on our side. And if it turns out he's not, we can take him. It's three against one, right? Roll with it, for now, okay?"

Mariah nodded fiercely at her.

"Go ahead, cut her loose, Christian," she said.

Christian cut loose her bonds, hands first, then her feet while she pulled the tape from her mouth. Charlie stood close. Killian did too, ready to react if she started screaming. But she didn't. She said, "*He* was in the brig. There was another one, came to get him out. Knocked me out somehow, and I woke up right where you found me."

Killian nodded, not denying a word she said. "That was Roland, my friend. He knocked you out with a mental trick, because that was the only way he could make sure you wouldn't get hurt," Killian said. "He planned to take you out of there when he left. Unfortunately, he was captured before he could."

"It's true," Christian told her. "He told Killian to get you out of there, but there were too many people shooting at us. So we came back for you."

"And for them," Charlie said, just to keep things honest. "Roland and Rhiannon, the pair of vampires who were captured."

Mariah blinked from one of them to the other, finally settling her gaze on Killian. "I don't know what happened to your friends," she said, like she was afraid he'd blame her and hurt her or something.

"How long ago did you wake up?" he asked.

"An hour, give or take," she said.

"At least I know Roland was alive an hour ago, then."

She frowned. "How?" "

"He had to tell you to wake up, or you'd still be out."

Mariah shifted her questioning eyes to Charlie, who only shrugged. If their will was that strong, why was there anything they couldn't do? Why didn't Killian just *will* her to believe his side of things? she wondered.

Because that would be meaningless, his voice whispered through her mind. *Because I want you to believe me for real, Charlie. I want you to know I'm telling you the truth.*

Then he focused on Mariah. "Can you walk?"

"I...think so." She cleared her throat then rubbed it with one hand. "Thirsty. Been tied up like that all night long. Fucking vampires." She shot him a quick look, like she wanted to take the words back.

He laughed. He actually laughed. Quietly, softly, but he laughed, and Charlie saw it erase a lot of the fear from her friend's eyes and found herself feeling grateful. Then he extended a hand to help Mariah up.

She sat there for a long moment, then with a decisive nod, she took hold and let him pull her to her feet. Olive soared down out of the trees to land on Charlie's shoulder, and they all started walking back.

"You said you'd been awake for an hour," Charlie said. "Did you see what happened to the other recruits?"

She looked back at the camp, her eyes haunted, and shook her head rapidly. "No. When I woke up, everyone was leaving. LT, the other officers, the medical staff. I couldn't get anyone's attention. They were probably all too freaked out from what happened. I tried. Jesus, I thought I'd lay there until I died of thirst or starvation or something." She looked around. "We really ought to get back, report in," she said.

Killian shot Charlie a look, and she read it. It wasn't going to be a good idea to let her go anywhere and start talking about the odd threesome she'd encountered in the woods.

Charlie thought it would be in Mariah's best interests to find out the truth before putting herself back into service with the BD-Exers. Or what was left of them. "Get back to where?" she asked her friend. "Report in to whom? You don't even know where they went. Do you?"

Mariah sighed. "You're right. God, Charlie, we're going to be AWOL—"

"Or presumed dead, like the others back there," she said. "Don't worry. After all that, no one's gonna hold it against us if we don't know where to report in. We'll wait it out, give things time to settle down, and then—"

Mariah's eyes got huge, and Charlie turned to follow them. Pandora had come trotting up behind them.

"It's okay, she's a pet," Charlie said.

Olive launched from Charlie's shoulder, swooped down at Pandora, who reared up and took a swipe at her. Killian looked horrified, but Charlie just smiled as the owl landed on a nearby limb. "Relax. They're playing."

"How can you be so sure of that?" he asked her.

"How can you not be? Olive's practically smiling. Aren't you Olive?"

"Who?" Olive asked.

"You," Charlie said. "You're a tease."

Mariah looked at her like she'd lost her mind, shook her head in disbelief or maybe frustration, and kept on walking.

They walked in silence for a long time, then spotted something out of place in the forest—a Jeep, that same green color of leaves in shadow. Mariah lifted a hand and started to run forward, about to call out, but Christian grabbed her, one hand around her mouth and pulled her down low. "We don't know who it might be," he whispered near her ear. Then he let go, and she sent him a look that should've set his hair on fire.

Slowly and silently, the four of them moved closer to the vehicle. It was in a clearing, part of a well-worn trail that wasn't quite a road, through the very forest whose signs forbade motorized vehicles. As they drew closer, they spotted two bodies, one on either side of the Jeep. Recruits, lying face down on the blood soaked forest floor. No one was around, so they jogged closer. Killian knelt beside the nearest one, touching his shoulder, rolling him over. There was a gaping hole in the guy's chest, even his shirt was ripped open, as if a bullet had exploded through him from back to front. Only there was no hole in his back. His back wasn't even bloody.

Charlie tore her gaze away, but it fell on something else, a purplish-red, fist sized blob a few yards ahead of them on the path. She went closer, not wanting to look but unable to keep herself from looking anyway. Then she saw it, and her hand flew to her mouth.

"What, Charlie? What is it?" Mariah asked, running closer.

"It's a heart," she said, unnecessarily because by then Mariah was beside her, staring down at it too, and could see for herself. "It's a human heart," she said, turning to stare in shock back at the body near Killian. "And I'm pretty sure it used to be his."

The sun was near to rising by the time they got back to the farmhouse. Killian had been paying attention along the way, though, and had spotted an abandoned and falling down barn that would make a decent shelter for him for the daylight hours. Olive flew ahead of them and headed inside through her attic entry. Pandora found a sunny spot to stretch out for a long nap.

Killian took Charlie aside, into the living room while Christian and Mariah raided their meager supplies for something to make for breakfast. "I've got to go," he told her without preamble.

She frowned at him. "Go where? And why? You don't trust us here alone, do you?"

He searched her face and wished he could say he did, but it would've been a lie. "It's almost dawn, Charlie. I need to get someplace safe before the day sleep takes me out."

"If this is one of my grandmother's places, shouldn't there be some kind of secret room in the basement or–"

"Yeah, and I'm gonna rest real easy with three super-humans trained to kill vampires walking around over my head."

She blinked. "Wow. You trust me even less than I thought."

"About as much as you trust me right now. C'mon Charlie, do you blame me? You've said repeatedly you're only goal in life right now is to kill whoever murdered your mom, and you still seem pretty sure it was me."

She lowered her eyes, but not before he'd seen the flash of hurt in them. He hated hurting her, and he had just now. That must mean she felt something for him, right?

"I'll be back at sundown. It would be best if you all got some rest, too. We've got a big night tonight. We've got to locate and rescue Roxy, Roland, and Rhiannon. And we've got to figure out what the hell is going on with the other Exers. With their hearts."

Charlie's eyes told him that she thought she already knew, and it killed him that he didn't have time to stay and talk it out with her. He thought he knew, too. He'd already seen her clutching her chest while her heart beat so hard she couldn't catch her breath. A side effect of the drug, the BDX. A side effect that led to hearts exploding right out of peoples' chests?

God, he hoped not.

"Maybe it would be best for you to try to relax," he told her. "Don't exert yourself too much today. And try not to get upset over anything. Just–"

"Just go back to being the fragile, overprotected little thing who might break in a strong wind?" She sighed, shook her head. "I'd kind of rather explode, Killian."

"Don't say that." He moved closer, sliding a hand into her hair, turning her face to his. "If your heart explodes, I feel like mine would, too."

She lowered her eyes fast, but he saw the moisture spring into them all the same. "Sappy, much?" she asked in a tight voice.

"Not till I met you."

She looked up again, a tentative glance, then a longer one. "Hurry up and prove yourself to me, Killian. I can't be all fucked up like this much longer or my head'll explode instead of my heart."

"One more night," he said. "I just need one more night." He hoped.

She nodded. "I'll hold you to it."

She was still looking up, still holding his eyes, so he bent a little and kissed her, even though he had no idea what her reaction would be.

She didn't pull away, but she didn't kiss him back, either. She just stood still, allowed it. Maybe her lips trembled, and maybe a soft breath whispered from them.

It would have to be enough. For now.

Killian left the house and jogged away as the sky began to turn to a paler shade of gray.

Having been up all night long, Christian fell asleep right after serving everyone a breakfast of instant oatmeal and coffee. The coffee was heavenly. As for the oatmeal—well, Charlie would've preferred a steak, but whatever. Apparently, being bound and gagged and held in a vampiric thrall was also a tiring proposition, because Mariah passed out on the sofa an hour later. Charlie propped a board over the attic window to keep Olive, who was also sleeping, from following her, then slipped out of the farmhouse.

There was a black bag full of all the stuff that Killian and his mysterious vampire friends had stolen from the lab at Fort Rogers, sitting in plain sight and beckoning her. But she ignored that. Her mother was lying in a funeral parlor in Portland. And while she knew the services tonight would be crawling with armed militia, she thought if she got there early enough, before the place even opened, she could at least have the chance to say goodbye in peace. And she had to do it. She had to.

She walked down the hill, across the grassy meadow. It was so early the sun was still sitting on the eastern horizon, and the air had that too-fresh-to-believe taste to it. A million birds seemed to be singing their brains out, dozens of different songs, maybe hundreds, but they fit together perfectly. It was soothing to her torn up soul. She walked through the dewy grass and down to the road beyond and looked longingly east. According to Killian, Roxy's truck was a mile or so back in that direction. She wanted to see it. She wanted to see if it was full of bullet holes, like he said it was, and she wanted to see if there was a phone under the seat and try to recover the deleted voice memo Roxy had allegedly left on it.

But more than that, she wanted to find Roxy. And she wanted to see her mother, and tell her...tell her what?

She closed her eyes and thought back to the last time she'd seen her mom. She'd argued with her about going away with Roxy. But just like always, Trish had been trying to protect her, and she'd responded by acting like a child.

She'd aged years since then. Decades.

"I wish she could see me now," she said. "Outrunning slow Jeeps and jumping tall fences. God, what would she think?" She sighed, shaking her head. There was no point. It was never going to be.

She turned left instead of right and started hoofing it in the direction she hoped was Portland. When a trucker pulled over to offer her a ride, and just over an hour later, dropped her within three blocks of her apartment before seven a.m., she decided fate was on her side for once.

She wanted to go home. She wanted to poke around and investigate the scene of her mother's death like some kind of forensic detective until she found proof that Killian had not murdered her. She wanted to gather up some of her things. But she was short on time, and unsure whether the apartment was being watched. So she didn't go further than the parking lot out back. And even then she felt wary.

God, Roxy had rubbed off on her, hadn't she? Yeah. Clearly she had, because Charlie found herself running her hands under the wheel wells and bumpers of her mother's mini-van, checking it inside and out for anything that didn't belong, before fishing the spare key from its magnetic holder in the back. She drove to the funeral home, watching her rearview mirror all the way in case she was being followed.

CHAPTER SEVENTEEN

It wasn't, Charlie discovered, very hard to break into a funeral parlor. She didn't imagine too many people tried. The place was in the suburbs and surrounded by trees and hedges. The window lock in the back broke with minimal effort. She just pulled and the little clasps on the inside snapped off, and she crawled inside, then closed the window behind her. Then she turned to check the place out.

It was a big old Victorian style house that had probably had an ordinary family living in it a century or so ago. It was completely lined in wallpaper—roses and vines in crushed red velvet on a gold background. A big brass and glass chandelier hung in the center of the room. There were folding chairs stacked on a cart, pushed up against a wall, and stands of all sizes and shapes for holding flowers. The place smelled like lilies, even though there were no flowers currently on display. Their heavy scent lingered. But no coffin. No body.

She tiptoed through the main room, which had doors off both ends and one off the side, but that just went to a restroom. The first door led to another room just like the one she was in, and the second, marked "staff only", led to an office. The office wasn't of interest, but the door that led from the far side of it was. It wasn't locked, and she walked through it slowly, the silence like a blanket around her, into what looked like a treatment room at your average medical clinic. A table with a concave headrest sat beside a tray littered with a bizarre mashup of medical instruments and cosmetics. Suture needles, combs and hairspray, eyeshadow, glue.

Her gaze got stuck on that table for a minute, wondering if her mom's body had been lying on it. Who had picked out the clothes she would wear? Who had told them how she liked her hair? Those things were *her* job. She should have done them.

She gave herself a mental shake and moved on, through yet another door in the back of this room, a door unlike the others. It was heavy and made of stainless steel, and when she opened it, the air that hit her was chilled. A walk-in cooler. Oh, hell. God, she didn't want to step inside that room. And yet she forced herself.

Three steps in, she paused to let her eyes adjust. It was dim, no windows in there, and she didn't dare turn on the lights. She left the door open though, for some reason creeped out by the idea of closing herself in with the dead.

Caskets, four of them, stood side by side like soldiers awaiting inspection. She moved closer, walking up to the first one, a cream colored box with gold trim. Very fancy. Gripping the side, she stiffened her resolve and lifted the lid.

A little old lady with too much rouge on her cheeks lay as peacefully as if she was sleeping. "I'm sorry," Charlie whispered and closed the lid and moved on.

The second casket was huge, dark cherry wood with black enamel hardware that looked like porcelain. Bracing herself again, she opened it. Wide open eyes stared at her from a purplish blue face. She dropped the lid and jumped backward, banging into the coffin behind her. Her heart started banging against her ribcage, and she pressed her hands to it and ordered it to calm the fuck down.

Okay, okay, he just hasn't been prettied up yet. Look again, he's not a vampire. He's not a zombie. He's just a dead guy.

She made herself open the lid again, just a little bit, then a little more. No, he was not a vampire. His face was blue and his eyes were shrunken and filmy. Completely dead. She replaced the lid with a full body shudder, and just for good measure, turned the oversized, T-shaped key that was sticking out one end of the gleaming box, which she thought locked the lid.

It crossed her mind that maybe morticians knew more than the rest of the world, if they felt it necessary to lock the dead inside their caskets.

She tried the lid to make sure, and it didn't budge. Nice. Blue-boy wasn't going anywhere.

Still clutching the giant key in one hand, she went to the third coffin, gleaming black with silver handles. She didn't think her mom would be in a box like that. Tucking the turnkey into her back pocket, she opened it and found she was right. This one was occupied by a dignified, silver haired man with a perfect mustache to match. He looked like a wax figure, or maybe a mannequin. Not natural at all.

Charlie turned to the final casket. It was oak, and the handles and trim were copper. It looked like something her mother would've liked. She didn't see one she thought would've been a better choice for her, which was probably why she'd saved this one for last.

Let her makeup be finished, she prayed. *Don't let her look like that blue guy.* She put her hands on the lid and paused for a minute, because tears welled up and made it impossible to see. "I'm so sorry I wasn't there, Mom. I could've saved you. I know I could have." She sniffed, wiped her eyes with the back of one hand. "I'm sorry I was so rotten so much of the time. I love you, Mom. I really love you. I always did. Always will."

Then she lifted the lid.

But the coffin was empty.

"She's not in there, Charlie."

Damn near jumping out of her skin, she spun around, her back to the casket. Lieutenant Lucas Townsend was standing there, only a few feet behind her. Holy hell, she should never have come here.

"What are you doing here?" he asked. "I thought that vampire had you."

"Where is my mother, LT? What did you do with her?"

He frowned as if puzzled by her hostile attitude. "We had to have her cremated. When there's a vamp attack, you just never know. Sometimes...sometimes they come back."

She didn't think that was true. In fact, she was certain it was a lie, but she made a note to ask Killian about it later. If she could get away from this asshole, anyway.

And just when, she wondered, had she become so sure Killian was the good guy and LT the bad one?

"The casket is just for show," he said. "For the funeral, you know."

She nodded and tried to make herself seem a little more friendly, a little less angry. "That was generous of you. Thank you for that." She ran a hand over the wood, leaving the lid open and getting her words in order before speaking them. "You were right. The vampire had me. I got away. I intended to head straight back to camp, but...I just had to come here first."

He was watching her closely, and she couldn't tell if he believed her or not. "I don't blame you. How did you manage to escape?" he asked.

"I just bided my time until daylight. I knew he'd have to sleep. When my chance came, I took it."

He nodded, coming a little bit closer. "I've been waiting. I figured you'd come here."

"I guess I'm more predictable than I realized." She took a

step backward.

He stopped moving. "He's filled your head with lies, hasn't he Charlie? I can see it in your eyes. You don't trust me anymore. Am I right?"

"He said some things, yes."

"He'd say anything to get you away from us."

"Because he wants to...feed on me, you said. Because of the antigen."

"Yes, Charlie. Yes, that's the only thing any of them want." He came another step closer, was standing in between two caskets now. She stayed just out of his reach but tried not to be obvious about it.

"Then why didn't he?" she asked, wondering just what he would say.

He frowned, gave his head a shake.

"Why didn't he just do it? He had all night. See, that's what I can't figure out."

"I don't know. Maybe he was full, from all the recruits he murdered on his way in to get to you. We lost twenty-three last night, Charlie. Twenty-three."

She lowered her head and didn't have to fake the emotion. This place was filled with it, and so was she. She couldn't even see her mother one last time. Emotion was easy. "Whoever did that should die," she said, and she meant it. Whoever killed all those recruits, whoever killed her mother, deserved death. Worse than death. "But how did he do that? One vampire? Against all those Exers? How did he kill them?"

"He had help. Two others were with him."

"Still, twenty three—"

"They just lunge from one to the next, ripping their jugulars out, drinking their fill and tossing them aside. It was a bloodbath."

It was. She'd seen it. But it hadn't been their throats torn open. He was lying to her. She kept sidling sideways, and so did he.

"We wounded one of his cohorts, captured them both. We'll get him, too. Come with me," he said. "We had to bug out. Camp is deserted now. They'll burn it soon."

Bug out to where? And were the vampire captives in the same place? Killian's friends, Rhiannon and Roland? And if that was where they took prisoners and if they were the ones who'd taken Roxy, would she be there too? She moved a little more, keeping him across from her. He did too. Soon he was in front of the empty coffin, and she was facing him.

"I'm exhausted," she said. "A long car ride will have me puking, I swear–"

"It's not far. Fifteen minutes."

"Don't bullshit me, LT. There's no way you have a secret military base hidden within fifteen minutes of Portland." She made her smile big and ironic, shaking her head like she knew he was playing with her and was playing right back.

"Fifteen minutes by chopper. It's an–" He stopped himself, looked at her. "Come on, Charlie. Just come with me. I'll take care of you, I promise." He held out a hand.

She sighed, nodded heavily. "You're right. I need some rest." She held out her hand, and he took another step to close the gap between them. She punched him hard, an uppercut to the chin. His head snapped back, hit the open coffin lid. He stumbled, started to straighten, and she grabbed the lid and brought it down hard, hitting him in the head again. Then she shoved him right into the box, closed the lid, and holding it down with one hand, she yanked the turnkey from her pocket with the other and locked him in while he pounded and yelled.

"Apparently, you didn't take your own cure, LT. You could've fought me if you had. But I doubt you'd have beat me anyway."

Her mom had always left an emergency credit card tucked in the back of her glove compartment, and it was still there. Charlie used it to buy some fast food burgers to fill her empty stomach, and then visited a grocery store for supplies for the farmhouse, human food, heavy on the protein. Then she drove back, arriving by noon, certain she hadn't been followed. And since everyone else was still sleeping, she put the groceries away, took that little black satchel to the van, and drove off again to satisfy her curiosity.....

She was sick of waiting for Killian to provide proof of which side he was on. She needed to make up her mind—either believe him or don't. Period. This uncertainty was maddening. And if what he was saying was true, unfair.

And in her heart, she thought it was true. She couldn't wrap her mind around the image of those hands that had touched her so tenderly, murdering anyone. Or those lips she so wanted to kiss again, draining her mother's life away. She couldn't. He couldn't have done it. He couldn't have.

She wanted to believe him. But her brain wanted proof.

So she drove east, the way he'd pointed when he'd mentioned Roxy's pickup, because she had to see it for herself.

The truck was not wrapped around a tree as Killian had told her it would be. It had been moved off the road into a weedy field. The debris that was supposed to have been scattered everywhere was gone. The road and roadsides were clean. Someone had come back here and cleaned up the scene. They would probably come back for the truck, too.

Pulling the van off to the side and taking a careful look around, Charlie thought it might be safe, at the moment. She got out and left the van running, its door open. The sun pounded down, and the pavement reflected it up into her face. She wished for a pair of sunglasses and shielded her eyes as she walked closer.

There were black marks on the road, rubber left behind from skidding tires. She walked past them, jumped the ditch on the roadside, and then moved toward the pickup truck. There was no glass in it. Every window had been shattered, and the truck was riddled with bullet holes. She pushed a hand into her hair, and a chill ran up her spine at nightmare images of Roxy, her grandmother, sitting behind the wheel while that many bullets were being fired at her. Or at her truck. Seemed like if they'd wanted to kill her, they'd certainly had the ammo to do it, whoever they were.

She went to the truck, opened the driver's door, looked underneath the front seat. But there was no phone there. She checked the other side, too, but nothing. Even the glove compartment was empty.

She flipped down the visors, and a pair of sunglasses fell out. Aviators. Old fashioned, like Roxy was. Just what she'd been wishing for. It made her eyes tear up. "Thanks, Roxy," she said softly, and she put them on and walked back to the van. From there she went off in search of the barn where Killian was resting, so she could read the files from the lab at Fort Rogers and wait for him to wake up.

R hiannon woke all at once, her head coming upright, her neck stiff and sore from its bent position. She wasn't lying down. She was upright, in a chair, her arms held to the chair's arms by thick metal cuffs that covered her from elbow to wrist. Tugging at them to test their strength, she quickly looked around her. *Roland? Where are you?*

No answer came. And he was nowhere in sight. She was in a large square room that resembled a gymnasium. There was a gleaming wood floor with red paint marking a large circle for some sport or other. It took up most of the room. Only the room's corners were outside the painted circle. She and her imprisoning chair were situated in one of those corners. There was a door in the corner opposite her. She tried hopping, chair and all, but its legs were apparently bolted to the floor.

"Dammit." She looked down to see for sure, but stopped when she saw that her legs were covered in some sort of form fitting spandex cat suit. Her own clothes, she recalled, had been torn by the bullets that had ripped through her and soaked by her own blood. She had healed during the day sleep. Her clothing, apparently, had not. Her boots, thank the Gods, remained, ankle high and black with potentially deadly heels.

Lifting her head and looking around, she called out, "All right, mortals, whoever you are. You have me. Now what?" She wasn't sure what sort of building she was in. She could smell the sea. The air tasted of it.

There was no sound, but she could feel that she was being watched. As her keen eyes scanned the entire room, she saw how high the ceilings were. Way up along the topmost parts of the walls, there were two panes of darkly tinted glass, one on either side, opposite each other. Like sky boxes for watching whatever sport took place here. She squinted to see through them, strained her mind to sense Roland's presence or anyone else's for that matter. And then, suddenly, that door across from her slid upward from the floor, and Rhiannon saw movement in the darkness beyond. Squinting, she leaned forward, for now she sensed a presence.

And since when can't I pick up on someone just because they're on the other side of a door, she wondered. But she knew the answer. In the past, DPI had used some high end technology only Eric could understand, to block telepathic transmissions. Vampires couldn't communicate or sense each other, or anyone else for that matter, through it. This place must be built with that same sort of construction. Which meant she would be unable to call out for help or let any other vampires know where she was being held from within the walls that surrounded her.

So Roland could be near, behind some barricade through which she could not feel.

The movement in the darkness drew her attention back to

the open door. Whatever was in there was inching through the darkness, ever closer to the opening, and Rhiannon renewed her efforts to break free of her bonds.

Something crackled, electricity, deep in the shadows, and the creature howled in pain and jumped out into the open, an elf-sized body with a tangled mass of black hair.

By the Gods, it was a girl. A human little girl. Ten? Twelve, perhaps. Too skinny to tell. And she emanated an essence that was completely foreign to Rhiannon. She didn't feel quite human. There were traces of The Chosen about her, but not quite. She was something different. Some kind of hybrid creature. Manmade, no doubt about that.

As soon as she had cleared it, the door slammed closed behind her, and the child jumped, startled.

A voice came, like the voice of God, if God were male, Rhiannon thought. It filled the room from some hidden speaker and echoed off the walls. "It's a vampire," the disembodied voice told the child. "Kill it."

Rhiannon lowered her head to hide her smile, lest she embarrass the girl. But the little thing let loose a growl and came charging at her. As she looked up in surprise, the metal cuffs holding her arms sprang free without warning, and Rhiannon surged to her feet out of pure instinct, and quick as a flash, put one hand on the child's head to hold her at arm's reach.

The girl closed her hand around Rhiannon's wrist, turned herself around like a dervish and flipped Rhiannon over her back, flinging her bodily halfway across the room.

She landed face-up on the floor, shocked to her core. "What kind of child are you?"

The girl pounced on her, moving beyond human speed, her hands flying, long nails tearing into Rhiannon's face and neck, ripping through flesh. Pain followed the raking path of those claws, and Rhiannon flung her off and sprang to her feet again, crouching this time, ready to fight.

"You're no ordinary girl, that's certain. What are you then? Another DPI experiment?"

The girl's eyes were blue, but they flashed with a golden-yellow light from behind her tangled hair for a moment as the two circled one another.

"You are, aren't you?" Rhiannon looked up toward the observation windows. "Have you no moral compass whatsoever? That you would use a child as a weapon?"

The girl threw herself forward, doing a sort of flipping hand spring and nailing Rhiannon in the chest with both of her dirty, bare feet. It was a crushing blow. She felt her ribs crack as she flew backward, crashing into the wall behind her.

She pushed herself up again, one arm hugging her own waist. The pain was excruciating, heightened, as was every sense in her kind. She got upright, looked at the child. "I cannot harm you, girl. Not only because you reek of the antigen that makes you family to me, but because...." She let her lips pull into a half smile. "I like you."

With a loud, terrifying growl, the girl came again, throwing a series of punches and kicks so rapidly that it was all Rhiannon could do to block them. She had to shut her mind down, stop thinking, and react from sheer instinct, her arms moving as fast as the child's to block every blow, but then the little thing jumped up high and head-butted her, taking her by surprise. Pain exploded behind Rhiannon's eyes, and she dropped to her knees, pressing the heel of one hand to her forehead. The girl jumped into the air and came down, elbow first, jamming it down onto Rhiannon's nape. The blow would've snapped a mortal's spinal cord, Rhiannon thought. She tried to move, but the child brought a knee up to her chin so hard it lifted her right up off the floor. She landed on her back again.

Breathing hard, furious and hurting, Rhiannon pushed herself upright, into a sitting position. Then she clutched the wall behind her, climbing her way up onto her feet again. The pain would soon become debilitating. And she was bleeding from several places now. Just scratches, but still...anything deeper could kill her.

She clung to the wall, hunched and hurting, but forced herself to straighten to her full height. The child, huffing and puffing and red-faced with anger and exertion, clenched her fists and came at her again.

Rhiannon flung out her hands and shouted, "*Enough!*"

The girl halted in her tracks as the powerful vampiric voice echoed off the walls.

"I am not a mere vampiress, little one. I possess far greater powers than those of the Undead. I learned to wield magic at the feet of those who first mastered it. The Priestesses of Isis. And I, Rhianikki, say to you, *Enough.*"

"Kill the vampire!" boomed the voice from beyond.

Rhiannon held her hand up, casting a shield around her, and though the child took a step or two closer, she stopped, though she probably had no idea why.

"You might want to cover your ears, child. Auntie Rhiannon is angry now." The girl frowned at her, and Rhiannon cupped her palms over her own ears in demonstration and nodded at the child to do the same. She quickly cast an invisible circle around the child, in hopes of protecting her from what was to come.

"Kill the vampire!" the booming voice said again.

"Oh, do shut up!" Rhiannon took a deep breath, opened her mouth and screamed. It wasn't a horror movie victim sort of scream. It was a bestial shriek, much like that of the legendary *Ben-sidhe*, or so she liked to imagine. The wild child staggered backward, fell to the floor and clamped her hands over her ears. Only then did Rhiannon crank up the volume.

The room vibrated. The two glass panes up above shattered into a million glittering shards and came raining down as she leaped forward to shield the child with her own body, covering her completely as she let the powerful cry die out.

That corner door shot upright again, and the girl squirmed

out from beneath Rhiannon and ran toward it.

"No, wait!" Rhiannon lunged after her, but the door banged down behind her. An instant later, Roland landed on the floor from somewhere far above, still bound to a chair that demolished on impact. He'd been behind that glass, Rhiannon realized. They'd been forcing him to watch. He'd flung himself through once the impenetrable glass had been shattered. The chair was in pieces, its metal cuffs open and useless as he got to his feet.

He gripped her arm, and she winced, but before she could protest, he'd leapt upward again, carrying her with him, jumping back through the broken window and into a room with seats, for viewing. When he landed, he yelped in pain.

"Roland?"

"Broken leg. Wrist, too, perhaps. No matter. You?"

"Ribs. Skull, perhaps. That little demon gave me what for, didn't she?" Rhiannon looked across to the window on the other side, but whoever had been there was long gone now, and Roland was pulling her toward a door, an exit she hoped.

"She practically flayed you alive," he said. He delivered a blow with the heel of his hand that sent the door off its hinges into the wall on the opposite side, then, still holding Rhiannon's hand, raced into a corridor and down it.

Armed men–DPI thugs–came toward them, bearing rifles in their arms, so she and Roland pivoted and headed in the other direction. When more came from that way, Rhiannon kicked in the first door she saw, and they entered a room with a large round window on the far side. Turning quickly, she bolted the door.

"Well it's about time. I thought I'd be stuck on this tub forever."

Whirling, Rhiannon widened her eyes. "Roxanne!"

Roxy got to her feet, brushing off her hands. She limped slightly as she came closer and was clearly tired and worried. "Do you know anything about my granddaughter?" she asked.

Men were pounding on the door. "Killian took her from the camp," Rhiannon said. "There's more, but we have no time."

"Less than none," Roland said. "You're going to have to trust us, Roxanne." Then he ripped the round window out of its wall as men started hitting the door with something harder than their hands.

Rhiannon looked out and saw a long drop and a lot of dark water. "I knew it. It's a porthole. Roland, we're on a ship!"

"You're just figuring that out?" Roxy asked. "And I thought vampires were perceptive."

"Yes," Roland said, "a ship, and we'll live to get off it if you will kindly launch yourself through that porthole before they get in here and kill us."

"We can't leave the child, Roland."

"What child?" Roxy asked. "They have a child?"

"We're both injured. We'll come back for her. I swear to you, my love, I will not rest until we have fetched her out of this vessel. Now please, go! Roxanne, you too, and cling to Rhiannon's back so her body takes the brunt of the impact. Go."

The door was shuddering now under each blow. Alarms were sounding. Rhiannon had no choice. She put her hands on the edges and pulled herself through the porthole, giving a final push with both arms to launch her on her way. Roxanne dove right out behind her, wrapping her arms around Rhiannon from behind and then holding on. Roland dove out last of all. Rhiannon stretched out her arms, aiming with her hands, and making her body as arrow-straight as she could. She rocketed past a name painted on the hull, upside down and backwards from her perspective. Then she hit the water hard. She sliced through it, Roxanne with her, but the impact was painful all the same on her already injured head. Bullets torpedoed through the depths around her as she descended downward. Roxanne let go at some point. Then Rhiannon opened her eyes to search frantically for Roland.

Out of the murky deep, he appeared, stroking toward her. She caught his hand, and they surfaced, side by side, finding and grabbing hold of Roxanne and pulling her along with them as they sped away from the ship.

CHAPTER EIGHTEEN

When Killian woke from his nest beneath the musty old hay in the barn, he knew immediately that Charlie was near. And something was wrong with her.

He dug his way out and brushed the hay from his hair and his clothes, searching the dim interior of the barn. Pigeons cooed from somewhere overhead, flapping from one perch to another every now and then. Velvet blue sky with fingers of deep purple cloud showed through the missing windows high in the barn's peak. And she sat near the broken door that hung from one caster, her eyes red and wet, her heartbreak as palpable to him as the scent of old hay and older wood.

"Charlie?" He hopped from the pile of hay onto the floor as she looked his way.

She wiped at her eyes quickly, reached down to shove a laptop computer back into the satchel they'd taken from Fort Rogers, then got up on her feet. "It's dark already. Time got away from me."

He went right up to her, put his hands on her shoulders.

"What's wrong?"

She sighed. "It's been an emotional day," she said. "I went to Portland. I wanted to see my mother before...you know."

He wanted to tell her that was a risky and dangerous thing for her to have done, but what would be the point? She wasn't a disobedient child. She was a powerful woman, intelligent and capable of making her own choices, taking her own risks. "That must have been hell," he said. "I wish I'd been with you."

She nodded. "I do, too." And to his surprise, she leaned close to him, laid her head on his shoulder. He put his arms around her and held her gently.

"Did you get to see her?" he asked.

She shook her head against him. "She wasn't there. LT was. Lieutenant Townsend, I mean."

That startled him. She must've felt it, because she hurried on. "He told me they had to cremate her, because sometimes the victims of vampires...turn."

"That's not how it works," he said.

"I didn't really think it was."

She was quiet for a minute. Waiting. So he said, "To change one of The Chosen into one of us, a vampire would have to drain them to the point of death. They actually have to be right there, at the end. The final heartbeat has to beat. Then the vampire cuts himself and feeds the mortal with his own blood. It only works with The Chosen. If you tried to change an ordinary human, they'd just die. At least I think they would."

"I had all but bled out at the hospital. You fed me your blood," she said.

"You weren't at the point of death. Would've been if it had been much longer, but you weren't. All drinking my blood did was keep you alive."

"It did more than that, Killian." She lifted her head, looked into his eyes. It was obvious again that she'd been crying. A lot. "It made you a part of me. You're inside me, all the time."

"And you're inside me," he told her. "I feel exactly the same. It's overwhelming. And it's not because we shared blood, Charlie, and I think you know that. It was before. As soon as I was within a hundred miles of you, all I could think about was getting closer. I could feel you. Like I knew you. Like I always had."

She nodded rapidly. "For me, too. I'm sorry I doubted you, Killian."

He blinked. Did that mean she didn't doubt him anymore? "What happened that changed your mind?"

"I don't know. I just decided to believe in you. That's what you do when you love someone, isn't it?"

"I guess so."

She relaxed against him again, and he said. "How did you get away from the lieutenant?"

"I knocked him over the head and locked him inside my mother's empty coffin. Bastard."

He smiled a little, tightened his arms around her.

"I went to see Roxy's truck. The bullet holes were there, just like you said, but everything else was gone. Including the phone that was under the seat."

He nodded.

"LT...he told me you'd been positively identified by an eye witness who saw you leaving my mother's apartment the night of her murder. Said they showed him a photo of you, and he was sure you were the one."

He laughed softly, and this time he pulled free of her, reached behind him, and pulled a cell phone from his back pocket. "This is Rhiannon's phone. I used it to contact her scientist friend Eric Marquand, and I emailed him the files from that computer you were just looking at."

She looked up sharply. "You read them?"

"Not yet. There wasn't time. I just located the formula for the BDX and sent it to him." He frowned. "You were reading them today while I rested, though."

She looked away.

"What did you find, Charlie?"

Shrugging, she said, "Not much. Go on, why did you get out your phone?"

He searched her face for a long moment, but not her mind. She'd closed it on him. There was something she wasn't telling him. And it scared him. He'd have to dig in and read those damned files, and soon.

Sighing, he looked again at the phone, then handed it to her. "Take a picture of me."

Charlie frowned. "Why would you want me to—"

"Trust me. Just do it, take my picture."

"All right," she said. Then she looked at the phone, found the photo feature, and aimed it at him. "Smile." And she took a shot. Tapping the phone to bring the photo up, she frowned. "That's odd."

"Nothing's there, right?"

Her eyes narrowed, and she leaned closer. "Everything but you is there. Even the wall behind you."

"Take a dozen more, and they'll come out the same way. We don't cast reflections and we don't show up in photographs."

A knowing look came into her eyes. "Then there's no way anyone could've identified you from a photo."

"No. But for what it's worth, thank you for deciding to believe me before you had proof that Townsend was lying."

She smiled and leaned closer, kissed his lips. He'd been craving this for so long, and he wanted to pull her back into the pile of hay and spend the next hour or so wrapped around her there.

But they still had people missing, and they had to save Roxy.

"We'd better get back," she said. "I'm afraid Mariah will take off if we're gone too long."

He nodded, took her hand, and they stepped out of the barn and into the night. When he saw the van, he tensed, but she said, "It's okay, it's Mom's. Mine now, I guess."

"We can use it." He squeezed her hand. "That was good thinking, Charlie."

"Yeah, well, I guess it's about time I did some kind of thinking."

"None of this is your fault," he said, looking her in the eye.

"We're gonna have to agree to disagree on that one," she said. "But I'm gonna make it right now. All of it."

She had a strength in her that he hadn't seen before, way beyond the physical strength that the BDX had given her. It was something inside her, something mental, emotional, maybe even spiritual. And it made him love her even more, even though he'd thought what he felt for her couldn't possibly get any bigger.

Rhiannon's phone, the one Killian had used to contact Eric Marquand, rang while they were finishing their dinner. The others were sitting around an old fashioned table eating as if they'd been starved for a solid week. He was eager to be out of the farmhouse and looking for their missing friends, but the humans were hungry and they all needed to be at their strongest for whatever lay ahead. Charlie had even bought a large beef roast for Pandora, who was outside tearing into it.

"How is the weather in the States?" the vampire asked without preamble.

Killian blinked before realizing what he was really asking; whether it was safe to talk. "It's perfectly clear." He started to move into the living room, but when he saw Mariah's eyes on him, filled with suspicion and mistrust, he thought better of it. Moving the phone away from his ear, he touched the speaker icon and stood close to the table so they could all hear both ends of the conversation.

"Good," Marquand said. "I've run some preliminary tests

based on the formula for BDX. I will be more certain once I've had a chance to examine the samples you've sent, but at this stage, I'm afraid the news is not good."

Killian looked around at the three who'd been injected with the stuff and wished he hadn't put the phone on speaker. Christian and Mariah looked nervous and were listening intently. But not Charlie. And that was when he realized that whatever Eric was about to say...she already knew. She'd read it in those files he hadn't had the chance to go over. Swallowing his fear, he said, "Go on."

"Among other things," Eric said, "the drug boosts the body's production of epinephrine, basically turning it into an adrenalin factory. In normal humans, this would result in a heart attack in pretty short order. What has the effect been on The Chosen?"

"It makes us strong," Charlie said.

"I'm sorry, to whom am I now speaking?"

"Charlie O'Malley."

"Roxy's granddaughter. Ah, then you've been rescued!" he said and his relief was evident in his voice. "I've been a friend of your grandmother's for many years, Charlotte. I'm sincerely relieved that you are all right."

"Thanks."

"Tell me, Charlotte, how strong are you?"

She looked at Killian. "Not as strong as you, but way stronger than a normal human. All of the BD-Exers—that's what they call us—can run faster, jump higher, hit harder, and last longer."

"Charlie's stronger than any of us, though," Christian said. "It's like it was supercharged in her."

"Did they do anything different when they administered it?" Marquand asked.

Charlie swallowed, and Killian knew the memory was hard for her. "They gave me all three doses at once. I was told they usually do it over the course of three days, with some kind of extra booster shot or something at the end. An additive. I don't think I got that."

"Have you experienced any tachycardia?" Eric asked through the phone's speaker. "Sudden incidences of rapid heart rate?"

Killian felt his stomach clench up and answered for her. "Charlie and Christian both have." He sent Mariah a questioning look. She just looked away. She was a hard sell, that was obvious. "And then last night," he went on, "when we went back to that camp again, BD-Exers were lying dead, everywhere." Lowering his head, he said, "It looked as if their hearts had exploded right out of their chests."

When he spoke again, Eric's voice was broken. "How many of The Chosen died?"

"More than twenty," Killian said.

"Twenty-three," Charlie said softly. She didn't ask if the two things, the rapid heartbeat and the exploding hearts were from the same cause, and Killian feared it was because she already knew.

Eric sighed, and it was a long moment before he spoke again. "There's a second drug they called Protectol. It's a supercharged combination of heart rate stabilizers, blood pressure lowering drugs, and anti-anxiety medications. All in extremely toxic doses. This cocktail would drop a horse in its tracks, but DPI claims it can be used to temporarily avert the side effects you witnessed. There was a note in the files about the BD-Exers needing to be treated with Protectol prior to battle to ensure they survive it."

Killian closed his eyes. "We have one vial of the Protectol, Eric. And we have three of The Chosen with us, all of whom have been treated with BDX. They were told it was a cure for the effects of the Belladonna Antigen. That they wouldn't die young, but would live a normal lifespan. From what you can see, is there any truth to that?"

He watched Charlie's face. While the others were leaning

nearer the phone, their eyes glued to it as they awaited his answer, Charlie had walked a few steps away, and was gazing silently out the window into the darkness.

"I don't see how. It would far more likely—" He stopped, cleared his throat. "I need to run more tests before I can say anything for sure. I should receive your samples by tomorrow."

Charlie turned and said, "Be honest with us, Mr. Marquand. We've earned that, I think. We deserve to know. These are our lives, our bodies we're talking about here. Please finish your thought. It would be far more likely to do what?"

Eric sighed into the phone. Killian heard it and heard another voice, a female. "Tell her, Eric. She's right, they deserve to know."

"Every indication is, dear Charlotte, that this drug acts upon the body like turning a thermostat to its highest setting would act upon its furnace. In layman's terms, doing so would burn up the fuel faster, not slower. I'm afraid this drug will have the same result on your bodies. It cannot extend your lives. I think it more likely that it would shorten them. Dramatically."

She closed her eyes. "So we're doomed either way."

"Not necessarily. You can postpone the side effects by staying as calm as possible and using the Protectol. The notes in the DPI files call for ten milligrams for every hundred pounds of body weight, given once daily, prior to extreme situations such as combat."

"The vial we have is fifty milligrams," Killian said.

"Good. Use them sparingly."

"And then what?" Charlie asked. "When we run out of this crap, what happens? The next time we get excited, our chests explode?"

"You can still become what we are, providing this BDX hasn't altered your body chemistry too much," Eric said. Mariah and Christian exchanged horrified looks. "We all had the antigen as humans," Eric went on. "Me, Killian, Roland and Rhiannon....where are they, by the way? I haven't heard from either of them. Aren't they still with you?"

"They were captured last night," Killian said. "It's only nine-thirty here. We're about to go out and search for them now."

"Do you have any idea where they've been taken? Do you need us to come out there?"

"To tell you the truth, Eric, I—"

"No," Mariah said. Killian shot her a look, but she kept on talking. "The last thing we need is more vampires here."

"I'm afraid you've got them, either way, child. Devlin and his gang of rogues have arrived on US soil. Larissa, Rhiannon's mole, reported to me since she couldn't reach Rhiannon. They're already in Portland, and they're out for blood. Human blood."

Mariah jumped to her feet. "A gang of vampires is in Portland? You knew about this?" she accused Killian.

"Rhiannon told me they were on their way. She and Roland's purpose in coming out of hiding was to stop them. Helping us was a sidebar."

"We must stop them at all cost," Eric said. "So if anything has happened...." He stopped there, cleared his throat. "If anything has happened to Roland and Rhiannon, you must let me know immediately so we can send others to eliminate this rogue band."

"Eliminate them?" Charlie asked. "What does that mean? You mean...kill them? Your own kind?"

"We have laws, young one," Eric said softly. "We do not harm innocents. We do not murder humans. We police ourselves. If a vampire does violence against innocent mortals, they must be removed. It is the way it has always been. I only wish the mortal world policed itself as diligently." He sighed. "Killian, call back if you need me. Please let me know the moment you've heard from Roland and Rhiannon."

"I will. Thank you, Eric." Killian depressed the cutoff button, lifted his head and looked right into Charlie's eyes. She looked back for a long moment, then closed them and turned away.

Mariah was staring at her, her eyes wide, stricken, shaking her head slowly, she said, "I can't do this. I need....Charlie, I'm sorry. I need to go."

"Stay calm, Mariah," Killian told her.

Charlie frowned at her friend. "Honey, did you get what they just said? This shit they gave us could kill us."

"But they have the Protectol!"

"So do we," Charlie told her. But Killian knew it wouldn't work. Mariah was in shock, facing her own mortality, shut up in a house with a vampire. She was going to run, and there wasn't a damn thing they could do to stop her, and her heart was already pounding, picking up speed in her chest.

"Please, Mariah, please stay calm."

"There's not enough," she countered, backing away, shaking her head. "Not enough for all of us. One dose each and one to spare. And we all know who'll get that."

"All the Protectol in the world didn't help the other recruits, did it?" Charlie demanded. "You saw the same thing I did back there."

"I'm going. You...you can't stop me." She ran to the door, whipped it open, and took off, racing across the meadow and looking back as if she expected pursuit. And then it happened. She came to a stop, dropped to her knees, her hands going to her chest.

"*Damn* it, no!" Charlie surged out the door after her, and Killian followed,

When they got to her, her heart was beating so loudly he could hear it, feel it. It was worse than Charlie's had been. And he didn't think she had much time.

"Oh, God, oh God," she whispered, gasping for air. "I can't...I don't..." She reached up, grabbed Killian by the front of his shirt. "Do it. Do...what you said. Change me."

"That's what you want?" Killian asked.

"Don't...let me die."

He sent a look Charlie's way, and she met his eyes and nodded. So he bent over the girl, sank his teeth into her throat. The blood gushed from her jugular into his mouth like a soft drink bottle that had been shaken up. And when it surged into his mouth, it was like drinking battery acid. It burned! He jerked his head away, yelping in pain and staggering backward, falling on his ass in the tall grasses.

And then there was a splattering pop. Charlie screamed, but Mariah was silent at last, lying still in the blood-spattered grasses, a great big hole in her chest where her heart should've been.

"No! No, dammit, Mariah, no!" Charlie was kneeling over her friend, shaking her shoulders, screaming in her face. But then she let go, straightening, wiping her tears away. "Dammit. Dammit, this isn't fair. It's not fair."

"Killian?" Christian asked. "Are you okay?"

Charlie turned his way, then came to where he knelt in the grass, and knelt down in front of him. "Are you all right?"

He lifted his head. His mouth was on fire, his tongue swollen, tears running from his eyes due to the burning. "I don't know," he tried to say, but his tongue was so swollen that it sounded as if he was speaking through a mouthful of cotton.

"Come on," she said, helping him to his feet. "Let's go inside, get you some ice, rinse your mouth with water. Christian, will you see if you can find a shovel? We need to bury her."

Charlie sank into a chair, pushing her hands through her hair. Her one and only hope of not dying, not having her heart blast its way out of her chest, had been in letting Killian make her what he was. But LT and his DPI cohorts had made sure that couldn't happen, hadn't they? They'd put something into the BDX...it must be what had caused the burns in Killian's mouth. Thank God he hadn't swallowed, had pulled away at the first touch of Mariah's blood to his tongue. She wasn't sure, but she thought it might have killed him otherwise.

Christian was staring at the closed door and looking stricken. She'd helped him bury Mariah, and then she'd stood beside the mound of fresh earth and said the only prayer she knew, one her mother had taught her in childhood. "Now I lay me down to sleep. I pray the Lord my soul to keep." Olive came flapping toward her, and she held up her arm for the bird to alight, and stroked those comforting feathers. "If I should die before I wake, I pray the Lord my soul to take."

"Amen," Christian said.

Killian had held ice cubes in his mouth to cool the burns to his lips and tongue. He whispered "Amen" as well, but it was still a little off. And then suddenly, he went very still, lifting his head, frowning, as if he was listening to something. And softly he whispered, "Rhiannon?"

Charlie widened her eyes and moved closer. Pandora, who'd been sitting nearby watching all the activity, did as well, as if she knew. She leaned into Killian's legs, head up, eyes alert.

"Yes, we have Charlie," Killian said. "Tell me where you are." He listened for a moment, then nodded rapidly. "We'll find you, Rhiannon. Just hold on. We're on our way."

CHAPTER NINETEEN

There were too many boats speeding around for it to be just another summer night on the Pacific, Rhiannon thought. It seemed every time she, Roland and Roxanne emerged from the salty, cold depths, another one came shooting by, forcing them to dive under again.

She opened her consciousness to receive the images and sensations in the minds of the passing humans, which her own mind then translated. This was how the reading of mortal thoughts was accomplished. One did not think in words. One thought in feelings and pictures. The words were only their mirror.

They were military and Coast Guard vessels, and they'd been dispatched to search for two vampires who had attacked the cargo vessel of a private government contractor, leaving several humans dead in their wake.

It was a lie. They had killed no one.

Roland was a lead weight. She hoped the salt water was having some impact on the bleeding, but was unsure, and there had been little time to stanch the flow any other way, though she had chanted the blood stopping spell she'd known from earliest childhood nonstop in her mind.

He'd taken a bullet. Maybe more than one. The sorry bastard had made a point of keeping his body between the rain of gunfire and her back as they'd made their escape.

Always protecting her. Always getting hurt doing it. Hadn't he learned by now that she could take care of herself?

She surfaced again, pulling him in her wake. As they broke the surface, she flipped her hair back with a toss of her head, then floated there, treading water, and holding him by one arm, floating on his back, his face strikingly pale in the moonlight. Even more so than usual. His eyes were closed, black lashes beaded with moisture. Her heart ached with love for him.

"He'll be all right, Rhiannon. He's always all right," Roxanne said.

Rhiannon nodded hard. "And you? How are you, my mortal friend?"

"Fine. They treated me fine. No torture, nothing like that. I think they intended to study me or maybe to use me to force Charlotte to dance to their twisted-up tune. Maybe both. Thanks for getting me the hell out of there. How did you know where I was?"

"We didn't. We were captured during our rescue of your granddaughter."

No boats were in sight at the moment, so Rhiannon took the opportunity to help Roland. She moved his body in time with the waves. Thank goodness the seas were calm tonight and the swells were gentle, lifting and lowering them like a mother's rocking chair. She moved down his body to his feet and unlaced one of his shoes. Then she moved back up again until she got to his upper arm, where the bullet had torn through, and knotted the shoelace tightly around his bicep, above the wound.

The blood, which had still been seeping despite her spells,

stopped.

She sighed in relief and lay her head upon his chest. "Roland, if you die and leave me to face eternity alone, I will follow you into the Underworld and make you pay."

Something sent a chill up her spine, some keen awareness that a predator felt when another was near. Rhiannon lifted her head from her lover's chest and scanned the dark waters in every direction. Wispy black fingers of cloud crept over the face of the moon, and a light rain began to fall, blurring the horizon until the dark sea and dark sky were as one.

"Roxanne," she whispered. "Don't move any more than you have to. Be still."

Eyes widening, Roxy looked around. And then the still waters were pierced by the slick gleam of a dorsal fin as it broke surface and submerged once again.

"I've often wondered how I'd die," she whispered to Roland. "But becoming a meal for a shark is one I never even imagined."

"Hell and damnation," Roxanne muttered.

The fin appeared again, far closer this time, and off to the right. It was, she realized as she continued to watch it, circling, moving ever closer.

Rhiannon closed her eyes and projected an image of herself as Pandora, ripping a great white to shreds with her fabulous white fangs and deadly claws.

Whether the shark received that image, whether it was even capable of sensing her threat, she did not know. She heard boats, then, several of them, speeding nearer from one direction, and one deeper, louder motor that came from another.

She was about to submerge again when suddenly Roland shot like a missile, straight up out of the water, his arm wrenched from her grasp. The gleaming great white surged upward as well, with Roland's leg clamped in its hungry jaws. Rhiannon screamed his name as the man and the shark parted company in midair. Roland splashed back into the ocean to her left, and the shark, with Roland's severed leg still held clamped in its jaws, to her right.

Her shock was so thorough that she forgot about the boats, about Roxanne, about everything. She scrambled after Roland, ignorant of the people who were shouting and diving off a fishing boat and into the water. They grabbed for him, as she fought them off, her mind only focused on Roland. There were too many. They were strong. They were vampires.

They were vampires! She stopped fighting.

Roland was hauled up a ladder and onboard a small fishing boat with machine guns mounted at intervals along its deck, and Rhiannon clambered up after him to see Roxanne already aboard.

"We need heat! We have to sear the leg before he bleeds out!" The desperate shout brought her head around to see the powerful young vampire who was giving the orders.

Devlin? The rogue she had intended to kill? Yes, and his gang. All of them. Larissa, the fledgling female, was wrapping a blanket around Roxanne, speaking softly to her, drawing her away from the rail.

Other boats were speeding toward them now, but vampires manned the guns and began firing as Devlin knelt at Roland's thigh, his own belt wrapped there and yanked tight. She stared at the stump of Roland's leg. It wasn't bleeding. But she didn't think it was due to the tourniquet.

Rising to her feet, clenching a fist and shaking it at the heavens, Rhiannon shouted, "Do you truly dare to take him from me? Do you think I will not rip apart the very heavens and tear out the jugulars of the gods themselves?"

"Rhiannon!" Devlin's voice was as sharp as a whip crack. "He's not dead. Do that magic you do to keep it that way."

He had an emergency flare in his hand, and as she watched, horrified, he struck it, and it lit. "Soak the leg in water," he told the others around him. "And keep soaking it. If I fuck this up, he goes up in flames."

Vampires obeyed, pouring buckets of sea water over the already soaked leg, and Devlin moved the torch, touching the stump and drawing it quickly away as the water poured over the spot. Over and over he did this, as gunfire shattered the night all around them.

Her enemy, Rhiannon realized, was fighting for the life of her beloved.

One of the military boats approaching them exploded under the hail of machine gun fire as Devlin applied the blazing flare to the bloodied stump of Roland's thigh.

Roland did not even moan, but the stench of his burning flesh was too much for her, and her mind was rebelling. She met Devlin's eyes as he burned her beloved's flesh, and said, "You were right, Devlin. I was wrong. I want you to kill them. Kill every last one of them." And then Rhiannon passed out cold on the deck.

"Shall we continue the pursuit of the *Anemone*, Devlin?" one of his followers, a young male named Jeremy asked.

"No." He said. They had sent a pair of vampires out on a speedboat in pursuit with orders to affix a tracking device to the *Anemone's* hull if they could get close enough without being seen. Their chances of success were slim to none, but it was all he could do.

He was below decks, staring down at the Diva bitch who had ruined his entire plan and her all but lifeless companion. Elders of his kind. But not the leaders his people needed. Not in these times. They were too ethical. Too moral. Too good. He had none of those flaws. And yet he couldn't leave them to die.

Their mortal friend was asleep, exhausted from her ordeal

at sea. He knew who she was, but had never met her before. The oldest living Chosen, Roxanne O'Malley, a living legend among his kind.

"Devlin?" Jeremy asked, prompting him for an answer.

"No, we can't pursue. Head for shore. Look for an isolated place. If they catch us, they'll kill us."

Rhiannon and Roland lay stretched out side by side on a table. There were no beds on the vessel. Just a galley and a head, neither of which Devlin needed. He had a bandage wrapped around his wrist, as did several others of his vampiric crew, each of whom had voluntarily given of their own blood, their own strength, their life force, to Roland. Most of it had dribbled down his chin, wasted. But he thought some might have made its way into his body to help him heal.

Devlin was angry, but he hadn't yet given up hope, and as they neared shore, running without lights, he had his crew shut off the engines. Three of his gang dove overboard, ropes in their teeth to pull the boat silently toward shore.

"How are they?" asked the pretty one. The fledgling vampiress, Larissa, had, he suspected, been reporting his actions to Rhiannon all along. And yet he'd done nothing about it.

"Rhiannon will survive," he said. "She's been drifting in and out, calling out both audibly and mentally to someone named Killian each time. If he's a vampire, and can hear her, I imagine we'll meet him soon."

"And what about Roland?"

Devlin pressed his lips, but said nothing.

Someone from above called down that they were as near to shore as the boat could go without running itself aground.

"Drop anchor," he ordered. "I'll take them in the dingy from here. I want everyone else to abandon ship and go on foot to our hideout. Stay there, out of sight unless you hear from me. I'll take our three castaways elsewhere. At sundown, we meet right here again."

"I'd prefer to stay with you," Larissa said softly. Her eyes were huge and searching his face.

"Why? We both know you've never believed in the cause."

She looked at Roland, lying there, white as the face of the moon and nearly as lifeless. "Maybe I do now."

He held her eyes for a long moment, then nodded. "All right. Get Roxanne and let's get going. We need to find a place where Roland can rest and recover.

K illian and his mortal band, Pandora and Olive included, had piled into Charlie's vehicle and followed Rhiannon's infrequent and increasingly confused-sounding calls to a private dock owned, apparently, by some incredibly wealthy mortals. Their mansion was some 70 miles from Portland on a wooded hilltop that looked down onto the ocean, boathouse and docks below. The entire property was surrounded by fence and patrolled by dogs.

The fence hadn't been a problem. They'd all jumped it easily. The dogs hadn't been a problem either. One snarl from Pandora sent them running for cover, whimpering as if she'd already attacked.

Charlie, Olive riding on her arm as had become the usual, spotted a camera mounted to the side of the redwood boathouse, picked up a pebble and expertly put out its lens.

Killian gave her a nod of approval, but she just looked away. She was strong now. Far stronger than she'd been when he'd first met her. But there was a sadness that lingered behind her eyes. Didn't she know that he would not let her die? No matter what.

They walked down the hill to the dock and out onto it, standing side by side. Christian remained on the shore.

"This must be them," Charlie said, standing on the end of the dock in the rain, watching a dinghy's slow approach.

"There are coast guard patrol boats everywhere tonight," Christian called from the grassy shore. "What if it's one of them?"

Killian shook his head. "No. It's vampires. Several of them." His skin tingled with awareness, and he felt Charlie tense up. Olive felt it too, ruffling up her feathers then shaking them hard, before letting them lie flat again. "It's all right, Charlie. Remember, you're Chosen. Vampires can't hurt you," he assured her. "Not even strange ones."

The boat came closer, and as it did, Killian became aware of more vampires, a dozen at least, all of them coming out of the water without the aid of any boat. They slogged up onto shore at various locations, dripping seawater, and loping away without so much as a greeting. The little boat, though, kept coming, and when it neared shore, its pilot got out, walked up to the prow and pulled it up onto the shore, ignoring the dock.

As the boat passed by him, Killian got a look inside. "Holy mother of God," he whispered.

"Oh my God." Charlie clutched his arm. Olive flew up into the air, then circled over the little boat.

Pandora came running, chuffing and switching her tail, lunging into the surf, then dancing back again.

"Easy, girl," Killian said, jogging back off the dock arm in arm with Charlie, then heading for the dinghy. Roland was lying there in the small boat, maybe dead, missing an entire leg. Rhiannon lay soaked and unconscious beside him. A girl, a young vampiress sat between them, her eyes wide and wary. Another woman sat nearby, with a blanket wrapped around her like a monk's hooded cowl. One of The Chosen.

Killian looked from the pair of them to the man who was pulling the dinghy up onto the shore. "Who the hell are you, and what in the name of God happened to them?"

The unidentified woman lowered her hood. "His name's Devlin, and he's the fellow who just saved our asses, so I'd suggest you speak more kindly to him, Killian."

"Roxy!"

"Gram!" Charlie broke away from him as her grandmother climbed out of the dingy onto the shore, and the two met in an embrace that almost brought tears to Killian's eyes.

"You're okay, oh, God, you're okay," Charlie said over and over. "You were hurt, Killian thought. Are you hurt?"

"Ah, bullet took a chunk out of my thigh. I lost a lot of blood, but our friends at DPI were good enough to patch me up. They injected me with something, too. Wouldn't tell me what, but my suspicious nature tells me it wasn't anything as simple as an antibiotic." She sighed. "Damn, Charlotte, I was afraid I'd never get you back from those bastards." Smiling, hugging her, Roxy looked up at Killian over Charlie's shoulder. "Thank you, Killian. You're a helluva man. Thank you."

Charlie lifted her head and turned to look back at him, telling him the same thing with her eyes. Then Olive swooped down to land on Roxy's arm, and leaning near, blinked into her eyes as Roxy stroked her and told her it was all going to be okay now.

"Time is short," Devlin said. "We're being hunted. Do you have a vehicle?"

Killian nodded. "I think we can all crowd in."

"Good. Let's do it, then. DPI knows we're out here somewhere." Devlin lifted Rhiannon from the boat and handed her limp body to Killian. Then he picked Roland up and carried him up onto the shore.

"This way," Killian said, starting off. Pandora was trotting along so close to his legs that he nearly tripped over her. She stretched her neck to sniff at Rhiannon, eager, he thought, to see if she was all right.

The stranger turned back briefly, staring out at the ocean. "They got away. We risked everything to find them, and they got away."

He sighed heavily, nodded, and then joined the rest of them.

Charlie had her grandmother back. She'd also had some more time to look through the stolen computer. To do more investigating. She'd already known the horrifying news that the vampire scientist Eric Marquand had delivered by phone earlier. She'd spent the afternoon in the barn, poring over files while waiting for Killian to wake. Now she dug into them even more deeply, searching for an answer to what had happened when Killian had tried to turn Mariah. It was there, too. The injection of a toxin known to be deadly to vampires, was usually given with the third and final dose of BDX. Had they given her that as well? She tried to remember her day long bout of agony while they'd pumped that chemical death sentence into her veins. She remembered the pale doctor injecting three doses of BDX into the IV bag and cranking up the flow. She did not remember a fourth injection. But she'd also been in screaming anguish and tranquilized into oblivion for much of the time.

One thing was clear. The BDX was dangerous, deadly, and DPI knew it, had known it all along, and had given it to all those recruits anyway. The average life expectancy of a BD-Exer was three months. Three fucking months. That was why LT hadn't taken the cure himself. And that was what had killed all those recruits at Fort Rogers.

What she still didn't know was why. What was the point of creating a race of super charged Chosen to kill vampires, if they would only live for a few months? What good were they?

The growing band had made its way to an abandoned warehouse on the docks where they intended to rest. It was near daylight, had taken them a few hours to get to the coast, and a few more to get far enough away from those searching for them. Roland was lying in a wooden crate. There were dozens of them scattered around this place, some packed with straw, others with some kind of mechanical parts inside. A big rusty flatbed truck was parked in the back and looked as if it had been there for decades. They'd pulled the van right inside and parked it beside the aging beast to keep it out of sight.

Rhiannon was awake now, kneeling beside him, silent tears rolling down her cheeks. Pandora had prowled the place until she'd found a satisfactory corner and was stretched out there, keeping her narrowed eyes always on her owner. And Olive had taken to the rafters and seemed to be content.

Christian was in the back near the vehicles by himself, and Charlie thought he was probably still grieving for Mariah. Roxy and Killian seemed to be sticking close to Charlie.

As Charlie sat there on the floor, leaning back against a metal wall, shell-shocked, exhausted, hungry, wrapped in her grandmother's arm, and wondering what the hell was in store for her next, Devlin walked up to Rhiannon, put a hand on her shoulder and said, "We should talk."

Rhiannon didn't look away from Roland. "You saved his life. I owe you."

He nodded. "I don't abandon my own kind if I can help them, Rhiannon. I'm not entirely evil."

"And yet you led your little gang in a raid that annihilated an entire village. A dozen humans. Maybe more."

Charlie leaned forward, listening. She'd recognized the name when she'd heard it, knew this was the rogue Eric had mentioned, the one Roland and Rhiannon had come here to stop. To kill.

"They were a village of spies, Rhiannon."

That drew Rhiannon's gaze. "What's this now?"

"Unlike you," Devlin said, "I never trusted the mortals to leave us alone in our haven. I kept tabs. I had informants. I crept about that village by night and listened to their thoughts. They were no ordinary villagers. Most of the locals had quietly been gathering evidence against us and were planning to send it to their DPI contact the next day, to collect a sizable reward.

You know there's been a price on our heads since the war ended."

She nodded. "I know."

"We had to move quickly to prevent it. It was us or them, Rhiannon."

She sighed, lowered her head. "I wasn't aware—"

"I probably should've told you."

"Yes, you should have. There was a child—"

"I went back for her. But you had already seen to her well-being. Erased the memory of the attack. Sent her off to safety."

She sighed. "I need to warn Eric and Tamara to get the rest of our people out of there," she said softly. "If anyone survived, or wasn't there the night of the attack...."

"That's probably wise."

"I meant what I said, Devlin. I will no longer try to stop you. Not after what these bastards have done. And on that ship...on that ship I saw...." She lowered her head, closed her eyes. "Dawn approaches. Leave me with my love a bit longer."

Devlin nodded, and went away from her, into the shadows where Larissa waited for him.

Sighing, Roxy said, "I'm going to scout around for something to eat," and with a final squeeze of Charlie's shoulder, she went off, leaving her alone with Killian.

"I don't blame Rhiannon for wanting to kill them all," Charlie whispered. They sat side by side near a shadowy wall. "I'll bet she'd just as soon kill me, too. They got into this mess trying to help me. If I'd just listened to you, to Roxy—"

"It's not your fault, Charlie."

"Yeah it is, Killian. It's completely my fault. Roland might die. He's the leader of an entire race, and he might die because I was too stubborn to listen and too prejudiced to believe. And yet they risked their lives for me. And what's the use? All this, to save me, when I'm going to be dead before long anyway."

"Don't say that."

"Why not? It's the truth. You heard Eric Marquand on the phone. He said this stupid drug isn't a cure for the early death sentence that comes with the Belladonna Antigen at all. It's a booster shot for it. It speeds it up." Something she hadn't yet told her grandmother. There hadn't been time. But she knew she had to. And soon. "Why the hell is everybody getting themselves shot and killed and burned and maimed just to give me a few more months?"

Killian was quiet for a long moment. Then he took her hand and said, "They're doing it because they haven't got a choice. We protect The Chosen. That's just the way it is. But I'd die trying to save you even if that wasn't the case, Charlie, and I think you know that."

"Don't." She got to her feet, shaking her head. "This is no time for that. Our lives are at stake. And besides...." She lowered her head, almost stopped herself from saying it, but then decided she had to. "I'm not going to live long, Killian, there's no point."

"Yeah there is. And you can live as long as you want to."

She knew what he meant. "If you try to change me, you could die."

"I would drink battery acid for you. And I'd do it happily."

"But I couldn't live with that." ·

"Then I'll find another way."

"What other way?" she whispered. "Cut me, let my blood run out of me until the last? Then refill me with your own?"

He nodded fast, but his eyes didn't hold hers.

"Tell me the truth." She put her hands on his face, turning it to hers again. "I've put my trust in you, Killian. Don't disrespect that by lying to me now."

He sighed heavily, but he met her steady gaze. "It would be risky. I wouldn't know exactly when your heart beat its last. And giving you enough of my own blood to bring you over, without having your blood to make up the loss, could be... dangerous."

"It could kill you," she interpreted. "That's about what I thought."

He held her eyes for a minute, and she stared right back at him, letting him see that she meant everything she was about to say to him. "I owe you an apology bigger than I'll ever manage to give. I'm sorry I didn't trust you, Killian. I'm even sorrier that I didn't trust what I felt and still feel for you. I should have, because it's the most real thing there has ever been. I'm sorry I almost got you killed, and got your friends hurt. I'm sorry, Killian. But my biggest regret is that my own mother died because of me, and I just...I don't know how to live with that. I don't know if I'm supposed to. I think I'm just supposed to...to go. Whenever it's time, you know? Just go." Tears choked her, and she got up and ran through the nearest door into a dim and dusty office to cry her tears in private.

Killian didn't let her, though. He followed her inside, locked the door behind him, and when he turned her around and pulled her into his arms, she didn't even try to resist. "If this is all we have, Charlie, than at least let's be together now. Let's relish whatever time fate gives us, and I promise you, if there's a way to save you, I will. I'll turn over heaven and earth to find it. I...I love you, Charlie. I love you."

"I love you, too."

He kissed her, and when she tasted the salt of tears, she couldn't tell if they were his or her own. He cleared off an old desk with a swipe of his arm and laid her down there, his body covering hers, kissing her, holding her, making her forget, for a while, that this love of theirs was doomed. This might be all they had. She pushed everything else from her mind and opened her heart, giving herself completely to him and to this.

He pulled her blouse over her head, baring her breasts to his hungry eyes. She saw the way they glowed red, and when he closed his eyes, she touched his cheek. "Don't hide anything about yourself from me. I want all of you, Killian."

So he opened them, and she watched the glow of lust, like

a fire behind his eyes as he fed at her breasts and licked at her belly. When he shoved her pants lower, she grabbed at his jeans, tugging them apart and pushing them off him. He peeled his own shirt off, and then he was pushing her legs apart and sliding inside her.

She closed her eyes in sheer ecstasy as he filled her and clutched at his back and his buttocks as they moved together. He kissed her endlessly, deeply, and he let her explore with her tongue, even touching those incisors that had felt so good sinking into her neck so long ago. Was it really only days ago? It felt like years. It felt like centuries.

God, she wanted to stay with him!

His kissed his way to her neck as his pace increased, and she felt him reaching for the pinnacle and knew his hunger was raging inside him. She felt it. She matched it as her own body tightened and tingled. He sucked the skin between his teeth, and she grabbed his head and moved his mouth back to hers. She didn't want to hurt him. Not for all the world would she hurt this man.

She loved him. She loved him like no one had ever loved anyone before. And what was more, what was both thrilling and heartbreaking, was that she knew he loved her just as much.

Her mind stopped working then as he made love to her, pushing her near the edge, then letting her settle back again, over and over, until at last she clung to him and rode the waves of ecstasy that washed over her. He held her to him as her body trembled and her tears flowed, and he moaned her name and then wrapped his arms around her and held her as if he'd never let her go.

CHAPTER TWENTY

Charlie stayed alone in the little room to think when the sun started to rise and Killian had to find a nice dark place to rest. It was an office or had been once. Old papers with curling corners were scattered on rusty file cabinets with a quarter inch of undisturbed dust on them. A few of their drawers were open, empty except for the small piles of litter some tiny rodent had probably been using as a nest.

She spent an hour in there, maybe a little more, all alone, feeling the deepest and most profound sadness she had ever felt over everything that had happened and everything that would. It wasn't death that got to her, it was the idea of leaving Killian. Of not being with him. Even heaven would be hell to her if he wasn't by her side. It was so unfair! She'd only just found him.

There was a tap on the door before it opened, and Roxy came inside. She offered a small bag of potato chips and one of the two cans of Diet Coke she carried. "Found a stash of junk food in a boat docked nearby. Got a bag for each of us non-blood-drinkers. It's not protein packed, but it's better than nothing."

"Thanks, Gram." Charlie took the bag, tore it open, and perched herself on the edge of the desk, because she was too grossed out to sit in the chair. Little creatures had chewed holes through its leather and were probably nesting inside. She glanced casually over her shoulder at the desk's surface, wondering if Roxy could tell by the shape of the dust free parts what had so recently transpired there.

Roxy sat on one of the file cabinets and munched on her own chips. "It's been a rough few days for you."

"Not as rough as for you. Or Rhiannon, or poor Roland. God, his leg...."

"If he lives, it'll heal. I mean, I assume it will. Then again, I've never seen a whole limb grow back before. Never saw one torn off like that. But that's only if he lives. God, I hope he lives." She bit her lip, lowered her head.

"You really care about him, don't you?"

Roxy seemed to search for words, taking her time before speaking again. "I love him. I love them all. I've fallen for Killian too, you know. They are true friends. Family, really."

Charlie lowered her head, closed her eyes. "Mom was family. She's dead because of me. DPI killed her, made it look like Killian did it, and I believed them–"

"So I've gathered." She sighed, lowered her head. "Your mother was a good woman, Charlotte. She's dead because the government's terrified enough to want to annihilate an entire race just because they don't understand them. They're willing to kill anyone, no matter how innocent, if it serves their purpose. You are a victim in all of this. And you're gonna keep on being one until you're tired of it. Tired enough to stand up and say *no more*."

Charlie picked her head back up, looked her grandmother in the eye. "I'm not feeling sorry for myself, if that's what you're getting at. I'm gonna die young. Maybe younger than we even thought. Now, with the BDX–"

"I know, Charlotte. I know. Your Killian and I had a nice talk before the sun came up. He told me what happened, how all those recruits died, and what Eric had to say about the drug."

Charlie took a big breath, nodded. "I've accepted it. I'm not whining about it."

"And he told me what happened to Mariah, too. How he couldn't help her." She waited, like she wanted to test Charlie's reaction to that.

"So you see why there's no hope. I can't let him try to change me into...one of them."

Roxy shrugged. "I want you to remember something, Charlotte. You're different from all those other recruits. Those...Exers. You're different. Everything about it went differently with you, that's what Killian told me."

She nodded. "So maybe there's a chance...that would be different, too."

"There you go."

"But it's a chance you never took, Gram." She searched her grandmother's eyes. "I've been dying to ask you. Why?"

Taking a deep drink from her cola can, Roxy swallowed, nodded. "I was in love once. I wasn't much older than you are now."

The admission distracted Charlie, momentarily at least, from her own misery. "Did he love you, too?"

"Oh, yeah. We were...we were passionate. Crazy about each other. It was beyond anything I ever thought I could feel."

Roxy's voice seemed to thicken a little with emotion, and Charlie's heart knotted up for her. "What happened?" she asked softly.

"I don't know. He just...he disappeared. He stopped showing up for work. He was a bartender. I asked the owner, but he said he never even came to pick up his last check. His car was gone, but all his stuff was still in his apartment." She sighed, and Charlie could feel the pain in that sound. "I never heard from him again."

"God, that's awful. Did you report him missing?"

"Of course I did. And later, when I could afford it, I even hired a PI to search for him but...."

"Was he like us? You know...a BD?"

"I didn't even know there was such a thing back then. Didn't know there was anything unusual about my blood. Much less whether he shared it." She shrugged. "I still hope I'll find him again someday, if he lived. And if he didn't, well then I'll see him on the other side. If I take that old Dark Gift, neither of those things can happen."

"Dark Gift," Charlie repeated. "Is that what they call it? Seems more like a curse to me." But it would be worth it, she thought. It would be worth anything to be with Killian.

"Yeah, being eternally young, immortal, growing stronger and more powerful with every passing year. That's a real hardship. Wouldn't wish it on anyone."

"Now you're being sarcastic," Charlie said.

"You're right. I'm sorry. It's a huge decision, and one you have to make your own damn self. But girl, I'm telling you, consider all your options before you choose death. Explore every possibility. And don't you dare give up on life until you're dead, you hear me?"

Charlie couldn't help but smile. "I hear you."

"Good. So while I'm on a roll, I'm gonna shoot for one more. You remember how pissed you got when you thought Killian had used you, tricked you, and killed your mama? So mad you let them shoot you up with their poison to make you strong enough to kill his ass?"

Ashamed, she looked at her feet. "I remember."

"Get that mad again, Charlotte."

She shot her grandmother a puzzled look.

"Get that mad about what these bastards did to your mother. To Roland. To me. To all those kids whose hearts blew out of their chests at Camp Crazy back there. Get that mad again, Charlotte. Stop crying, and start fighting."

Roxy popped another chip into her mouth and left the office. Charlie sat where she was, turning her grandmother's words over and over in her mind.

Charlie got a few hours of sleep. When she woke, she did more reading, ate more chips, wished for an actual meal. She sifted through files on the DPI computer, files about BDX and its side effects and all the various "samples" that had been taken from each of the "subjects" during their treatments. Nothing specific, but she assumed it was to compare cells or whatever before and after BDX. She racked her brain to figure out what the government had to gain by creating a bunch of super-thugs who were unlikely to last more than a battle or two before their hearts exploded, even with the help of the Protectol. There had to be more to it. There had to be.

She was pacing the bowels of the warehouse. Olive had found a little corner in the rafters and was apparently sound asleep. So were all the vampires. At least she hoped they were, but she wasn't so sure about Roland. How did one tell a sleeping vampire from a dead one?

There were crates and boxes everywhere, tossed haphazardly, lids pried off, straw-like packing material scattered all around them. The mice and birds in this place probably thought they'd hit the nest-building-material jackpot.

Roxy and Christian were napping, or so she thought. It was only when a throat cleared nearby that she looked around.

Christian stood there, drinking from a water bottle. "You can't sleep either, huh?"

"I managed a few hours. Been reading ever since. You?"

He smiled, but it was sad. He'd lost a good friend in Mariah. "I can't stand it in here. All cooped up like this. It's freakin' depressing. And it's still three hours till dark," he said.

"You're right on all counts."

"I was thinking of taking a walk." He looked a little longingly toward the nearest exit. There were several doors on the warehouse. Giant ones at the front and rear, but a couple of smaller ones too, for people rather than vehicles.

"Do you think it would hurt anything?"

"No one's looking for you, as far as we know."

He took his sunglasses from his pocket and put them on. His hair was a little longer than it had been, and he'd let his whiskers come in over the last couple of days. His clothes were street, not camo. She had no idea where he'd got them. A pair of too big jeans and a Ford Racing T-shirt. She didn't think Christian would be recognized.

"There are seals just offshore," he said. "I heard them earlier."

She smiled. "Maybe I'll come with you."

"I was hoping you'd say that." He went to the van, reached in and plucked out the sunglasses she'd left on the visor.

He handed them to Charlie and she put them on. "I can do even better," she said, and turning, she headed through the warehouse to the small office area. Inside, she snatched a truck-driver hat off the wall, complete with a bulldog logo. After smacking it against the desk to shake out most of the dust, she twisted her hair up into a knot and plopped the cap down over it.

"There. Do I look badass?"

"Redneck Lara Croft," he said.

"You're a funny guy, Christian."

He smiled at her, and they headed out a side door. Charlie blinked in the brilliant sunlight, despite the hat and glasses. It had been dark in that warehouse. When her eyes adjusted a little, she took a careful look around her, but nothing looked out of line. There were seagulls bickering, a few dockworkers further along the shore, but no one anywhere near them. She didn't see any conspicuously parked cars or newspaper-reading spies. They picked their way among cargo containers, barrels and fishing nets down to the shoreline, then walked along it a little ways. The late afternoon sun was beaming down, and the waves tumbled in. She wanted to take off her shoes and walk barefoot in the surf. But if she had to run, bare feet might be a detriment.

Shame she had to think of everything that way. But maybe not for much longer.

"What are you gonna do, Christian? Now that this is all over."

"You really think it's over?" he asked.

She shrugged, inhaling deep. The air smelled fishy and salty and clean all at once. "Well, we got Rhiannon and Roland back. We got my grandmother back. We've got a friendly vampire scientist with a sample of that stuff DPI uses to keep our hearts from exploding too soon. With luck he can whip us up a batch. I mean, what else is there?"

He shrugged. "That vampire, Devlin...he's still planning some kind of...attack."

She shrugged. "I don't think Rhiannon's gonna let that happen." She shrugged. "I mean, yeah she said otherwise, but she was upset. Either way, it's not up to me. I just want to get away from all of this. Try to live out whatever time I have left in some kind of...normalcy."

"What about Killian?"

She took a deep breath, let it out slow. "Whatever time I do have left, I'm hoping to spend it with him."

"Are you gonna let him change you? I mean, if he can?"

"I don't know. Would you?"

He shook his head. "I couldn't." It seemed like an admission. Then he nodded out at the water about the same time she heard the seals barking.

She looked at them, a couple of hundred of them at least, some long and sleek, others fat and powerful, basking on pallets tied together on top of floating barrels for a makeshift dock. It had probably been put there to keep them from climbing all over the actual docks. Their smell was pungent, but she didn't care. One big animal pushed a slightly smaller one right off into the water, barking ferociously before claiming the vacated spot as his own. He posed as if he thought someone might want to take a picture to memorialize his triumph. She laughed, not taking her eyes off them.

"Cute, aren't they?"

That was *not* Christian's voice.

It was LT's. She turned slowly, staring him down, then looking past him for Christian and not seeing him. "What the hell are you doing here? Where's Christian?"

"On his way to the new base by now. We had a Jeep waiting."

Maybe she was dense, but her brain wasn't processing this. "Was he working for you all along?"

"Why does that matter?"

"He wasn't. I know he wasn't."

LT shook his head, then tapped his own shoulder. "The tattoo. The ink doubles as a tracking device. Once you get your ink, you're ours for life. I'll see to it you get yours just as soon as we get to the new base."

"I'm not going to any new base or anywhere else with you, Lieutenant."

"Easy, Charlie. I'm just here to make you an offer, that's all."

"I don't want to hear anything you have to say. You lied to me. You told me this BDX shit was a cure for the side effects of Belladonna. You told me I would live a normal lifespan, when the truth is just the opposite."

"You don't know the whole story."

"I know you robbed me of years I would've had otherwise."

"No–"

"Bullshit. I saw what happened to the other recruits. Their

hearts exploded. Jesus. That's what I have to look forward to. Because of you."

He nodded, looking genuinely sad. "We were unprepared for attack. If the doctor had treated them prior to the battle, they'd have been all right."

"With the Protectol, you mean."

He blinked, clearly surprised by how much she knew.

"But the Protectol doesn't stop the BDX from burning us out faster than the Belladonna ever would have, does it LT?"

"You've been getting a lot of classified information. Doc didn't clear out the lab as ordered before we evacuated the base. Am I right?"

"Didn't even take his laptop," she said. "So I know. I've seen through the bullshit. If you're gonna try to take me back, try it so I can kick your ass. Let's get on with this. Thanks to you, my time is extremely limited."

He looked at her for a long moment, then nodded. "We'll get on with it. But I'm not taking you anywhere. In fact, I'm letting you go. You, and your grandmother both."

She frowned hard, watching his face, trying to read him the way she could so easily read Killian. But it didn't work the same way with anyone else. "Go on. Tell me the catch."

"No catch. Just walk away. Go back to that warehouse where you're holed up, wake your grandmother, and walk away."

He knew where they were staying. Hell.

"And then what?" she asked.

"Then we walk in and take the five vampires you've got sleeping in there before they wake up."

"You're crazy. There aren't any vampires in that–"

"Don't bother, Charlie. I know everything."

She lowered her head, shook it. "Why do you say you'll take them? When what you mean is, you'll kill them?"

"No. I mean we'll take them. We didn't know who they were before, Charlie. You don't even understand, Rhiannon is *ancient.* One of the few truly ancient ones to survive the war. Roland is only a few centuries younger. We need them alive."

"That's only two. What do you plan to do with the other three?"

He shrugged. "We have uses for the others as well. They won't be killed. I promise. And whether you leave or not, we're coming for them before sundown. If you're in the way, you're going to die, and so is your grandmother."

She stared into his eyes and wondered if he even had a soul. "I'm not gonna hand them over to you just to save my own ass. Who the hell do you think I am? *You?* A fucking traitor?" She leaned in closer, chin coming up. "I am going to stand there between you and my friends, and the only way you're going to take them is over my dead body, *Lucas.*"

He held her eyes, then said, "We have an antidote, Charlie."

She blinked. Didn't mean to, but the words hit her hard.

"Yeah, that's right, an antidote," he went on. "It reverses everything the BDX did to you. Takes away the strength, the power. Lets you go back to what you were before. An ordinary BD destined to weaken and die over time. A little more time though. It'll give you back the years you say I stole."

"What part of 'I won't betray my friends to save my own ass' did you not understand?"

She turned on her heel and started to walk away.

"How about to save your mother?"

Charlie stopped, suppressing a chill that felt like ice cubes melting down her spine. She didn't turn around because she couldn't move.

"We didn't cremate her body. Her body wasn't in the casket because she's still alive."

"Don't lie to me, LT. Not about that."

"It's not a lie. We don't kill anyone we might be able to use as leverage. It's DPI policy."

"I saw the crime scene photos."

"We drugged her. Laid her out on the floor, used some

body paint and special effects blood. One of our experts retouched her eyes. You gotta love technology."

She turned slowly. He pulled out a telephone and dialed a number. Then he spoke. "Put the prisoner on the phone."

Then he held it out to her.

"Hello?" said a voice. Her mother's voice.

It hit Charlie in the gut like a wrecking ball. She didn't touch the phone, just stared at it like it was a snake that would bite her. "You faked this, too. It's a recording or something."

"Hello?" her mother's voice said again. "Is that you, Charlie?"

"Ask her something," Lieutenant Scumbag said. "Something only you and she would know."

She took the phone, tears welling. "M-mom?"

"Charlie? OhmyGod, Charlie, baby, are you all right?"

"Yeah, I'm fine Mom. Are you?"

"No. No, I'm not. These people have....have kidnapped me, and they won't let me go. I'm being held on–"

"Shut up!" There was the sound of a slap and her mother's whimper.

Charlie's eyes flashed to LT's. "You hurt my mother, you son of a bitch, and I swear to God–"

He snatched the phone from her. "Just ask her the question Charlie. You've got five seconds, then we disconnect. Understand?"

She nodded, and he handed the phone back to her. "Listen, Mom I need to ask you something. You remember that puppy I had when I was little. The one with the watch-eye?"

"God, Charlie, why are you asking about Buttons at a time like this?"

Charlie closed her eyes as relief washed over her. It was her mother. It was for real. She was alive. "Listen, Mom, you just do what they say. I'm gonna get you out of there, okay?"

"Don't put yourself at risk, honey. Just run away. Get as far away as you can."

"I love you, Mom."

"Love you too, baby."

LT took the phone, ended the call, pocketed it. "We're coming in hot, Charlie. Eight PM. An hour before sundown. That's all the time I can give you. We need to have time to get them contained before they wake. You and your grandmother get the hell out of there before eight." He looked at his watch. "You've got just under two hours. I suggest you move your ass."

She lowered her head, closed her eyes. "You'll let my mother go?"

"By nine tonight, she'll either be safe and sound back in her apartment, or she'll be occupying that casket we bought for her. I'll kill her myself if you try to fuck me over."

"I believe you."

He nodded. "This isn't sanctioned, Charlie. *I'm* making this call. The powers that be want you almost as bad as they want the vampires. Letting you go, that's all me."

She narrowed her eyes on him. "Why?"

He looked away. "We're coming in hot at eight. Get yourself clear." Then he turned and walked away.

Charlie went back to the warehouse as casually as she could, in case LT was watching. She couldn't appear to be hurrying, because if she was going to comply, she had no reason to hurry. She had two hours. It would only take two minutes to wake Roxy and take off.

Once inside, she picked up the pace, jogging to where her grandmother slept and shaking her. "Gram. Gram, wake up."

Roxy came wide awake slow, then seemed momentarily disoriented when she did. "What's going on?"

"We're in trouble. Get that computer booted up. I've got a cell number. Can you triangulate it and get us a location?"

"Of course I can." She was rubbing her eyes and opening the good doctor's laptop before Charlie finished speaking. She fished a pair of reading glasses out of a pocket and put them on, then her fingers were flying over the keys. "What I wouldn't give for a cup of coffee. Give me the number."

Charlie gave her the number she'd seen on the cell phone and memorized. The one she'd used to talk to her mother. Roxy typed it in, hit a few more keys.

"It'll take a minute. Who's at this location?"

"Mom," she said. "She's alive."

Roxy stared at her, wide eyed.

"Christian had a tattoo. All the Exers get them at some point in their training. Turns out it's a tracking device."

"I knew it," Roxy gasped.

"I don't think Chrisitan did."

"Where is he now?"

"They got him. He and I took a walk and my former fuckwad lieutenant was waiting for us."

"How the hell did you get away?"

"He let me. Says they're coming for the vamps at eight o'clock sharp. That's how long we have to vacate or we're going down with them. If we get away, Mom lives. He says they'll let her go. If not, they take us out when they come for the vamps, and she dies. Anything yet?"

"Not yet." She hit more keys. "You know he's lying. They won't let her go. They'll use her to force you to come in. If he loses you now, he's in deep shit with his bosses. They're not going to let you walk, Charlotte. You're too valuable to them."

"You really think that?"

"You descended from the oldest living member of The Chosen. And there's more, more than that. They want more than just your service in the military. They want your genes. Your cells. Your DNA."

Charlie blinked. "I believe you."

Roxy nodded, seeming relieved that she didn't have to

work hard to gain Charlie's trust anymore. Charlie wished she'd been more trusting all along.

"So how are we going to get our friends out of this one, Charlotte?"

Charlie licked her lips and paced the warehouse, looking around aimlessly and pushing a hand through her hair. Her gaze fell on the minivan and the old truck parked beside it and froze there.

"You think that old thing runs?" she asked.

"I have yet to meet the engine I couldn't make run," Roxy said.

By seven forty-five everything was ready. Their plan would either work, or they were all dead meat. Charlie sat behind the wheel of the ancient truck. It had half a tank of gas in it at first, but they'd used all but a gallon or so. She wouldn't need even that much.

Five long narrow wooden boxes were lined up on the flatbed, their lids on tight, a huge blue tarp stretched over them and tied down at the corners.

At five minutes to eight. She gave herself the last shot of Protectol. There had been one more, but they'd sent it off to the scientist, Eric, somewhere in Romania, so he could make more. Then she took Olive, who was perched on Roxy's arm watching her, and the bird came eagerly, landing on her shoulder and bunting Charlie's face gently with her beak. Charlie smiled, a tear welling up in her eye. "Yeah, I love you too, bird. Now go on, go with Roxy. Be safe." She shrugged, but Olive didn't move.

"I'll take her." Roxy came closer, sliding her hand under Olive's feet and lifting her away. Then she leaned in, and hugged Charlie hard. "Watch yourself. Stay alive. That's an order."

"I'll do my best."

The truck's motor was running, popping and skipping, but running. Charlie kissed her grandmother's cheek, then turned and climbed behind the wheel. She put the shift into first gear, thanking her stars that she'd learned to drive a stick back in high school, because her driver's ed teacher made it a part of the curriculum. She'd done pretty well in that class. But this was different. A truck, not a car. If she stalled the damn thing, it was over. And it might be over anyway, because they were going to start shooting the minute she crashed through the door. She was starting from the other end of the warehouse, hoping to nudge it up into second gear by the time she hit. Maybe even third. Couldn't afford to lug it, though. She had to be going fast. She'd found a pair of old welding helmets in the office, and was wearing one of them on her head in hopes it would deflect bullets. The other one was rigged to the passenger seat at head level to convince them she had a passenger.

She took a deep breath, checked her watch, waited until two minutes before eight, then revved the motor and released the clutch.

The truck moved forward on bald tires she was surprised could still turn. Halfway across the floor, she caught second gear and pressed the accelerator all the way down. Almost to the door, she let up and caught third beautifully, no lugging. She hit the door with the pedal down and burst through it. A rush of adrenaline surged through her blood, and her heart sped up beating fast, then faster, despite the Protectol.

Gunfire rained, and she ducked instinctively, but never slowed, shifting into fourth and taking a corner so fast she almost rolled it. Faster, fifth gear. It was as high as the thing went. She was doing sixty along the waterfront, but it felt like ninety. Glancing into the side mirrors, she saw LT's men diving into vehicles and speeding after her. Some of them were still firing at her, and the gap between them and her was narrowing way too fast. The pier was up ahead, just past where the seals lounged. It was huge, held up out of the ocean by concrete pylons.

The seals dove into the water as the noisy old truck sped past, followed by all those Jeeps and sedans, and the rat-a-tat of automatic weapon fire. They scrambled off their perches in a massive display of the survival instinct. The truck's rear window blew out. Then a tire, sending her skidding to the left. She gripped the wheel, fighting it back on course, forcing it to the right.

They'd almost caught up. It was now or never. She passed a tower of shipping containers, giving her a brief second when they couldn't see her. Aiming the truck at the pier's middle pylon, about twenty feet out from shore, she yanked off her helmet, opened her door and dove.

The truck sailed out over the water, arching downward, and hitting the pylon nose-first. The gasoline she'd poured into the radiator exploded on impact.

Charlie had hit the ground hard, but there was no time to pay attention to the pain that rocketed through every freaking part of her body, or to worry about the way her heart was hammering hard enough to break her ribs. She rolled into the water, arrowing deep in spite of the pain and swimming below the surface to the next pier up, then swimming under it. On the other side, she emerged, crawling up onto shore, keeping boats, pylons, and anything else she could find between her and her pursuers.

They were swarming around the blazing pier. Flames floated on the surface and all around the truck, whose nose had sunk into the sea. All the crates had flown off and into the water, sinking due to the weight inside them.

No one was looking her way. Charlie pulled herself up onto the shore, and dashed across an open area to get lost among the buildings further in. And then she was beyond them.

The white minivan came out of an alley, pulled up beside

her, and stopped. She jumped in, and Roxy stepped on it, driving them quickly and calmly away.

Charlie glanced into the back, her entire body shaking. They'd folded down the back seats to make room. Five vampires lay still as death. Roland still with only one leg. And Killian, looking so beautiful she wanted to crawl back there and curl up beside him. And the way she felt, it might be the last chance she ever had. Pandora was crowded into a corner, but close enough to Rhiannon to keep her content. Olive roosted on the console in between her and Roxy.

Roxy kept sending worried looks her way. "Are you okay?"

The pounding of her heart got worse. Doubling over, hands pressing to her chest, gasping open mouthed breaths as her heart jackhammered her chest, she panted, "I don't think so, Gram. I really don't think so."

CHAPTER TWENTY-ONE

Killian came awake as if someone had fired a shot of adrenaline into him. He sat up with a ragged gasp and found himself on the deck of a fishing boat.

Charlie appeared above him, backed by the star-dotted sky, and everything inside him felt good just looking at her. She reached down for him. "We don't have much time." Her voice seemed off. It had a catch to it.

He clasped her hand and let her pull him up, noting they were no longer in the warehouse. They were on Devlin's fishing boat. Devlin and Larissa were already up. She stood by the rail, staring out at the sea as they sped over the waves. Devlin paced, rubbing his chin.

Rhiannon was up as well, sitting on the deck, Pandora beside her, as always, Roland's head rested on her lap as she stroked his hair, her cheeks wet with tears.

He still only had one leg.

"He didn't regenerate?" Killian whispered in alarm.

"No," Charlie said. "He hasn't been awake yet either. We

don't know what that means. Rhiannon's never seen a vampire with an amputated limb before. She doesn't know if that sort of thing heals during the day sleep, or over many days' sleep, or never." She lowered her gaze and her voice, "She doesn't even know for sure if he's going to wake at all."

"He'll wake!" Rhiannon said. But her tone of command was missing. She sounded unsure, almost broken.

"Of course he will, Rhiannon. We know that," Killian said quickly.

"Devlin and his band tried feeding him from their own veins," Rhiannon said softly. "It didn't work. Human blood might do the trick, if we had one around."

"I'd offer my own, if I wasn't afraid it would poison him," Charlie said.

Roxy shook her head. "He wouldn't want it from you when you heart's hammering like it is. Could kill you. I, on the other hand–"

"You're still recovering from a gunshot wound, a kidnapping, and a significant lack of nutrition," Rhiannon said. "Besides, I heard you tell Charlotte that DPI had injected you with something after stitching up your leg. For all we know it could be the same drug Charlotte's friend Mariah was given–the one that made her blood toxic, corrosive, probably deadly to us. We cannot risk it."

Killian tore his gaze away from Roland's sad looking, blackened stump, and met Charlie's eyes. "Your heart–"

"It's been racing for about forty-five minutes, now. Gram's had me doing deep breathing and meditation to try to slow it down. It hasn't exploded yet, so maybe it's working."

"She needs another shot of that Protectol," Roxy put in. "And she needs it soon."

"What the hell happened while we slept?" Killian put a hand on Charlie's shoulder, walking her to the nearest deck chair. He didn't have to urge her to sit. She was shaking. He felt it. Too much adrenaline coursing through her veins.

294 | MAGGIE SHAYNE

"They found us at the warehouse," she told him. "Christian's tattoo was some kind of tracking device." She leaned back in the seat, taking a deep nasal inhale and blowing it out slowly, before going on. "They took him. DPI was about to raid the warehouse, but we gave them the slip and made our way straight to Devlin's boat. Gram and I hauled you onboard and headed us out to sea."

"That's as much of an explanation as we've had so far," Devlin said, "I was just asking where the hell the rest of my group are. I've been unable to reach them mentally. They were supposed to meet us onboard at dusk."

"I know, I heard you tell them," Charlie said. "We're still within sight of shore, Devlin. Have been since dusk. They haven't shown." She reached for a pair of binoculars she had sitting nearby, but when she held them out to him, he waved them away. Preternatural eyesight was far beyond the capability of the spy glasses. "Maybe DPI found them, too," Roxy whispered.

"Then they're dead," Devlin whispered.

Killian lowered his head, and Larissa put a hand on Devlin's arm and whispered, "No."

"I found out–" Charlie stopped there, pressing a hand to her chest, and taking another of those long, deep breaths, then blowing it out slowly. "I can't." She looked to Roxy.

"Deep breaths. Deep and slow," Roxy said, crossing the deck to stand beside her, one hand stroking her hair off her forehead. "Lie still. Silence your mind. Focus only on your breaths."

She did, and nodded as if it was better, but Killian didn't think it was. "Tell them the rest," she whispered.

Roxy nodded. "Charlotte's former lieutenant told her that her mother is still alive. That they're holding her, and he let her talk to her on the phone to prove it. But our girl managed to spy the number he'd dialed on the phone's screen, and I was able to triangulate and get a location, about fifty miles southwest. Which means they're at sea. Since they threatened to kill Trish unless we walked away and let them take you all, we're in an understandable hurry to get there."

"Probably that same ship where they held us prisoner," Rhiannon said. "The *Anemone*."

"I don't think so, Rhiannon," Roxy went on. "We've checked the maps, and there's an island within the area where that cell phone is pinging. Ships tend to move. That phone hasn't."

Rhiannon took her gaze from Roland's, briefly. "We need to get back to the *Anemone* all the same. They have a child there."

"A child?" Charlie lifted her head. "Rhiannon, what *happened* on that ship?" She looked at Roxy, but she only shrugged.

Rhiannon returned her gaze to Roland's face. "I was placed into a sort of...arena-like room and this wild eyed little girl, more animal than human, attacked me." Shaking her head, moving her fingers over Roland's forehead, she said, "I thought it was a joke at first, but she was strong. As strong as you, Charlie. Perhaps stronger. And I couldn't fight back. She was one of The Chosen. But...different."

"They gave the BDX to a child?" Killian asked, dumbfounded.

"No. No, she was different from the Exers as well. Very different, but similar. I don't know how else to describe her. She felt like...a hybrid. A new kind of being." Then she closed her eyes slowly. "I will find that ship again and take that child out of there. She'll fight me every step of the way. But I will do it."

She fell back into chanting something mystical and foreign. A spell, maybe, or a prayer, over Roland, her hands constantly stroking, caressing him as she did.

Devlin said, "We were trying to catch up to the *Anemone*, certain it was the heart of this DPI operation, which I intended to wipe out of existence." He sent a glance at Rhiannon, at

296 | MAGGIE SHAYNE

Roland, a resentful one.

"But you stopped to pull us from the sea," Rhiannon said. "That says more about your character than you probably care to admit, Devlin."

Devlin turned his head and spat into the water. "I won't lift a finger to help a mortal. The Chosen, yes, because I have no choice, but I don't like it. I can't, however, let one of my own kind die if I can prevent it."

"It's a unique sense of honor," she said. "It surprises me to learn you have any at all."

"Go fuck yourself, Rhiannon."

She lifted her brows. "I'd kill you for that if I didn't owe you. Roland would be dead if not for your twisted moral compass."

"Roland is dead already, for all you know."

Rhiannon did no more than move her head and Pandora pinned her yellow gaze on Devlin, crouching deep and growling.

"Keep menacing me with that overgrown feline, and I'll throw it overboard. This is *my* ship. You're not in charge here."

"I'm in charge anywhere I happen to be, Devlin. And you have pushed me as far as is wise. My nerves are raw. My temper, frayed. One more nudge from you, and my fragile grip will break."

"I'm going to find that ship, lady. And no matter what you say, when I get there, I'm going to kill them all."

Rhiannon looked down at Roland and said, "You will *not* kill them all, Devlin. You will only kill the ones I don't kill first."

Charlie sat up a little. "You aren't going to kill any of them. Neither of you. We're going to the island, not the ship, and we're going to get my mother back. Alive."

"Your mother is none of my concern," Devlin said.

Charlie sprang off the chair and onto her feet in front of him so fast he almost stumbled backwards, and she grabbed him by his shirt. "You can't hurt me, fuck-face, because I'm one of The Chosen. But I can hurt you. Might do you some good to remember that." She let him go with a little shove.

Killian's eyes damn near popped their sockets, he was so surprised. She was fuming, and pissed, and he didn't doubt she meant every word she said.

Devlin turned and strode away, up to the bridge and the helm, away from all of them.

Rhiannon sent her a look of surprise and approval.

"You should stay still," Killian told her.

"I can't stay still. I've been injected with fucking speed, how am I supposed to stay still?"

"I need to talk to you."

Rhiannon was occupied with Roland. Roxy nudged Larissa with her elbow, and the two of them walked around the deck, toward the stern. "So talk," Charlie said.

Killian heaved a sigh. "I'm worried about your heart."

"It's *my* heart. Let me worry about it."

"If it starts to feel like it's going to—"

"It's not."

"Not yet. But if does—"

"If it does, then I'll die." She bit her lip and cast a glance skyward, like she was looking for help somewhere, but then she clenched her jaw and faced him again. "I won't let you risk your life for me, Killian. I couldn't live with it if you traded your life for mine. That's my decision. I'm not going to change my mind. I'm sorry."

At sunset, Lieutenant Lucas Townsend gathered the troops to the parade grounds at New Fort Rogers, also known as Location 2. Commandant Barnaby Crowe stood right beside him, his bulldog face unreadable.

"First, recruits, my apologies," LT said. He clasped his

hands behind his back as he spoke, but he wasn't making eye contact with any of them. He was looking at the horizon beyond them. It made Christian want to turn around and see what the hell he was looking at, but of course, he couldn't do that.

"What happened at Fort Rogers shouldn't have happened. No recruit should have died the way your colleagues, my men and women, died back there. It's unacceptable." His eyes seemed to well a little. He blinked the moisture away, glanced at Crowe, who nodded once, firmly. LT pulled a folded scrap of paper from his pocket and read from it in a voice that was strangely robotic.

"We now have an antidote to the BDX. It will reverse all of its side effects, and restore you to the way you were before the treatment. You'll lose your enhanced strength and endurance, but your life expectancy will return to that of any other BD. The Exer Program has been terminated." He crumbled the paper in his fist, and looked at them slowly, eyes lingering on every one of them for a second. "It's been an honor to serve with you. You're good people."

People muttered, but Commandant Crowe held up his hands. "Save your questions for later, recruits. We're eager to get this antidote into your systems before any more of you die the way your comrades did at Fort Rogers. Report to the Infirmary immediately."

Everyone started heading for the infirmary, and Christian didn't have a choice but to follow along. As they passed by the tent where Charlie's mother was being held, Christian tried to catch a glimpse of her again, but it was too dark inside. He was racking his brain to figure out a way to get word to Charlie. He knew she and Killian and the others had got away. Someone had heard LT trying to explain that to the commandant, and word had spread through the new camp like wildfire. Christian was glad. He wished he was still with them, but he had to pretend otherwise, bide his time here until he could figure a way to get off the island.

Everyone was gathered in front of the medical tent, and he could see inside. The place was lit, but dimly, and the flaps were tied back. Beds were lined up in rows and rows, as many as they could fit in there. Dr. Mariner and a handful of nurses were taking the Exers from the front of the crowd to the furthest beds, having them strip down to their skivvies and lie down. Arms were swabbed, IV lines inserted.

Christian was uncomfortable in more ways than one. His shoulder hurt like hell, because as soon as he'd been alone long enough here on the island, he'd taken a sharp blade and cut away the tattoo LT had used to track him down. There was a white bandage over the spot now. He figured he'd be in deep trouble for that when LT saw what he'd done, but no one had said a word about it. And that made him even more nervous. On top of that, he wasn't too happy about the notion of letting them inject him with yet another untested mystery drug. But he didn't know how the hell he was going to get out of it, either. LT stood on one side of the crowd of Exers, the commandant on the other. Christian was near the back, but things were moving pretty rapidly. There were only a few dozen of them left, after all.

Rhiannon gently lowered Roland's head from her lap, got to her feet, and walked over to Charlie, taking the deck chair beside her.

"Any improvement?" Charlie asked.

"Not yet." She stared back at Roland.

Pandora had stretched out beside him, close enough to touch. Every now and then she would turn and give his face a lick, rocking his head to the side as she did. Trying to wake him, Charlie thought. It was sweet.

"Would you like to know how Killian would feel if you

died?" Rhiannon asked her suddenly.

Surprised by the question, Charlie looked at her. "I already told you what happened when he tried to turn Mariah. It burned him, Rhiannon. Like acid, he said. I can't risk that my blood will do the same to him. No more than you were willing to risk that Roxy's might poison your Roland." She shook her head. "Besides, it's my life. My decision."

"It is. But still, you should know. Here, let me show you."

Rhiannon pressed her palms to either side of Charlie's head and stared into her eyes. "Feel what I'm feeling right now, young mortal. At least make an...informed decision."

It started to wash over her then, a grief that only a being thousands of years old could feel. It was the darkest despair, and that was only the edge of it. She couldn't bear to feel more, but she sensed there was a black hole of it swirling inside the ancient vampiress. It welled up in Charlie's chest, tightened her throat too much to let her so much as swallow, and filled her eyes with tears. Her entire soul seemed to go black with the most hopeless feeling conceivable. Complete devastation. Utter loss. Endless, crippling grief.

With a strangled sob, Charlie pulled her head away.

"He loves you," Rhiannon told her. "And you love him, you little idiot. Love like that is worth any risk. Anything. It's worth anything. You have to try. Believe me, he'd rather die trying than to live on without you." She looked back at where Roland lay on the deck. "And if he does die trying, the option to join him will always still be there."

Charlie was stunned into silence. First, by the sheer power of the pain Rhiannon was in. And then too, she was stunned by what she'd said, which made Charlie think the ancient vampire queen was considering a morning walk herself, should her beloved not return to her. A walk straight into the sunrise.

God she hoped Roland survived. No one deserved the kind of pain she had just now glimpsed. No one.

"Oh my God," Charlie whispered. She pressed both hands

to her chest, then poked around her neck in search of her pulse. "It's normal. My heartbeat has gone back to normal."

"I thought it might," Rhiannon said, and she resumed her former position, pulling Roland's head into her lap. "The heart can only focus on so much at one time. I gave it more than any heart should be expected to bear. It couldn't sustain the episode, too." And then she went back to stroking Roland's head and chanting.

Charlie was exhausted. She had to be, after having her heart pound at such a powerful rate for more than two hours. Killian wished he could convince her to sleep, but he didn't see it happening. She was at the bow, staring out over the water in search of the island, her hair blowing behind her. A sea goddess on her way to exact vengeance upon those who had wronged her.

"They'll know we're coming," Killian said. "Even Rhiannon's *glamourie* can't hide us from sonar." He was standing on the elevated bridge beside Devlin at the helm. And he couldn't take his eyes off Charlie.

"If so, they know it already. We're only a couple of miles out." Devlin pointed. "Keep watch. The island should come into view soon."

Killian saw easily through the night, but even then, it was tough to tell the ocean from the night sky—there was no separation. And then, just gradually, there was. The shape of the island rose in the distance, darker than the rest. "I see it!" he said, pointing.

Devlin adjusted the motors. They quieted substantially, and the boat slowed.

"It feels abandoned. Doesn't it?" Killian asked.

Devlin nodded. "There's something...it's weak."

He guided the boat nearer. Rhiannon had carried Roland

below decks and had remained down there with him. Pandora was down there as well, and so was poor Olive, shut up in the galley where she couldn't panic and fly out over the ocean. Killian was afraid to give voice to his thoughts...that if a vampire didn't wake by night, he was probably dead. He supposed Rhiannon wouldn't be able to remain in denial once his body showed signs of beginning to...decompose. But maybe it was better not to bring it up until then. Or at least until after they did what needed doing here tonight. Rescuing Charlie's mother.

After that, Rhiannon had her own ideas about what came next, and so did Devlin. But all Killian wanted was to take Charlie, her mother, her grandmother and her owl, and get them the hell out of here, to someplace safe.

As if thinking of her summoned her, Rhiannon came up from below and joined the three women who'd gathered at the bow. Roxy and Larissa stood on either side of Charlie, and had spotted the island as well. Killian jogged down the steps from the bridge and went to them, watching as the island took form from the darkness, tall and broad and craggy. It was bigger than it had looked from far away, but the feeling it emitted was one of emptiness. Almost...lifelessness.

No birds called. No insects or reptiles buzzed or chirped. Devlin killed the motor, and the only sound was the water slapping against the hull as momentum carried them nearer an empty dock. There was only one other boat in sight, a small speedboat.

Killian hurried to the starboard side, and grabbing one of the tie lines, jumped over the rail to land on the dock. He tied it off and caught a second line thrown his way by Charlie. She had a determined, stubborn look about her. Not scared. What was there to be afraid of? She'd already lost her mother once. And she'd apparently made up her mind to accept her own death. Not that he intended to put up with that.

As soon as the ropes were tied, the others joined him on

the dock, with the exception of Roxy, who stood near the rail, and Larissa, who was piloting the boat back out to sea. Roxy was neither a BD-Exer, nor a vampire. Her place was on the boat, standing guard over Roland. She had two rifles with two 30-round clips for each of them. 120 shots. And as an added precaution, they were leaving one vampiress behind to help her. Larissa. They would take the boat out away from shore and wait for their signal to bring it back.

"No welcoming party," Charlie whispered. "I'm beginning to wonder if there's anyone here."

"Someone's here," Rhiannon whispered.

They walked inland from the dock, and it was easy to see the well-worn trail that led to the camp. Three hundred yards later, a village of army green tents. A flagpole with no flag. A backpack on the ground. A feeling of death hung heavy over the island, and more weakly, a sense of waning life, and the summons of one of The Chosen who was dying.

"That one," Killian whispered, pointing at the big tent with the red cross marking it as the infirmary. "Someone's alive in there, but in trouble."

"Check it out," Devlin said. "The rest of us will fan out, look for any other signs of life."

Killian took Charlie's hand as she started to move away from him. "Not you," he said. "I need you with me."

"I need you right back," she told him.

Rhiannon and Devlin had split off in separate directions. Killian and Charlie approached the medical tent. He opened the flap and felt the cold, heavy energy of death hit him squarely in the chest. He could see perfectly in the darkness, but knew she probably couldn't. And it was for the best. Rows of beds stretched from the front of the tent to the rear of it, every single one of them with a dead person in it.

"Oh my God," she whispered. "They're recruits. Exers. All of them. My God."

And he realized she could see after all. She could see the

bodies of every young, twenty-something man and woman in the place, all of them freshly dead. Each with an empty IV bag attached by a piece of tubing. They walked slowly among the beds, and Charlie was whispering names. Tom and Kendra and Nikos.

Something crashed to the floor, and Charlie jumped out of her skin and right into Killian's side, where his arm went around her automatically.

"Help...." The tortured whisper came from down low.

A man dragged himself across the floor toward them.

"Christian!" Charlie ran to him, kneeling. "Christian, what the hell happened here?"

The big man looked up. His arm was bleeding, and Killian realized he'd torn out the IV that must've been there. "I got it out in time. I think...it was in time."

"In time for what?"

"They said...it was an antidote." He gasped a few shallow breaths. "To the BDX. They said...we'd go back to normal. But I didn't believe them. So as soon as they left the tent, I yanked my line. Maybe too late, though."

"Christian, what happened to everyone else in here?" Killian asked.

"They just started...dying. They thought I was dead, too. They didn't know I could hear them, outside."

"Hear who?" Charlie demanded. "What did you hear, Christian?

"The commandant. He told LT...we'd served our purpose. Said it was kinder this way. Something about...focusing on the offspring now."

"The offspring?"

He nodded, gripped Charlie's arm. "They're killing us. They're killing us all. We have to–"

"They're already dead," Charlie whispered. "I'm sorry. We checked every bed."

"Come on, let's get you out of here." Killian put his arms

under Christian's and tried to help him to his feet. He noticed the white patch on his shoulder, realized what he must have done to get rid of that tattoo, and shivered.

"Your mother was here, Charlie," Christian said, his voice weak and choked by grief as he struggled to stand. "She was alive."

"Where?"

"I'll show you. Just...don't leave me."

"We're not gonna leave you," Charlie promised. "You're our friend, Christian."

Killian walked Christian to the door, and Charlie came along too, but slower, looking at the beds, at the people in them. Dead, all of them, and he could see it was getting to her.

He put his free hand on her shoulder while keeping the other firmly around Christian. "They're at peace, Charlie. Let them go."

She turned and mashed her face into his chest, crying audibly. And he held her, one-armed, kissed her hair. "I'm sorry, baby. I'm so sorry."

She sniffed, finally pulled it together, glancing toward a walled off section of the infirmary. "Be right back." Stepping away from him, she hurried into that section. When she came out again she had a rucksack over her shoulder.

"Where was my mother?" she asked Christian as they stepped out of that place of death and into the night. It was heavy, the death energy. Like a cold wet blanket weighing down the very air, and weighing Killian down with it.

Weakly, Christian lifted a hand and pointed at a smaller tent some fifty yards away. Killian moved quickly. He didn't know where Rhiannon and Devlin were, and he didn't like this. They were walking around in plain sight. And there was still someone alive on this island.

Please, let it be her mother. Let her be okay.

When they got a little closer, Killian felt the presence more keenly, but it wasn't what he expected. "Charlie, does your mother have the Belladonna Antigen like you do?"

"No. Why?"

"Because whoever's inside that tent does." He helped Christian sit down in front of a tree. "Just rest a minute, okay? I'll come right back for you."

He nodded, looking as if he couldn't move if he wanted to.

Killian and Charlie continued toward the tent. He didn't have a gun and wished to hell he did. When they got to the front of it, he reached for the flap, pulling it back the tiniest bit, so they could peer inside.

That bastardly lieutenant sat in a chair in front of a desk, with a handgun, its barrel pressed to his own temple.

Charlie flew at him like she'd been shot from a cannon, taking the gun and knocking him and his chair over, landing on top of him. She reached back, gun in hand. "Take this."

Killian took it.

Charlie got up, lifting the man by the front of his shirt. "What the hell is this, LT? You gonna kill yourself over all those kids who died? It took you this long to figure out what a fucking blind idiot you were, and you can't take it?"

He lowered his head, shaking it slowly. "I swear to God, I didn't know."

"You knew they were making super fighters out of BDs."

He nodded, closing his eyes in abject misery.

"And you knew the side effects would kill us sooner instead of making us live longer," she said.

"Not at first. Not until it started happening. Then we developed the Protectol, and they were working on an antidote."

"Working on an antidote?" She asked softly. "Then you lied when you said there was one."

He couldn't look her in the eyes. He just nodded. "I didn't know what was really going on, Charlie. I didn't know they'd just...just kill them all once they had what they wanted from them. Not until it was too late."

"And what, exactly, did they want from them?" Kilian asked.

"Fuck that. Where's my mother?" Charlie demanded.

LT looked up at her, making eye contact for the first time. His were bloodshot and red-rimmed. His despondence was not false, Killian thought. It was real. He wanted to die. He almost felt sorry for the man, but Charlie didn't seem to have a bit of pity for him.

"They took her with them. They want you alive, Charlie. They want your DNA. Because of your grandmother."

"Took her with them where?"

"The ship."

"The *Anemone*?"

He nodded at her, not even registering a hint of surprise that she knew its name.

"Come with me. Now."

He shook his head. "I'm not going anywhere. I'm not leaving this island. I'm dying with my recruits."

"No you're not, Lucas." She reached out and snatched the gun from Killian, worked the action, aimed it at him. "You're coming with me. You're going to help me get my mother back and put a stop to whatever these mad scientists you're working for are up to. Do you understand? You're doing that right now. Tonight. And if you still want to die when we're finished, then I'll fucking help you. You got me?"

He just shook his head. "What are you gonna do, shoot me? That's what I want."

"Is it?" She lowered the barrel to his groin. "Cause I will shoot you, Lucas, but I'll make *damn* sure I don't kill you. Get. The Fuck. *Up.*"

He got up. She put a hand on his shoulder and shoved him out of the tent. When they got to the tree where they'd left Christian, she made Lucas pick him up and carry him, leaving Killian free to fight, if necessary.

"Call out mentally to Rhiannon and Devlin," she said,

glancing over at Killian as they headed back along the path to the shore. "Have them meet us at the boat, and I'll signal Roxy."

She was amazing. She was evolving right before his eyes. Taking charge. Becoming a leader. Feeling empowered.

He did as she asked while she continued talking to Townsend.

"Do you know where that ship is heading?"

"Out to sea," he said. "There's no real destination, they just keep moving. They know there are vampires onto them, hunting for them. They're just trying to stay one step ahead."

"And why did they leave you behind?"

He lowered his head. "To wait for you, so I could bring you to them. They knew you'd come after your mother."

"And they also knew I would have my friends with me. What were you supposed to do about that?" She asked again. They were on the dock now, and the fishing boat was chugging back toward them at full power. "Why didn't they just stay and kill them, themselves?"

"The only ones left were the commandant and his staff. They don't do battle. They give orders."

"But they expected you to take on five vampires all by yourself?"

He shook his head slowly. "I'm supposed to call them as soon as you're all here. Once I do, I have three minutes to get you into the last boat and get us clear before the missile strikes wipe this island out of existence, and the vampires with it."

"And conveniently incinerate all those bodies," Killian said softly.

"And then what do you do?" Charlie asked.

"I bring you to them," Townsend said.

"Well then that's exactly what's going to happen." Charlie untied the speedboat and held its rope.

The fishing boat slowed as it approached the dock. Rhiannon and Devlin came off the path from the camp, in time to see Charlie take Christian from the lieutenant and hand him into Killian's arms. Then she grabbed LT by his collar, and flung him up and over the rail. He landed sprawling on the deck. She jumped onboard behind him, tied the speedboat's tow-line to the stern, then went to stand over him, staring down. "As soon as we're far enough away from this island, you make that call, Lieutenant. Tell them you have me, and we're on our way."

Rhiannon watched as Killian carried Christian, unconscious now, up the gangplank Larissa and Roxy had quickly extended. "My goodness," she said softly. "The more I see of this girl, the better I like her." She walked up the gangplank behind Killian, and Devlin came behind her.

"Devlin, pull up the plank behind you," Charlie said. "I tied that little speedboat to the stern. We'll tow it when we leave here. Rhiannon, take this." She pulled the bag off her shoulder.

Frowning, Rhiannon looked inside.

"Human blood. For Roland. I took all they had in the infirmary."

Rhiannon's brows rose and she blinked as if stunned by Charlie's actions. Then she turned and hurried below decks to where Roland was.

CHAPTER TWENTY-TWO

The little island exploded behind them, as drone planes bombed it into oblivion. Charlie hadn't even looked back, Killian noted. She'd stood in the bow looking straight ahead, and she stood there still, an hour later.

Killian couldn't take his eyes off her, watching the wind in her hair, the straightness of her spine, the new power and strength he sensed in her. She'd changed since he'd first met her. But the change only made him love her all the more.

Devlin was at the helm, guiding them toward the *Anemone*. He'd made Lieutenant Townsend put his cell on speaker so they could all listen as he'd made his call to Commandant Crowe to say that he had Charlie and was on his way. The commandant gave the coordinates, and Devlin had taken the helm from Roxy to set their new course.

Rhiannon was below, trying to get some of that human blood into Roland. Lieutenant Townsend was sitting near the stern, silent and pensive. They hadn't bothered tying him up. He wouldn't try anything, partly because he wouldn't stand a chance against them, and partly because he was so filled with self-loathing and regret. He'd be more likely to hurt himself than any of them. But Larissa was staying close, watching over him. Despite what he'd done, he was still one of The Chosen.

"It was smart thinking, grabbing that blood for Roland," Killian said, because he needed to say something. He moved up to stand beside Charlie, looking out over the nighttime sea with her.

"It was selfish. We need all the help we can get to save my mother. Besides, I thought I might find some Protectol for Christian and me in there."

"Did you?"

She pulled a capped syringe from her pocket. "One dose. We'll have to split it. I hope it's enough to keep my heart inside my chest when we attack the *Anemone*."

"And what about after that?" he asked.

She drew a deep breath. "I can't think about anything beyond getting my mother out of there alive, Killian. I just can't."

He sighed. It was a deep, heavy sound. "I want you to live, you know."

Meeting his eyes, she held them, and he tried his best to read her emotions, her thoughts, and wasn't sure he still could. There was too much going on in his own head, too much he wanted to see in her eyes, clouding his perceptions. She said, "I want to live, too."

He lowered his head, trying to come up with an argument he could win, but she kept on talking. "I've been horrible to you, Killian. I judged you because of what you are. And I regret that. If I'd trusted you, none of this would've happened."

"How could you? I wasn't honest with you."

"Still—"

"And if none of this had happened, Charlie, then all the shit the government was trying to pull, whatever they're up to now, it would've just gone unchecked."

She nodded. "I guess that's true."

"I'm in love with you," he told her. "And it's not because you're one of The Chosen, and it's not because of the bond that sharing blood caused in us. I'd love you even without all that. I know you as well as I know myself. It's like our souls were entwined before we even met. I just...I want you to know that, before we face this battle. Just in case...." He paused, took a breath. "Just in case."

She lowered her head and her eyes. "I didn't want that to happen."

"Didn't want me to love you?"

She nodded. He cupped her chin and lifted her head, and he saw tears welling and then spilling over.

"It's heartbreak for you, Killian." Tears made her voice low and tight. "I'm going to die. Soon. And it'll hurt you so much when I do."

He nodded. "I haven't given up on you, so you shouldn't either. And I don't want to think about that right now anyway. You're right, we need to focus on the fight we're facing right now. We'll figure the rest out after. But until we do, I just want to be with you, to relish every second that I have you in my life, to love you with everything in me. I'll worry about hurting later on, if and when I have reason to."

"I love you, too, you know," she whispered. She let herself drift closer to him, let her eyes fall closed. "And it's not because you're my vampire guardian. And it's not because you fed me back to life from your own veins. I'd have loved you even if we were two ordinary people. I'd have loved you the first time I looked into your eyes. Because I'd have seen your soul, Killian, and I'd have known that it's the other half of mine."

He kissed her, tasted her tears, felt her love for him, unreserved and endlessly deep. There was nowhere for them to be alone, to make sweet love the way they had before. No privacy on this tiny boat. And yet, the kiss held all of that inside it, and for right then, it was enough.

"Ten minutes," Devlin called.

Killian lowered his forehead to hers. "We'd better tell the others."

Charlie walked below decks, trying to distract her heart from breaking by thinking of the things she and Killian would do together after this was over. It would be just the two of them, alone, making love and basking in each other, finding joy wherever they could, for as long as they could. He came with her, naturally. He didn't seem to want to be too far away from her, even for a moment. And that was fine with Charlie.

Rhiannon turned as they came down the steps, beaming a full throttle smile their way. "It worked," she said, and then she stepped aside, so they could see Roland. He lay on his back on the table that was his makeshift bed, eyes open only slightly, but enough so Charlie could see the life in him. His lips were stained crimson and one bag of the four she had brought, lay empty.

A blanket was over him, but Charlie could see the shape beneath it. He still had only one leg. His right thigh stopped above the knee. Nothing seemed to be growing back yet.

"The burn is healing," Rhiannon said, tugging the covers aside to show them the healthy pink skin that had grown over the end of the stump, where before it had been blackened. "That's progress."

"Has he spoken?" Killian asked.

She nodded. "He said my name." Her smile wavered, but she forced it back into place. "Only once, but he said it."

"It's incredible" Charlie said. "And he drank."

"Drop by drop, but yes, he drank." Rhiannon let her smile fade and looked directly into Charlie's eyes. "I owe you a debt I shall never be able to repay, Charlotte O'Malley. You have my protection, now and always, for as long as you live."

"You'd have thought to look for blood in the infirmary if I hadn't," Charlie said.

"What would have or might have happened isn't the point. What *did* happen is the point. And what *did* happen is that you saved my Roland for me." She narrowed her eyes. "I think your grandmother and those DPI bastards must be right about you, Charlotte. There is something very worthy, very special, about you."

Charlie felt her chest swell when Rhiannon said that. But she swallowed any reply. She wasn't sure there was a right thing to say.

"Devlin says we'll reach the *Anemone* in ten minutes," Killian said, as he squeezed Charlie's shoulder from behind.

Rhiannon nodded. "And when we do? What is the plan then, Charlotte?"

Blinking, Charlie looked up at her. "You're asking me?" And she looked at Killian for help.

He shrugged. "It's your mother. This is your operation, Charlie. You seem to be the team leader here, and you've been doing just fine so far."

"Some team leader. I've been wrong about everything."

Rhiannon shook her head. "But brave about everything. And strong, and determined, and smart. If I believe you can do this Charlie, trust me, you can. I am never wrong."

"You...are sometimes....wrong," Roland whispered. And as they all turned to stare at him in surprise, he smiled very slightly. "But not, I think...about this."

Rhiannon's hands pressed to her face as tears streamed. "My love, my love, you're coming back to us."

"I am. Is there, by chance...any more of that lovely O-negative to be found?"

Charlie shot a look at Killian to see him smiling as broadly as she was, while Rhiannon helped Roland sit up and handed him another pint.

"Before he drank, he said, "I wish I could be more help. In

my current state, I fear I'm not much use."

Killian closed a hand on Roland's shoulder. "I can make you such an amazing prosthetic leg that you won't even miss the one you lost, Roland. It'll be better than the original."

Roland's brows lifted. "How?"

Killian shrugged. "It's what I do. Used to do, anyway."

Roland nodded. "Then I accept. Providing, of course, it doesn't regenerate on its own." Then he looked at Charlie. "Go on, go make your plan. I believe in you."

Charlie could've cried. How had she ever thought these beautiful beings were monsters? She must've been so blind.

"Charlie?" Killian prodded.

"Okay, okay. Roxy must be in the galley with Christian and Olive. Will you get her and then meet me on deck, Killian? We'll figure this out together." She left the room, ran up onto the deck, and then up onto the bridge. "Cut the engines, Devlin."

He did so, then sat looking at her expectantly as Roxy, Killian and Rhiannon gathered. Larissa came to join them when she saw the huddle, tugging LT along beside her, her small hand gripping his forearm. They all gathered around, looking to Charlie to lead. To decide. It was almost too much pressure.

Roxy moved closer, put her hand on Charlie's arm. "This is what you were born for, Charlotte. This is the moment when you live out your destiny. Trust in that."

Rhiannon was nodding. "It's why your grandmother lived so long. Her genes are special so that yours would be special. It's why they treated you with this BDX nonsense in a different way than any of the others, and why it worked more strongly on you than it did on them—so that you would become the strongest of anyone they have ever given it to. All of that has lead you to this moment. You are important. And every bit as special as DPI believes you are."

The weight on her shoulders grew heavier. Killian was

standing beside her, and he closed his hand around hers. "You're the only living descendant of the oldest living Chosen. You're one of only two surviving Exers, stronger than any of the others ever were. You hear the thoughts of vampires, even though you shouldn't be able to. And vampiric blood runs in your veins. My blood. You're different, Charlie. It's true."

Drawing a deep breath, she looked at each of them. Devlin nodded. "When they took Roxy captive, when they took Roland and Rhiannon captive, they took them aboard that ship. The *Anemone*. It's logical to think my people are there as well," he said.

"How many?" Charlie asked.

"Fifteen, when I left them." He lowered his eyes. "I just don't know why I'm not sensing them. We're so close, I should—"

"DPI has technology that can block telepathic signals," Rhiannon said. "It wouldn't be the first time they used it in construction. We've encountered it before."

Charlie nodded slowly, then went on. "What do we have for weapons?"

Devlin said, "Plenty of weapons, but we're low on ammo. We also have a pair of harpoon launchers and some flare guns."

"Okay." Charlie had ideas pouring into her mind and took a leap of faith, just spouting them as they came to her and hoping they were right, that she was somehow intended for this task. "LT, you're going to take me to the *Anemone* on the little speedboat. Bring me to them just like you promised you would. Killian, Devlin, you'll have to swim to the ship, otherwise they'll see this boat and blow it out of the water. Bring the harpoon guns. You can use them like grappling hooks to get onboard."

"What about sharks?" Rhiannon asked, wide eyed.

"It's rare for a shark to attack like that," Roxy said. "Roland had gunshot wounds, he was bleeding. That's what drew it."

She didn't look reassured and stroked Pandora nervously. The poor cat looked miserable. Charlie figured she was seasick as hell. But she was still better off than Olive, shut up in the galley below decks.

"Larissa, Rhiannon, Roxy, you'll have to stay behind to care for Roland and Christian, and to protect them in case you're discovered. Also, so that we have someone to rescue us if we all end up in the water again. As soon as Killian and Devlin leave the boat, you should head a few more miles away, just to be safe. All right?"

Everyone nodded except Killian. Charlie knew he wasn't comfortable with her going off with LT on her own. "Rhiannon, can't you cloak the fishing boat with some of your magic?" he asked.

"The boat, of course. The living beings aboard? Not so easily. There are too many and I'd have to maintain it for too long," Rhiannon replied.

Killian looked like he wanted to argue, but gave up. He trusted her, Charlie realized. They all did.

She hoped to God she could live up to that trust.

It was time. LT was in the little speedboat, waiting for her. Charlie stood on the deck of the fishing boat, face to face with Killian. Leaving him behind was one of the hardest things she had ever done, or, she thought, ever would.

He held both her hands, staring deeply into her eyes. "This isn't goodbye. I'll be right behind you."

"I know."

"Stay alive, okay? Wait for me," he said.

She nodded hard, trying to smile through her tears. "I'll do my best."

"I love you, baby."

"I love you back." She tipped her head up for his kiss. He

318 | MAGGIE SHAYNE

wrapped her up in his arms and kissed her deeply, tenderly, and for a long, long time. When they parted, there were tears in his eyes.

She pressed her palm to his face, then turned and jumped over the side, landing in the little speed boat. As soon as she did, LT undid the tow line, and put the smaller boat into motion.

Charlie kept the little fishing boat in sight for as long as she could while LT piloted them toward the *Anemone*. For a few precious seconds she could still see them. Roland, sitting up on a deck chair now, having polished off all the human blood they'd had, waving her off as its regenerative power coursed through his body. He was regaining his strength quickly. Rhiannon was close beside him, her watchful eyes scanning the waves. Devlin, holding one of the harpoon guns, was near the rail, watchful and tense. And Killian stood away from the others, cradling his harpoon gun, holding her eyes with his even after she could no longer see him.

Be safe, he told her softly. *When you give us the word, I'll be there. As fast as the ocean can carry me, I'll be there.*

I know you will. And she did. Not even a dozen sharks, not a thousand armed men, would keep him from her. How had she ever doubted him?

"It's necessary," LT said. "They'll be searching the water. Even now, it's going to be almost impossible for them to board the *Anemone* without being seen."

"Don't worry about it. We'll distract them."

He held her eyes for a second. His were dull, almost lifeless. She didn't think he cared whether he lived or died, and that meant he didn't care whether anyone else did, either. He'd damned himself. He didn't see any hope of redemption. He just wanted to be done.

"Turn around," he said, letting go of the helm and picking up a length of rope. "I have to tie you up, make it look real."

She didn't like it, didn't trust him, but she turned around, put her hands behind her back. The speedboat had slowed way down, was still moving through the waves, but slowly. He tied her hands behind her back, taking his time about it. When he finished, she gave a tug to test them. Nice and tight. Very convincing.

"There's a loose end near your hands," he said. "If you take hold of it and pull, the knot will come loose."

"Nice," she said. "Good thinking."

He resumed steering the boat, and it picked up speed again. She looked back, but the little fishing boat was out of sight, now, swallowed by the darkness of sea and sky that melded into one far behind them. She sat still, because with her hands behind her, she was likely to fall if she didn't.

"What did they really want with us, Lucas?" she asked.

He looked at her as if she should already know the answer. "A bunch of super humans, brainwashed to think the vampires were their enemies, eager and able to kill on command." It sounded like a rehearsed line to her.

"Yeah, that's what they admit to. To us, anyway. But once they realized that our life spans would be severely shortened, that going into battle could cause our hearts to explode in our chests...they still kept making more of us. Why?"

He looked at her. She thought he'd deny it, but it wouldn't have done any good.

"Christian overheard the commandant say something about focusing on the *offspring* now. What did that mean?"

"I don't know."

"But you have an idea."

He shrugged, kept his gaze focused on the horizon, then pointed. "There it is."

She looked, saw the huge hulking shape of a large ship emerging from the darkness up ahead. It was running dark. No light emerged from it. "I don't care. Tell me, or I'll tell Commandant Crowe you helped me."

He swallowed hard, took a breath. "I really don't know,

Charlie. I only know that Dr. Mariner had orders to take samples from every Exer after the third treatment. Ova from the women. Sperm from the men. The women's rations were spiked with fertility drugs to ensure an abundant supply." He couldn't even look her in the eye when he said it, and Charlie was too shocked and horrified to reply.

A spotlight came on from the ship, sweeping across the waters and nearly blinding her when it stopped.

LT raised a hand and waved.

The light stayed on them, and she heard the buzzing of motors drawing nearer. Soon a couple of small, fast boats pulled up alongside. Someone, a male voice, shouted, "Kill your engine and throw out a line."

LT obeyed, shutting off the engine. He tossed a rope over to the closest of the boats.

"You chose the wrong side, Lucas," she said softly. She could see the remorse in him, and she could feel it. "You made mistakes, serious ones, but you can make up for them."

"Not in a hundred years," he said. And he looked her in the eyes. "For what it's worth, I'm sorry."

"Don't be sorry. Be right. This time, LT, be right."

He frowned a little, but then soldiers were hauling the boat right up close to theirs. "Untie her and get her aboard," one of them said.

Nodding, LT untied her, taking longer than he actually needed. Then he nodded, and she climbed a short rope ladder up onto the larger boat and got herself over the rail. He came up behind her. A man in unmarked olive drab sat in the rear, manning an outboard motor, and heading them back toward the *Anemone*. The other boat had sped around, shining its spotlight on the waters. It was a damn good thing they'd left the others far behind in the fishing boat.

LT started to tie her hands again, but one of the other guys yanked the rope away from him. "I'll do that."

Hell. This wasn't good. The man tied her wrists so tightly

it hurt, and within minutes, her hands were tingling from lack of circulation.

"It's too tight," she said.

The DPI thug faced her again, pulled something from his pocket, a roll of duct tape, ripped off a piece with his teeth, and smacked it over her mouth. It didn't matter. They were at the *Anemone* within a minute or so, and the smaller boat was piloted right into a waiting sling, then the boat was slowly lifted up and up. It was so high, Charlie wasn't sure whether Killian and Devlin would be able to get onboard.

As soon as the smaller boat was lowered into its rightful place aboard the *Anemone*, the men piled out, the mean one taking her arm. She could kick their asses without breaking a sweat, she thought. But instead, she looked around. There were other boats, like the one she'd just been in. They were mounted above the water in those mechanical slings all the way around the entire ship.

A big man with sagging jowls stood on deck, waiting. Charlie remembered the first time she'd seen him on TV in her mom's apartment a hundred years ago. Commandant Crowe.

"Well done, Lieutenant Townsend. Welcome aboard, recruit." He said to Charlie. "You'll be happy to know I've decided not to court martial you for desertion." He nodded at the man nearest her, who reached out to rip the duct tape off her mouth so she could reply.

It felt like he'd ripped part of a lip off with it, and she licked them to be sure they were intact. Then she met the bastardly commandant's eyes. "So you court martial deserters? And loyal recruits only get murdered. Weird policies you have." She didn't give him the satisfaction of holding his gaze, and instead continued her inspection of the ship. It was large, but not ocean liner large. Not battleship large. More like a cargo ship. She counted every man she saw, even knowing it wasn't going to tell her much. There would be more on the other decks, below.

I'm onboard the Anemone, she told Killian, praying he could hear her. She was on an upper deck, in the open, sea wind whipping her hair. She presumed whatever technology was in place to block telepathy could only be maintained in enclosed places. *There are six men walking around the deck, armed, watching the water. Two on each side, one bow, one stern. You should head this way now.*

Got you. Be safe.

She sighed, relieved to hear his reply inside her head. Then she was led down several levels of stairs, a man on each side of her, holding her arms, Commandant Crowe leading the way, LT following behind them. She was taken into a room that looked like a doctor's office. Sheet draped table, instruments. One step inside, she stopped and her blood chilled in her veins.

"You remember Doctor Mariner," The commandant said.

Her eyes shifted to the doctor she remembered so well from Fort Rogers. She didn't think she'd known his name until LT had said it on the way here. Jesus, what were they going to do to her?

"Commandant," LT said, "all due respect, sir—"

"If you don't have the stomach for this, get below." The old man nodded at his cohorts. "Strap her down for Dr. Mariner. You, Smith, show the lieutenant to his quarters."

Two men grabbed her, one at each arm. She tensed, ready to bust them up, but the doctor caught her eye, held up a familiar looking tranquilizer gun.

She couldn't allow herself to be sedated. Bonds, she could fight. But not drugs. She'd just have to bide her time. So she stopped fighting.

They shoved her toward the table with the straps on the sides and at the feet. The commandant closed the door. LT's horrified expression was the last thing she saw as he was led away. They pushed her onto the table, forced her to lie down, because she resisted just enough to make it look good. Then they untied her hands, and quickly strapped her arms down while Commander Crowe stood at her feet.

"This is mainly a research vessel, Recruit O'Malley. And you are going to be a very valuable specimen. We need to know what makes you special," he said. "We need to know why the BDX was so much more potent in you than in any of the others, and why your grandmother has lived so long, seemingly escaping the side effects of having the antigen. The early weakening and premature death. And of course, we need to harvest some samples "Your lieutenant didn't allow Dr. Mariner to do so before. He said things got too crazy due to your...unusual reaction to the treatment. But I'm beginning to suspect he has a soft spot where you're concerned."

No fucking way are you taking eggs from my ovaries, you sick bastard, she thought.

"Now I want you to make sure not to get upset or to struggle, dear. I know you've seen what happens when you do. Your heart could explode, and we'd be left with just a corpse to work on. And really, while we could make due, we prefer a live subject."

She let them strap her arms, her legs. She had no choice, she was outnumbered four to one, and they had the tranquilizer ready to use if necessary.

God, she prayed, *let Killian get here before they do this. Let him get here.*

CHAPTER TWENTY-THREE

Killian was relieved when it was finally time for them to move. Rhiannon insisted on coming with them, despite her fear of another shark attack. She owed Charlie, she kept saying. And besides, there was a girl on that ship, an innocent, monster child that needed rescuing.

Roland was supportive of her decision, even encouraging of it, and insisted he would be fine now, that the blood he'd imbibed was restoring him more with every passing minute. And yet he was frustrated, wondering what good he was to anyone right then.

The three vampires slipped into the water, dove deep, then shot through the Pacific like missiles toward their target. Killian and Devlin each had a harpoon gun. Rhiannon said she didn't need one.

Killian emerged from the waves near the starboard side of the large ship, far enough away that he could see the two men far above, patrolling that side. He could also see Rhiannon, near the ship's bow, climbing the slick hull like a drenched and angry spider, her long black hair dripping water down her back. He had no idea how the hell she was doing that.

He aimed his harpoon gun at the hull, about midway between the two soldiers up there, and let fly. The spear sailed, dragging its rope behind it like a comet's tail, and embedded itself in the ship with a dull "thunk" only a few yards below the rail. Killian swam closer to the vessel's side and began climbing the rope. He used his feet on the ship's slick hull to help push him, pulling himself higher. He reached the top, the harpoon gun still in hand, wrested the harpoon from the hull, and reloaded it, minus the rope this time. Gripping the bottom rung of the rail right in between two lifeboats, he pulled himself up high enough to see the man near the stern, leveled the harpoon gun and crept closer. But he didn't fire. He reached the fellow without being seen, snatched a flotation ring hanging from the rail and moved closer. Then he lowered the ring over the guy's head, pinning his arms to his sides, and bending, sank his teeth deeply into his throat. He drank rapidly and deeply, until his victim lost consciousness in his arms, and then lifted his head and tossed him right over the side.

He watched the man fall, saw him hit the water, and opened his mind to gauge his condition. He was unconscious, but still alive. Meanwhile, his blood was coursing through Killian's veins, strengthening him, giving him energy and vigor he hadn't had enough of before.

The second man was still gazing out to sea as if nothing had happened. He hadn't heard a thing. He shook a cigarette loose from a pack, lit it and stood there smoking for a moment. Odd, how they were dressed. Not in military garb, but more like paid assassins. Mercenaries, maybe.

Killian waited until the smoking man turned to pace along the deck and was just about to go after him, when, as if sensing something, the thug turned. He spotted Killian and opened his mouth to shout and alert the others to his presence. Killian moved too fast for that, though, so fast that to the human, it probably looked as if he'd disappeared, and reappeared right in front of him. Toe to toe.

He clapped a hand over the smoker's mouth, bent his head, sideways, and once again, sank his teeth deep and drank in the power, along with a hit of nicotine. When this one passed out, he put a floatation ring around him and threw him overboard to join his comrade.

Two down.

He headed to the bow of the ship to see how Rhiannon was faring, and found her just as she lifted her head from a dead man's throat, licked her lips, and tossed his spent body over the side.

He was still staring at her in a mixture of awe and horror when Devlin came from the other side. "I took out the two on my side and one in the bow."

"Don't kill any more unless you have to," Killian said.

Devlin looked at Rhiannon. She rolled her eyes. "No wonder Roland likes him. He's got that same irritating sense of honor. By the Gods, it's maddening."

It sounded like a slam but felt like a compliment. There was no time to analyze or ask, because she went on. "Devlin, your people are likely far below, possibly on what I believe is the lowermost deck. There's a room with an arena. A sliding door in one side raises up. That seems to be where they were keeping the girl-creature captive. It stands to reason other prisoners would be held in the same area. Particularly if they've been brought aboard for her...training." Rhiannon pulled her hair around to one side and wrung the seawater from it. "Where is Charlotte?"

"I don't know," Killian said. "Haven't heard from her in a while."

"Below decks, then," Rhiannon said. "Where the telepathy is blocked."

"What's our next move?" Devlin asked.

Killian swallowed hard. "We find Charlie. We find her

mother. We find your people and the girl Rhiannon saw, and then get all of us the hell out of here."

Devlin looked at Rhiannon. She lowered her head, sighed, but nodded.

"What?" Killian asked. "What am I missing?"

"They're not going to let us off this ship, Killian. And even if they did, we haven't the means to rescue that many people and get them all safely back to the fishing boat. Especially Charlie's mother, a mortal, and that child, whatever she is."

"What option do we have?" he asked.

"We can't leave anyone alive," Rhiannon said softly. "I know it goes against your sensibilities, but we're at war. We wipe them out, and we take this ship."

He shook his head. "I'm not killing anyone unless I have to."

Devlin clapped a hand onto his shoulder. "You *do* have to. All of them. No mercy. This has to end. Using The Chosen as guinea pigs, as weapons against us? You think it will stop if we leave any of them alive, Killian? We need to wipe them out."

"All we need to do is get the innocent out of here and escape alive," he said again. "And right now, all I need to do is find Charlie."

Commandant Crowe stayed, but the others left as soon as they had her strapped down. Dr. Deathly, which was a far more fitting name than Mariner, not to mention it was the one she'd got used to calling him, leaned in so close she could smell his breath.

"Now, you need to stay calm, Charlotte," the doctor was saying. "I can't inject you with the Protectol or the results of my testing will be skewed. So I want you to breathe deeply and evenly, and try not to get upset."

"I've been taken prisoner by a bunch of armed goons,

strapped down to a table and now you're going to experiment on me like a lab rat. And I'm not supposed to get upset?" She didn't bother telling him his testing was already screwed, since she'd had a half dose of Protectol only an hour ago.

The doctor lifted his brows. "I'm not going to harm you. But you must understand, what we can learn from you could help thousands born with your unfortunate condition."

"Help them how? Like you helped my comrades? By killing them? No way. No fucking way." She thrashed and tugged at her bindings, deliberately breathing hard and making it clear that *calm* was not an option.

"Charlotte, you'll only hurt yourself. Your heart—"

"Let it explode! At least I get to go out fighting!" She twisted from side to side, lifting her shoulders one at a time from the table, then arching her back, flipping like a fish on dry land.

Crowe put his hand on her chest and flattened her back to the table. "You will calm yourself down and cooperate, Charlotte."

"No I fucking won't!" she shouted. Because she needed them to play their trump card. If Protectol would skew their results then so, she guessed, would that tranq they were threatening her with. So they'd have to use something else to force her cooperation. "I'd rather die than help you bastards!"

"Would you rather your mother die?" Commandant Crowe asked.

She stopped struggling and glared at him. "My mother's already dead. You should know, you murdered her."

Looking so smug she wanted to tear his face off, Crowe said, "You spoke to her. Lieutenant Townsend said—"

"Lieutenant Townsend is a liar, and that phone call was a cheap trick. I'm not an idiot."

Shrugging, Crowe went to a telephone on the wall, picked it up and spoke into it. "Bring Trish O'Malley to Infirmary Two."

He hung up again without waiting for a reply, then went to the giant mirror on the wall and pushed a button. The mirror faded, becoming a window instead, and she could see another exam room just like this one, but empty.

Seconds ticked by. And then that other room's door opened, and a blond woman was shoved through. She stumbled and fell to her knees, unable to catch herself with her hands tied behind her back. But then she sat up again, scuttling into a corner, lifting her head, looking fearfully around.

"Mom," Charlie whispered.

Her mother looked terrified. She had a bruise on one cheek and a swollen lower lip. Her hair was a wild, tangled mess. But it was her. It was her mother. She was alive.

Tears burned in Charlie's eyes. She blinked them back, but they spilled anyway.

"Now I think you can see your position a bit more clearly, recruit," said Commandant Crowe. "You'll follow orders, or we'll hurt your mother. You don't want that, do you?"

She shook her head. "I'll do whatever it takes to keep my mother safe," she said, and she looked at the man, looked into his eyes. His living, lying, evil eyes. And she said, "Unfortunately, that means I have to kill you both."

He frowned. Charlie flexed one arm and snapped the strap holding it. She grabbed Crowe by the throat before he even knew what was happening. He clawed at her small hand with his, but she ripped the other arm free and sat up, grabbing him with both now.

The doctor scrambled, opening a cabinet, grabbing for a needle, a vial. His hands were shaking, his tranquilizer gun standing in the corner, forgotten. He was in a panic. Charlie crushed the commandant's larynx and dropped him to the floor, then reached down to rip the straps from around her ankles.

Just as the doctor came at her with a loaded syringe, she hopped off the table and grabbed him up by his wrist, squeezing until his bones snapped. The syringe fell. She caught it in her other hand, turned it toward him.

"No, no, please, it'll kill me. It's too big a dose for an ordinary—"

She jammed the needle into his neck, depressed the plunger, and he sank to the floor. "What the fuck were you planning to do with my ova, you amoral bastard?"

He didn't answer, already out. Dead, maybe. Furious, Charlie picked up the stool he'd been sitting on and hurled it through the glass of the two-way mirror, then jumped through behind it, avoiding the broken shards and landing on her knees in front of her mother.

"Charlie?" The way she was looking at her, Charlie would've thought her mom barely recognized her, and she couldn't imagine why. She didn't look any different.

She grabbed her mom by the shoulders. "Get up, turn around," she said, moving her mother where she wanted her instead of waiting. But before she could untie her, the door burst open and two armed men came in.

Charlie reacted instantly, moved her mother behind her, and kicked the gun right out of one guy's hand as he aimed it at her. She let the momentum of the kick carry her around, grabbed the stool on the way, and came the rest of the way swinging it at the other one's head.

As he fell, out cold, she picked up the dropped gun, pointed it at the first attacker. He backed up, shaking his head, hands up in surrender.

She leveled the gun at his head.

"Charlie, no!" Trish shouted, drawing Charlie's eyes her way.

He used her distraction to pull his gun and fire, but Charlie saw the movement from the corner of her eye and rocked sideways, lifting her gun and firing back. His shot hit her in the shoulder and hurt like hell. Hers went right between his eyes.

And then she stood there, looking at the two men on the

floor, one dead, one unconscious. Two more dead men on the other side of that broken two way mirror. She'd killed three people, and the shock of that was rippling through her soul, thick and black and leaving its stain forever.

"I didn't have a choice," she whispered, but it didn't wipe that stain away.

She closed the door, turned to her mother. "Turn around." Her voice sounded hard and cold.

Trembling and wide-eyed, Trish turned around, and Charlie untied her hands. Then she spun back, and threw her arms around her, holding her hard. "Charlie, Charlie, baby, I'm so glad you're all right. God, where did you learn how to fight like that?"

"They taught me." Charlie hugged her back, but only briefly.

"C'mon." Charlie pulled free, wiped her eyes. "We don't have time for this. Later, Mom."

Her mother frowned. "Charlie, are you okay? You're... you're different."

"Yeah. I'm different." She led her mother back through the broken glass into the treatment room and avoided looking at the two dead men on the floor. "Grab some gauze and shit and let's get out of here."

Nodding rapidly, her mother opened cabinets, grabbed handfuls of supplies, then finally noticed Charlie's wounded shoulder. "You're bleeding!"

"Don't panic. I'm okay, Mom." She took some of the cotton, wadded it up and crammed it into the bullet hole, wincing. Her mother wrapped some tape around it, and Charlie put a hand over hers to keep her from trying to apply another layer. "We have to move. Now."

Nodding, still looking worried as hell, Trish followed Charlie out the door and into the hall. She didn't know whether to go left or right, so she went right and thought as hard as she could, *Killian! Where are you?*

Killian heard Charlie's call, but just barely. He stopped what he was doing. He, Rhiannon and Devlin had already descended to the lower decks and were currently crouching in some kind of observation deck overlooking an arena far below. The door was open into the hallway behind him, so he stepped through it, held up a hand for silence, and focused on Charlie. *Where are you?*

Deck Three. The hall outside the medical unit. You?

They were both in the hallways, and there were no closed doors between them. No walls lined with whatever technology DPI used to construct thought-proof barriers.

Deck Six. Way below you, but also in the hallway. That must be why we can communicate.

I have my mother. We're heading topside. I need to get her out of here.

I'm on my way, Charlie. Wait for me.

He turned to Rhiannon and Devlin, who were looking at him expectantly. "Charlie's on Deck Three, and she has her mother," he told the other two. "I think she's hurt, but she didn't say. I felt it."

"Go after her, then," Devlin said. "I need to try to find my people."

"And I, the girl," Rhiannon said. "We'll join you as soon as we can, Killian. Be careful."

Rhiannon pointed downward at the arena below them, returning her attention to Devlin. "Those panels in the wall open upwards. That's where the girl came from. I got the impression they were using me as some kind of training lesson for the child."

"A vampire for her to kill."

"Precisely."

"Apparently, they didn't know just what vampire they had."

"They will now," she said.

Devlin jumped from the viewing deck and landed on the floor of the arena below.

"Go to her, Killian," Rhiannon said. "Devlin and I will meet you on the upper deck." And then she jumped, too.

Shaking his head in frustration, Killian went back the way he had come, waiting for another message from Charlie, but not getting one.

Charlie led her mother along the hall, up a set of stairs, but there were men on the landing. They saw her, raising their weapons before she had a chance to lift her own. They had the drop on her, point blank too.

"Just why are you standing there blocking the passage like a bunch of raw recruits?"

That voice came from right behind her, and it belonged to LT. She glanced over her shoulder and saw him standing there with his sidearm fully loaded, she hoped, in his hand.

She met his eyes, smiled a little in gratitude. He almost winked but not quite.

"Well?" he demanded. "Get the hell out of the way. Can't you see our most important prisoner is injured?"

"But sir, the infirmary is–"

"I know where the infirmary is! She needs help we don't have down there. Get your asses to the commandant's office for new orders. Pronto!"

The men looked at each other, shrugged, and moved out of the way, hurrying back along the corridor.

"You're hurt," he told Charlie.

"Yeah, I'm aware of that." She gripped her mother's arm and headed up the final flights to the main deck.

"She was shot," her mother said. "She'll bleed to death. We need to stop it."

"It's fine, Mom," Charlie told her. "We've slowed it down.

Stopped it, maybe." They emerged onto the main deck and looked around. It was still deserted. Of course it was deserted, it was the middle of the night. "There," she said. "We'll take one of those lifeboats."

The three of them ran to the nearest lifeboat, suspended just off the deck in a sling. Following the ropes and pulleys with her eyes, Charlie spotted the lever that would release the lifeboat into the sea. "Climb inside, Mom. Hurry. You too, LT."

"I'm not leaving you, Charlie!" Her mother grabbed her shoulders and held on. "You have to come too, you're hurt."

A herd of men were thundering up the stairs. "Mom, if you don't hurry, you'll get us all killed. Now go!"

Her mother climbed into the boat, probably too shocked by Charlie's tone of command to do otherwise.

"You want to make up for what you did to me, LT?" Charlie asked. "Then get my mother the hell out of here." She shoved him so hard he flipped over into the launch, because men were spilling onto the deck, surging her way. She lunged for the lever, hitting it as she flew past and then sliding across the deck. The ropes whirred like dragon-sized mosquitos, and she heard the splash when they stopped and hoped the little boat had stayed upright.

Its motor started up, and it sped away. Hearing that flooded Charlie with relief as she pushed herself up from the deck. Her hand slipped in her own blood. Hell, Trish had been right about that, hadn't she? The bandage job hadn't been good enough to stop it.

"That's far enough, lady."

She lifted her head and realized that she was completely surrounded.

"Okay, okay, easy now," she said. "Your people want me alive, and I'm bleeding out, here."

"Shove the gun away from you and put your hands up."

She shoved the gun across the deck toward the men, and

held her hands up as best she could, still lying on her chest. It was over, unless someone showed up to help her, and soon. *Killian, the deck's crawling with assholes. Don't come up here alone.*

D evlin and Rhiannon smashed through one of the two panels in the wall. As soon as they did, Rhiannon felt a rush of sensations. Every mental impulse that had been blocked from her before now came flooding into her mind. So many thoughts, feelings. So much anguish! So many vampires!

There were two rows of cells on either side of a long hallway. At the end of the hallway was a black steel door, and she felt the crackling energies of something awful beyond it.

As she hurried forward, though, she felt more and stopped to pay attention to what was all around her—the vampires in the cells on either side of this hallway.

One vampire in particular. One she knew very well.

"Reaper?" she asked, turning in the direction where she felt him and meeting his eyes. Then she raced toward him.

"Rhiannon, wait–"

She gripped the bars of his cell. A powerful jolt rocketed through her body, launching her across the hall, so that her back slammed into the cells on the other side, and they jolted her too. She found herself face down in the center of the floor. Pushing herself up, she lifted her head and looked at him and then around him. Five cells on each side of the hall. A half dozen or more vampires in each one. More than just the fifteen who'd been with Devlin.

Devlin knelt beside her, gripping her shoulders. "Are you all right?"

She was shaking all over from the blast of electricity, but she nodded. "We have to find a way to shut it off," she said.

"There's control panel at the end of the hall, Rhiannon," Reaper called. His deep voice was familiar, but it lacked its former power. And as she looked up, she saw his young friend Seth standing at his side.

She scanned the cells in search of others she might know, but most of the vampires were strangers to her. Many of them fledglings, barely months Undead.

"Where is Briar?" she asked. "And Vixen and the others?"

"We don't know," Seth said. "We haven't heard from Jack or Topaz in months. Briar and Vixen were captured with us, but they took them somewhere else. We don't know where."

"We can talk about all of this later, Rhiannon," Reaper said. "The control panel is back there." He nodded in the direction he meant.

Devlin let go of Rhiannon and ran that way. Trying to shake off the effects of the jolt, Rhiannon got slowly to her feet and watched him. He opened a small metal door, looked inside for a moment, and then pulled a lever.

The sounds of locks disengaging echoed in the cavernous space. The wall panel they'd broken through to get in here started to raise, only to get itself stuck partway, due to the damage they'd done to it. And the cell doors all slid open.

"We have friends in trouble above," Devlin said. "Come, all of you." He turned to run back the way they had come.

As the vampires surged from their cells, a river of them flowing toward the broken panel and through it, Reaper came to Rhiannon, put a hand on her shoulder. "Come on. If you're weak from the jolt, I'll help you."

She met his eyes, shook her head. "I can't join them. Not yet." And she looked toward the black metal door.

Reaper looked as well, and with a deep breath that sounded like one of regret, he said, "Are you sure you want to see what's in there, Rhiannon?"

"No," she said softly. "But I'm sure I have to."

CHAPTER TWENTY-FOUR

Killian emerged onto the uppermost deck to see a nightmare. Charlie was lying face down on the deck in a spreading pool of blood, and no less than twenty armed men surrounded her, aiming weapons and closing in. He was unarmed, one vampire, against twenty armed mortals. He didn't think his chances were very good.

She couldn't see him. So he spoke to her from his mind. No. From his heart. *I'm going to get their attention, Charlie. As soon as I do, pull yourself up and over the side.*

No! Don't, you'll be killed!

Roland and the others are still out there somewhere with the boat. Call to them and they'll find you. It's your only chance.

I don't have a chance, Killian. I'm dead either way. We both know that.

I love you, Charlie. There was never a moment when I didn't. I love you. And I'll damn well save you, or die trying.

Killian, please, don't—

He lunged forward, grabbing the first man he came to,

338 | MAGGIE SHAYNE

ripping the weapon from his grasp, and slamming its butt into his chin. Spinning, swinging the rifle like a baseball bat, he hit a second one, and then a third. That was as far as he got before the others turned to see him there and raised their weapons. He dodged, hit the floor, rolled as gunshots rang out, and listened for the splash of Charlie hitting the water.

He couldn't see her anymore, and as he lunged at full vampiric speed from one position to another, he felt fire rip through him, and knew he'd been hit. Why the hell wasn't she going overboard?

When the men turned their attention Killian's way, Charlie got up onto all fours, scrambled forward and grabbed the gun she'd dropped. Its barrel was slick with her blood, but she picked it up, leveled it, and started firing at their legs, loath to kill anyone else. Her fury had made her do murder below. And she didn't like the way that felt, didn't want to feel that way again, not ever, if she could help it. These men were not evil. They were misled, lied to, and following their employer's orders. And they probably believed they were fighting on the side of right. Fighting to protect their entire species.

Men dropped, others turned her way and lifted their weapons. She felt it when Killian was hit, and it drove her to keep on fighting.

But there was no way they could win. Killian was down, in pain and bleeding on one side of the deck, and she was in the same condition on the other. She kept firing, and so did he, and then she squeezed the trigger and heard a hollow *click*. Out of ammo. It was over.

I love you, too, Killian. I'll meet you on the other side.

One of the DPI thugs came walking up to her, raising his weapon and looking her right in the eyes. She knew it was over. She *knew* it.

And then someone came sailing over the side, onto the ship, airborne and dark, with black fabric flapping like wings behind him. He landed on her would-be assassin. Then he bounded from the fallen man, landing on one leg and then leaping off again, sailing over the tops of all of them to land between Killian and his attackers.

Roland!

Devlin's voice came from the top of the stairwell, "Attack!" And vampires surged onto the deck.

Charlie pulled herself upright and let loose a screech that split the night. When everyone was looking her way, she shouted, "We're not killing them!"

Roland stood across the deck from her. "Men, lay down your weapons. We are not your enemies, nor the bloodthirsty beasts you've been led to believe we are. Take the lifeboats and go. Pluck your comrades from the waters as you do. You will not be attacked."

There was a long, tense moment of silence, and then Killian stood up on the far side of the deck. "You're outnumbered. Abandon ship or die. Those are your only two options."

One man, all dressed in black, tossed his rifle away as if it was polluted. "They don't pay me enough for this shit. I'm out of here."

Then, one by one, the others dropped their guns and made their way to the lifeboats, carrying their wounded along with them. And the very vampires they'd held captive and tormented, manned the levers that lowered the vessels, and set them all free.

Charlie collapsed. It was getting harder to see. She wasn't sure if it was the blood loss or the pounding of her heart, which was faster and harder than it had ever been before.

"You're gonna be all right."

She looked up fast, as Killian gathered her into his arms, holding her head to his chest, his fingers threading into her hair. She put her arms around his neck clinging. "You're okay?" she whispered.

"I'm fine. And so are you."

She lifted her head a little, looking him over, one hand pressing to his face. He had a rag knotted tight around his upper arm, and the wound didn't look as bad as she'd feared.

"Roland bound me up. I didn't lose much blood. It hurts like hell, but I'm fine." But he was examining her just the same way she'd done to him. "You're not, though."

"I....I don't think I've lost that much blood. But my heart—"

"I can feel it. It's like it's my heart too." He stared into her eyes and deep into her soul, she thought. She felt him there, almost melding with her. And yet her heart was pounding faster and harder. So hard it hurt her chest now. "Let me go," she whispered. "Don't risk your life for mine."

"Without you, I don't have a life, Charlie." And then he bent to her neck, and he sank his teeth into her.

She closed her eyes, in a twisted combination of fear for him and the most intense pleasure she could imagine. And when he didn't cry in pain or back away, she knew there was no toxin in her blood. He wouldn't die. "Oh, God, Killian, it's so good," she whispered, and her hands clutched his head, fingers tangling in his hair as she pulled him harder to her. She arched her neck toward him as he suckled her there, taking her into him, taking her very life inside him.

And then the pleasure peaked, even as she felt herself begin to fade. And the pounding of her heart, she realized, had slowed. Was still slowing. And then beating just once, and then after a long pause, beating just once more. The darkness beckoned her, but she didn't fear it. She embraced it, knowing that on the other side of it, there was life, endless life...

...with the man she loved.

Roland hobbled through the broken wall panel, using a discarded rifle for a crutch, and went almost limp with relief when he spotted Rhiannon at the end of the hall in front of a large black door. He'd had no easy time getting down there, once he'd run into the swarm of Undead heading up. But most of them recognized him for what, if not who, he was. An elder. An Ancient One. And they parted to let him through, casting horrified looks at his stump.

He'd hopped, for the most part, keeping his left hand braced on a wall as he made his way, rapidly down flight after flight of stairs. He'd made it into the observation room and from there had flung himself to the floor below, landing heavily on one leg, and then falling on his face rather gracelessly.

But he'd felt her near and picked himself up with the help of the rifle he'd found lying on the floor, and hobbled on.

Her hand was on the iron door as she turned, and beside her, a man he knew well.

"Jesus, Roland, what the hell happened?" Reaper asked with a horrified look at his missing leg.

"Roland!" Rhiannon ran to him, wrapping him up in her arms and kissing him repeatedly. "You were supposed to wait in the fishing boat."

"And you believed I would do so while you faced armed killers and death? Honestly, Rhiannon, how long have we been married?"

She smiled when he repeated her own favorite sarcastic comment back to her, but then pulled away a bit, tearing her eyes from his. "The little girl. She's beyond that door, Roland. I know she is. We have to take her with us."

"The little girl?" Reaper asked, and he opened the door. "There's more than one, Rhiannon, and not all of them female."

Rhiannon turned and Roland put his arm around her and made his way through that open door with her. There were thirteen of them. Wild-eyed, matted haired children ranging in age from somewhere near two to possibly thirteen. They were kept one to a cell, their cages much smaller than the ones the vampires had been in. And all of them snarling and growling and lunging at the bars as the vampires moved slowly inside. They were children. Innocent children.

"The Offspring," Rhiannon whispered. "This was what they were talking about."

Reaper nodded. "I've heard enough to know what's been happening. They've been bred using the sperm and eggs of parents who were referred to as Exers. Do you know what that means, Rhiannon?"

"Exers are members of The Chosen who have been treated with a drug called BDX that changed them into super-humans, but cut their short lives even shorter. This must be what their true purpose was. To provide the genetic material to create a new race."

"They're like animals," Reaper said. "And they're trained to do one thing and one thing only."

"Kill vampires," Roland muttered. "By the Gods."

Rhiannon was eyeing them, and she found at last, the little girl who'd fought her so fiercely. "It doesn't matter what they were trained to do. They're The Chosen. At least, partly. We must protect them." She blinked the moisture from her eyes before facing either of the men and spoke clearly and firmly. "We must find a place for them. Or create one. They're our responsibility now."

When Charlie awoke, she was on the deck of The *Anemone*. And she was in Killian's arms. But everything else was different.

Everything.

She lifted her head to stare into his eyes and then past him at the deck, where no battle raged, no bodies laid, and no blood stained the wood. The ship was plowing through the water at a powerful pace, and the sky was the unmistakable purple of twilight.

"It's a new night," she whispered.

"Yes," Killian said. "It's a new beginning. I took you below when the sun rose, but I brought you up here when it set again. I thought you'd enjoy the view...when you first felt your new nature."

She frowned at him. "We're still on the ship?"

"It's our ship now. Lucas is back. So are your mother and Roxy, Christian and Larissa, even Olive and Pandora. Lucas told us that what was happening here was a Black Op. Very few people knew about it. We put all the DPI personnel off in lifeboats, and every vampire onboard joined together, and sent out our will to erase their memories. We replaced them with the memory of a storm at sea, their ship going down. Whether it worked, we can't yet know. But if it did, it could be days before anyone realizes the ship is missing, and we've disabled everything that might send out a signal and give away its location. We have time."

"Time...to do what?"

He shrugged. "Get away. Find a safe place, to live. Rhiannon mentioned something about finding a brand new Hotel Transylvania, but I think she was joking." He lowered his head, kissed her lips softly. "Do you remember what happened?"

She tried to remember, but it was hard. There was so much competing for attention in her brain. The smell of the water, the sounds of the large fish swimming beneath the waves, the stars in the sky sparkling so much more brightly than they had before, the feel of Killian's cheek beneath her hand, and the power of his arms around her, and the love overflowing in her heart for him. She tasted the salt in the sea air and the lingering flavor of his lips. She picked up a thousand scents on the wind.

And then that wind seemed to blow the clouds from her mind, and she whispered, "I'm a vampire."

"Yes."

She smiled, her eyes racing over his face. "God, Killian, you're so much more beautiful than I could see before." Blinking, she looked beyond him. "Everything is."

He laughed, and she laughed with him.

"Where is Olive?" she asked.

"There's a gigantic arena type room on Level Six. She's got full run of it, and lots of room to fly. I think Pandora misses her though."

"The owl and the pussycat went to sea," she said softly.

He nodded. "That they did. But the owl's not going to be happy until she sees that you're okay."

She smiled, happy the poor bird was out of the fishing boat's cramped galley. "And everyone else?"

"They're below, waiting for us. Roxy and your mother are with them."

"A victory party?

"More of a Charlie party. You led us to this victory, Charlie. Thanks to you, dozens of vampires who were captives on this ship are now free. Not to mention the children, but I'll tell you about them later on. You're not just a vampire. You're respected among your kind. You'll be legend before long."

"That's ridiculous."

"No it's not. You were born for this. Roxy's always known it. And now we all do, too."

Lifting her head she met his eyes, basking in the praise and letting it sink deeply into her soul. He watched her every moment of that time, feeling what she was feeling, she thought. Just the way she could feel what he felt. Love...the biggest most amazing love imaginable...and all of it for her.

"We should join them," he said softly, his eyes dancing over hers.

She twisted her arms around his neck, pulled herself up

and kissed him long and deep and slow. And then she said, "Maybe we can let them wait just a little bit longer."

EPILOGUE

The demon child who had beat the living tar out of Rhiannon was doing her best to repeat the process as Rhiannon knelt beside a bathtub, trying to wash the grime from the little beastie. Other vampires aboard the ship that was their temporary home, had taken on the challenge of the others, and she couldn't help but wonder if they were having more luck than she was.

"I know you can understand me," she said, holding the powerful child's arms as she kicked and splashed water everywhere. "I don't know if you can speak, but I know you can understand."

The girl wrenched one hand free, swung it and hit Rhiannon in the jaw. Rhiannon flew backward into the wall, but sprang to her feet again as the little girl launched herself out of the tub and landed in a ready crouch in front of her.

"I do *not* want to fight with you. I am *not* your enemy. The people who raised you were liars. And you will never be made to fight, nor kept in a cage ever again."

The child's frown was deep, her lips trembling, and her breaths came rapidly. "What mean...cage?"

"Your room. Where you lived. Where I found you." Rhiannon edged toward the bathroom door and opened it. "You get to live here now. With me. Until we find an even nicer place."

"I no live with vamper," she said. "I *kill* vamper."

"Vam*pire*," Rhiannon corrected.

Roland hopped into the doorway, and when Rhiannon turned, she saw him holding one hand over his eyes, and extending a hand with a chocolate bar in it. The little girl attacked her while she was looking the other way, but Rhiannon caught the top of her head and held her at arm's reach.

"Enough!" she shouted, and the vampiric power in her voice stunned the child into stillness.

Rhiannon pulled her arm away, looking down at the claw marks and shaking her head. Roland came hopping in, keeping his eyes averted until he'd tossed the girl a towel. "Wrap that around you. I have something for you."

The little girl obeyed, which shocked Rhiannon to no end. She wrapped up in the towel, staring at Roland's leg.

"Where gone, you leg?" she asked.

"A big fish ate it. Here," Roland said, unwrapping the chocolate bar. "This is for you. To eat."

"Hungry," The girl said.

"Well, take it then."

She looked suspiciously at Rhiannon as she edged forward, one hand holding up her towel, her black hair soaked and still tangled, but clean, dripping down her back. She snatched the chocolate bar from Roland's hand and brought it near her face, sniffing at it, before taking a bite.

And then the look on her angry little face turned into one of rapture. Her eyes widened, and she gobbled the rest of the bar, then licked her fingers and chocolate coated lips.

"Now," Roland said, "If you will try to be a good girl and

do as we say, I will give you one of those every single day for the rest of your life. Would you like that?"

She nodded.

"We're not going to hurt you," he said. "Not ever."

She lowered her head. "Hurt...when don't fight well."

"You never have to fight again."

The girl lifted her head. Rhiannon noticed how dark her eyes were. Almost as dark as her own. And her hair, just as black. Like the wing of a raven. She might even have a bit of Egypt in her poor, mixed up DNA.

"Your life will be good now," Rhiannon said, moving closer to Roland, sliding an arm around his waist. "You will have anything you desire, from now on."

The little girl blinked as if trying to understand, and Rhiannon thought the poor child probably couldn't even think of a thing to ask for. Then she saw something beyond Rhiannon, and her little eyes rounded. "Who is it?" she asked, pointing at her own reflection in the mirror.

Rhiannon moved beside her. "That's you. See? Wave your hand, like this." She demonstrated. The child copied, her eyes widening when her reflection did the same. "It's just a piece of glass people made so they could see what they look like. It's called a mirror."

"But...I no see you."

"Mirrors don't work on vampires, child."

She didn't seem to understand that, but Rhiannon thought it was all right. The little girl touched her own tangled hair, then turned to look at Rhiannon's.

Rhiannon smiled. "Would you like your hair to be like mine?"

She nodded, wary, untrusting.

"I can do that," Rhiannon said. "Come with me. I'll tell you a story while I comb your hair. And you can meet my friend, Pandora. She's going to love you." She held out a hand.

The little girl looked at it for a long moment. And then she lifted her own little hand and slipped it into Rhiannon's.

Something in Rhiannon's heart seemed to hiccup as she closed her hand around the much smaller hand of the little girl.

Her little girl.

"I think I shall call you Nikki. Short for Rhianikki, which was my name long ago. Would you like that? Nikki?"

Staring into Rhiannon's eyes for a long time, the little girl seemed to think on that. And then, very slowly, she smiled.

The End
For now....

TWILIGHT VENGEANCE
COMING SEPT. 2015

Devlin is a loner who doesn't like humans, except as sustenance. He'll help The Chosen, of course, but only because he has to. He doesn't enjoy it, resents them for their power over his kind, even though he was once one of them. But when a snoopy little aspiring horror writer discovers the vampires' new haven, one they are determined to keep secret from the mortal world, Devlin wants her dead. And he doesn't much care if she's one of The Chosen or not.

If you liked TWILIGHT GUARDIANS, you might also like
Eternal Love: The Immortal Witch Series

ABOUT THE AUTHOR

New York Times bestselling author Maggie Shayne has published more than 60 novels and 23 novellas. She has written for 7 publishers and 2 soap operas, has racked up 15 Rita Award nominations and actually, finally, won the damn thing in 2005.

Maggie lives in a beautiful, century old, happily haunted farmhouse named "Serenity" in the wildest wilds of Cortland County, NY, with her husband and soulmate, Lance. They share a pair of English Mastiffs, Dozer & Daisy, and a little English Bulldog, Niblet, and the wise guardian and guru of them all, the feline Glory, who keeps the dogs firmly in their places. Maggie's a Wiccan high priestess (legal clergy even) and an avid follower of the Law of Attraction

Connect with Maggie

Maggie's Website	www.MaggieShayne.com
Maggie's Bliss Blog	www.MaggiesBlissBlog.com
Twitter	@MaggieShayne
Facebook	Facebook.com/MaggieShayneAuthor

Made in the USA
Lexington, KY
23 September 2014